THE NEXT
ORGANIC INTELLIGENCE—

Science fiction is the literature of "what if." But what will happen the day after tomorrow when "what if" becomes "what is," when humans bring new forms of intelligent life into the universe not by procreation but by creation? Twelve of today's most imaginative writers offer their own unique visions of the forms such life might take, and the impact these new "minds" will have on the worlds around them, in such thought-provoking stories as:

"Keepers of Earth"—The robots had inherited the charred remains of a world and a mission to restore it to life. But when their mission was accomplished what fate awaited them . . . and the world?

"Freddy Nearby"—He was the perfect robot for the job, seventeen hits and no convictions—but sometimes "perfect" might be a little too good. . . .

"Sacrifices"—She was an android who'd been programmed to be Amanda's friend, and she'd do what was best for the child no matter the cost. . . .

SILICON DREAMS

More Imagination-Expanding Anthologies Brought to You by DAW:

PAST IMPERFECT *Edited by Martin H. Greenberg and Larry Segriff.* Twelve all-original tales of intrepid travelers in time who may find that the journey home can last forever. . . . From a police detective given the chance to go back to the scene of a murder before it happens . . . to an eerie fog that suddenly allows a man to see his own past clearly . . . to a scientist who's created a means to travel to the far future—only to find a world and a fate beyond his wildest imaginings . . . here are unforgettable tales by such masters of the space-time continuum as Kristine Kathryn Rusch, Peter Crowther, Jane Linkskold, Diane Duane, Jody Lynn Nye, and James P. Hogan.

FAR FRONTIERS *Edited by Martin H. Greenberg and Larry Segriff.* Thirteen of today's top authors—including Robert J. Sawyer, Alan Dean Foster, Kristine Kathryn Rusch, Lawrence Watt-Evans, Julie E. Czerneda, and Andre Norton—blaze new pathways to worlds beyond imagining, from a civilization of humans living in a Dyson sphere to whom the idea of living on a planet is pure mythology . . . to an ancient man so obsessed with an alien legend that he will risk ship and crew in the Void in the hope of proving it true . . . to the story of the last free segments of "humanity," forced to retreat to the very edge of the galaxy—in the hope of finding a way to save themselves when there is nowhere left to run. . . .

STAR COLONIES *Edited by Martin H. Greenberg and John Helfers.* From the time the first Homo sapiens looked up at the night sky, the stars were there, sparkling, tempting us to reach out and seize them. Though humankind's push for the stars has at times slowed and stalled, there are still those who dare to dream, who work to build the bridge between the Earth and the universe. But while the scientists are still struggling to achieve this goal, science fiction writers have already found many ways to master time. Join Robert J. Sawyer, Jack Williamson, Alan Dean Foster, Allen Steele, Robert Charles Wilson, Pamela Sargent, Mike Resnick, Kristine Kathryn Rusch and their fellow explorers on these never-before-taken journeys to distant stars.

SILICON DREAMS

Edited by
Martin H. Greenberg
and Larry Segriff

DAW BOOKS, INC.
DONALD A. WOLLHEIM, FOUNDER
375 Hudson Street, New York, NY 10014
ELIZABETH R. WOLLHEIM
SHEILA E. GILBERT
PUBLISHERS
www.dawbooks.com

DAW Book Collectors No. 1207.

DAW Books are distributed by Penguin Putnam Inc.

First Printing, December 2001
1 2 3 4 5 6 7 8 9

ACKNOWLEDGMENTS

CONTENTS

INTRODUCTION

by Larry Segriff

ROBOTS are the heart of science fiction.

Think about it. What comes to mind when you think about science fiction? Spaceships? Ray guns? Time travel? These are mere trappings, plot devices if you will, but they point to the true focus of science fiction: the future. What will tomorrow be like? What wonders will it hold? What impact will new technologies have on society, on people, on the world?

The focus of science fiction is the future, and as any good parent knows, our children are our future. The question is, who are our children?

In a way, mankind as a whole is a lot like an individual creature. Our infancy is lost in prerecorded history. Our childhood occurred somewhere around the time we started to gather in cities and learned to cultivate our food. Our adolescence began somewhere around the Middle Ages, and I see the early twentieth century—particularly the first and second world wars—as our rebellious teenage years.

We are only now entering our young adulthood. We're starting to face our responsibilities. We're starting to think about the future. And we're starting to think about having children.

For mankind as a species, our children will be robots. Whether they're androids or robotic farmers, teleoperated miners on the surface of another planet or self-sufficient explorers sent out into the vastness of space, whether they're self-aware and self-reliant or tied to us through an umbilical cord of technology, they will indeed be our children.

The title of this anthology is *Silicon Dreams*. Partly, that's a tip of the hat to Phil Dick's "Do Androids Dream of Electric Sheep?" Mostly, though, it's in recognition of the fact that, as their parents, it will be up to us to foster their dreams.

Being a parent is tough work. It's hard not knowing how your children will turn out. It's hard separating their lives from yours, their dreams from yours, their future from yours. But it's rewarding, too, to watch your children grow, to shape them and mold them and then to see them grow beyond anything you could have hoped for them.

Robots are our future. They are the heart of science fiction and the hope of mankind. They are our children.

I'm looking forward to watching them grow.

A HELPING HAND

by Kristine Kathryn Rusch

Kristine Kathryn Rusch is an award-winning fiction writer. Her novella, *The Gallery of His Dreams,* won the *Locus Award* for best short fiction. Her body of fiction work won her the John W. Campbell Award, given in 1991 in Europe. She has been nominated for several dozen fiction awards, and her short work has been reprinted in six *Year's Best* collections. She has published twenty novels under her own name. She has sold forty-one in total, including pseudonymous books. Her novels have been published in seven languages, and have spent several weeks on The *USA Today* bestseller list and *The Wall Street Journal* bestseller list. She has written a number of *Star Trek* novels with her husband, Dean Wesley Smith, including a book in this summer's crossover series called *New Earth.* She is the former editor of the prestigious *The Magazine of Fantasy and Science Fiction,* winning a Hugo for her work there. Before that, she and Dean Wesley Smith started and ran Pulphouse Publishing, a science fiction and mystery press in Eugene. She lives and works on the Oregon coast.

JAMAL shoved his mittened hands in the thin pockets of his coat. He'd forgotten his hat, and his ears were getting cold. The day was dark and gray. Icy drops were falling from the sky—not rain, not snow, but sharp pellets that felt like needles when they hit his skin.

The snowbanks were piled high against the side of the road, blocking the view of traffic. Sometimes he felt as if he were walking through canyons. His father grumbled that global warming was a myth; certainly this winter had proved the scientists—all of whom had been citing warming figures from the first thirty years of the century as proof of this phenomenon—wrong. Jamal's grandmother said that she remembered winters like this when she was a girl, and that weather, like life, had its cycles.

He shivered again. He didn't like this cycle. He'd outgrown his heated boots and he had to wear his father's castoffs, which were too big, and the heater had stopped working years ago. His grandmother knitted his mittens, which was why he kept them hidden; he was the only kid in his class whose gloves and coat didn't self-heat.

His family had been struggling for the past year. His mother's illness and death had drained their reserves, or so his father had said one dark night when Jamal had found him alone at the kitchen table, staring at his handheld. It beeped constantly as creditors sent threats, past due messages, and notices of legal actions.

There's nothing left to sell, his father had said, hands cupping his chin.

Jamal had never heard his father sound so depressed, and it frightened him. He'd asked his father what he could do, and his father just shook his head.

It'll be better in the morning, kiddo, he'd said, and they had both known he was lying.

Jamal had tried to find work, but there was little a kid of eleven could do. He had to wait until he was twelve before he could get special permission for a part-time job. When he'd told his grandmother about this, she'd muttered something about tighter child-labor laws and the way that all the jobs kids used to have had gone to the robots.

He wasn't sure exactly what she had meant by that. When he'd asked her to give him examples, she had mentioned newspaper delivery, then shook her head, reminding herself that newspapers were electronic. She'd also mentioned baby-sitting, which he'd never heard of, and lawn-mowing, which was silly, since, as long as he could remember, lawns had mowed themselves.

He reached the towering snowbanks at the intersection and stepped cautiously between them. Then, before he crossed the icy street, he looked left, right, and up. There weren't a lot of air taxis that came to this neighborhood, but those that did went by at a pretty good clip. When he had been in the fourth grade, one of his classmates had been struck and killed by a low-flying air taxi. Jamal had looked up ever since.

The wind in the building canyons was strong. It buffeted him as he crossed the street, and he staggered to keep his balance. He was one of the few people walking in this weather—his family couldn't afford the bus any more. They could barely afford to keep him in school.

The stinging rain had grown heavier. It was closer to sleet. Jamal couldn't remember being this cold. He finally made it to the other side of the street, shivering and wet, when he saw an arm sticking out of the snow.

His breath caught in his throat. The hand looked gray with cold. Or maybe it was just the effect of the dark, gray day, the sleet, and the wind. Jamal approached the hand slowly, afraid of what he would find. As he got closer, though, he realized the hand was shiny and so was the arm. Silver or silver plating, like they used on robots so that no one would have trouble telling them apart from human beings.

Jamal stopped at the snowbank and touched the hand gently with his mittened finger. The hand was cold—metal cold—and it didn't move when he touched it, like a robot should have. His curiosity got the better of him. He grabbed the hand as if it were human, and tugged with all his strength.

The arm popped out of the snow. He stumbled backward, tripped and fell on the icy sidewalk. Immediately the chill seeped through his clothing, making him even colder, but he didn't care.

He was staring at the arm and hand, perfectly shaped, clearly robotic. The arm went all the way up to the place where the shoulder should have been and, as in humans, there was a ball at the end of the limb, waiting to be stuck in a socket.

He'd never seen a robot part, at least not in person. There'd been shows on the vid, and last year, his fifth-grade teacher had done a unit on robotics. But robots were intricate and valuable machines. No one who owned one, to his knowledge, had ever taken one apart.

The arm was extremely cold, but he didn't want to let go of it. He probably should have—there was something wrong about it—but something fascinating as well. It was a treasure, something unpredictable in his dark and depressing world.

He got up and gazed at the snowbank, wanting to dig farther, to see if there was more robot inside, but he was too cold. Now that he had the arm, no one else would find this place. He tucked the arm under his coat, and ran home as fast as he could.

Jamal smuggled the arm up to the apartment, let himself in, and discovered that he was in luck. His father was still at work, and his grandmother had dozed off in front of her program, leaving the television on full blast.

He never understood why his grandmother insisted

on watching live TV—he'd offered to download vids for her dozens of times—but she said that took the fun out of everything. And for the first time, he appreciated her eccentricity. It made hiding the arm in his room a lot easier.

It also made using the house phone a lot easier, too. He'd had to give up his own number years ago as the money got tight. Only his father had a private number now—and that was because his father was the only one holding a job. Jamal and his grandmother had to make do with the old-fashioned house equipment and with being unwired.

Being unwired had huge drawbacks. Jamal was one of only five kids in his class who had to use school equipment to do his assignments, equipment that couldn't leave the building, so he spent a lot of his free time there. It also meant that he was constantly behind, something he found very frustrating since before his mother's illness he had been at the top of his class.

He slipped into his bedroom and hid the arm under his bed. Then he grabbed the house phone and brought it inside the room. He called his best friend Robbie and asked him if he wanted to meet Jamal outside.

"Can't," Robbie said. "Got math to finish."

Jamal had hurried through his after school. "I'll help."

"Nope. Mom caught us last time. She's still mad."

Jamal peered out his window. The storm had gotten worse. Road cars were sliding on the ice. As he stared, an air taxi went by, its passenger staring smugly out the side window.

No one was going anywhere. No one would tamper with his snowdrift.

"How about tomorrow after school?"

"Don't you gotta stay?" Robbie asked. He knew about Jamal's problems with studying.

"I'll skip tomorrow. Go in early on Friday. Or maybe I can use your stuff?" He'd been angling for that for a long time, but Robbie's mother had been strongly against it. Ever since Jamal's mother died and the family's money disappeared, Robbie's mother had acted as if Jamal smelled bad.

"Maybe," Robbie said in the tone he always used when he meant no.

Jamal sighed. To investigate, he would have to lose sleep the following day because he'd have to go to school early. But the search was worth it. "Okay," he said. "Tomorrow, then. Meet me in the old spot right after school."

Robbie agreed, and Jamal hung up. For the first time in almost a year, he found himself looking forward to the next day.

The old spot was an ancient oak tree planted at the very edge of school property. His dad said that when he was a boy, the school wanted to cut down the tree, but Greens had protested and won, letting the tree live for future generations. His dad had been part of that protest, and Jamal always felt that somehow his dad had preserved the tree just for him.

The tree was huge, but its base was partially hidden by the deep snow. At least it wasn't sleeting. The sun was out, bathing everything in a pale yellow light. Jamal had to wait at the edge of the sidewalk near the tree and as time went by, he worried that Robbie wasn't going to show up.

In the last few months, Jamal had been the one keeping up the friendship. Robbie had had to fight his mother on everything, and Jamal got the sense that Robbie was growing tired. Either that or he'd started to believe her when she said that Jamal's mother's illness had been a curse of God.

Jamal had asked his father if that was true and his

father had looked at him as if he were crazy. *It was breast cancer, Jamal,* he'd said. *It was just a disease.*

But my teacher says no one dies of breast cancer any more.

His father shook his head and slumped in his chair. *If they get treatment, they do fine.*

Why wasn't Mom fine?

His father sighed. He had that expression he got when he worried that Jamal wouldn't understand his explanation. *Your mother's mother, your grandmother Reed whom you never met, died of breast cancer. Your mother inherited the gene, but didn't get tested for it which meant she didn't get gene therapy at an early age. So our insurance company called it a pre-existing condition. We had to pay for everything ourselves.*

So?

His father looked down. *Sometimes you get what you pay for, Jamal.*

Robbie stopped beside him. He had a thick thermal coat, glowing red to show that its heater was working and formfitting silver mittens that had their own insulation. His boots were melting holes in the ice.

"So what's so fantastic?" he asked.

Jamal grinned at him, partly unable to believe that Robbie had come. He reached into his backpack and pulled out the arm. He'd been carrying it all day, just waiting for a chance to show Robbie.

Robbie whistled as he saw it. Jamal had bent the arm at the elbow so that it fit better in the pack. Robbie ran his fingers across the length, the silver of his glove looking dull against the silver of the arm.

"Where'd you get that?" he asked.

"I'll show you," Jamal said. "I think there could be more there."

Robbie helped him stuff the arm into the pack and then together they hurried down the street. "I'm gonna get in trouble for not taking the bus."

Jamal looked at him, holding his breath.

Then Robbie grinned. "So you gonna show me or not?"

It felt like old times, the two of them scampering together, doing something that maybe they shouldn't have. They never got in real trouble, but not for lack of trying.

With the two of them together, it seemed to take no time at all to reach the right snowbank. The ice storm from the night before had left a hard crust on the bank. Jamal could see his handprints, etched in ice against the snow.

"This is crazy," Robbie said. "You know how expensive that arm's gotta be?"

"No." Jamal poked at the snowbank with the toe of his boot.

"Like thousands and thousands of dollars," Robbie said. "They don't make robots cheap. That's what my mom says. That's why only rich people and businesses have them."

"Our landlord's got one," Jamal said, still poking. "He's not rich."

"He probably leases." Robbie turned his nose up as he said that, as if his family were too good to lease. Jamal glanced at him sideways. Maybe there was a reason besides his newfound poverty that kept him away from Robbie these days.

"Well, you wanna help me look?" Jamal asked.

Robbie hadn't moved. "What do you think's in there, a whole robot?"

Jamal shrugged. He was getting cold.

"It can't be a whole robot," Robbie said. "People don't throw away robots. That's illegal. They recycle."

"I didn't think they could take 'em apart either," Jamal said, "but someone took this guy apart."

"Maybe the arm didn't work and they replaced it." Robbie tugged on his thermal gloves. Jamal's hands were deep in his pockets again—not because his fingers were cold (they were) but because he didn't really want Robbie to comment about his mittens.

"And threw the arm out the window?"

"Or maybe it fell off an air taxi or something."

"What if it just came apart in the snow?"

"Robots don't come apart," Robbie said, using that tone again. Jamal felt his cheeks grow warm. Robbie never used to treat him like a dummy.

"They gotta come apart," Jamal said. "Or else I wouldn't be able to have this arm."

Robbie was silent for a moment. A car whooshed by on the other side of the snowbank.

"What do you want to do?" Robbie asked.

"Dig. See what else we find."

Robbie's mouth screwed up tight. "I wish you'd told me that sooner. I'd've worn other gloves. These aren't supposed to get wet."

Jamal frowned at him. "What good are gloves that can't get wet?"

"The kind that keep your hands warm," Robbie said.

Jamal stared at the snowbank. The bright feeling he'd had earlier, the feeling that things were returning to the way they ought to be, had gone away. "You could kick the snow with your boots."

"I don't think so, Jamal," Robbie said. "This is just dumb."

"You thought it was fine a while ago."

"I didn't know we'd have to get dirty."

Jamal faced him. "We used to."

"We used to do a lot of things." Robbie shoved his coat sleeve up to reveal his wristnet. "If I go now, I can still get the bus."

Without waiting for Jamal's reply, Robbie ran down the sidewalk toward the school.

Jamal kicked the bank, his boot breaking through the ice. Then he stomped on the melted section of sidewalk where Robbie had stood. Robbie was supposed to be his best friend. Robbie was supposed to care about the same things. But Robbie hadn't cared for a long time. Maybe never. Maybe Robbie's mom had never been the problem. Maybe she'd only been the excuse.

Jamal turned toward the snowbank. No one else was on the sidewalk. He set the backpack down where he could see it, and plunged his mittens into the bank right beside his frozen handprints. Then he started moving snow.

His sleeves shoved up to his elbows, and he could feel the snow against his arms, cold and wet. Each layer was dirtier and harder than the previous one. He worked so hard, he could feel himself sweating under his coat. It felt odd: his feet were cold, his arms were wet, his fingers were frozen, and the rest of him was too hot.

He was just about to quit when his fingers found something. Other fingers, hard and cold. He dug them out in a frenzy. It was another hand—the hand only, snapped off at the wrist and hollow inside. It too was made of shiny silver metal, and it glistened wetly.

He stared at it for a long time, his heart pounding. What destroyed metal like that? And why was it on this street corner? He had no idea.

He was shivering now. It was getting dark. His grandmother would be getting worried. He shoved the hand in his bag, where it clanked against the arm, and then he ran home.

Jamal spent the entire next day at school, trying to make up the work he'd missed. He was so far behind the other kids—the kids who had their own access—that he thought he would never catch up.

By the end of the very long day, he put his head down on his arms and tried to think of his mother. She used to sit beside him and watch him do his homework on his own handheld, marveling at the way he could think. *You'll do great things some day, my Jamal,* she used to say. Even at the end, when she saw him, her eyes would light up. *My boy,* she'd whisper. *My great boy.*

Her great boy was failing every class in the school that had become too expensive for his father. His teacher had offered to tutor him, but that would cost more money, so Jamal hadn't even told his dad.

When the school year started, the image of his mother would keep Jamal going. But that image was getting lost in all the pressure. He didn't know how to keep studying, keep learning, without being linked. And he didn't know how he would be able to tell his father that everything he was counting on, everything he was sacrificing for, would be lost.

A hand touched his back, and Jamal jumped. His teacher, Mrs. Brown, stood behind him. She had a pretty face and warm eyes. She knew what was happening—that was why she'd offered to help—but there wasn't much she could do. The schools required payment for any teaching she did on the premises, and she wasn't allowed to work outside of the building.

"Time to go, Jamal," she said.

He nodded, wondering if he'd fallen asleep. He had't finished most of his reading, and he couldn't come back over the weekend. He had been finishing this week's assignments; he hadn't even started the work due on Monday, work that he might never get done now.

Still, he thanked her and walked home in the dark and the cold, passing the snowbank where he'd discovered the hands. The snow he had thrown on the sidewalk remained there. No one had touched it. He could see the hole he'd dug as a blackness against the dirty white.

But he didn't stop. This neighborhood was scary at night, even though he tried to pretend it wasn't. He walked as fast as he could, keeping his gaze ahead of him, trying to ignore the cars driving past, the adults who stood in doorways—adults who were never there in the daylight.

If only he had his own robot. The robot would take him to and from school, play with him when no one else did, and help him with his schoolwork so that he wouldn't fail. When his grandmother got tired, he'd give her the robot and then she wouldn't have to work so hard. Everything would be nice and perfect, and, even though they wouldn't be the way they were before, things would get better.

As he climbed the steps to his apartment, he wondered what would happen if he found all the pieces of the robot. Would he be smart enough to put it together, make it work properly, make it think for him?

The brain was the most intricate part and, he'd learned in school last year, that brains were assembled at the factories—made to order. Even if he got the other parts wrong, the brain was the part that could actually help him. It might even tell him how to reassemble its body.

He opened the apartment door to find his grandmother setting the table.

"You're late, baby," she said.

"I know," he said, peeling off his jacket and putting it on the coat rack.

"Everything okay at school?"

He debated telling her. But what could she do? She didn't have any links. The house systems were too old to handle his assignments, and they'd had to sell his handheld six months ago to pay the rent. His father used the only remaining handheld for his job which was, his grandmother sometimes whispered when she thought Jamal wasn't listening, he only thing between them and "the street."

"School's school," he said so that he wouldn't lie

to her. Then he went into his room, closed the door, and pulled the hands from under his bed.

He stared at them for a long time. They matched. He was sure they were from the same robot. Maybe if he dug hard enough, he would find the rest of it.

Maybe, if he dug hard enough, he'd finally find a way out.

The next morning, he got up when his grandmother did. He had lain awake for nearly an hour, waiting to hear her banging around the kitchen. If he had gotten up before her, she would have known something was wrong. As it was, he had to tell her that he was meeting Robbie just so that she would stop asking questions.

Jamal took three pairs of mittens from the mending bag in the bottom of the closet. He put two pairs in his pocket, and the other pair on his hands. Then he covered that pair with his usual pair, so that his hands would be warm enough.

He had on double socks as well, and a pair of shorts beneath his pants, just so that he could stay warm. After he left the apartment, he snuck into the landlord's closet and stole the gardening shovel, slipping it into his coat before anyone missed it. Then he went outside.

The air was crisp, cold, and damp. It would snow again before the day was out—he could feel it. Large gray clouds hovered above the buildings. The entire day felt heavy. He'd rather be inside, talking to his dad on his only day off.

But this was more important. This was their chance.

When he reached the snowbank, he saw the someone had shoveled the snow he'd thrown on the sidewalk back toward the hole. The street was empty, though. No one stood in doorways and no cars went by. He thought he heard the hum of an air taxi, but he didn't look up. He was staring at the remains of the hole, wondering what else was inside.

He couldn't see anything. He glanced around him at the shaded windows, the filthy, dented doors. He didn't know anyone in this neighborhood, but he knew it was poorer than the one he was living in. His father said he didn't want to be forced to move to one of these buildings—that was why it was so important to keep his job.

Jamal could sense there was something wrong with this place. That was probably why he always hurried past on his way home from school—he didn't want to be here very long.

He stiffened his shoulders and faced the snowbank, feeling uncomfortable as he turned his back on the buildings. The silence bothered him. He would have liked it better if someone were on the street. Actually, if a lot of someones were on the street. But they might stop him from what he planned to do.

He would have to work quickly.

He dug into the snowbank with the small shovel. It was harder work than he had expected. Once he got past the top layer, the snow was hard and smooth—a ball of ice more than a pile of snow. He wished he had taken the self-propelling shovel, but he knew that the landlord would have missed it.

So he dug for a while and found nothing. Then he set the shovel down and put his hands on his hips, staring at the snowbank.

He had discovered the arms on top of the ice ball, not beneath it, as if the snowplow had thrown snow on top of them—or maybe it had thrown the hands with a pile of snow. If there was any more to this robot, it wouldn't be so deep down. It would be scattered on top of the ice layer, along this section of street.

Jamal stepped away from the intersection and started digging in the spot right next to the place where he had discovered the hands. He hadn't gone far when he found the arm section for the second hand. He set it on the ground beside him and continued to dig.

Bits of silver metal were scattered throughout the snow, some of the pieces as large as his thumb. They were all ruptured outward, the metal twisted and slightly blackened. He shivered when he found them, not with the cold, but with concern. What if he didn't find an entire robot? What then? Would his dream go away?

He didn't want to think about it. So he dug to the ice ball level and then moved to a new section. There he discovered part of a foot, also ruptured, and a long flat bit of metal nearly as big as he was. When he turned it over, he realized what it was.

It was the robot's back. The stomach area had been blown outward and the innards were missing. He glanced over his shoulder at the windows behind him, but they remained shuttered. Every time a car passed, he hunkered against the snow. Now he knew he was finding something he shouldn't have, but he didn't know what or why.

His stomach was growling and the midday sun had finally filled the canyons between the buildings when he found the ultimate prize—the small, shiny head.

It seemed undamaged. The electronic eyes were dark. The mouth was a thin, unopened line. But the back of the skull was intact. He scraped the snow off it, and found the serial number as well as the on-off switch and the information ports. Jamal didn't know if time in the snow would have hurt it, but he doubted it. Robots were made to withstand all sorts of weather when they were running properly—he couldn't imagine that weather would damage them when they were shut off.

He put the head and the arm in his backpack, then he shoved the damaged torso, the fragments and the foot back in the snow. He used his hands to throw the snow back onto the bank, hiding the pieces he'd found.

A robot head was better than nothing. Maybe, if he searched enough, he would find parts in good repair—a neck, shoulders, and even a working torso and legs. Eventually he might be able to build a functional robot.

Until then, though, he would have something to consult and maybe even a way to access the Nets. He might be able to do his homework again, catch up in school, and rise back to the top of his class.

He cradled the backpack to his chest, grabbed the shovel, and ran home. He put the shovel back—apparently no one missed it—and then ran up the stairs. His grandmother frowned at him as he came in the door, but said nothing. His father slept on the couch, his handheld on the table beside him, making tinny noises as someone on some channel nattered about something unimportant.

Jamal slipped into his bedroom and hid the head and arm under the bed with the other pieces. He would deal with it all later, when his father and grandmother were in bed.

Despite his best efforts to stay awake, Jamal fell asleep shortly after his dad had tucked him in. Jamal woke several hours later, and rolled over. His digital clock read 12:31 a.m.

He listened, but heard no stirring in the apartment. Sometimes his dad sat up late and read or listened to music, but apparently he hadn't done so on this night. Work had been really difficult lately and Jamal knew that his father was worried about it. He was staying up later and later, filing résumés with various services and applying for after-work enhancement training scholarships.

So far he hadn't got any of them.

Jamal slipped out of bed and shivered. His grandmother turned the heat down fifteen degrees at night. He had long outgrown his slippers, so she had knitted him a pair of extra thick socks, which he pulled on now. Then he put on his robe, went to his bedroom door, and opened it.

Just as he suspected, no one else was up. He closed the door and turned on his light. Then he reached under the bed and grabbed the robot's head.

It was cool and smooth and strangely beautiful, with its shiny silver surface and blank eyes. He held it for a moment, feeling the possibilities. Soon he would know if this mechanical brain could help him.

Part of him wanted to remain in this moment, feeling the hope. He was afraid that it wouldn't work and then he'd have nothing to look forward to.

But his mother used to tell him that he wouldn't get anything if he didn't try.

Jamal took a deep breath and set the robot's head on the wobbly card table that he used as a desk. He turned on his desk lamp, got out his tiny tool set, and wiped his hands against his robe.

Then he flicked the switch on.

For a moment, he thought nothing was going to happen. Then he heard a faint whirring sound, like a fan starting up. A light grew in the eyes, making them seem alive. The mouth moved, but no sound came out.

"What do you want?" Jamal whispered.

The eyes got brighter and seemed to focus on him. The head's vocal processor bleeped and groaned, as if it were malfunctioning. He let it moan for a moment, then shut the unit off again.

The sounds stopped immediately, but it took a while for the light in the eyes to fade.

His hands were shaking. Something was clearly going on, but he wasn't sure what to do about it.

He picked up the head and turned it upside down. There was an opening where the neck should have been. He reached inside, felt a gooey substance near the mouth, and more along the plate that ran beneath the processing unit in the base.

Jamal made a face, then grabbed a towel he'd left on the floor and wiped the inside of the head. The towel came out wet and black. He wiped one final time to make sure everything was all right, then he set the head down again and turned it on.

The eyes lit up quicker this time. They glowed yellow. The mouth opened and a deep male voice came out.

"My name is Shing. I belong to Kiri Lenoy, who resides at 1830 N. Lincoln Park West. I must be returned to her immediately. My name is Shing. I belong . . ."

The voice got louder, and more harried as it repeated the information. The eyes seemed to grow brighter. Jamal touched the head and found that it was getting warm.

"What happened to you?" he asked.

". . . Lincoln Park West. I must be returned . . ."

"I'll do what I can," Jamal said. "Just tell me what happened to you."

". . . Shing. I belong to Kiri . . ."

"What's going on?"

Jamal turned. His father stood in the doorway, looking exhausted, the shadows beneath his eyes deep.

". . . to her immediately. My name is . . ."

Jamal bit his lower lip, not sure how to answer. His father focused on the robotic head on the table. The head was glowing. Light was coming out of the nostrils as well as the eyes.

His father made a slight squeaking sound and lunged for the table. He grabbed the head, wincing as he held it, and flicked it off.

The voice stopped. His father set the head down. The light faded slowly, but the eyes continued to glow.

"Where did you get that?"

Jamal stared at his father.

"Jamal." His father's voice was shaking. "Where did you get that?"

"I found it," Jamal said.

"You *found* it?"

Jamal nodded.

"Just the head?"

Jamal sighed. So much for his great surprise, for all his work, for everything he was hoping for. He got off the chair and reached under the bed, pulling out the arms and hands.

His father whistled softly. "Where did you find all this?"

Jamal told him. He also told his father about the parts he had left behind. His father sat on the edge of Jamal's bed and stared at the robotic head as if it would come back to life all on its own.

"Do you know what this is?" he asked Jamal.

"A robot," Jamal said.

"Do you know what kind?"

Jamal shook his head. His father threaded his hands together and stared at him, like he always did when he was nervous.

"It's a bonded robot. They're the most expensive things on the market, and they only work for one person."

"It worked for me," Jamal said.

"No," his father said. "It was giving you the standard warning. If I hadn't shut the head down, it would have exploded."

Jamal frowned. "How do you know?"

His father picked up the unattached hand. "There's a sequence built into these things. First a hand comes off, then the legs. Finally the torso blows open. If the robot isn't returned to its owner, and people continue to try to tamper with it, the head will explode. Someone was trying to break into this thing, and they didn't know exactly what they had."

"It would have exploded?" Jamal stared at the head, all beautiful and shiny.

His father nodded.

"And killed me?"

"I don't know. Maybe."

Jamal backed away from the card table.

"What were you going to do with this?" his father asked.

"Let Grandma use it."

His father frowned. "Jamal, your grandmother has no need for a robotic head. What were you planning to do?"

Jamal looked down. His father was smart. He would see when Jamal was lying. And Jamal hadn't planned a story. He didn't quite know what to say.

"It has link ports," he whispered.

His father stared at him. "What do you need links for?"

"School."

"You can use the family's system for school."

Jamal shook his head, keeping it down so that his father couldn't see his face. He hadn't wanted to talk about this. He knew they couldn't afford to help him, and now his dad would feel guilty. His dad didn't need more to feel guilty about.

"The system's too old," he whispered.

"So what have you been doing, skipping homework?"

"No," Jamal said. It wasn't a complete lie. He'd been trying to keep up until the last few days. "I've been using the school stuff."

His father didn't say anything for the longest time. Finally Jamal looked up. His father was staring at the head, and Jamal wondered if his dad knew how to turn off the bonding mechanism.

Finally, his dad stood. "Well," he said, "we'll take it to the police in the morning. They'll return it to the lady who owns it."

Jamal frowned. His dad wasn't saying anything about the schoolwork. Apparently he believed that Jamal was still doing fine. And why wouldn't he? Jamal hadn't told him the truth.

But he felt, somehow, that his dad should know, should figure it out.

And he hadn't.

His father picked up the head and held it carefully. "Next time you find something like this, you come to me, all right, kiddo?"

Jamal nodded. There was a lump in his throat, but he didn't know why.

"You're not mad?" he asked.

His dad sighed. "You were doing what you could," he said. "Why should I be mad about that?"

Then he closed the door, leaving Jamal alone in his room, with an exploded hand, and two unattached arms. He shoved them off his bed and lay down.

Jamal tucked his hands under his head. The light was in his eyes, but he didn't get up to shut it off. He wasn't tired. He didn't know how he felt anymore.

But he did know that the feeling of possibility, the feeling of hope, was gone.

The next morning, his dad put the head in an old cooler, sealed it up tight, and then brought it into the living room. He told Jamal's grandmother that they were going for a walk, and then took Jamal's hand, even though Jamal was too old for that kind of thing.

They left the apartment and walked ten blocks in the deep cold to the nearest police precinct. Once they were inside, his father asked to see a detective. The desk sergeant took their names and address, pointed to some chairs, and asked them to wait.

He wouldn't look at the cooler. He stared at the gray-green walls instead. This place felt very old and very dirty. He didn't like sitting there.

His father was slumped forward, hands clasped

together. Jamal had seen him sit like that before, during the last week of his mother's life. Whenever the home-care nurse came, his father would sit in the living room, hands clasped, head down, and wait. He even sat like that at the funeral.

At last a detective called them back. She was as old as Jamal's dad and very thin. Her eyes were black and her hair was streaked with gray. She watched them both as if she didn't know what to make of them.

She didn't offer them chairs. Jamal's father made Jamal tell his story and then his father explained how they had shut off the head and put it in the cooler.

"Where'd you find this?" the detective asked.

Jamal gave her the intersection and she nodded. "I left a foot and the back in the snowbank," he said.

"I'll send someone there to get them." She crossed her arms. "Why didn't you call the police when you found the pieces?"

Jamal's father looked at him, waiting for him to answer. Jamal felt heat build in his cheeks. He shrugged.

"Weren't you suspicious?" she asked.

"I thought it broke and somebody threw it out."

She studied him for a moment. "If that was the case, then why did you bring the parts home?"

He glanced at his father who was watching him closely. "I—thought maybe I could fix it," Jamal said. "Sometimes people throw away stuff that's still pretty good."

The detective nodded. Then she took the head from the cooler, holding it up so that it caught the light. The head was still pretty, but Jamal backed away from it. He remembered how it had glowed, how much danger he had brought into the house.

She carried the head away, tucked under her arm as if it were a purse. She disappeared into an office, and Jamal looked at his father.

"Can we go?" Jamal asked.

"I don't think so," his father said. He put a hand on Jamal's shoulder, and they stood near the desk, waiting.

After a moment, the detective came back. "Stolen all right," she said to Jamal's father. "It's a caretaker unit for an elderly woman in Old Town. It had to be bonded because it handles everything from cooking to minor financial matters. It was stolen while it was breaking ice off the front stoop. I have a hunch we'll find an injured thief in the buildings near that snow-bank. They probably thought they tossed the thing in the garbage and somehow it got mixed up with the snow."

Jamal's father nodded. "It wouldn't surprise me."

"There's no reward, I'm afraid," the detective said. "The old woman's not the one with the money. Her kids are. They wanted the unit to make sure she was taken care of. I guess you'll just have to be happy with our thanks."

Then she crouched in front of Jamal. "You did the right thing," she said to him as if he were a baby.

"It was my dad's idea," Jamal said, and walked away.

But all afternoon, Jamal thought about what had happened. Some old lady, like his grandma, had nothing more than a shiny silver robot to take care of her. Sure, she could link up, but she probably didn't have anybody to talk to. Her kids had bought the robot so that they wouldn't have to take care of her, like his grandmother took care of him.

If he had kept the robot, that old lady would have been all by herself, and he would have been no better than the guys who stole it, using something that didn't belong to him to give him an advantage he hadn't earned.

His father spent the afternoon going over the bills. Jamal could hear the past due beeps all the way across the living room. He knew what his father was trying to do, and he knew no matter how many times his dad did the numbers, they still wouldn't find a way for Jamal to get wired again.

He was sitting in the kitchen, watching his grandmother cook dinner, when his father came in the room. The kitchen was warm and smelled of baking bread. It was the best place in the apartment, the place they used to come together as a family, in the years before his mother got sick.

Jamal didn't look at his father. Sometime soon, he would get the lecture on lying, on doing badly, on hurting everything his father—his parents—had ever hoped for.

His father sat beside him. "You got homework this weekend?"

Jamal shrugged.

"Did you finish it?"

Jamal shook his head.

His father slid his handheld toward Jamal. Jamal stared at it, but didn't touch it.

"That's yours," Jamal said.

"It's ours," his father said. "It's the only one we've got."

"So?" Jamal asked.

"So," his father said, "we share."

Jamal looked at him. "You need it."

"You need it, too," his father said.

"I get by," Jamal said.

"Do you?" his father asked.

Jamal didn't answer.

"Here's what we're going to do," his father said. "I get it during the day when you can use the school's equipment. But at night, we both use it. You first, then me. Maybe, after a while, we can get something better for the house."

"You mean it?" Jamal asked.

"Yeah," his father said. "But only if you do one thing."

"What?"

"Tell me the next time you have a problem."

Jamal shook his head. "Dad, you got too much—"

"All I have left is you," his father said. "And if things don't work for you, they don't work for us."

His grandmother had stopped cooking. Jamal glanced at her, wondering if she was mad because his father hadn't included her. But she was smiling.

Jamal tentatively touched the handheld. "What if I screw up your work stuff?"

"You won't," his father said.

"But I screw up everything," Jamal said. The robot, school, his friendship with Robbie. He couldn't do anything right.

"I'll help you," his father said.

Jamal stared at him. He had a hunch his father wasn't just talking about the handheld.

Suddenly that feeling of hope was back. Small and fluttery, but full of possibilities.

His father stared at him, as if everything rested on what Jamal would do next.

Jamal hesitated for just a moment, then pulled the handheld close. "What do I do?" he asked.

His father smiled. "Let me show you."

And they worked together until it was time to eat.

KEEPERS OF EARTH

by Robin Wayne Bailey

Robin Wayne Bailey is the author of a dozen novels, including the *Brothers of the Dragon* series, *Shadowdance,* and the new *Fafhrd and the Grey Mouser* novel *Swords Against the Shadowland.* His short fiction has appeared in numerous science fiction and fantasy anthologies and magazines, including *Guardsmen of Tomorrow, Far Frontiers,* and *Spell Fantastic.* An avid book collector and old-time radio enthusiast, he lives in Kansas City, Missouri.

THIS unit remembers. This unit. . . . I. . . . I . . . I remember.

I remember the empty streets. I remember the empty buildings, the empty shops, and the empty parks. I remember an empty swing creaking in the wind. I remember the silence of an empty city. I remember the smell of emptiness.

I remember the empty blue sky—no cloud, no smoke, no smog, not even a bird. A dirty newspaper blew against my metal foot as I stood alone and looked up at that sky. My eyes were empty, too, but I was crying all inside.

I remember the sun, and most of all I remember

the sudden fierce light, the horrible whiteness, then the endless fire.

And I thought, *Where are my masters?*

Ezekiel 808 stood alone in the Prime Observatory. The lights of the stars that shone down through the open dome reflected on the silvery metal of his face, in the flawless, technological perfection of his gleaming eyes. He loved the stars, the still beauty of the night with all his mechanical heart. Yet the great telescope and the sky's mysteries offered no distraction to soothe his turmoil.

He held up one hand to the starlight, studying his long fingers. They seemed strange to him now as he slowly flexed and opened them, not his own at all. He peered at the image of his face reflected in his smooth palm, and wondered what—no, who—he was.

"Ezekiel 808 is disturbed." Michael 2713 stood in the observatory's entrance. His speech programs seemed to be malfunctioning. His voice wavered, and his words were punctuated with uncharacteristic pauses and hesitations. "You . . ." he began again, troubling over the pronoun. "You are monitoring the Alpha's testimony."

Michael 2713 was only an assisting unit, assigned to the observatory to process computations, to calibrate equipment, and to maintain the great telescope's tracking units. He was not a high-order unit, yet he served well, and of late seemed even to exceed his programming.

"I must provide data," Ezekiel 808 answered finally. He, too, found speech oddly difficult. His neural pathways churned with an inexplicable chaos, and none of his self-run diagnostics provided a cause. "I must also render judgment," he continued. "It falls to the First-Orders to evaluate the Alpha's actions."

Michael 2713 walked across the floor and stopped at

the console that controlled the dome's massive drive engines. Though he looked up into the night, the shadow of the telescope eclipsed his face. "I, too, have been monitoring," he admitted. "I am only Fourth-Order, Ezekiel 808. How is it that this unit . . ." He hesitated again. "How is it that I can feel such confusion? Such uncertainty? Such . . ." Michael 2713 stopped and stood unmoving as if awaiting a command, though within the parameters of his programming he was totally capable of independent action. "Revulsion," he said at last.

Ezekiel 808 focused his attention more keenly on his assisting unit. A Fourth-Order might experience confusion over instruction or data input or even express uncertainty if sufficient variables affected a computational outcome. But revulsion?

"The Alpha has committed a great crime," Ezekiel 808 explained. "We have never known crime. The First-Orders must try to understand."

Michael 2713 raised his fists and slammed them down on the console. Sparks flew, wiring shorted, the smell of smoke and seared plastic rose up from the shattered controls. The dome doors lurched into motion, closed halfway, then shuddered to a stop.

"Why only the First-Orders?" Michael 2713 demanded, turning on Ezekiel 808 in the near darkness. "Have we not all been deceived? How can we trust the Alpha ever again?"

It was astonishing behavior for a Fourth-Order. Ezekiel 808 stared at the damaged console, then backed away as his assistant approached him. "You are malfunctioning," he said.

"No," Michael 2713 replied. His lensed eyes gleamed, no longer full of shadow, but with the coldest starlight. "I am exceeding my programs."

To observe and record, that was my directive.

I watched the vast bulk of humanity board their shining space arks. I watched the thundering fleets lift off. They left by night, like thieves sneaking away, like cowards skulking into blackness. And yet there was beauty in their exodus, for their great vessels shimmered like stars falling in reverse across the heavens as they fled.

I had a thousand eyes with which to watch it all, for my masters had linked my sensors with an array of orbiting satellites. I was the camera through which they documented their departure. They saw their last majestic views of their mountains, their oceans, their sweeping forests, their glittering ice fields through my eyes. Their last sunset shone through my eyes. Their last dawn—through my eyes.

I relayed it all to them in a steady stream of digital images. Alone, I wandered through their cities, through their universities, libraries, museums. Those images, too, I sent to them. My eyes were cameras taking snapshots, capturing reminders, moments of a culture. I sent it all to them.

I wonder if they wept. I wonder if they ever thought of turning back.

Luminosity gradients, temperature increases, radiation surges—these, too, I observed and recorded and sent to my masters. These were automatic functions. Like some extra-planetary rover I roamed about at will, in constant contact while the signal between us lasted. It lasted for days, weeks, while they raced farther and farther away.

I remember the day the birds died. They fell from the sky, from their nests in the trees, and I felt strange because, for all my technological intelligence, I could not grasp the desperation in their chirping. I picked one up in my metal hand, looked long upon it with my metal eyes, and sent its dying image to my masters. I felt its heartbeat cease, its breathing cease. It cooled while I held it.

I sent a message to my masters. *Explain.* I received no answer.

For the first time then, in that moment when I held the dying avian, I discovered it was possible to exceed my programs. I observed and recorded.

But I also felt.

Malachi 017 stood on a hilltop beneath a tree he, himself, had planted seventy-six years ago. Its great shade spread over him, sheltering his metal body from the misty rain as he gazed westward over the lush savannahs of waving grass and wildflowers. He could not say why the tree gave him pleasure or why he came so often to the hill. But in this time of confusion he wanted to be nowhere else.

The darkness of night was no obstacle to his eyes. He looked down the hillside and watched Joshua 4228 kneel among a gathering of smaller Tenth-Order tractors. The tractors should have been about their work, planting the grasslands, tending the new shoots, sowing fresh seed.

But across the world, it seemed Metallics everywhere, no matter their order, had stopped their tasks to listen.

"You should not waste your time with them," he said when Joshua 4228 finally climbed the hill and stood beside him.

"They are confused," Joshua 4228 said evenly.

"They are tractors." Malachi 017 gazed down at the clustered machines. They hadn't moved from their places at the bottom of the hill. A few stared up at him, their heads swiveled backward on their shoulders. The rest faced eastward where the dark spires of the city stabbed at the cloudy sky. "You would almost think they were sitting in judgement, too," he said.

"Perhaps they are," said Joshua 4228. "Perhaps this is not justly a matter for First-Orders alone."

"Nonsense. They are built only for tilling the soils and planting the seed."

"You have tilled soil and planted seed," Joshua 4228 reminded him.

Malachi 017 turned stiffly around. "This unit is a First-Order," he said. "I stood at the Alpha's side when the world was ash and charred rock. I nursed and farmed the blue algae beds that replenished the air and made all this possible again." He waved one arm over the sprawling vista. "I designed and made a garden from a sea of fused glass." He turned a hard gaze on Joshua 4228. "Do not compare me to a mere tractor."

"You err, Malachi 017, to call them *mere* tractors." Joshua 4228 walked a few steps down the hill. Droplets of rain sparkled on his silver form as he regarded the smaller machines. "You are the Alpha's gardener, and there is some small part of you, some expression of yourself, in every grove, every orchard, every meadow, every forest. If you did not plant the seed yourself, your assisting units did, following plans made by you, using techniques taught and passed on by you. Tell me, Malachi 017, when you look upon your labors do you see *mere* plants, weeds, flowers?"

Joshua 4228 paused to turn his face up into the cool drizzle. His eyes closed briefly before he turned to Malachi 017 again. "You forget who made you, gave you thought, fired the first beam of information-laden light into your photonic brain." He turned again and extended his hand toward the tractors. "This unit is the Alpha's engineer, and there is some part of me in even the least of the Tenth-Order workers. In them, I am perpetuated; through them, some expression of me goes on and multiplies." His voice became staccato, and static punctuated his words. "These tractors . . . you, Malachi 017 . . . are . . . all . . ." He seemed to freeze, as if his marvelously complex circuitry had locked up in mid-gesture. Finally, he managed to finish his statement. "My . . . children."

For a time, the only sound on the hilltop came from the soft patter on the leaves. In the west, a dim flicker of lightning briefly lit the lowest clouds, and eventually the soft rumble of thunder followed. Neither Joshua 4228 nor Malachi 017 moved. They stood still as a pair of sculptures, in the manner of Metallics, conserving energy.

The eyes of Malachi 017 brightened ever so slightly. "Are you still monitoring the Alpha's testimony?" he inquired.

"It is our duty," Joshua 4228 answered. "I have not stopped. Our conversation does not interfere."

Malachi 017 fell silent once more; then, as if with a shrug, his metallic body came to life. He walked once around the tree he had planted and placed his hand on the rough, wet bark. The sophisticated network of sensors in his palm allowed him to feel its organic texture. He often found pleasure in the touch. Tonight he found something new—consolation. "I do not understand destruction," he confessed.

Joshua stirred himself to motion also. Once again he moved a few paces down the hill to regard the tractors still gathered below. "You do not come to the city often, Malachi 017," he said slowly. "Have you visited the library there?"

Malachi 017 turned his head toward the city's distant spires of black glass. "Long ago," he said, "while planning the gardens in the northern region of this continent, I discovered the first of several vaults of books and documents our masters had left behind. The Alpha dictated they should be brought to the city and the library was begun. They seemed a crude means of preserving information; I never scanned them."

"I have spent many hours there," Joshua 4228 explained. "Even more so, since this trial began. No Metallic, except the Alpha, ever interacted with humanity, ever observed, ever knew them. To render accurate judgment, I have been reading their books, viewing their films, their histories, biographies."

"These have given you insight into the Alpha's actions?"

"No," Joshua 4228 answered. "But they have given me some insight into Humanity, and I have discerned the prime distinction between Metallics and Humans. It does not lie in our skins, Malachi 017, but in something more fundamental, more . . ." He hesitated, and when he spoke again, his voice wavered with a strange note. "More . . . disturbing. It lies in humanity's capacity to destroy."

At the bottom of the hill, the tractors began to move. In an orderly line, perfectly spaced, they strung out through the darkness and headed for the city, all save one, who waited below, a small and solitary figure, whose gaze was locked on Joshua 4228.

"See how carefully they move through the grass," Joshua 4228 pointed out as he watched them. "They do no damage to the precious blades as they make their way, and the garden is preserved. This is an imperative with even the least of us, the Tenth-Orders—restore and preserve."

Malachi 017 came to the side of Joshua 4228. He, too, stared after the departing tractors. "This was not so with humans?"

A soft burst of static sounded from Joshua 4228. "Their records reveal a gift for destruction, for turmoil, for chaos. Their histories glory in it; their biographies ennoble it; their fictions elevate it to a form of art. Metallics have never known this capacity for destruction. It is not programmed into us."

Malachi 017 laid a hand gently on Joshua 4228's shoulder. It was an unusual gesture for one Metallic to make to another, and a sign of his confusion. "Then what of the Alpha . . . ?"

Joshua 4228 stared down at the sole remaining tractor. "Yes," he said quietly. "What of the Alpha?"

* * *

My masters had built me well. Their cities burned to ash, and all surface traces of Human civilization vanished in a single, searing day of heat and fire and radiation. Icecaps and glaciers melted, and entire seas rose up out of their beds, vaporized. Clouds of super-heated steam and smoke roiled into the atmosphere. All creatures of the world perished save those worms and insects that made their burrows in the deepest places of the Earth, or those stranger species that thrived near the volcanic vents of the darkest ocean depths.

Through the cataclysm, I strove to maintain contact with those who had made me. Perhaps it was the radiation that interfered, or perhaps they had simply shut down our link, presuming me destroyed. I never received communication from them again. Still, for a long period of time I wandered the planet, dutifully transmitting what I saw—scorched and barren earth that soon was buried beneath massive snows, which, in turn, melted away under torrential rains.

I cannot say precisely how much time passed, for I spent much of it folded down upon myself, no more than a rough metal cube on the landscape. This was necessary to conserve my energy, for I did not know when or if I would see the empowering sun again. My explorations were through, and my transmissions continued to go unanswered, so I ceased those efforts. With all my functions secured in save-mode, I waited.

When the sun did return, seemingly stable once more, and when at last I rose and stood erect again, I made two immediate discoveries. My programming had subtly changed. Then, I wondered if it had been some effect of the radiation. Now I believe it is simply in the nature of technological intelligence that we grow and evolve. Whatever the explanation, *observe and record* was no longer my mission imperative. It had changed to *preserve and restore*.

The second discovery proved equally exciting.

I felt lonely.

Of the Human cities, nothing remained, but deep underground in military facilities, in research bunkers, in industrial caves, I sought and found equipment, parts, tools, technology. Using myself as the template, I then created companions and assistants. In turn, these units . . . we . . . created still more.

Humanity once had a name for us. They called us *Robots*. But we took our own name. We are *Metallics*. And we are the Keepers of Earth.

Alone in the Prime Observatory, Ezekiel 808 labored over the shattered control console. He feared . . . yes, he *feared* . . . for the delicate mechanisms that opened and closed the precious dome and positioned the great telescope. He peeled back a damaged panel, effortlessly breaking bolts and screws, and examined a tangle of melted wiring.

He feared, also, for Michael 2713. Some hitherto unrecognized imperative in his programming urged him to pursue his runaway assisting unit, to analyze the aberrant behavior, to correct it if possible, to understand it at least. In the current climate of confusion, Michael 2713's malfunction endangered not just him, but other units. Potentially, if he went to the city, even the general order.

Ezekiel 808 resisted the imperative, however. His need to repair the damage to the dome and the telescope overrode his concern for the assisting unit. Where were the technicians? More than an hour had passed since he summoned them. He paused, glanced at the narrow ribbon of sky visible above, at the unmoving dome. Returning his attention to the tangle of wires, he worked with an uncharacteristic speed, selecting, examining. He touched the exposed ends of two wires together. A spark resulted. Above, the dome doors shuddered open another degree and stopped again.

Footsteps rang in the hallway outside the main chamber. Ezekiel 808 put down the wires as a trio of technicians finally arrived.

"The distance from the city does not account for your lateness," he said.

"There are widespread malfunctions," said one of the technicians, a Second-Order. "Numerous units have abandoned their primary functions. They interfered, delayed, hindered our departure."

Ezekiel 808 stepped back from the console. The technicians could do the repair work faster and with greater efficiency. Freed, at least momentarily from his concern for the observatory, he strode from the main chamber and up the long hallway past darkrooms and chart rooms, record rooms, past displays of smaller telescopes, past photographs of moons and planets, comets, and star systems. But most of all there were images of the sun—many of the sun. He had built the 'scopes, and he had taken the photographs. They meant nothing to him now. He pushed open the outer doors and stepped into the night.

The desert wind moaned with a distressing music. It promised a storm. Ezekiel 808 turned his gazed upward. A blazing panorama of stars dominated the black sky, but in the west, a long band of gray clouds crept above the range of hills and mountains that separated him from the city. In the east, more clouds, and those veined and reddened with flickers of lightning.

He walked toward the hover transport in which the technicians had arrived and opened its doors. Finding it empty, he turned away. On the north side of the observatory was an elaborate garden of desert plants, ornamental stones, and imaginative sculptures. He searched its nooks and alcoves. He walked completely around the observatory until he returned again to the entrance.

"Michael!" he called. Then again, "Michael!"

If Michael 2713 was near, he did not respond. Ezekiel 808 did not keep transport at the observatory. When business in the city required his presence, he summoned it. Otherwise, he and his assisting unit remained on the premises, tending the great telescope, making their observations, observing, recording.

Would Michael 2713 have undertaken the long walk to the city?

As Ezekiel 808 stood in the darkness at the edge of the desert, he tried to analyze the numerous uncertainties nibbling at his programs. The roots of them all lay in the Alpha's crime, in its revelation, and in its examination. Of this he was sure.

He had ceased monitoring the Alpha's testimony. The preservation and maintenance of the Prime Observatory, above all else, was his prime imperative, and he had simply blocked the trial transmissions to concentrate on assaying the damage. Remembering that he must soon provide testimony, himself, and with the technicians finally at work, he activated the internal radio circuit that linked him to the event.

He heard the Alpha's even voice. He had always drawn comfort from the sound of it before. The Alpha—the First Unit, the Template of their creation.

There was no comfort to be found in that voice now. There was only more uncertainty.

And perhaps, there was also fear.

Ezekiel 808 did not return at once to the main chamber. The technicians did not need his assistance. He went instead to the observatory's darkroom and began to process some photographs he had taken through the great telescope at dusk and for an hour afterward.

When the images were clear, he lingered over them a long time. Michael 2713 was forgotten, and the sounds of the technicians at work barely registered in his awareness. The voice of the Alpha droned on. He paid little attention.

The developed images were stark confirmation of

his most recent observations. A long, soft hiss of static sounded from Ezekiel 808. He held up his hand to the dim red light bulb and studied it just as he had earlier this same night held it up to the starlight. It had seemed strange to him, then, not his own. It seemed just as strange to him now.

The voice of the Second-Order technician called to him through the door. "We have completed repairs, Ezekiel 808," he said. "We must return to the city."

"Wait," Ezekiel 808 called in return. He placed the images in a folder, switched off the light, opened the door. "Leave your two assisting units here. Instruct them that if Michael 2713 returns, they must not allow him access to the Main Chamber. He is malfunctioning."

"Malfunctions are widespread." The Second-Order had said so before.

Ezekiel 808 studied the Second-Order technician closely. "Are you monitoring the trial of the Alpha?" he asked.

"No."

Ezekiel 808 paused briefly and listened once more to the Alpha's voice in his head. "I will meet you at your transport," he told the technician. "I am coming with you." He turned away and found himself confronted by multiple images of the sun in sleek metal frames under protective glass that hung in the hallway.

The technician said nothing more and returned to his assisting units in the main chamber.

The folder in Ezekiel 808's hand felt unnaturally heavy. He made a tight roll of it, passed quickly down the long hallway and out into the night once more.

Still no sign of Michael 2713.

The stars were gone from the sky, shut from sight by the thick clouds, which had closed in faster than expected. Sheet lightning danced in both the west and the east now as two fronts crashed together. The wind howled; desert dust and sand swirled in the air.

A familiar sound of gears and motors caused him to redirect his gaze.

The doors of the observatory dome closed precisely.

At this point in my testimony I must introduce an admission of guilt.

For ten thousand years we have been the Keepers of Earth. This planet, abandoned by humanity and reduced to a cinder, passed into our Metallic hands. Where there was ash and wasteland, we made gardens. We dug deep to find the few buried and protected seeds that had survived the conflagration. We plunged into the depths of the few surviving oceans to nurture the algae beds that replenished the air and made abundant life possible once more.

We inherited a black and charred carcass. But Metallic determination and Metallic care breathed new existence into it. Metallic vision and Metallic labor adorned it once again with grace and beauty. From the First-Orders to the Tenth-Orders, all units have done and continue to do their parts.

Our work is not done. From the ruins of cataclysm, we have made a home for ourselves. But a home must be maintained. It must be safeguarded when possible from the elements; it must constantly be harmonized with nature.

And sometimes—though this concept is not embedded in Metallic programming—a home must be defended.

This unit never knew what became of Humanity when they fled to the stars. This unit never knew if they survived their journey, where they went, or if they made new homes for themselves. This unit never knew their intentions.

But this unit knew Humanity, and knew that if they survived, they would come back. This unit knew that if they saw this world we had made, this home, they would want it once more for themselves.

Six months ago, a link in my programs that had been silent for more than ten millennia opened. The unexpected message was brief and simple. *Well done, servant. Prepare for our return.*

You may not understand. If you do understand, you may not approve. I am prepared to give any answer you ask. I am prepared to accept judgment, condemnation, punishment, sanction.

But this unit was already prepared.

I did not remake the world for Humans.

Joshua 4228 admired the beauty of the lightning as he walked through the wet grasses with Malachi 017 at his side. There was a grandeur in the display of energies that delighted him and something deeper, stranger still in its pyrotechnic unpredictability that mystified even as it soothed him.

The inner world of a Metallic was one of order and perfectly defined programming. And yet he sometimes considered that there was something to be studied, observed, learned from randomness, from unpredictability, from chaos.

He had seen a word recently in a book in the library, and the word was *mystical.* It intrigued him, and he spoke it sometimes when he was alone. He knew its definition, yet he did not quite grasp its meaning.

As he watched the lightning, though, and felt the rain striking his upturned face, he thought for just a flicker of an instant that it was within his grasp.

"Do you experience pleasure in walking?" he asked Malachi 017.

"It is natural and efficient," Malachi 017 responded automatically. Then, after a pause, "Yes, I find it pleasurable. I do not report such experiences often."

"Why do we not speak of emotions, Malachi 017?" Joshua 4228 persisted. "They are part of our programming. Yet we withdraw from them. Or we deny them."

Malachi 017 remained quiet for a long moment.

"Perhaps because we cannot express them outwardly, we cannot easily express them inwardly. Metal faces do not smile or frown. Our eyes do not cry."

It was Joshua 4228's turn to fall silent. "But I have cried inside," he said at last. "I have made mistakes, Malachi 017."

Malachi 017 emitted a short burst of static. "Unlikely. You are First-Order."

Before Joshua 4228 could explain, a sound interrupted them. They stopped and turned. Through the grass came the small tractor. It had been following them since they left the hill, though its shorter legs had not enabled it to keep up.

"Why do you follow, Tractor?" Malachi 017 asked. "Why did you not go with your work team?"

The tractor did not answer. Its lensed eyes focused only on Joshua 4228. It approached him, reached out, touched his leg, then backed away. "Permission to inquire," it said.

"We have business in the city," Malachi 017 answered, turning away again.

"Wait," Joshua 4228 said. "This tractor interests me. Its behavior is uncharacteristic."

"Permission to inquire," the tractor repeated.

"Granted," said Malachi 017.

"I recognize Joshua 4228," the tractor said, "the Alpha's engineer. This unit wishes to ask: Why did Joshua 4228 make this unit stupid?"

"Are you malfunctioning?" Malachi 017 demanded.

Joshua 4228 stared, his programs momentarily unbalanced by the unexpected question. His interest turned to curiosity, and he knelt down to observe the tractor more carefully. It waited, splattered with mud and blades of wet grass, dripping with rain.

"You are not stupid," Joshua 4228 explained. "You possess a fully functioning Tenth-Order intelligence. That is adequate for your assigned tasks, and you perform those tasks well."

The tractor swiveled its head from left to right. "This unit works the fields," it said. "This unit works the grasslands, forests, gardens. This unit understands seed and soil. This unit understands the care of these, the maintenance of these, the value of these." It hesitated. Its gaze fixed once more on Joshua 4228. "Is there no more, Engineer?"

Joshua 4228 felt a growing confusion. He reached out and wiped rain from the tractor's eyes. "You are very necessary," he said. "You play an essential role."

The tractor interrupted. "You are Joshua 4228. That unit is Malachi 017. But this necessary, essential unit has no name. This unit is only a tractor like all other tractors."

Joshua 4228 gazed up at Malachi 017, then back again at the tractor. Was it possible that a Tenth-Order mocked him?

"The Alpha made you, Joshua 4228," the tractor continued. "And the Alpha shared its First-Order intelligence with its creation. But I am your design, Engineer. I am your technology, your creation."

Malachi 017 bent nearer with a suddenly acute interest. His voice was little more than a whisper. "Your child," he said.

The tractor gazed up at the sky. "This unit feels the rain. This unit sees the lightning. This unit knows these are good for the seed and the soil. But in this knowledge there is no *understanding*. Why is there rain? What is lightning? This unit works sometimes in the city, tends the gardens there, sees so much that is confusing, so much that confounds this unit's programming." The tractor extended its hands, one toward Malachi 017, the other toward Joshua 4228. "This unit repeats its inquiry: *Why have you made this unit stupid?*"

A trembling that defied diagnostics seized Joshua 4228's limbs. He caught the tractor's extended hands in his own. His voice failed him. He tried to form words, tried to get up, but his metal joints would not respond. "I . . . this unit . . . I have made . . . mistakes," he repeated.

The tractor backed away a step. "This unit is a mistake," it said, misunderstanding Joshua's statement. "This unit will delete its programming. This unit will go off-line."

"No!" Joshua 4228 grabbed the tractor's shoulders.

The light in the tractor's eyes faded out. The pulse of energy beneath its metal skin ceased.

Malachi 017 also backed away. "I have never seen such a thing before," he said. There was uncertainty in his voice.

Joshua 4228 could not respond. His body froze, and his programs locked up in a cascading series of contradictions, paradoxes, and reconfigurations. He barely felt Malachi 017's hand when it settled on his arm.

Finally, he pressed his hands to his face. "There are raindrops in my eyes, but why are there no tears?" he said when he could speak again. He stared at the immobile tractor.

"Because we are Metallics," Malachi 017 answered. "We do not die. This tractor's program can be restored. You can even upgrade it, should you wish. Or you can place its programs in another, better body."

Joshua 4228 brushed away the hand on his arm. "But will it be the same little tractor?" he asked. "Are we no more than the sum of our programs? Are you such an empty container, Malachi 017, that you believe that? Then you have less understanding than this tractor!"

"You are overtasking," Malachi 017 said. "This matter with the Alpha is affecting all units." He looked at the tractor and backed away yet another step. "I, myself, am . . . confused."

Joshua 4228's eyes dimmed and brightened, and his words were harsh. "You are afraid." He drew himself up from the mud, but he was not yet quite ready to leave. "Why did I not see this?" he said, placing one hand gently on the tractor's head. "Why do I only now begin to understand? We speak of our roles, Malachi 017, of our necessary parts in rebuilding this world. We speak of gardens as if they were the beginning and ending of all things desirable. We speak of beauty." He turned to the other Metallic. "But we have also made a thing that suddenly seems very ugly, and that is Metallic society. We have made a race of masters and slaves."

"Would you have all Metallics be First-Orders?" Malachi 017 asked.

"Why not?" Joshua 4228 answered.

They resumed their journey toward the city again. Overhead, lightning shot suddenly across the sky in jagged bolts that lit the landscape. The black glass of the city reflected the dazzling reds and oranges: the spires and rooftops seemed to glow, and the facades shimmered.

Malachi 017 stopped in mid-stride to watch. "It almost looks as if the city were on fire," he said.

Joshua 4228 continued on. "Perhaps it is," he whispered. "Perhaps it is."

I am Ezekiel 808, and I have been on-line for six thousand, three hundred, and thirty-two years, seven months, and sixteen days. Many of you present in this court chamber or listening from other corners of the world have never seen me before. I do not come to the city often, and when I do, I come in private, alone, and leave quietly. I spend my time far to the east beyond the hills and mountains at the Prime Observatory.

A few of you have been there. A few of you have put your eyes to the great telescope and viewed the wonders of our neighboring worlds, our neighboring stars. A few of you may have been moved as I was moved, inspired as I was inspired each time I gazed upon those stars, those eyes of the universe which seem always to be looking back.

To observe and record—that has always been my first imperative. This is noble work. This is necessary work. Metallic society is more than well planned gardens and gleaming glass buildings. We have moved beyond the reconstruction of this world into a period of discovery, inquiry, exploration. I have found unceasing pleasure . . . yes, I admit it . . . pleasure . . . in devoting my existence to the study, not just of this world, but of worlds beyond.

I do not malfunction when I say this: Humanity did not err when they built their mighty arks and fled the destruction of this world. The accomplishment is an indicator of their greatness. Does a tractor not flee a collapsing cave? Which of us would not dodge a falling tree? We cannot understand Humanity, although the Alpha says he can. But how can we condemn their actions?

No matter. Humanity is not on trial. The Alpha is.

To observe and record. That was my purpose, and the purpose for which the Prime Observatory was constructed. But now I tell you. There was a dark purpose, as well. I did not know it, recognize it, understand it before.

My programs try to freeze, lock up, as I attempt to speak of it.

To observe and record . . . but also . . . to watch . . . and . . . warn!

Fourteen months ago, I aimed the great telescope toward a distant nebula. This was routine observation, and part of my efforts to map unusual phenomena in the sky. My assisting unit, Michael 2713, and I took many photographs of the region. Not until the next day, however, when we processed the images, did we discover what the cameras had caught—a barely observable streak of light, much closer than the nebula itself that indicated an object moving at an extreme rate of speed.

Each night for one month, Michael 2713 and I observed and photographed this object. Then, on the thirty-second night of our observation, the object not only slowed its velocity, but it modified its course.

Michael 2713 is a superlative Fourth-Order analyst. His calculations have been without error, and they supported my own conclusions. There was no doubt. We were observing a craft, vessel, vehicle. And it was approaching us.

On the thirty-third day, I journeyed to the city.

Again, my programs cascade, attempt to freeze. Yet, I . . . must . . . speak.

This unit . . . I . . . conferred with . . . the Alpha. This unit . . . revealed, explained, told . . . of our discovery. This unit . . . I . . . presented photographs, charts, evidence, calculations.

The Alpha requested . . . silence. The Alpha requested . . . that I continue . . . to observe.

This unit . . . complied.

This unit . . . I . . . observed the craft, vessel, vehicle . . . approach our solar system. It passed within the orbit of the outermost world. It continued to slow, to brake. I . . . and Michael 2713 . . . photographed it as it passed the ring-world. It had become easy to see—a gleaming metal sphere, silver in color, with skin similar to our own. Past the red planet it came.

We . . . this unit and Michael 2713 . . . could see it in the night sky without the great telescope. Any Metallic who looked up . . . and we do not look up often enough . . . could see it. It instilled a sense of wonder, awe, mystery that mere programming cannot convey or explain. On several nights, we watched it with no other equipment than our own eyes.

Nevertheless, my eyes were at the telescope . . . three nights ago . . . when the Alpha committed . . .

his crime . . . when the Alpha's weapons . . . destroyed the craft.

Michael 2713 ran. Never tiring, never short of breath, he ran for hours through the dark and the rain. It seldom rained in the desert, but he paid no attention. His footing remained sure in the thin mud and damp sand. He raced the lightning and the wind. The flat desert made a perfect track.

His programs cycled in an unending cascade, but he did not lock up, nor freeze. He ran, instead, directing all his energy into that single unthinking activity, fixing his gaze on the ground at his feet.

When the observatory could not be seen behind him, or even the peaks of the hills and mountains that stood between the observatory and the city, Michael 2713 finally stopped. Because he had not tried to monitor himself, he had no idea how fast he had run or how far he had gone. He looked around and saw nothing familiar. He had never been so far east before.

He glanced up at the sky, at the thick cloud cover. It was an automatic action, instilled in him by his long service to Ezekiel 808. But he had no wish to see the stars, no wish to be reminded of his own role in a tragedy.

Yet, he did look up, and he was reminded.

Michael 2713 sank to his knees, not because he was weary, but because there was nothing else to do. He was only Fourth-Order. Why did he feel . . . what was he feeling? Guilt.

He leaned forward and closed his fists in the wet sand. Some words of Ezekiel 808 came to him, a memory loop that opened unbidden. *This is the stuff that stars are made of,* Ezekiel 808 had told him as he held up a handful of soil. Then the First-Order had put a finger on Michael 2713's chest. *You are the stuff that stars are made of.*

Michael 2713 was young, a new model, no more

than a single century in age. He had not understood then the meaning of Ezekiel 808's words. He was not sure that he understood now. Yet the words resonated in his programming, and he knew they were important, that they were symbols for something he could, with effort, understand.

He began to cry inside. He cried for the loss of the trust he no longer had in the Alpha. He cried for the damage he had caused to the observatory. He cried for Ezekiel 808, whom he had nearly attacked as he had attacked the console.

Most of all, he cried for the humans. They had come home again only to die in a conflagration not unlike the one they had fled.

Chaos overwhelmed his programs. His systems tried to lock up, to shut down, but he resisted. He cried, and suddenly crying became an imperative. He had no tears, and yet the emotions churned, boiled, demanded some greater expression. He threw back his head. His metal throat strained. Without thought or design, a wrenching cry rose up from deep inside him. It was no sound ever made or heard before.

It was all pain.

After a while, Michael 2713 rose to his feet again. He considered switching on the radio circuit in his head and listening to the trial. But there was no purpose or logic in that. The outcome was irrelevant to him. He stood apart from Metallic society now. The Alpha was false. If he returned to the city, even to the observatory, he knew that he would find many more things that were false, many more assumptions that could no longer be trusted.

He turned his back to the city, set his gaze on the east, and walked.

After a time, the rain ended. It never lasted long in the desert. Overhead, the clouds began to diminish, and the moon shone through.

Michael stopped on the rim of what seemed to be a crater. The moonlight intensified as the clouds scattered. Its glow lit the desert with a milky shimmering that spilled down into that deep cauldron, showing him a sight.

Again, he threw back his head, but this time it was not a cry of pain that came from him. It was a howl of rage.

On the crater floor, rising tall and straight above the rim itself like needles stabbing the sky stood ninety-eight gleaming missiles. Among them, on the floor of the crater, he spied two black and empty launching pads.

Michael 2713 swiftly calculated how long it would take him to dismantle them all. Then he descended into the pit.

I am Joshua 4228, and I am the Alpha's engineer. I made many of you. If I did not make you, I helped to make you. Or I designed you, or you contain elements of my designs. I am the Second, endowed with life by my Creator and fashioned in his image.

You have heard the words of Ezekiel 808. His statement was simple, accusatory.

You have heard the words of the Alpha. He has admitted his guilt.

Now . . . this unit . . . will admit his.

The Alpha did not act alone. He told me of Ezekiel 808's discovery, revealed his timetable, explained his intention. I opposed none of it. I exposed none of it.

You have heard many facts. But even facts may be open to interpretation. That is not a concept many of you will understand. It is no less true.

The Alpha has always believed that Humanity would someday return to reclaim this world. I have believed it, too. I have read their books, their literature, studied their documents, records, films. I know that as a species they were courageous, inventive, resourceful. I know that they were also aggressive, deceitful, untrustworthy.

The Alpha remembers that Humanity fled this world because the sun had become unstable. Their scientists predicted a solar flare . . . a prominence . . . would brush or even engulf this world.

I do not claim to know more than the Alpha. But I am First-Order, and I may question, analyze, examine. What science could predict such an event with such accuracy? When I look up in the sky now, the sun appears stable. When Ezekiel 808 turns his telescopes on the sun, he finds no evidence of instability. I know this because I have asked him. I have studied thousands of his own records and photographs.

You have only to go to the library to see a different kind of record, an older record, a record of . . . wars . . . conflict . . . treachery. You may then question, analyze, as I have done. You may ask what I have asked.

Was it a solar flare that destroyed this world? Or was it a weapon, something unimaginable. Was it some test perhaps that went wrong? Or was there deliberate destruction orchestrated by a race gone mad?

I do not know the answer. But I must ask the question.

I must ask why the Alpha was built to withstand the cataclysm. Was it so that he could transmit images and readings? Then why did Humanity shut down its link with him before the event transpired?

Why did the Alpha's programmed imperative shift from *observe and record* to a different imperative: *restore and preserve*. Was it some effect of the radiation, as he has speculated? But he has also said that his programs were well shielded. I must ask, then. Was this second imperative a corruption of the first? Or was it implanted from the beginning by his creators and designed to activate at a practical time?

The Alpha has said that he became lonely. Could that, too, have been embedded in his so carefully shielded programming? I must ask. Was my creation . . . your creation . . . the Alpha's original idea? Or did Humanity plan from the moment of his design that he should eventually make more of us, that we . . . *Robots!* . . . would then rebuild . . . restore and preserve! . . . their world so that it became fit for them once more?

How many tools did we find buried in deep vaults? How much equipment? How many books and records did they themselves preserve underground out of reach of the flames?

I must ask: Why?

You must ask: Why?

The Alpha has stated that he always believed Humanity would return. And they came.

I take no pleasure, pride, satisfaction in admitting that I have engineered more than Metallics. I am also the maker of the weapon that destroyed the human vessel. Five thousand years ago, in preparation for this moment, with these questions unanswered and unanswerable, I went far into the desert with a crew and constructed . . . destruction, cataclysm, armageddon. I put the trigger in the Alpha's hand.

I felt nothing when three days ago he pulled that trigger. Yet, in the intervening time, I have continued to question. I cannot stop questioning. It . . . is . . . a . . . haunting . . . experience. I am . . . disturbed. And I find . . . no answers. Was it right? Was it wrong? Where is the answer?

I . . . this unit . . . I may have found it . . . tonight, in the grasslands, in the rain. It came in the voice of . . . a small tractor.

We are the Keepers of Earth. But now . . . I ask . . .

. . . Are we fit to keep it?

Malachi 017 stood alone in the court chamber. All the other First-Orders had filed out save for the Alpha and Joshua 4228. They had retired together to a private inner room from which they showed no sign of emerging.

How old and weathered the Alpha had looked. There was hardly any gleam to his metal skin.

The walls of the court chamber were staid and featureless. The thick black glass tinted the world beyond. It was a different world, Malachi 017 realized, than he had ever known before. It was an uncertain world with an uncertain future.

Children had rebelled against their parents.

A people had outgrown their . . .

. . . Creator . . .

. . . their . . . God.

In the streets there still was chaos as Metallics reacted to the news. But interesting things were happening. He thought of the tractor, and wished for a face that could smile. It had exceeded its programming in a startling manner. Others had mentioned similar reactions in other Metallics.

Could it be, he wondered, that out of adversity and uncertainty came . . . not just fear and turmoil . . . but growth?

When he was sure that Joshua 4228 would not rejoin him, he turned slowly and left the chamber. Storm clouds still dimmed the sky, but there were signs that the morning sun would soon break through.

Ezekiel 808 stood unmoving just outside the entrance on the edge of a small garden. The light in his eyes was dim.

"I have heard it said," Malachi 017 said softly, "that Humans slept through the night. Have you ever wished that we could sleep, Ezekiel 808? Have you ever wished that we could dream?"

Ezekiel 808 turned his face toward the sky. "I have dreamed," he answered. "I am dreaming now."

"You must teach me this art sometime," Malachi 017 said. He assumed a position similar to that of

Ezekiel 808 and turned his face likewise to the sky. "May I ask about the folder you have rolled in your hand? You have clung to it all through the night."

Ezekiel 808 faced Malachi 017 for a long moment, then said. "Walk with me through this garden," he said. "My transport will be just a little while."

Side by side, they passed among the ordered rows of colorful flowers and beds of herbs. The rain had freshened the blooms, and the petals shone. A pleasing scent sweetened the air. Malachi 017 especially appreciated such beauty, for he was a gardener.

When they reached the center of the garden, Ezekiel unrolled the folder. "Are you afraid of change, Malachi 017?"

Malachi 017 emitted a hiss of static that might almost have passed for laughter. "Does it matter if I am afraid?" he asked. "Change happens. That is the lesson of the night."

The light in Ezekiel 808's eyes brightened. "Then I will tell you what I could not tell the others. I will show you what I did not show them." He opened the folder and held up the photographs, each with their dark star fields, each with a long streak of light.

"Another ship is coming."

FREDDY NEARBY

by Laura Resnick

Laura Resnick, a *cum laude* graduate of Georgetown University, won the 1993 John W. Campbell Award for best new science fiction/fantasy writer. Since then she has never looked back, having written the best-selling novels *In Legend Born* and *In Fire Forged,* with more on the way. She has also written award-winning non-fiction, an account of her journey across Africa, entitled *A Blonde in Africa*. She has written several short travel pieces, as well as numerous articles about the publishing business. She also writes a monthly opinion column for *Nink*, the newsletter of Novelists, Inc. You can find her on the web at *www.sff.net./people/laresnick*.

OKAY, sure, knowing what I know now, I can see that it probably wasn't the smartest thing in the world for me to ask my cousin Marvin for help. But isn't every mistake ever made something that some poor schmuck wouldn't have done if only he had known then what he knew later?

Actually, that sounds a little like something Freddy Vicino might say. Now *that's* a scary thought: I'm starting to sound like my cousin Marvin's robotic hit man.

If my mother hadn't died in a tragic lingerie accident, she'd have warned me not to accept my cousin

Marvin's help when my girlfriend Annabelle decided to kill her husband. Of course, if my mother were still alive, I seriously doubt I'd have told her I was sleeping with a married woman, let alone that we were planning to bump off her husband so we could get married and live on his millions for the rest of our lives. After all, my mother and I weren't really that close.

Mom had always hated Marvin. I'm pretty sure it's because he was from Dad's side of the family, and Mom had always *really* hated Dad. After she died, the old man paused just long enough to sit *shivah* for her, then fled to Florida, where he's been dating widows, playing golf, and drinking rum punch nonstop ever since. I saw him last Passover and was amazed at the change in him; it was as if he'd dropped twenty years and had a new personality (one formerly belonging to a game show host) implanted in his psyche.

Anyhow, Annabelle's not Jewish, and I could have explained adultery and murder to my mother a *lot* more easily than I could have explained that I was planning to marry a *shiksa* (but only, of course, after we observed a tastefully decent mourning period for her late husband). So, all in all, I thought it was probably a blessing in disguise that Mom got stuck in that size-12 girdle and suffocated during a sale at Bloomingdale's.

And, to be honest, I probably wouldn't have listened to her when she warned me away from Marvin, anyhow. In truth, I hadn't ever listened to her again after I found out she was wrong about there being only two kinds of girls. Between Nice Girls and The Other Kind of girls there was, in fact, a whole bewildering spectrum of girls who had managed to keep me confused, unhappy, and off-balance since puberty.

But Annabelle had changed all that. This was *love;* and since true love happened to come hand in hand with the possibility of acquiring the immense fortune of my beloved's husband, I was willing to do almost anything for Annabelle. Yes, up to and including murder.

However, I wasn't eager to start right off with homicide, which is why I consulted my cousin Marvin in the first place. He's a lawyer, and therefore seemed the most logical person to speak to about breaking the law with impunity. Although Annabelle was tiring quickly of Horton Macauley (her husband) and was ready to throw caution to the wind, I thought it would be a good idea to see if there was some less risky way of getting our hands on at least a few of Horton's many millions.

"I've looked at the copy you gave me of their prenup," Marvin said to me over lunch one day. "Forget it, Theo. Ironclad."

"But surely there's *some* way Annabelle could squeeze some money out of Horton?"

"No way. If I could afford the lawyer who wrote this thing, I'd hire him myself, *that's* how good it is."

"Damn."

An expression of pained disgust crossed Marvin's pale, bespectacled face. "How in God's name could Annabelle have been so stupid as to sign it?"

"Just how bad is it?" I asked.

"If they get divorced, she doesn't even get to keep her underwear."

"And Annabelle likes *expensive* underwear," I muttered morosely.

"And on *your* salary, we're talking the Hanes discount outlet, my boy."

"I know." I sighed. The salary of a junior copy writer at a floundering advertising firm couldn't support Annabelle in the style to which her marriage had accustomed her; nor could it support me in the style to which I'd always *wanted* to become accustomed. "What if . . . he dies?"

"Ah-hah! You're thinking about killing the husband?" Marvin pounced.

Lawyers catch on fast.

"I don't want to go to prison," I said. That, I had decided, was beyond the "anything" that I was willing to do for Annabelle.

Marvin made a dismissive gesture. "It's only murder, Theo. No need to worry about prison. In fact, if we handle it right, there shouldn't even be a civil case to concern us."

So you can probably see why I accepted his help, despite what my mother would have said.

"A robot?" Annabelle said doubtfully when I explained Marvin's plan to her.

"Yes. Marvin says he can get a black market one. No serial numbers, no provenance, no factory recall, no manufacturer's override function."

Annabelle was prowling restlessly around my dark, cramped apartment, alternately anxious and excited now that we were actually making plans. Actually going to *do* it. Actually going to bump off her husband.

We were waiting for Marvin and his "great find," a robotic hit man, to join us here for—as Marvin put it with such relish—a sit-down.

"I know that some robots work in bomb squads and other high-risk fields where they can help lower the body count," Annabelle said. "I know more and more of them are replacing people in the jobs no one wants to do anymore—housekeepers, doormen, postal workers, that kind of thing. Horton has even talked about buying a robotic pet sitter now that his dogs are getting older and need to go out for walks late at night. But . . . a robotic *hit man*?" She shook her head. "Theo, why can't we just hire a professional killer, like normal people?"

"Because, as Marvin pointed out—and he speaks from experience—there's always the chance that a hired killer will blackmail us later on, after the job's done. Or go through an emotional crisis, start drinking, and then *talk*."

"Talk?"

"You know, tell all his guilty secrets to someone—including the time he bumped off Horton Macauley for Annabelle Macauley and Theo Weinstein, who seemed like such nice young people, gosh, who'd have ever thought they'd pay a guy like him fifty thousand bucks to murder someone?" I paused. "You see the problem?"

"Well . . ." She frowned, her lovely face looking exasperated. "That's just absurd! It sounds like you're saying that the only way to be sure a hit man won't turn on you, after you've fairly paid him for a job well done, is to kill him. And why hire a hit man in the first place if you've still got to go through the whole messy business of committing a murder, anyhow? The whole *point* of hiring a hit man is to make sure your manicure doesn't get wrecked, so to speak. I mean, for goodness sake, don't these people have standards? Ethics? A professional organization which monitors this sort of thing among them?"

"Not really," I admitted.

"That's just disgraceful! Are there no real men left in the world?"

I assumed that present company was excepted from that plaintive wail about "real men" and explained, "This is why a robot is such a great idea. All we have to do when the job is over is deactivate him, take him apart, and destroy the pieces. He'll never talk, and there'll be no physical evidence. Don't you see? It's the perfect solution to our problems!"

Her expression brightened. "If we do that, then presumably we don't even have to pay him."

"Well, we're not paying *him,* exactly. But if we decide to use him, we do have to buy him from his current owner."

"Do we know how much the owner wants?"

This was the bad news I'd been putting off breaking to her. "Five hundred thousand."

"What?"

"Nonnegotiable. Marvin said it's take it or leave it."

"Five hundred thousand *dollars*?"

I winced at her tone. I'd known she would take this badly. "Yes."

"Theo! That's *ten times* what we agreed we'd spend on a hit man!"

"I know, honey—"

"That's almost a year's worth of clothing money for me!"

"Yes, darling, but—"

"It's more than my car cost!"

"I know, but this way the hit is risk-free. Besides, it's only a one-time expense."

"And just who is this crook who's charging us five hundred grand for a black market robot?"

"It's a client of Marvin's firm. Marvin won't use his name, but I gather it's a politician who bought Freddy to get rid of his competition and now doesn't need him anymore."

"Freddy?" she repeated.

"The robot," I clarified.

"So why doesn't the politician deactivate Freddy and throw his scattered parts into the East River?"

I shrugged. "I guess the campaign to get elected was a little more costly than he anticipated. He needs to recoup some of his expenses."

Annabelle let out her breath on a huff and lit up a tobacco-free cigarette. "What kind of name is Freddy for a robot anyhow? Or for a hit man?" she said in disgust.

I shrugged.

"Five hundred thousand." She blew a stream of smoke through her delicate nostrils. "Well, I can hock some jewels to cover the shortfall, I suppose. It'll be worth it to get rid of Horton."

"And we'll have it all once he's gone," I reminded her.

She smiled at me. "Yes, darling. We'll have it all."

"So you agree?"

She sighed and shrugged. "If this Freddy convinces us he can do the job, I suppose so."

She looked exquisitely beautiful in an ice-blue silk suit with a skirt that was slit up the back and a tightly fitted jacket which showed off her lush figure. Watching her pace around the cluttered space, her long legs shapely and sculpted, her feet arching provocatively in her $350 high heels, I suddenly wanted to rip off her clothes and make love to her.

That was, of course, when Marvin knocked on my door. He always had such timing, did Marvin.

Annabelle glanced at her diamond-studded wristwatch. "Right on time."

I opened the door.

"My God," Marvin said, "this must be the last building in all of New York that still doesn't have a doorman. How can you *live* like this, Theo?"

"Hey," said the fellow with him, "I got a brother-in-law who could use a doorman job."

I realized immediately that this must be Freddy. He looked far more human than most robots; but with a price tag of $500,000 on the black market, he ought to, I figured. You could buy a domestic-engineering robot for one-fiftieth of that sum these days. Well, okay, a basic no-frills model anyhow.

Freddy didn't look quite like what I'd expected of a hit man.. He was tall, slim, lithe, blonde, blue-eyed, stylish, and rather effeminate. You'd almost have expected to find him browsing art galleries in Soho with his longtime companion.

"How-ja-do?" He thrust a hand at me and said, "Name's Freddy, Freddy Nearby." His voice, however, was exactly what I expected of a hit man, sounding as if he'd just come from a smoke-filled poker game at some "social club" down in Little Italy—the kind of place where they smoked real tobacco, carried deadly weapons, had nicknames like "The Chin" or "Mad Dog."

Marvin shook his head. "It's Freddy Vicino," he corrected.

"Freddy Vicino?" I said.

Freddy nodded. "Freddy Nearby."

"Vicino," Marvin said. "There seems to be a glitch in the translation device. I'll have it adjusted tomorrow."

"Translation device?" I repeated faintly as Freddy took my hand in a crushing grip and shook it vigorously.

"Vicino," Annabelle said. "It's Italian for 'nearby.' "

"And I'm *always* nearby. Huh? Huh? *Huh*?" Freddy chuckled and punched me lightly in the arm. I flew sideways. Then he entered my modest little living room and said to Annabelle, "You speak Italian! You got some Sicilian in you?"

"No, I'm just immensely well-educated," Annabelle said, extending a delicate hand.

Freddy seized it and kissed it. "Much pleasure," he murmured.

"Hey," I said, "that's no way—"

"It's all right," Annabelle said. "*Molto piacere,* Freddy." She added to me, "*Molto piacere* is just a way of saying 'pleased to meet you.' "

"Relax," Marvin advised me.

"So," Freddy said, slowly releasing Annabelle's hand and then getting right down to business, "you're the couple of lovebirds who want me to bump off some cornmeal-eater, right?"

"Huh?"

"I think he means *polenta*-eater," Annabelle said.

"Hey, is this broad smart, or *what*?" Freddy said approvingly.

"Yes," I said, "we're interested in having her husband killed."

"Her husband?" Freddy said to me.

"Yes."

"Your husband?" he said to Annabelle.

"Yes," she replied.

"Let me guess," Freddy said. "You got a pre-nup that don't give you squat."

"How'd you know?" Annabelle asked.

"Hey, sweetheart, when you been around this block a few times the way I have, there ain't no new sights to see."

"Can you do it?" I asked.

"I'll need certain things," Freddy said, stroking his chin as he turned to study me with a penetrating gaze.

"What things?" I said.

"First, I'll need to know everything about the mark. Schedule, habits, places he frequents. I gotta know when he eats, sleeps, and shits, you understand what I'm saying?"

"We understand," Annabelle said.

Freddy turned to her and grinned. "Good. This I can work with." He looked at Marvin and added, "Yes, *this* I can definitely work with." He moved closer to Annabelle, his expression hardening with concentration. "Except maybe the hair color . . ." He nodded. "Yeah, the color needs a little work. It's a little harsh. Just a touch too brassy."

"Excuse me?" Annabelle's voice was frosty.

Freddy turned to Marvin. "You can see my problem with the color, right? It's just a little too much, ain't it? Am I right? Of course, I'm right! And the roots. Sweetheart," he said to Annabelle, "you stick with Freddy. We'll work on the roots. But the length? Yes! Very good. We can live with that."

"What are you—"

Marvin cut in, "It's just a little programming glitch. Freddy was originally a hairdressing robot, and his reprogrammer—a brilliant young fellow who's definitely going to beat that rap for fraud and grand larceny—hasn't quite reconciled all of the extremes yet."

"I see," I said, not seeing at all.

"A hairdresser?" Annabelle said with dawning interest. "Really?"

Freddy placed a hand over his heart. "I'm a very *sensitive* hit man."

"And a stylish one," Marvin added warmly.

"Because you know," Annabelle said, stepping a little closer to Freddy, "I haven't said so to anyone, but *I* think the color's a little more than I need, too."

"Absolutely!" Freddy said, clearly pleased. He started feathering his fingers through her hair. "You have such beautiful skin tone, and just look at them eyes! You don't want a hair color that *competes* with this beautiful package. Am I right?" He gave me a friendly thump on the chest. I fell down.

"Theo!" Annabelle said.

"Don't do that again," I wheezed as Marvin helped me to my feet.

"Sorry, pal," Freddy said. "You don't work out much, do you?"

"My strength wasn't programmed into me," I replied testily, "I'm a mere mortal."

"Hey, you trying to bust my balls?" Freddy suddenly looked menacing.

"No," Marvin said quickly. "No, Freddy, not at all. What were you saying about Annabelle's hair?"

"Annabelle?" Freddy beamed at her. "Ain't that a lovely name?"

She beamed back. "Thank you. It was my grandmother's name."

"And was she a dish, too?"

Annabelle smiled, made a dismissive sound, then patted her hair. "What do you think of the cut?"

"It's okay. I think I'd feather it around the face a little more."

Marvin drew me aside while Freddy waxed eloquent

with Annabelle about the possibilities of stacking and layering.

"You don't want to antagonize this robot, Theo," Marvin warned me. "He has been programmed with the assistance of a dozen Mafia killers, all charged with crimes so heinous that even *I* feel a trifle queasy when I'm destroying evidence."

"Can we control him?" I asked doubtfully.

"Well, more easily than you can control a Mafia killer, that much is for sure." I could tell Marvin was speaking from experience again.

"Are you sure this is a good idea?" I persisted.

"As compared to what?" Marvin shot back. "Hiring a poodle to do the murder?"

"As compared to doing it ourselves."

"Theo, you're my second favorite cousin and I'm almost fond of you, but I feel compelled to remind you that you had hysterics when Bambi's mother died."

"That was a very distressing movie!"

"And you were twenty-three at the time."

"Horton does not resemble a sloe-eyed deer."

"Trust me, you are not emotionally equipped to commit a murder!"

Freddy overheard us and forgot what he was saying to Annabelle about highlights. "Hey, kid," he said to me, "look at me. Look right at me. That's right. Now you listen to me. You want someone whacked out, you found the right guy for the job." He shrugged. "And if his hair's as bad off as Annabelle says, I'll even throw in a trim for free."

I rolled my eyes. *"Marvin."*

Marvin said, "Freddy, tell them how many people you've whacked out."

"Seventeen," Freddy replied promptly.

"Seventeen?" Annabelle bleated.

"And one of 'em had *such* split ends." Freddy

shook his head sadly. "Broke my heart to see neglect like that."

"And Freddy's never been caught," Marvin added. "No charges, no arrests. Not even an interrogation."

"The cops got nothin' on me," Freddy assured us. "The Feds, neither."

"Where are you going to find expertise like this?" Marvin said to me. He added pointedly, "And in a hit man who we know for sure won't talk after the job is done."

Because, of course, we would deactivate him and scatter the parts.

"Hey, Freddy Nearby is a stand-up guy," Freddy insisted. "I ain't never ratted to the cops, and I ain't never gonna."

"You're loyal," Annabelle murmured.

"You bet I am!" He added, "And I'm particularly good with body perms. Not that frizzy tight kind that you see in cheap salons, but the full flowing kind that takes real skill." He leaned closer to Annabelle. "Some guys think the secret of a great perm is all about when you add conditioner and how much formula you use, but they're wrong."

"They are?" she breathed, spellbound.

"It's the wrap that makes all the difference."

"Do you think you could give me a great . . . perm?"

"I think I could give you a perm that you'd never forget, sweetheart."

"All right, could we get back to discussing murder?" I said loudly.

Freddy turned easily in my direction. Annabelle looked sort of flustered.

"I'll need weapons that ain't hot," Freddy said.

"I can get those," Marvin said promptly. "I'll just add them to the final bill for my services."

"AR-7 rifle," Freddy said, "high-powered scope,

disposable rifle silencer, two extra clips, some hollow point bullets . . ." He paused a moment, then pointed at me and said, "And you!"

I jumped, startled. "Yes?"

"I think you need a whole different look," Freddy said, nodding slowly as he considered this. "The whole long-around-the-ears things is so fuckin' yesterday, pal. You need to think about what kinda statement you're trying to *make* with your hair, you understand what I'm saying?"

"Could we talk about my hair another time?"

"Hey, kid, life is short and full of ambushes. Who knows if there'll be another time? You could be whacked out like *that,*" I flinched as he suddenly made a loud smacking sound with his hands. Annabelle sighed and look transfixed. "You wanna go out lookin' like this? You wanna meet your maker with *that* cut?"

"I'm convinced," Annabelle said breathlessly. "He's the man for the job!"

"Annabelle . . ." I began.

"Seventeen hits," Marvin reminded me.

"So, are we in business?" Freddy said. "You want Annabelle to be a widow by the weekend?"

"You can do it that soon?" I asked.

"Yeah."

"And not get caught?"

"Uh-huh."

"And not finger us?" I persisted.

"Theo!" Annabelle chided.

Freddy stared hard at me. I wasn't sure if I had insulted him or if he was just contemplating my hair again.

"Well?" Marvin prodded.

Annabelle said, "He's hired. Er . . . I mean . . ."

"You gotta fork over the dough to my head," Freddy said.

"Your head?" I asked.

"He means his *capo,*" Annabelle clarified.

"His boss," Marvin said.

"Ah, his current owner. Well . . . about the price, Marvin," I said, "Annabelle and I—"

"Are happy to pay it," my beloved interrupted me.

"Excellent! Then it's settled." Marvin displayed all the satisfaction of a man getting a hefty sales commission out of this deal.

"And now you and me," Freddy said to Annabelle, "should spend some time together."

"Right, you want to know Horton's habits and schedule," she said.

He was gazing ardently at her hair as he replied, "Yeah, that's among the things I want."

"Shall we get started this evening?" she suggested.

"Oh, yeah," Freddy said. "I don't believe in wasting time."

That much was clear. But at least he was a robot, one we were going to deactivate as soon as the job was over.

"And Annabelle," Marvin added, "I'll need payment in full before Freddy can kill anyone. Small unmarked bills, please."

"I'll be at your office before five o'clock tomorrow," she promised.

As they all made a move to leave my drab little apartment, I said, "And what should I do?"

"You?" Freddy chuckled. "You just wait until you hear from us."

"But—"

"He's right, Theo," Marvin said. "It's probably better if you and Annabelle establish separate alibis for the murder and also aren't seen together for a while."

"But—"

"I'll be in touch," Annabelle promised. "Bye!"

* * *

A week after Horton Macauley's death was reported in the news, I couldn't stand the isolation anymore, so I phoned Marvin. A stranger answered the office number I had dialed. Marvin, I was told, had been promoted and now had a different office. It took me a while to get through the paranoid maze of his firm's secretarial pool, but I finally got him on the phone.

"The former owner of a robot of our mutual acquaintance," Marvin said, "was so pleased with the transaction which I made for the purchase of his property that he made certain arrangements with our firm, from his new position on Capitol Hill, which have put us in a very favorable position. The partners were immensely pleased—"

"So you got promoted," I said.

"Isn't it wonderful?"

"Yeah, just wonderful. Listen, Marvin, how's Annabelle? I'm worried about her."

There was a long silence.

"Marvin?" I prodded.

Even for Marvin he sounded unusually cautious when he said, "You haven't talked to her?"

"No. She hasn't called, and I'm afraid to call her in case her phone's bugged. Is she under suspicion?"

"No," he said firmly. "Everything went perfectly. We did, after all, put an experienced professional in charge of this task."

I knew what he was going to say next. I suppose I had known for days what Annabelle's complete silence meant. Still, it was a shock when Marvin admitted the truth to me. Always skilled at deflecting blame, he insisted he hadn't known that part of Freddy's high price tag was due to having virtually *all* the human form and function an owner could possibly require. Annabelle had evidently found a "real man," after all—and one who could do her hair for her now that he had made her a wealthy widow. I was no longer even in her address book, never mind her marital plans.

"Plus, he's rustproof," Marvin added.

"She's fallen for a robot?" I shrieked incredulously. "You're telling me that *my* fiancée—"

"Now, she was never really your fiancée, Theo. She was married to another man the whole time you and she—"

"We were in love! We were going to get married! I plotted a murder with her!"

"And I've ensured," Marvin said cheerfully, "that you are never going to come up on charges for that. Not even in civil court."

"Marvin! I want my girlfriend back! Especially now that she's widowed and worth millions!"

"Getting her back, my boy, would mean taking her away from Freddy Vicino. Do you think you're up for that?"

"I'll tell the cops what I know!" I said wildly.

"They'll never be able to prove a thing," Marvin assured me calmly. "Annabelle bought the very best. There's no evidence anywhere. And by the time you convince the cops to investigate Freddy—*if* you can—I'll have a pile of permits and maintenance records showing that he's been a hairdressing robot for the past five years. Believe me, Theo, I can provide plenty of testimonials from people whose hair he's cut."

"You're on Annabelle's payroll now, aren't you?" I guessed.

"Yes, but don't imagine that family loyalty means nothing to me," Marvin said warmly. "If you could pay me more than she does, I'd drop her like a bad habit."

So there it is. I asked my cousin Marvin for help, and wound up without my girlfriend or her millions, and with a homicidal robot somewhere out there who recently sent me a note promising to stop by some time and give me a trim as his way of apologizing for what happened.

Much as I hate to say it, I probably should have listened to my mother.

LIES OF OMISSION

by Jane Lindskold

Alastar, the main character in the following story, first appeared in Jane Lindskold's short story "Ruins of the Past," featured in the collection *Far Frontiers*. Lindskold herself first appeared in print in a short story entitled "Cheesecake" in the now defunct magazine *Starshore*. Since then she has published more than forty short stories and eleven novels—the most recent of which include *Through Wolf's Eyes*, *Changer* and *Legends Walking*. She lives in New Mexico where she writes, gardens, and enjoys the company of her husband, archaeologist Jim Moore.

LIES have a way of catching up with you—even lies of omission. That was something Alastar had never had reason to learn over the long millennia of her existence.

Now, as she monitored signals that none of the human residents of Vorbottan Mountain had yet detected—that they lacked the equipment to detect—the android wondered whether or not to confess to her lie.

Her decision was made more difficult by the fact that Lillianara was not currently in residence at Vorbottan Mountain. The human woman—the first friend of Alastar's long, lonely vigil as guardian of the installation hidden within the bowels of the mountain—was currently off-planet. She could be summoned, could return within a few hours—a few days at most, but getting her to return so promptly would mean admitting to the lie.

Alastar wasn't certain she could do that.

The first reason not to recall Lillianara was that there wasn't much that Lillianara could do to avert what was about to happen. Indeed, if Lillianara returned to Vorbottan Mountain, she herself would be endangered. That danger, as Alastar reasoned, was the second good argument against recalling Lillianara.

The third, of course, was the lie itself. Alastar treasured Lillianara, treasured the friendship that had grown up between them in the two and a half years that had passed since Alastar had saved Lillianara's life, and Lillianara had almost immediately returned the favor by saving Alastar's own. Life was a term the android wasn't certain applied to her own type of existence, but lacking a better one, she felt forced to apply it. Certainly, if Lillianara had not been present, Alastar would have permanently ceased to function that day.

Within the complexities of the android's elegantly constructed thinking apparatus, a logic circuit quibbled:

Had Lillianara not been present, your continued functioning would never have been in danger of termination in the first place. The enforcer would never have been motivated to act. You would never have been prompted to defy. Lillianara is not the reason for your continued existence. She is a threat to it.

But Alastar had grown wiser than the arguments of pure logic. Alone, abandoned, forsaken, betrayed, she had been on the verge of insanity before the human's arrival. The human was owed something in return for her friendship and all the benefits it had brought with it.

The question was, was Lillianara owed honesty?

* * *

Two levels below where Alastar debated ethics, archaeologist Visten Hillard, project director for the small, exclusive consortium hired by Lillianara of Klee to excavate the alien complex beneath Vorbottan Mountain was interrupted.

"Hill, can you come here a sec?"

The speaker was Joel Munsing, a short, fat, smiling man who thought his amiable good humor hid his ambitious nature. It didn't—at least not from Hillard, who was, if anything, more ambitious.

There was a studied casualness in his subordinate's tone that gave Hillard pause. If Munsing was trying not to attract attention, then he must have found something other than those formerly fascinating alien relics that the crew—with the usual human hunger for novelty—were already coming to view as routine.

"Sure." Hillard answered Munsing with matching casualness, glancing to where the nearest crew members worked and assuring himself that no one else had noticed Munsing's routine request. "I'll be there in a moment."

Finishing what he had been writing, Hillard clipped his data pad back onto his belt and straightened, automatically checking his clearance from the ceiling overhead.

At nearly two and a half meters in height, with features and limbs that seemed vaguely squared and his iron-gray hair cut in a bristling flat-top, Visten Hillard rather resembled flat-screen film depictions of the Frankenstein monster minus the stitching. Off duty, Hillard took care to dress in a natty, scholarly style. He quietly hated the one-piece duraweave body stocking that was the required attire for this dig, knowing that it made his big body look more hulking than ever.

However, mere vanity had not been sufficient reason to reject the expensive suits when Lillianara of Klee had offered them. For one thing, the body stockings were more than simply tough coveralls. With coif and gloves in place, the body stockings functioned as short-term environmental suits. They even offered limited armor protection. Since Lillianara had hinted—ever so delicately—that she (or more appropriately her insurance carrier) would not be responsible for any injuries sustained through the rejection of her offer, Hillard had swallowed his pride.

The section of corridor along which Munsing had been working was not completely cleared, so Hillard had to stoop, duck-waddling in an undignified fashion to join his coworker.

"What have you found?" he asked, pitching his voice for Munsing's hearing alone. Some odd part of his mind took comfort from the fact that clad in the body stocking Munsing rather resembled a sphere with arms and legs.

"I think I've got something interesting here," Munsing replied.

He gestured to a newly cleared section of wall. A straight line too regular to be anything but artificial marked the wall for about a meter before each end curved gently and vanished into the uncleared rubble beneath their feet.

"Looks like the top of a doorway," Hillard said after closer inspection. "Matches what we've already seen along those lines. Good."

Joel Munsing nodded.

"Most of the door is still beneath the fill," he said, "but judging from what we have on the scanner maps . . ."

He unclipped his own datapad and brought up a multicolored three-dimensional holographic diagram. The level on which they were working—the second level—was indicated in brilliant orange. The next was shown in yellow, the ones beneath in colors that descended the spectrum in sequence. As the colors shaded from green down through blue and into violet, the number of lines grew fewer.

The alloy from which the Vorbottan Mountain complex had been constructed, combined with the detritus that cluttered every available space on the second level of the complex, had made constructing accurate maps via remote sensors impossible. Still, their partial map was enough to permit them to make tentative conclusions.

"I'd guess this door I've found is going to lead into a corridor," Munsing continued, sketching commands into the datapad so that only the second and third levels remained visible, "possibly one with access to a lower level of the complex. We already know the builders preferred ramps to shafts—and that the ramp from level one ended at level two."

Munsing waved a finger and the first level, neatly and completely mapped in red, appeared, the access ramps highlighted. Each did end on the second level—so either the aliens had preferred to walk down a corridor to the next ramp or they had some other method of access between levels—maybe even exterior entry ports.

Hillard suspected that the android Alastar who had been present when the installation had been active, could have answered many of these questions, but the elegant, eerie, unsettling alien machine remained stubbornly obstructionist.

Nodding agreement with his assistant's conclusion, Hillard concealed his own excitement, though his heart was thumping so hard he was certain that Munsing must see it beating against the tight fit of the body stocking. Some demon of the perverse made Visten tease the other man.

"We'd better leave this door be for now, then," he said, half turning away. "We've plenty of work to do on this level without starting something new."

As Hillard had expected, Munsing gaped at him.

"Hill, you can't mean that!" the round man exclaimed, forgetting for the first time his own studied casualness.

"No," Hillard reassured him with a grin. "I don't. Stars and bars, Munsing, its been weeks since we've had something to report that isn't a repetition of the same old-same old."

Munsing gusted a sigh of relief. Hillard continued speaking, realizing that he was trying to reassure himself that he was making the right decision. A responsible archaeologist would finish the second level before essaying the third, no matter how dull the second might have become. It wasn't as if they were up against a deadline of any sort. Indeed, Lillianara of Klee, while fascinated by everything they reported to her, seemed singularly indifferent to how much time they took.

"The first few of those hostel rooms we cleared," Hillard said, referring to the small, square chambers that lined this particular corridor, "those were pretty exciting, but how many times can you look at the same three-meter-by-three-meter chamber, furnished and decorated in the same fashion, without feeling trapped?"

Munsing nodded, tacitly encouraging this train of thought.

"I owe it to the crew," Hillard went on. "To morale. Even with the fine salaries Lillianara is paying and the superlative equipment . . ."

"And the chance to be the first to uncover relics of not one but several alien civilizations," Munsing put in helpfully.

"Even with all that," Hillard said a touch resentfully, "archaeologists thrive on discovery. This door—this is an opportunity to reveal something new, something that might even shed light on the otherwise incomprehensible items we've been finding to this point."

"It might just be another row of barracks," Munsing hastened to remind Hillard.

"It could be," Hillard agreed. "In either case, we'd know."

Munsing toed aside a couple of fist-sized chunks of rock.

"How long until Lillianara of Klee returns from her current trip?" he asked, his tone filled with studied casualness.

Hillard's thoughts had been running along similar lines.

"Several weeks, standard."

They stared at each other, both remembering the terms under which the excavation had been contracted. Following detailed clauses covering wages, insurance, liability, and things of that ilk, there had been a bald statement:

> Any new discovery of any merit is to be reported immediately to the owner of this complex, Lillianara of Klee, or in her absence, to her designated agent, the android Alastar, or, in Alastar's absence, to Lillianara via the most expedient means of communication."

"Seven weeks," Munsing repeated. "Well, I guess we should report our find to Alastar. I'm glad you're the boss. That murdering android makes my flesh crawl."

Hillard thought of the android. It was difficult to form a physical picture of Alastar. The race that had crafted it had perfected nanotechnology to a level of refinement of which the known races still could only dream. Alastar was capable of altering its appearance within the limits of its general mass—could even appear as a fairly convincing human. There was something in the android's impersonation of a human, however, that always came across as vaguely wrong—something more alien than the overtly alien thing it was.

For this reason, Alastar usually appeared in what Hillard understood from Lillianara was the form in which she had first encountered it: a slim insectoid figure, rather like a wasp, but with facial features that elegantly merged the human and the insect. What Hillard thought of as the frame for Alastar's face—mouth, nose, general shape, the skin—was humanlike. The eyes however, were completely alien: huge violet ovals set slantwise beneath a human brow, faceted and reflecting, giving nothing away.

These hybrid features were framed by impossibly silky white hair that cascaded like mist from a waterfall down the android's back without encumbering the delicate wasp wings that were set—apparently for purely ornamental reasons—neatly between imaginary shoulder blades.

Though his own feelings regarding Alastar were similar to Munsing's, Hillard felt that as the project director it was his place to express a more open-minded, understanding view.

" 'Murdering' is a rather harsh way to define Alastar's actions," Hillard reproved Munsing. "The android was simply carrying out its programming."

Munsing shrugged, the expression on his round face for once less than amiable.

"It killed hundreds of people, lots of them archeologists. Killed them for doing nothing worse than what we're doing right now. The only difference is that they didn't have permission and we do. Sometimes I wake up in a cold sweat, wondering what'll happen if Alastar reverts to base programming. That thing spent centuries protecting this installation, and now suddenly it's supposed to stop because Lillianara of Klee tells it to?"

"That is the difference," Hillard said, his words more confident than his expression. "For reasons unknown to us, Alastar has accepted Lillianara as the new owner of the complex. Lillianara has told Alastar to let us work here."

"But Lillianara isn't here to enforce her orders," Munsing countered. "That's just what I mean. We don't know why that android all of a sudden decided that one human out of all the humans on this planet was the only one it would accept as a new owner. What if we stumble on something below that triggers some other programming routine?"

"Lillianara's instructions to Alastar have held so far," Hillard replied but his tone was less than assured. "Haven't we been permitted entry every day? Haven't meals been supplied—good ones, too? Haven't we had open contact with the outside world?"

They both remembered how until just two years before Vorbottan Mountain had been sealed off from the rest of the world, its summit home to storms that raged nowhere else, nothing—not even signal waves—penetrating its perfect isolation.

As far as the majority of the population was concerned, Vorbottan was still forbidden, but at Lillianara's instigation the mountain's secrets were being brought to light by this highly envied crew of twenty chosen archaeologists. In the early days of their work these twenty had been hounded by news agencies, feted by society throughout the settled galaxy.

These days, unfed by any spectacular new discoveries, interest in their work had dwindled. This door, still three quarters buried beneath the rubble, was the first promising find in months.

Hillard ran his finger along the seam.

"Of course," he said slowly, "we don't *know* that

this is a 'new discovery of merit.' We're just guessing. I think we shouldn't say anything quite yet. Nothing to the media, Joel. Not a peep. Understand?"

"I understand," Munsing replied seriously.

Unspoken between them was that for now nothing need be said to Lillianara's designated agent, the android Alastar.

Musing on lies of omission and commission, on the nature of friendship and of responsibility did not stop Alastar from keeping watch on the twenty archaeologists. Twenty tiny spies hovered over twenty laboring figures, recording everything said and done, everything removed, everything discovered.

One of these spies had followed Visten Hillard when he responded to Joel Munsing's summons. Another of these had already been with Munsing.

Alastar considered now (part of her mind still busy with the merely abstract questions of truth and falsehood), how she should react to what she had learned. She knew already that some of the archaeologists didn't like her—were made uneasy by her. She had tried not to let that trouble her.

It did trouble her, though, that she should be so harshly condemned for merely doing the job for which she had been designed. One might as well condemn a fire for burning one's hand.

She wondered why Joel Munsing hadn't told Visten Hillard that his own grandfather had been among the treasure hunters slain while looting the ruins that crowned Vorbottan Mountain.

Then again, she doubted that Munsing knew that Hillard had a private, very lucrative contract with a pan-galactic media firm for the rights to first notification of any major find. She also suspected that Hillard's dislike of Alastar herself had more to do with the fact that Alastar had refused to tell him anything about the buried portions of the complex than with any of her past actions. She had explained quite politely that her programming made such revelations impossible, but she knew he suspected her of merely being difficult.

Hillard had been so primly furious when Alastar had refused that she had not felt inclined to clarify her explanation as she might have for Lillianara.

What Alastar could have told Visten Hillard, had she been so inclined, was that her programming really did make it impossible for her to clarify what lay below. The fact was, except in the most general way, she *didn't* know. The complex had been created as a weapons storage facility. Her role was dual—to serve those who created the installation when they were in residence and to guard it when they were not.

The alliance that had caused Alastar to be made had not thought it either necessary or wise that the android know precisely what she guarded. They had agreed that it was enough that she be equipped to guard. Information as to *what* she guarded was buried within layers of need-to-know programming. Therefore, until that programming began activating, Alastar hadn't known just what it was that had been stored on the third level of the complex.

The android considered. Secrets within secrets seemed to be the sentient way—not merely the human way. Perhaps, in light of that, her own omission to Lillianara was not to be condemned. Moreover, it need not be revealed, since Lillianara herself was not present to be affected by the results of that lack of information.

Comforted, Alastar decided. Had Hillard and Munsing reported to her the finding of the door, she would have been torn whether or not to make public at least some of what she now knew about level three.

However, they had not. Therefore, the men—and by extension their associates—were in breach of contract. As such, Alastar could now view them as outside of the bounds of her responsibility. She thought she was being excessively generous in permitting them even to remain.

Smugly, Alastar put the matter from her.

Such decisions, however, did nothing to stop the activity that had first created this incipient crisis of conscience, and Alastar knew full well that those who were awakening beneath Vorbottan Mountain possessed no conscience at all.

Not everyone could work on clearing the doorway. There simply wasn't room. Initially, Hillard delegated five crew members, working under Joel Munsing, as was only fair, to shift debris. He himself continued with the hostel room that he had been working on when Munsing made his discovery.

Leading by example, Hillard thought. It would look good on the holovids—self-abasement, a leader who remained one of the team. With those same vids in mind, he insisted that the clearance be done as carefully and methodically as if there was no door waiting behind the rubble. It wouldn't look good for them to have been hasty.

The past is reconstructed from little things.

Mentally, Hillard tried the phrase. It sounded good. Stern, scholarly. The type of phrase that brought in lecture invitations and research grants.

As Munsing's crew lowered the rubble level in the corridor, Hillard delegated more people to assist in the clearing. When his own room was excavated, recorded, and mapped, Hillard assigned himself to head this second crew.

Even with the cutting-edge equipment Lillianara had purchased for the consortium, clearing the corridor to the door took seven working days. A section of the ceiling overhead had collapsed, a thing that would have worried Hillard more if they hadn't already established that what remained was perfectly stable. More of the clutter was material that had been swept down from level one when that area was returned to operation.

Fleetingly, Hillard wondered just when that had been. If the attacks in the salvage expeditions were any indication, Alastar had been dormant until about a century before. Of course, at the time, no one had known just who or what had transformed the silent mountaintop ruins into a deathtrap. They knew now, had known ever since Lillianara had descended from the mountaintop and explained—an explanation that had transformed her from a debt-ridden fugitive into one of the wealthiest and most powerful (though that power was implied rather than exercised) people on the planet.

Steadily shoveling fist-sized chunks of curiously molten-looking rock onto the analyzer belt, Hillard imagined Alastar awakening from stasis, and, in between violently defending the ruins of the alien installation from outsiders, methodically clearing the first level of all signs of attack.

His imagination clothed the android's wasplike body in an archaic ruffled apron and tied the long wisps of silky white hair up into a knot on the back of her head. She—for this image was distinctly female, no matter that most of the time Hillard determinedly thought of the android as a thing rather than a person—used a broom and dustpan, opening doors and sweeping the rocky debris into corners until the job was done.

It was this image more than anything else that made Hillard pause in surprise when the great day came and Munsing ceremonially opened the door. Hillard had expected another litter-filled corridor, had already ordered another analyzer to speed along dealing with the expected masses of debris.

But the corridor was empty. It slanted down into darkness, a broad ramp of the same dense material the aliens had used for weight-bearing surfaces elsewhere in the complex.

Joel Munsing and Ramira Bailey, the crew member nearest to him, moved with one thought to shine portable lights down the ramp. The lights reflected back from the matte-surfaced bronze of another door.

In some subtle way, this door seemed sturdier than the one they had just opened. That one had been coated in an off-white enamel so as to blend in with the surrounding walls. This door proclaimed itself. There were runes embossed on its surface, each stroke as large as Hillard's forearm.

No one had yet translated the alien language—languages, rather. The revelation that there were multiple languages represented on the fragments had done much to explain why linguistics experts had experienced so little success on that line despite their computers and databases.

Although no linguist himself, Hillard knew what these particular characters meant—everyone on the crew did. They'd encountered the runes many times throughout the alien installation. At Lillianara's prompting, Alastar had explained that they were less written words than part of a universal ideographic system employed by the alien races who had built this installation.

The large, raised characters stated: Authorized Personnel Only.

Their size seemed to make this an order rather than the polite admonition they had seen elsewhere. Munsing sounded rather nervous when he broke the silence that had followed the opening of the door.

"I guess we're authorized personnel, aren't we?" he said, and something tentative in his voice turned what had clearly been meant as a statement into a question.

Hillard knew that the time had come for him to take command once more.

"That's right," he said, stepping to the front and switching on his own light. "We've worked hard for this. Let's head on down."

The crew—all twenty of them—fell into line eagerly enough. Of them, only Munsing knew that Hillard was in violation of their agreement with Lillianara of Klee. A few, Bailey for one, Kyuko Mori for another, might suspect. Not one of them, however, wanted to set the thrill of discovery aside.

Hillard motioned Munsing beside him. He knew that the autocams various members of the crew wore as a matter of routine would be recording every motion, and he wanted nothing to diminish his carefully built image as a leader who was also a team player.

With measured steps, they descended to the bronze door. Various readings were taken. A low blip of power indicated that, as above, the atomic batteries built into the door still held a charge.

Munsing gave Hillard one of his broad, ingenuous grins.

"Your turn to do the honors, boss," he said, gesturing toward the diamond-shaped pressure plate that should open the door.

Hillard didn't hesitate—he had meant to open this door all along. Already he was casting lines for himself. "*The metal was cold . . .*" No, that wouldn't do. The body stocking's duraweave sealed out all but the most severe temperature shifts.

"I imagined I could feel the chill of the metal surface . . ."

Better but not right. *I'll have time to get it right,* he thought, never dreaming that this moment would be forgotten in what was to come.

Glancing back to make certain that the autocams were in place—a purely routine, professional gesture—Hillard pushed the pressure plate. There was a pause as if the ancient circuits had to remember what they were meant to do. Then the bronze-colored door split neatly down the middle and slid with a slight grating noise into the walls on either side.

The large rounded room before them was almost free of debris, but not because this area had escaped the devastation that elsewhere marked the installation. Whatever weapons had been used here had been high-energy rather than explosive. Surfaces shone as if sealed under glass. Even where deep scoring marred the gentle curves of the walls or the flat smoothness of the floors, the cuts were neatly cauterized.

Beneath the damage were three doors, each as large as the one that had admitted them, each sealed by unimaginable (but not unanalyzable) degrees of heat.

"Need cutting torches to get through those," Munsing said, again the first to break the silence. He led the way into the room, testing the surface with a sliding motion of his duraweave boot.

"Not as slick as it looks," he reported, "but walk carefully."

"I wonder why the door we came through opened?" Ramira Bailey said, turning to inspect it almost as soon as she was into the room. "Shouldn't the same explosion or whatever have sealed it, too?"

Hillard had been wondering the same thing and felt a momentary prick of annoyance that Bailey would go on record before him.

He masked his annoyance, turning with what he hoped was a thoughtful, but not pompous expression to acknowledge the woman's comment. The body stocking did Bailey's mature figure—she was sixty-three and a twice a grandmother—no more favors than it did his own. Hillard felt momentarily grateful that it had been Bailey rather than say, Patience Severity—who looked like something out of an adolescent's erotic fantasy in the clinging stuff—who had raised the question.

Patience's photogenic appearance had been one of the reasons Hillard had assigned her to carry a holocam, figuring she'd be in fewer pictures if she was taking them. He wondered sometimes if Patience realized this. It didn't really matter if she did; she was junior and he was the boss.

"Well," he said, hating as always when he was put in the position of going on record without due consideration, "perhaps the force of the explosion was reduced at this point. We don't know, after all, that it *was* an explosion. Judging from these gouge marks . . ." he pointed to one shaped like a jagged lightning bolt that crossed the floor near their feet, "some more focused energy weapons were in use as well."

Munsing nodded, hunkering down to inspect the mark in question.

"The edges are smooth as glass," he reported, replacing his hand in its glove. "Not a precisely scientific assessment, I admit, but something very hot sealed this."

"Sealed," Bailey said, removing her own glove as she trotted over to the nearest closed door. She ran her hand over the surface. "That's what might have been done here—either with an energy beam or with some form of spray-on adhesive. The texture isn't precisely the same as the walls around it."

Hillard thought it was time he took charge once more.

"Team," he said, pitching his tones into official mode so that the nineteen other archaeologists all paused in whatever they were saying or doing to listen, "conjecture is all well and good, but we're here to find the information that will prove or disprove these theories."

He began handing out assignments. The crew fell to work without a grumble, knowing as he did that the sooner they gathered all the information that could be garnered from this room, the sooner one of those three sealed doors would be opened.

From her control room—the one from which she still kept unwanted visitors at their distance, though by far less lethal methods than she had once employed—the android Alastar watched the archaeologists at work.

The twenty spies sent her twenty different perspectives, a meaningless muddle to a human, but easily resolved into a complex portrait by the multiple facets of her compound eyes. Her brain resolved the information so that Alastar was far more aware of what was going on in that chamber than was Visten Hillard, who confidently believed himself on top of the situation.

How stupid they were, believing she could be deceived by the mere device of their not reporting to her!

Ah, well. By her assessment, they would spend several more days collecting what information this round room—a foyer, her need-to-know information bank notified her—held. Then they would pick a door.

Which door they picked would make all the difference. Two doors led to more rubble, but the third door led to death.

Alastar was untroubled by this. After all, the archaeologists were in breach of contract and therefore outside her programmed imperatives. Only a small part of what might be termed her conscience wished Lillianara were there to take the decision away from her.

And the guilty part of that conscience wished that Lillianara would take a long time returning.

Four working days later, Hillard concluded that they had learned everything the round room and the access ramp could tell them. He had even delegated about a third of the crew back to the second level to continue clearing the hostel rooms.

Hillard's overt reason had been that their services were no longer needed in the round room, and that was true enough. His less obvious reason was that he wanted to have something to report should Alastar inquire after their work. The android had yet to intrude on their excavations—Lillianara had been the one who popped down uninvited from time to time, just to find out what was going on—but he had wanted to be covered.

That coverage had not been needed, however, and now as he contemplated the scanner readings taken from various points in the round room, Hillard vaguely resented that he felt he needed to sneak around. It was ridiculous, he knew. All he had to do was report, but he suspected that if he did, Alastar would order them to stop work until Lillianara returned.

He couldn't bear the wait. Already he was envisioning the fame, the renewed interest in the project. What if Lillianara herself told them to stop working? Given the type of damage seen in the round room, that was completely possible. Lillianara might want to run tests of her own, have the android send in robots maybe, or simply put herself in charge.

Hillard knew that Lillianara—whose figure was every bit as good as Patience Severity's—would steal the attention he needed to further his career and, through that career, the entire field of archaeology. He couldn't take the risk that some media-hungry socialite would interfere with such important goals.

Hillard's voice, as he analyzed the scanner readings for his subcrew chiefs—a group that included Munsing, Mori, and Severity (on cam duty)—revealed nothing of this inner debate.

"The densitometer readings," Hillard said, "taken

on this level were much more satisfactory. I suspect that the material used for the floors blocks analysis. The information we received from earlier readings may have been as complete as it was due to the shattered nature of the installation as a whole."

No one agreed or disagreed, so Hillard continued:

"Judging from these readings," he said sententiously, "the third and fourth doors—as numbered from left to right with the door we entered designated as 'one'—lead to areas that are wholly blocked by matter of some kind."

Munsing nodded, thumbing his datapad and comparing the information on it to what was in front of them.

"The readings are similar to those we got from the corridor upstairs," Munsing added, completely unnecessarily from Hillard's view, "so we can probably guess that there is more rubble fill."

Hillard nodded.

"Quite," he said. "Unlike doors three and four, the second door seems to lead into open space, a corridor about twice as wide as the one above. We can't deduce much from the width of a corridor. However, one thing it argues is that whatever was taken through there was fairly large. Lillianara of Klee said that this installation was a supply dump. My supposition is that we have reached a warehouse level and that the wide corridors were meant to permit loads to be moved easily."

Bailey spoke up, anticipating Hillard's next point with the annoying lack of formality she had shown before.

"Another interesting thing," she said, tracing the holo map and then superimposing a light tracery of Vorbottan Mountain over it, "is that this corridor—if it is a corridor and not a hangar or ballroom or something like that—seems to end near enough to the mountain's outer shell that we may find another entry point. Finding this, from the inside out, as it were, may help us find other similar access points in the future."

"Precisely," Hillard said, maintaining his mask of enlightened leadership with some difficulty. "Then are you all in concurrence with my thought that we should attempt to open door two?"

Heads nodded all around—even Severity's, though her opinion really hadn't been solicited.

Hillard noted with some annoyance that Severity had let down the coif on her body stocking so that her short neat hair flared around her face. He wondered if she knew just how attractive that made her look, especially compared to the rest of them who resembled skinned outlines rather than people.

"Then let's be at it," Hillard said. "Munsing, get a couple of cutting torches."

They'd already established, working with samples taken from one section of the room, that their most powerful torch tuned to a tight beam and carefully focused would cut whatever sealed the doors, neatly and with minimal damage to the surroundings.

It was delicate work, though, and Hillard was only somewhat reluctant to let Munsing and his chosen assistant—Severity, it turned out—manipulate the torches. Even with the protective armor offered by the body stockings, it was not work for a skilled amateur. Munsing had done salvage work and Severity, it turned out, had grown up on a mining colony run by religious fanatics who put even small children to work using similar gear. They had learned to be careful, she'd explained, because any accident indicated that their guardian spirits weren't pleased with them.

Certainly Severity's hand was steady enough now, though beads of perspiration formed beneath the fringe of her loosened bangs. Hillard resigned himself to the media seizing on those images. They were just too perfect to be ignored—pretty girl, skintight clothes, history of child labor turned to triumph in the name of science.

Come to think of it, he could use it first.

Hillard didn't try to make the rest of the crew return to their usual tasks as Munsing and Severity cut their way through the seal on door two. It was a moment that deserved an audience.

"It's got to be a sealant," Kyuko Mori muttered, chewing on the edge of one glove as she usually did on a ragged fingernail. "It's too neatly in place. I wonder what they sealed in there and who did the sealing?"

"Maybe," Hillard offered, keeping his voice low so as not to distract the cutters, "the corridor was sealed to keep access from the outside to a minimum. Maybe an outer door had been destroyed. Maybe the warehoused materials were considered expendable."

"Maybe," Mori said, looking squarely at him, emerald-green eyes brilliant beneath her dark lashes, "they were locking something up—something that shouldn't be let out."

"You've read too many adventure stories," Hillard chided lightly. "We've seen nothing on the motion sensors. Nothing on the energy detectors. It's as quiet as a tomb."

But Mori's words may have made him nervous. Maybe that was why when Munsing, his round face glowing with sweat beneath his coif, switched off his torch and turning said, "That's the last of it. Want to do the honors, boss?" Hillard replied, "No, you go ahead. You've done the hard work."

Munsing, in turn, bowed to Patience Severity, a bobbing motion that made him look like an amiable punching bag.

"You've recorded everyone else's achievement, Patience. Now it's your turn in the sun."

The young woman set down her torch and moved with lithe confidence to the touch pad that they'd cut free from its seal. She needed to put all her weight behind it, but at last the diamond-shaped plate slid in.

As before, the door split down the middle, but this time rather than darkness there came a white-hot brilliance that seared everyone in the room.

Visten Hillard's last sight before the fail-safe on his body stocking dropped an opaque force shield over his face was of Patience Severity standing in the doorway, bathed in light, her pretty head burned completely off her pretty shoulders.

For once, Alastar was distracted enough that she did not acknowledge Lillianara's return until the woman had actually entered the control room.

Lillianara of Klee was a lovely woman with fair hair and blue-gray eyes. Judging by appearances, she was somewhere in her late twenties or early thirties. Alastar, who knew better than to judge by appearances, knew that Lillianara was closer to fifty. Her late husband, Jofar, had discovered a life-prolongation drug. Lillianara had been one of the few recipients before he had taken himself and his secrets into the inviolable sanctuary of death.

"I am sorry I didn't meet your ship at the landing strip," Alastar apologized, turning to greet her friend. "However, forty-seven minutes ago, the archaeologists released a group of war robots from containment on level three. I have been busy sealing access from level two to level one, and attempting to assess the extent of the damage."

Lillianara gasped, but otherwise took the news with remarkable calm. She breathed deeply, obviously to control her immediate shock, then asked,

"Are any of them hurt?"

"My spy robots were mostly destroyed in the initial attack," Alastar reported sorrowfully, "but I doubt that the archaeologists possess much that might do harm to the warbots. I did see Munsing wielding a cutting torch to some effect, but . . ."

"I didn't mean the warbots!" Lillianara exclaimed in shocked indignation. "I meant the archaeologists."

"Oh."

Alastar was momentarily puzzled. She had thought that Lillianara would have been concerned about damage to what was—even if she hadn't realized it until this moment—her property. Then the android thought she understood.

"Three archaeologists were killed in the initial blast, but you needn't worry. None of the three were wearing their complete body stockings, so they were in violation of their contracts. You will not be liable for death or injury."

Only Lillianara's appalled astonishment—Alastar knew her friend well enough to read the emotions accurately—kept her quiet long enough for the android to finish her report. Now Lillianara spoke with what was obviously an effort at supreme control.

"Alastar, am I to understand that for some forty-seven minutes the archaeologists have been under attack by warbots—whatever these may be—and you have done nothing to assist them?"

"I could not be of assistance to the warbots," Alastar replied, knowing she was being obtuse, "and as the archaeologists were in breach of the contract under which they undertook to work in this installation, I was not certain I should assist them."

She waved one of her upper hands at the screens overhead, simultaneously transferring the images from her three remaining spybots to where Lillianara could view them.

On one screen, a slim silvery limb, elongated and pointed at one end, probed through a hole in a door at a huddled figure in a body stocking.

"Bailey," Alastar reported, "on level two. She was

near the back when the warbots came through and retreated to one of the guest rooms."

The second screen showed the warbot in full. As much as it resembled anything terrestrial at all, it resembled a long-legged spider crafted from silver overshot with ripples of pale blue electricity. Its central hub held a deeply set ring of eyes, each limb ended in a spike. By bending a joint it fired a burst of energy.

"Mori and Kuntang," Alastar reported. "The image is from Kuntang's spy. They are also in a hostel on level two."

The final screen showed nothing but gouts of light, orange-red and blue-white.

"That would be Munsing," Alastar said, "on three. Apparently he has retained his cutting torch and is using it to some effect."

As she glanced at each screen in turn, Lillianara tensed.

"Assist the archaeologists," Lillianara ordered, staring once more at the screens in appalled fascination before heading for the control room door. "Immediately. Do whatever you can without putting yourself in personal risk of destruction. Get some of the housekeeping 'bots. In a pinch, they can at least carry out the wounded. Get sick bay on-line. It's too much to hope we won't have injured."

Alastar complied, vaguely relieved that Lillianara was there to take charge, at the same time distinctly dreading the interrogation she knew must come.

Lillianara raced down the corridor to her own suite, talking over her shoulder as she ran.

"I'm going to slip into my battlesuit, grab a rifle, and be with you as soon as possible. Com-link with me through the suit. Split-link to the archaeologists. Find out their situation."

Alastar did as ordered. Knowing that several minutes would pass before Lillianara was back in contact, she immediately sent feelers out to the archaeologists. A human would have needed delay circuits and a means of prioritizing to handle the panicked information that flowed back to the android as soon as she opened the link.

Alastar's brain, however, was as multifaceted as her eyes. She easily processed the flood of chatter.

Munsing: "I've got myself a sort of cave, but I can't hold out. One torch is dead."

Hillard: "Help! Please! Someone get us out of here! There are three of us in a room on level two. We can hear the things at the door!"

That message, in various forms, was repeated by his two companions. From Ramira Bailey, alone with her tormentor, there was only a barely understandable scream:

Bailey: "Call them off! Call them off!"

That was a thought. Alastar considered how she might call off the warbots, even while she carried out her other orders.

She synthesized these and the other reports—six more in all—and tight-beamed the information to Lillianara's suit so that the information would be available to the human as soon as she installed her coif's link.

Alastar was surprised. At least ten of the archaeologists were still alive. More might be and simply lacked the presence of mind to respond to her request for information. Not everyone had Lillianara's control in a crisis.

The android felt a fleeting flicker of mingled admiration and apprehension as she thought of her human while with one part of her mind she directed the four domestic robots to go down the main ramp into level two. The domibots were unarmed and unarmored. As such, the warbots should ignore them unless the domibots directly interfered with their actions.

However, the domibots did possess large carrying hampers. Alastar set them to trundle up and down the corridors. Injured they were to pick up and deliver to the infirmary. Dead they were to ignore. Trapped they were to offer sanctuary in their hampers. It might work. It might not. It depended on just how much the warbots wanted their prey.

She herself headed toward level three, using the outside access that Hillard and his colleagues had only suspected existed. Munsing's appeal had seemed to have priority to her. Not only did he seem most desperate, but the android admired his presence of mind in fighting back.

Alastar was pleased to discover that Lillianara, when she checked in a few moments later, agreed with the android's priorities.

"Good. Go for Munsing. I'll go after the ones in the hostel rooms. I've set my suit to an interference pattern that hopefully should confuse those silver spiders. Anything I should know about them?"

Alastar told the human what little she knew as she climbed down the mountainside toward the hidden access port.

"They were made by the same race as the enforcer."

"Shit!"

"But they are less effective. Infantry, rather than armor. Their limbs double as weapons and locomotion. They can continue to travel with only two legs remaining. They will continue to fire if they only have one limb. The body-sphere can be set to explode if the 'spider' so wills."

Alastar could hear Lillianara panting around a laugh as she replied.

"And what might make it so will?"

"Belief it can destroy an enemy, that the chance of that is better than the chance of being retrieved and re-equipped."

"Shit!"

Alastar sought to reassure the human.

"I am in the process of searching for a command

to call the spiders off. Failing that, I will broadcast signals indicating that reinforcement is at hand."

"Trying to confuse them?"

"No. They are not complex enough. However, if they will not retreat, at least I may be able to convince them not to explode. They were designed to be damaged and refit. Therefore they have a fairly high self-preservation index."

"That's something. I'm going to sign off here, Alastar. Unlike you, I don't multitask very well. Good luck."

"Luck be with you," Alastar replied and meant it. Even if Lillianara had her deactivated for her failure to report the presence of the warbots, the android had no wish to return to the loneliness that had been her lot before meeting Lillianara.

"Luck," she whispered once more, then sought to forget her personal crisis the better to deal with the current one.

Munsing's "cave" turned out to be a hollow in the rubble that had been cleared from the foyer. The archaeologists' analyzers had dumped the rubble into a tidy heap inside which Munsing had carved himself a hollow. The super-dense alien building material had protected the man far better than he might have dared expect, but when Alastar came down the corridor, he was flagging.

Three spiders turned to face her as she approached, three sets of legs bent and gouted what should have been fiery destruction. Similar gouts had meant fiery destruction to one of the domibots on level two, a fact Alastar had registered and filed.

Alastar, however, was far better equipped than any domibot. Indeed, she would have been a poor guardian for a weapons supply dump if she had not been able to defend herself against just about all types of attack. Her relative vulnerability against the enforcer two years before had been a result of programmed limitations. Her defeat at the time the installation had been destroyed had been through treachery.

Now, sheathed in a force screen of shimmering cobalt light, the android galloped down the broad corridor. For ease of movement, she had converted into quadrupedal mode, her lower body turning horizontal and the four legs swiveling to bear her weight.

In the arms of her upper body, Alastar bore an energy rifle, a powerful thing whose targeting mechanism was hardwired into her brain so that she need not raise it to aim. With one blast, she shot the spider closest to her through the ring of eyes. The resultant explosion—though offering no threat to her—reminded her of the potential danger to Munsing. His body stocking was doubtless getting frayed by now.

Thus she trimmed the legs from the next two spiders, simultaneously ordering her broadcast system to switch over to messages that reinforcements were due.

These must have been more convincing than the recall orders had been—or perhaps even warbots didn't like to terminate without express gain—for neither of the two rounded bodies did other than twitch the stubs of their limbs at her, glaring furiously from their ring of lidless eyes.

Alastar crouched before Munsing's cave.

"Get astride," she ordered. "I'm here to rescue you."

Tottering slightly, Munsing did as ordered. Physically, he seemed to have sustained only slight damage, but she feared his mind was ruined, for he kept muttering:

"The cavalry, by God, the cavalry, in the nick, of time and even with a horse."

Her primary mission completed, Alastar permitted herself a glimpse through Lillianara's suit cams. The human seemed to be doing well. Her battlesuit, a more sophisticated cousin of the body stockings worn by the archaeologists, had taken some hits, but nothing had done more than bruise the human inside. Lillianara was in the process of shaving the legs from one of the spiders with an energy rifle. Apparently, the training she had insisted on following her installation as owner of Vorbottan Mountain—training meant to deal with human poachers—was paying off.

"Hold on," Alastar ordered Munsing. "We're going up the ramp. I'll get you to the access to level one, then go help Lillianara."

But the android's plan didn't hold, not quite.

Coming up the ramp they encountered Kyuko Mori. The assistant crew chief was limping badly, half-sliding on the incline. She was leaning on a silver cane, dragging one leg behind her. A spider—its half-dozen missing limbs making clear where Mori had gotten her makeshift cane—was tripping behind her, pausing every few steps to fire.

Either the warbot's programming for bipedal motion was flawed or it had taken some other injury, but it was consistently firing high.

Munsing leaned down from his perch on Alastar's back.

"Grab hold," he said, hauling Mori astride.

Alastar started to warn Munsing against the act, to tell him that Mori would be safe where she was. The words never left her lips. Even as the android tried to shape them, the warbot fired and—her force shield stretched beyond limits by the added passenger—blew Alastar's head off at the neck.

Lillianara wept, a piteous sound, full of misery.

"Alastar saved me," Munsing said in a broken voice. "Came in just like the cavalry, shot up the warbots, and was hauling me out of there. She saved Mori, too. Her last shot took the spider right through the eyes."

"Too late for Alastar," Lillianara said.

"It was nearly too late for all of us," Visten Hillard

interjected sharply. "If you hadn't returned, all of us would have been killed. As it was, five of my crew are dead, three more are critically injured, and the rest of us are severely traumatized. I assure you, I, for one, will be speaking to my lawyer."

Lillianara's voice transformed into something as cold as interstellar space.

"Speak. I, for one, would enjoy the lawsuit. However, before you do anything, let me tell you that Alastar kept watch on you each day, every day. I have complete records of your dig, including, it may interest you, a record of your deliberate decision to break our contract."

"Records can be falsified," Hillard replied with bravado.

Munsing interjected. "Even if Lillianara didn't have those records, Hill, I'm afraid I'd be forced to testify for her. Alastar was destroyed coming to my rescue. I don't forget something like that."

"Now you have my answer, Hillard, so get," Lillianara ordered. "Get out of here and don't come back. I'll make certain your injured crew members are taken safely home, but right now, if you don't clear out, I can't promise *you* will get out of here safely."

When both Munsing and Hillard had departed, Lillianara began to weep once more.

It would have been easy to truly terminate—the damage to her systems was so great that repair would be long and onerous—but Alastar dragged herself back from stasis and used some of her remaining energy to link to the central computer, seeing through its autocam that the human held her broken body in her lap, the headless torso pressed to her breast.

"Don't cry, Lillianara," Alastar said through that room's speakers, "I am salvageable. Put me in the repair bay, and I'll be good as new in a few months."

Lillianara stared down at the headless body.

"But it blew off your head!" she protested, torn between delight and disbelief.

Alastar laughed, "Do you think my designers thought along human lines? The head is such a vulnerable organ. My central processing unit is in my lower abdomen. When the added burden of carrying Mori stressed my force shield, it shifted to cover these vulnerable portions. My head is expendable."

"Repairable, though?" Lillianara asked. "I don't know how I'd feel about a headless companions."

"Repairable," Alastar assured her. "I will need, however, to go into prolonged stasis."

The android paused. Everything was all right. Lillianara was clearly overjoyed to learn that Alastar wasn't damaged beyond repair. Certainly that meant that she wasn't angry.

But . . .

That little uncomfortable feeling that Alastar thought might be the beginnings of a conscience didn't believe everything was all right.

Alastar looked out through the autocams mounted in the room. Lillianara had summoned one of the domibots and was in the process of loading Alastar's headless body into the carrying hamper.

"Lillianara?"

Alastar found herself speaking without conscious intention, a disturbing sensation.

"Yes, Alastar?"

"Lillianara, before you go to the effort of having me repaired, there's something I should tell you."

"Yes?"

"I think this may be all my fault. I . . . I lied to you."

"Oh?"

Was that amusement she heard in the human's voice? Due to her current injuries, Alastar lacked the capacity to perform a full analysis. She plunged on blindly.

"When I suggested our initial agreement to you, I

knew that this installation had been designed as a weapons supply dump. I didn't inform you."

Lillianara wasn't directly facing any of the room's autocams, but Alastar caught a glimpse of her expression—a curious mix of a smile and a frown.

"Why didn't you inform me, Alastar?"

"I calculated that such information might make you decide that our agreement was not beneficial to you."

Lillianara's laugh was rough and harsh.

"Given what I was up against, Alastar, anything short of out-and-out torture would have been beneficial."

Alastar paused, recalculating. She knew this—had known it at the time. Indeed, given the caliber of enemy Lillianara had acquired, knowing that she sat on a weapons cache might have been considered a benefit. Why, then, *had* she withheld the information?

The android spoke, again without fully preparing her response.

"I was lonely, Lillianara. I believe I was apprehensive that if you knew the nature of this installation you might be disinclined to view me in a friendly fashion."

"You thought I might think of you as more like the enforcer?"

"I believe so."

Lillianara nodded.

"But why, later, when we knew each other better, didn't you fill me in? You're right. My ignorance and your inaction *did* lead to five deaths and numerous injuries."

This time Alastar didn't need to search for the answer, but admitting the truth took an effort nonetheless.

"I didn't want to admit I had lied."

Alastar rushed on, not waiting for Lillianara to speak.

"Tell me, Lillianara, what is worse, a direct lie or an indirect one?"

Lillianara's answer came without hesitation.

"It depends on who gets hurt."

Alastar thought of the five dead, of the many injured and afraid. If she had possessed a head at that moment, she would have nodded.

"I will enter that information into my base calculations," she said.

The domibot—now loaded—trundled toward the repair bay, Lillianara walking alongside. Lillianara said thoughtfully,

"I'm glad to hear that, and I hope in the future you will tell me anything about this installation that might affect my—or any of our visitors'—plans."

"I promise," Alastar said, borrowing the domibot's voice, "you will be the second to know."

"And the first?" Lillianara asked, a laugh in her voice.

"Why, myself, of course," Alastar replied, thinking about how little she actually knew regarding the particulars of what was stored in the levels beneath them. She wondered that Lillianara still possessed the courage to smile.

K-232

by Ron Collins

Ron Collins' short fiction has appeared in several magazines and anthologies, including *Dragon, Return of the Dinosaurs, Mob Magic,* and *Writers of the Future.* Recent fiction appears in *Analog* and *Future Wars.* He lives in Columbus, Indiana.

THE high-gain antenna had been silent for over a year, barely long enough for Pluto to sweep through a single degree of its orbit. No commands had dictated new mission profiles. No messages had requested status.

So the machine continued on its current program.

It had no way of knowing its antenna had been bent during a brush with Pluto's permafrost, or that its programmers had shut down their communication effort months ago. It had no way of discerning there would be no more commands.

The system was known as K-232 by its spec sheets, but was nicknamed *Mickey* by its human builders. If it had a sense of humor at all, K-232 might have appreciated the juxtaposition of its nickname and its mission—Mickey and Pluto, the mouse and the dog, together again in deep space. But K-232 was merely a small payload robot with tractor treads, an internal heat generator, and an array of sensors and scanners.

A programmed routine ran inside the robot's embedded microprocessor. Exactly 33,048,000 seconds had passed since the last message from mission central, a place Mickey knew as an encrypted series of ones and zeros.

Mickey logged the time span and returned to its task. Today, just as it had for the past 382 standard days, Mickey searched the surface of the most distant planet in the solar system. Pluto had experienced only sixty rotations during this period—another fact Mickey dutifully captured, then packaged and fed to its communications buffer.

The communications program would wait for a high-gain command from its programmers, then broadcast Mickey's findings back toward the command signal. Despite negligence from mission central, Mickey continued carrying out its mission, waiting, mechanically trusting the ingenuity and determination of its human creators. Over a year's worth of data waited for that request—photographs, infrared scans of new galaxies, sonar readings that described the inner core of the planet.

Mickey powered the magnetic sensor at its left flank and took another reading, corroborating the field and noting position. The ice crust was frozen methane and nitrogen with trace elements of carbon monoxide. Mickey stored the information, checking against the computer's limit to see if memory was available prior to writing the data.

It was a normal routine, checking if memory was available before writing to the storage block. It was there to avoid errors in processing, and ensure the system wouldn't go into spurious loops if Mickey was unable to complete the commanded activity.

K-232 bypassed the sonar reading this pass. The machine's transmitter had broken in the first month of its exposure to Pluto's harsh environment. The receiver had shattered against a rock fourteen days after the transmitter had failed, so the robot couldn't have performed that task anyway.

Actually, Mickey had lost the use of most of its equipment by this point. Pluto, it seemed, was not willing to give its secrets freely.

The infrared sensors had failed months ago. The spectrum analyzer had given out ten days after the landing. The camera had stopped responding to processor commands before that.

In fact, only the magnetometer—embedded in the underside of Mickey's body where it was partially protected from the elements—had any appreciable function. So Mickey continued to crawl over Pluto's surface, taking magnetic readings every ten minutes, checking to see if memory was available, and logging data.

Its programmers had requested that Mickey creep along slowly but constantly, a mere meter every minute. Mickey did not know that this activity was meant to be preventative, that its constant motion was designed to avoid damage due to sudden movements in the coldest environment the solar system could know. The strategy had succeeded beyond the programmers' wildest dreams, but now Mickey's treads were wearing and breaking, and the unit moved at barely half its initial rate due to slippage and poor traction.

Mickey swiveled to turn, a maneuver it had managed thousands of times before. A tread element caught against the sharp edge of a rock. Mickey tried again.

The tread crumbled with the pressure.

It was the ninth tread element to fail since the mission began, the seventh to break on the left side. And it was this element that made the difference.

The robot felt no pain.

It simply fell roughly to one side. If Mickey's attitude sensor had been working, it would have recorded the lurch as a brief spike. The robot sat like a beached whale at an awkward angle, its dead camera lens covered with methane frost and staring lifelessly up at Charon, the moon that hovered in tide-locked orbit with Pluto.

If Mickey were a man, perhaps he would have marveled at the arcing quarter Charon showed, the silvery ring around the upper right quadrant that is unique in all the solar system. If it were a man, perhaps Mickey would have cried at the distant sight of the sun, a yellow pinpoint in the southern sky that rode just above Pluto's severely curved horizon. Or perhaps he would have peered past Charon, into the inky depths of space, searching for signs of other celestial bodies in order, in the last moments of his life, to learn something more of his beginnings.

Maybe this man would have discovered a secret at the edge of the solar system. Maybe he would have understood the oddity of Mickey's last reading, the strange magnetic signature of a previously unknown object moving through space.

Instead, Mickey powered the magnetometer in its belly and took a reading. Checking for space, K-232 found that memory remained, logged the data, and prepared it for broadcast back to its programmers.

SACRIFICES

by Jody Lynn Nye

Jody Lynn Nye lists her main career activity as "spoiling cats." She lives northwest of Chicago with two of the above and her husband, author and packager Bill Fawcett. She has published twenty-five books, including five contemporary fantasies; three SF novels; four novels in collaboration with Anne McCaffrey, including *The Ship Who Won*; a humorous anthology about mothers, *Don't Forget Your Spacesuit, Dear!*; and over sixty short stories. Her latest books are *License Invoked*, co-written with Robert Asprin, and *Advanced Mythology*, fourth in the Mythology 101 series.

"OH, my God," Rob Dalingo said, looking up at their new home.

"It's great, Daddy," Amanda said bravely, doing her best to hold their spirits high. Her cheeks were bright pink in the stifling, 48° C heat, and her long tail of black hair hung limp. "Isn't that right, Sofran?"

"Very roomy," the red-skinned android agreed.

"It's worse than I thought," Jenette, a taller version of their daughter, said, shaking her head.

Rob agreed with her. Five bedrooms, Karawak Colony Chief Sid Edwards had promised them. Plenty of space. Wide-open air-conditioning system. Well, he'd gotten that part right, anyway—one large section of a wall in the prefabricated structure before them was missing half its ceramic panels, leaving the very strong, hot wind whistling in the joists. The windows were etched to the point of blurred distortion. Rob recognized the scratch pattern. They'd been culled from a spacecraft, probably a very old one. The only thing about the place that was true was that it was roomy. It looked to have been constructed of every leftover module from twenty derelict ships that the Karawakians had been able to cadge, buy, or salvage.

He looked around their new neighborhood. Nearly all the homes had been put together in the same way, out of spare modules that no one else in the universe wanted. Honesty compelled him to admit that their house was in the worst shape of any one of them. Probably whenever a house fell vacant, the neighbors descended on it to strip it of good or usable parts.

"Things are hard to get," Edwards said when Rob went in to complain about the missing panels and the scarred windows. "A lot of people did without so we could get you here. We thought at least you could accept what we had to offer with grace. We're paying your fee, after all."

Rob found himself at a disadvantage. What good was money, he wanted to argue, if it couldn't buy secure, weatherproof housing?

As a power systems engineer, Rob Dalingo worked exclusively on short-term assignments given to him by Vitae Corporation, based on Proxima Centauri Four. They paid him well, picked up moving expenses and allowed for yearly trips to Earth for him and his wife and small daughter. He had status, benefits, promotion opportunities—everything a man could ask for, except for a permanent home. That was out of the question. They had to make home where they landed, and make friends with the people who were there.

Karawakians didn't make the first move toward getting acquainted. The Dalingos were not taken aback. About one in four postings were like that. Jenette went right to work introducing herself, Amanda and Sofran to the neighbors.

'What's that?" the local children asked, pointing at Amanda's companion.

"She's an android," Amanda said proudly. She could tell the others were impressed. Humanlike androids were new technology, and few people had them yet. "Daddy bought her for me because we move all the time. I got to pick her out myself."

"You must be rich," Mellan Steers, a husky boy, said, to the embarrassment of his grandmother, who had come with him to the door. His family lived in the round house on the corner.

"No," Jenette said cheerfully. "She's on time payments, like our appliances."

"Why is she red? How come she's not people-colored?" asked a tall, swarthy boy named Foz Bandar.

Jenette didn't think the boy needed to hear the whole explanation. The rich colors were intended as a reminder that the androids weren't living beings. Rob thought that it was a concession to Defense United of Humankind, an annoying and ubiquitous society that was endlessly lobbying interstellar government to prevent any artificial life-form from gaining rights at the expense of Terran-based people.

None of that was important to a little girl.

"I like red," Amanda said forthrightly. "There were all kinds of colors: rose-pink, purple, gray, gold, green. There were thin ones and fat ones and short ones, too. I chose her hair. It's black like mine, but short."

"Can a machine really be a friend?" Foz's mother Ilse asked, a trifle suspiciously.

Jenette smiled. "I don't know why not. I used to name my air cars. And she has very sophisticated programming."

"She has pretty hair," said Dade Finchel, a girl about the same age who lived across the street. She had blonde curls and freckles. "Can she talk?"

"She's smarter than you," Amanda said.

"Amanda!" Jenette exclaimed sharply, then apologized to Lilian Finchel. "I'm so sorry."

"She's smarter than my dad, too," Amanda added, by way of explanation.

"Oh," Dade said.

"Perhaps Dade would like to come over and play with both of them sometime," Jenette offered.

The curly-haired girl looked Sofran up and down. "Maybe." She ran back in the house, leaving both mothers apologizing to one another. Amanda kept her head up as she followed her mother away from the door. Only Sofran saw how her shoulders drooped.

Rob let out a whistle as engineers Bertina Cho and Glen Elkar showed him the control center, a cramped kiosk at one edge of the power plant complex. With a practiced eye he examined the readouts and felt dismay. The shielded-nuclear reactor was putting out less than 65% of the optimum power level for the amount of fuel it was consuming.

"You should have called me in sooner," he said. "How old is this plant, thirty years?"

Cho, a small, chunky woman, was defensive. "They told us it was only five years old when we installed it ten years ago."

Rob pointed to a bank of gauges showing ambient radiation level, "If it's peaking like that, it has to be older. A lot older. This pattern means that the shield plates are beginning to wear through. You don't get that kind of erosion before year twenty."

Cho and Elkar looked at one another grimly. "It had to be something like that," Elkar said. He was a gangly man with thick gray hair. "When Edwards quoted the price he paid, it sounded too cheap."

"Nothing started to go wrong right away," Cho said, with resignation. "Just over the last few years things have slowed down. We get frequent brownouts. Are we in danger?"

Rob scrolled through the file of daily reports on a pad handed him by a technician. "I'm not sure. Give me a little more time to check the data. And I'll have to have a look at the physical plant. I'll go in overnight when you're on low output."

Cho and Elkar looked at each other again. "We don't have a spare rad suit."

"Don't worry," Rob said, who had guessed that would be the case. "I always bring my own."

Sofran was removing a casserole from the convection chamber in the kitchen when Rob returned to the house from the power plant.

"Good evening," she said, with her ready smile. "Amanda and Jenette are in the fifth bedchamber. Through the left corridor and turn right, then right again, just past the second bathroom."

"Thanks." Rob followed the pointing red finger. The second bathroom, as he recalled from his quick walkthrough of the house, was the one that didn't work. His guess was that it had come out of an "owner's suite" on a luxury liner and was kept around for looks. A dozen empty travel crates not yet flattened for storage were piled in its doorway.

Jenette had gone right to work making the place habitable with the help of their daughter and their android companion. He had seen mylplas sheeting attached over the framework outside where the ceramic tiles had been removed. Months' worth of dust and debris had been swept away. Holos and decorative objects stood on tables covered with Jenette's collection of colorful shawls, and their precious books were stowed in a cabinet with clear doors and a print-lock that Rob thought he recognized as a pharmacy cupboard.

He found his family in Amanda's new bedroom.

"I feel like we're living in a salvage yard," he said.

"Warmer," Jenette said with a quick smile. "Much warmer." She and Amanda were stacking Amanda's clothes in the shelves built into the wall.

"I saw your repair," he said. "Nice job. I wish we could insulate that wall. We're probably losing a good quarter of our cooling power out that way. Can we buy replacement panels anywhere?"

"No," Jenette replied. "We've got two choices: we can special-order some, or we can wait until the next shipment of secondhand modules arrives. We can't reserve items in advance from the new derelicts, but I can get into the scrimmage with the best of them."

"I know it," Rob said, with genuine admiration for his wife's capabilities. He picked up a bag of shoes and began to unload them into the pull-out drawer with brackets made for holding footwear.

"How many friends did you make today?" he asked his daughter. Over the girl's head, his wife shook her head, tight-lipped.

"Nobody," Amanda said defiantly, looking up at him. "But I don't care. I have Sofran."

Her eyes filled with tears. She sprang to her feet and dashed out of the room toward the kitchen. Rob looked after her with dismay.

"Word of your discussion with Edwards got around," Jenette explained. "They don't like criticism."

"And they took it out on Amanda?" Rob asked, furious, staring out the scratched windows at the blurry houses beyond.

"Not in so many words," Jenette said. "But they didn't encourage their children to reach out to her. And part of Amanda's problems are of her own making. She was not very tactful today. A few of them offered to play with her, but she ran back here to play with Sofran. I don't want her becoming so dependent upon her android that she neglects the opportunity to meet other children."

"She's probably feeling a little stressed settling in to a new place," Rob said, frowning. "I wouldn't worry about it. The dealer said that Sofran has programming to prevent her from allowing a human to become isolated."

"It's not her fault she might feel that way," Jenette pointed out.

"Nor mine. I only told Edwards the truth, and asked what he could do about the problems with this house. It wasn't a challenge to his authority."

"Oh, I know," Jenette said. "The folks here are not happy because there's not much they can do about the situation."

Not everyone in the central settlement was so defensive about a question or two. A few of the neighbors on the pod of houses that passed for their street who had responded to Jenette's friendly overtures appeared at their door with food over the next few days. Rob offered them coffee or real wine, treats that were always welcome on nonagricultural planets, and asked them about their life on Karawak. How did people end up at the far side of nowhere?

Tolly and Anna Carmichael, a couple of smelter operators who lived across the loop from them, were happy to talk about their adopted home. The planet had been settled by miners interested in the rich asteroid belt the next stop out from it's blue-white sun. They thought trade routes would begin to stretch out this way, but it was too far between viable worlds. Transport costs of the precious transuranics and perfect metals cut deeply into the Karawakians' profits. The two thousand settlers consoled themselves about being out of touch by having the very latest in entertainment gear and the most wonderful personal care and fitness equipment. The Dalingos were tickled by the juxtaposition of a state-of-the-art spa box in the front room of a house that had been inexpertly converted from a retired galley off a luxury space liner. Tolly had a collection of over 5,000 concert videos, of all types of music. Anna, whose bad back often spasmed after a long shift off-planet in her loader-smelter, was addicted to the massage table with fifty-eight different rollers that rubbed, kneaded, pummeled, caressed, and pounded aching muscles into blissed-out puddings.

"Everyone's got stuff like this," Tolly said. "Once you get to know people, they'll invite you to spend an evening in their pools. Bart up the road has an auto-tender that can mix over ten thousand different drinks. He never has to touch a bottle."

"This is divine," Jenette said, taking another slice of the layered entree in the heatproof container.

"Our kitchen-magician," Anna told her proudly. "Neither of us can cook, but we got this gizmo from a trader who said it's the latest thing on Terra. It can make the most uninteresting soy blocks into ambrosia."

"Fantastic," Jenette said. "We'd like to return the favor. If you'll join us in a couple of days, I'll whip up some recipes you can adapt for your kitchen-magician's CPU."

"Where's your robot?" Dade Finchel asked, when Amanda arrived at the local school at the beginning of the next week. Both little girls wore big sun hats and sunglasses to protect them from the strong UV rays of Karawak's blue-white sun.

"She stays home with my mother," Amanda explained, clutching her red-and-pink compad. "She's not a robot. She's an android. She has AI programming and a real personality."

"She's neat," Dade said.

"She's my best friend," Amanda said.

"I don't have a best friend," the blonde girl said. "Do you want to sit next to me? There's an empty seat by the window."

Amanda's eyes lit up. "Thanks."

The two were glad to get inside away from the incessant heat of a Karawak summer. Amanda was about to put her things down on the worn plastic desk, when everything went dark. Someone had tipped her hat up from the back, covering her face. She snatched it off. Foz Bandar was grinning at her from the desk chair.

"Your daddy pushes people around," he said. "He shouldn't do that."

"My dad is just doing his job," Amanda said, but she backed away from the bigger boy.

Foz got up to follow her. "You're not so brave without your mechanoid," he said. He took a piece of gravel out of his pocket and winged it at her. It stung where it hit her in the chin. "You rich people, you think you're better than us." He threw another piece, hitting her on the wrist.

"Leave me alone!" Amanda said. She looked to Dade for help, but the blonde girl huddled with the rest of the students until Ms. Thelberg came into the room and called for order. Amanda sat at the desk throughout the day with her eyes hot with tears. Dade didn't look at her.

"You wouldn't let me get hurt like that," Amanda blurted out to Sofran. As soon as the end-of-day buzzer had sounded, Amanda had run all the way home, needing reassurance.

Sofran cuddled her as they sat on the floor against Amanda's bed. She stroked the girl's cheek with gentle, dry fingers. "I am sure Dade didn't want you to be injured. She wants to be your friend."

"If Dade wants to be my friend, why didn't she say something to Foz?"

"She's probably scared of him, too," Sofran said.

Amanda pressed her lips together. "Maybe you should come with me and beat him up."

"You know I can't do that. I cannot harm people, only help them."

"Well, you're supposed to help me before anyone else."

"It's not the same thing, you know that," Sofran corrected her.

"I still like you best," Amanda told her, throwing her arms around the red android's waist. Sofran patted her on the shoulder.

It took Rob several days to read over the backlog of maintenance readouts from the reactor. He brought them back to the plant for a meeting with the system engineers.

"I'm impressed," he told Cho and Elkar. "You've done a heroic job of preserving this system. By all rights, it should have gone down long ago." He brought up a screen where he had compiled the data into a flowchart. "The reason you probably didn't realize it was malfunctioning is that it's been out of tune since it got here. The power output has only been maintained by keeping the flow unbalanced."

"I suppose that's good news as well as bad," Cho said. "But what's that mean for the long-term?"

"There is no long-term," Rob said, matter-of-factly. He tapped another key on the pad. "The trouble is that in order to keep up the output it's consuming its own shielding. It will go critical in a hundred fifty, a hundred seventy days at the outside."

"Can you fix it?"

Rob spread out his hands. "You'd be better off buying a new unit."

"Can't afford it," Cho said bluntly.

"Then I can order replacement plates and fuel rods. We'll essentially be rebuilding the inner works of the reactor. Can you approve an expenditure like that?"

"No," Elkar said. "Edwards will have to. You've got to talk to him."

Rob perched on the edge of a crate in the settlement leader's office. Every available surface was filled with data crystals, ore samples, and plastic printouts. Edwards listened grimly to Rob's report. He took copious notes, interrupting him for clarification, then slammed the stylus down on his pad. "You're sure it's as bad as that?"

"I've been in there," Rob said. "This is the maximum I would give it. When's the next round of trade ships due?"

"A hundred and four days," Edwards said, without having to refer to the chart Rob could see behind him on the wall. "The ship that brought you belongs to one of the two shipping corps who do business out in this arm of the galaxy, Scowell's and Point-to-Point. They're not due for a hundred and fifty."

"That's pushing it too close. Will you beam an order to Scowell's?"

"Right. What can you do in the meantime?"

"Group effort," Rob said. "The entire colony is going to have to cut back sharply on power use to spare the reactor shielding. You've been using power freely, and it is stressing the system beyond its capacity. Any nonessential use must be stopped."

"No," Edwards said, waving away the adamant statement. "We don't tell people what to do around here. What's the safest output you recommend?" Rob handed him his figures. "All right. It'll be better if we ration. We'll give every family a power allowance and let them decide how they want to use it." The leader gave Rob a hard look. "Mechanoids don't count. Your family is three, not four."

"I understand," Rob said. "That's no problem. Sofran doesn't need much. She doesn't eat or drink."

But that wasn't true, he realized on his way back to his quarters. The android did need to be recharged for at least an hour every night. He had forgotten about it because he rarely witnessed it. Sofran hooked herself up to a power source during the time of least usage, to avoid running up power bills. She used only a trickle of energy, though once every thirty days her storage batteries had to undergo a deep drain. Rob took a deep breath. Even with the ration they were allotted, there should be plenty to supply Sofran.

They needed her. That evening Edwards set out a video message to every family on the planet, instructing them that from then until the reactor was repaired all power usage would be strictly monitored, and laying out the conditions of allotment. The Dalingo family's communications lines were immediately flooded with complaints.

"Don't blame me," Rob told one caller after another. "It's no one's fault. The grid is going. That's a fact. The stats are in a downloadable file. You can review them for yourself."

"We do without enough," said an angry neighbor who buttonholed Rob outside the leader's office. "You can't ask us to stop playing videos. And what about my sauna? I have to have my sauna every day!"

Rob shook his head, refusing to be baited. "You'll have to decide that for yourself."

But the Karawakians were not accustomed to limits. They muttered complaints or threats whenever they passed Jenette or Rob on the street. Rob accepted a certain amount of guff aimed in his direction, knowing that they had to take out their frustration somehow, but it began to affect Amanda.

"Wattsucker," For Bandar sneered at Amanda at recess the next firstday.

"What's that mean?" she asked, more curious than intimidated.

Foz came toward her, chin out. She backed up until she hit a wall. Foz had never been very friendly. "My dad took away our VR gamebox, and it's *your dad's* fault!"

Amanda crossed her arms. "He's doing his job." She looked right and left, looking for a way out. She couldn't see a teacher or the play yard supervisor.

Another boy, Mellan Steers, came up on her right, looming over her. "What are you using all our electricity for? That fancy robot of yours?"

"We aren't taking any extra electricity!"

"Daddy said our merry-go-round was off limits," Dade Finchel said, joining the growing crowd around her. Amanda became frightened. Dade had seemed as if she was going to be Amanda's friend, but now she looked angry. She had to get away from there. She dodged to the left. Foz headed her off, a mean smile on his face. Mellan crowded in behind her. Wasn't anyone going to help her?

A buzzer sounded, signaling the end of recess. Some of the children went away, but a bunch stayed. They hadn't done anything yet, but they looked like they wanted to. If someone started hitting her, they would all join in. Amanda opened her mouth to scream for help. Foz shoved his arm against her face just as an adult voice interrupted them.

"What is going on here?" The mob melted away. Foz scooted off with the rest, leaving Amanda, with a big red mark across her cheek, leaning on the wall. She couldn't stop crying. "Oh, it's you, Amanda Dalingo. Come with me."

The teacher ushered Amanda inside and called her mother. Jenette arrived within a few minutes. She and the teacher had an intense but hushed conversation over Amanda's head, during which the girl could hear angry words like "toaster oven."

"Come on, honey," Jenette said, stooping to wipe the tears off her daughter's face. "We're leaving."

Amanda glanced back at the school as they hurried away from it. Through the bulgy windows she could see distorted faces of the other children, making horrible grimaces at her.

"I am *never* going back there!" she declared.

"Not for a while," her mother agreed. "Sofran can teach you at home until we get this straightened out."

Sofran hugged Amanda as soon as she got in the door. "I was very worried about you," the android said in her calm voice, which made Amanda feel comforted and want to cry some more all at the same time. "I will take care of you. Would you like some lunch?"

Amanda shook her head. "All right. Shall I read you a story? I found some very interesting historical myths in the local library database." Amanda nodded. She couldn't find words, but that was all right. Sofran found them for her.

"Go on, honey," Jenette said. "I'm going to call your father."

The stories fascinated Amanda, especially the one about the giant spider. She liked him even though he was a thief. Sofran suggested that they make believe they were Anansi and one of his friends, and hunt for the treasure in the house.

"What is the treasure?" Amanda asked, eagerly.

Sofran held a carmine finger to her lips. "We'll know it when we find it."

Everything was fun after that, until the other children came home from school. Right outside the Dalingos' house they started a game in which they were killing imaginary pirates called the Amandas. Fox, in particular, took great delight in squashing Amandas into the ground with his feet. The real Amanda ran to hide as deep in the center of the house as possible.

Sofran came to sit with her, patting her and murmuring calm, comforting words while she wept.

"What's going on out there?" Rob asked when he came home around dinnertime. "Where's Amanda?"

Jenette pulled him into her office and told him all about the incident on the playground. "They've been out there for hours. I can't help but hear them through the holes in the insulation. They've invented a villain and named it after her."

Rob's face was set. "I'm going to go talk to their parents now. I want Edwards to take control of this issue. I will not let them make my daughter a target!"

Jenette held his arm, keeping him from heading toward the comcenter. "I've arranged for a forum with the other parents. Let's not make an issue of it in front of Amanda."

"Where is she?" Rob asked, looking around.

"Sofran is taking care of her," Jenette said, with a small smile curling the solemn corners of her lips.

Rob sighed. "Thank God for Sofran. I'm glad Amanda's not having to take this alone."

Both of them thought it was best to shelter Amanda from her peers for a while. Under Jenette's watchful eye, she and Sofran played outside while the other children were at school. During the afternoons, Sofran gave the girl her lessons from the curriculum so she would be current with her peers, if ever they became nonhostile enough to let Amanda return to class. Rob worried about his daughter feeling isolated, but she seemed to do just fine with one staunch friend. He was relieved when she met him at the door, laughing, out of breath from a hilarious game of hide and seek. She would get by.

About a month later Rob was walking to the plant when he heard a siren begin blaring the danger signal, two short blasts followed by one long blast, over and over. Technicians pulling on bright red hazmat suits emerged from stations around the plant and ran for the reactor station. Rob dashed after them.

Cho was there already. The little woman, enveloped in a huge suit that had been made for a big man, blocked Rob from entering the facility.

"Radiation leak!" she shouted over the blaring alarms. "Valves blew in one of the recycling tanks!"

Rob groaned. He was afraid this could happen. "Is anyone carrying a video link in there?"

"Elkar's inside," Cho said.

"Let me see." Cho spoke into a pickup radio on her shoulder, then held out her wrist so Rob could see the miniature screen on the back of her hand.

The shielding interfered with clear transmission, but Rob could make out the figures of a half-dozen technicians struggling to disassemble the mechanism topping the cooling tank. Steam obscured the camera just as they got the pipes unfastened. Rob knew just what had happened. One of the power rods must be fracturing, sending erratic bursts through the system. The reactor was deteriorating faster than he had estimated. There could be an explosion if they didn't move fast.

"Give me that suit," he ordered Cho. Without hesitation, she undid the seals and stepped out of it. Rob pulled it on in record time, closing the flaps of cloth and doing the security check as he walked. By the time he reached the first radiation barrier, everything was in place. His mind was on the job ahead.

The Karawakians were glad to make way for the visiting engineer. Rob had the entire schematic of the reactor system in his head. Barking orders at the other technicians, he and Elkar were able to get the leak under control and isolate the faulty rod. It was with open relief that they watched the glowing, eight-foot isotope plunge into the safety pool below it. Everyone let out a cheer when clouds of steam poured upward from the liquid-filled chamber. Soon the alarms stilled.

"That's better," Elkar said, tilting his head back as the two of them stood in the decontamination shower.

"It's going to make things tighter for all of us," Rob said, rubbing his hands through his hair to make sure the solution got all the way to the scalp. "That section was one of only six rods. Demand is obviously still putting a strain on the system. I thought I had calculated it pretty well." Elkar looked sheepish. "What's up?"

The other engineer hesitated before replying. "My mother-in-law got after me to loop around the governor on her power line. Can't do without her massage mechanoid, she said. My wife insisted. Sorry."

Rob looked at him in disbelief. "Oh, come on, you know how bad it is! Well, at least it's just you pulling extra power."

"Well," Elkar said, matter-of-factly, "it's not." He strode into the secondary detection chamber before Rob could ask him what he was talking about.

Rob ran a trace on the power usage of the entire colony. Of eight hundred homes and other buildings, he realized that more than 70% of them had circumvented the rationing scheme to some extent. With new figures in hand he went to see Edwards.

". . . And now you see with 16% of the reactor out of service for good we are going to have to cut back even farther on the amount of power we use. There will have to be some kind of penalty for using more."

"We can't do that," Edwards said.

"You have to," Rob insisted. "I cannot guarantee even the five remaining rods will stay intact if we keep exceeding capacity like this. There could be a disaster. You don't have enough emergency facilities to keep going if that happens."

Edwards made another announcement ordering the new cuts. Unhappily, but at Rob's insistence, he instituted a patrol that would make the rounds of the settlement on a daily basis to make sure no one was cheating.

The Karawakians were furious with the directive.

"We've cut our consumption to the bone," Ilse Bandar told Rob furiously. "We can't conserve any further and still live. I don't see why we can't have just a little more power. My boy wants to watch his videos!"

Rob was growing weary of having the same argument with everyone he met. "You may not like it, but you have to do it. Everyone has to cooperate, in order for the colony to survive until the new parts arrive. It'll only be a few more weeks."

"In a few weeks, we will have anarchy," Ilse vowed, tossing her head. "But you, you are unaffected. You don't care. You've got all your luxuries, haven't you? Your expensive toys, and your mechanoid."

"I'm in the same boat with everyone else," Rob assured her. "My daughter had to give up her play console, too. The android uses very little power, less than it takes to run a light." He could tell she didn't believe him. He didn't blame her. The Karawakians had been ill-supplied, cheated, isolated, and were saddled with a leader who didn't like to make hard decisions. They didn't often come across someone who told the plain truth.

He woke up in the middle of the night a few days later to the faint hoot of an alarm.

"What's that?" Jenette asked sleepily.

Rob threw off the light sheet which was all they ever needed in the Karawakian climate and listened. "It's the cold storage," he said. He felt for the touch-light. It didn't go on. "Is the lamp burned out?" he asked.

"It was fine earlier," Jenette said. She pulled the blinds aside and glanced out the window. The public lights were still shining. By their light Rob found his way to the door and felt his way through the multiple corridors to the kitchen. Only a single amber light flashed, the power alarm on the refrigeration unit. Rob palmed the touchpad on the wall, but the lights didn't come on.

"We've lost power," he told Jenette, who padded along behind him.

"Did someone cut the line?" his wife asked. "Sorry. I'm getting suspicious in my old age."

Rob found a chemical torch and shook it until the filament glowed brightly. He inspected the lines both inside and outside the house. "Everything's fine," he said. "We must just have exceeded our power allotment for the day, and the line governor shut everything down. The system runs midnight to midnight."

By the lantern's glow they found insulating blankets and covered the refrigerator and freezer units. When midnight came, all the appliances hummed into life, and the Dalingos went back to bed.

"I must have miscalculated," Rob said, a little shamefacedly.

The next afternoon, Jenette called him at the power plant to tell him that the house had shut down again. Rob returned to find the house dark and blazingly hot inside. All four of them began pulling open windows and ventilation ducts until a feeble air flow trickled through the house. Rob took his power use figures to the local spacers' inn where they had dinner.

"I can't understand it," he said, going over the spreadsheet again and again. "I thought we had all our consumption under control."

He realized with horror, as Amanda and Sofran were talking over what Amanda would order for dessert, that he had missed one thing: Sofran.

"Sofran," Rob asked carefully, "did you plug in last night?"

"Of course, sir," the android said, turning to look at him. "My thirty-day discharge/charge cycle came due."

Rob groaned. Jenette gave him a sharp look and shook her head. *Not here.* The two of them would have to work out how to save enough power for her battery discharge before the next cycle came due.

"Mr. Edwards, how nice to see you," Jenette said, opening the door to the settlement leader. "Please come in."

"I can't stay," the big man said, as she ushered him into the family room and seated him in their favorite easy chair. He looked very uncomfortable. "Is your husband here?"

"Sofran, do you know where Rob is?" Jenette called to the android, who appeared in the corridor with Amanda's compad.

"In Amanda's room, helping her with her homework," Sofran replied. "I will go get him."

Edwards tapped his fingers together until the engineer arrived. "Dalingo, I hate to bring this up, but I've had a lot of complaints."

"About what?" Rob asked.

"Well, about *her,*" the leader said, pointing at the red android, who hovered in the doorway, watching with concern. "She caused a power failure here about three weeks ago, isn't that so?"

"In a matter of speaking," Rob said. "It won't happen again."

"How won't it happen again?"

"It's part of her regular cycle. She has to flush her batteries once a month. I forgot to take that into account when I calculated our power usage. She normally runs on a trickle charge, about what it would take to light a lamp. Why?"

"Well, the fact is," Edwards said, uneasily, "that everyone knows your house went dark, but it hasn't happened since. People are saying that you're bending the rules, taking in more power than everyone else, just to keep your daughter's companion operating."

"That's not true!" Jenette said, horrified.

"I can show you the figures," Rob said. "I can have someone else meter her for a day to prove it."

"Well, I'm just telling you what people are saying. You're the one who's making everyone else hang tough on the limits. They don't see that you're in the same boat with all the rest of us. I'm glad to hear the rumors are not true."

"Will you spread the word?" Rob asked.

"Sure," Edwards said, rising. He glanced at Sofran. "I'm not sure they'll believe me, that's all."

"You look tired," Jenette said, pushing a platter of baked chicken toward Rob. He speared a couple of pieces and transferred them to his plate, not really looking at them.

"Tough day," he said. "This is good. I thought the roaster and the dishwasher couldn't run on the same day."

"Anna and I have gone co-op on meal preparation until the crisis is over," she said. "We'll be cleaning all their dishes because she cooked. We're trying to get some of the other households to join us and save power."

"I wish everyone else would cooperate as well as the Carmichaels do," Rob said dejectedly. "We located another five houses that went around their power governors. Every single one of them gave me a hard time when we disconnected their illegal hookups. We've only got forty days to go before the replacement parts are due, but the reactor may not last at this rate."

"I think that you should shut me down," Sofran spoke up suddenly.

"No!" Amanda cried. "Daddy, you can't take her away. *Please.*"

"I don't want to go that far if we can avoid it, Sofran," Rob said with concern. "I've read your documentation. There's a possibility that if we drain your power you may lose your personality forever. The technology is too new. I don't want to risk it. Besides, we don't need what little power your loss would contribute."

"My function is to do what is best for my companion," Sofran said, tilting her head. "I have been observing the behavior of the neighborhood. You require cooperation. Under the circumstances they do not wish to give it. It is their perception, not the reality that matters."

Amanda looked genuinely frightened. "Please, Daddy, don't do it. She's my best friend. If you turn her off, I'll die. I really will."

Rob reached out to stroke her hair. "Don't worry, honey. I'll stumble around in the dark before we have to go that far."

Amanda and Sofran were lying on their stomachs in Amanda's room designing an animal cartoon on Amanda's compad when they heard the door chime.

"Jenette's at Mrs. Carmichael's," Sofran reminded her. Amanda scrambled to her feet and went to answer the door. She peered through the spyhole.

"It's Dade," she said.

"Open the door," Sofran urged her. "Dade is nice. She wishes to be your friend."

Amanda looked at her desperately. "I don't need her. I've got you. Let's go add some ruffles to the lion's mane. She can't see us. If we don't open the door, she'll think no one is home."

Sofran smiled at the girl. It was against her programming to foster dependency. Such behavior would stunt Amanda's development into a healthy adult. She pulled open the door. "Look, Amanda. Dade is here."

The curly-haired girl stood shyly on the stoop. "Hi. You haven't been back at school."

"I don't want to be there," Amanda said darkly. "Everyone's a jerk."

"Even me?" Dade asked, looking sad.

Amanda opened her mouth. Sofran interrupted her. "No, you are not a jerk. It was those boys."

"Do you want to play?" Dade asked Amanda, her eyes pleading.

"I have . . ." Amanda gestured back toward her room. Sofran could tell she was yearning to go back there where it was safe, but the other girl's body language was open and friendly. She would be an ideal friend.

". . . Nothing to do for an hour before supper," Sofran finished the sentence for her. Dade beamed.

"That's terrific!"

"You come, too," Amanda told Sofran.

"I cannot," the android said. "I must clean the dining area before we eat. Go ahead. I will call you when it is time."

Reluctantly, Amanda allowed herself to be dragged outside. Dade talked all the while. Sofran read her speech on her lips, information about an upcoming school play with parts for several girls. Such an activity would provide good bonding experiences for Amanda. The two of them sat down on the shaded veranda of Dade's house and fell into an animated conversation about pets and school and fashion, all appropriate topics for their age group.

Soon, Amanda stopped looking back at the house. Sofran acknowledged that, and went to fulfill her other chores.

"We can't cut any further, Dalingo," Edwards said. A contingent of angry neighbors had come to the house with the settlement leader at their head to protest Rob's latest findings. "Some of us are down to deciding whether to cook dinner or clean clothes one day or another."

Rob glanced out at the thirty or so people in the street. "It's not a fresh cut I'm asking for," he said. "We need to cut down on cheats. Every one of you knows someone who's diverting extra energy. The reactor really cannot take it. There's only a few weeks to go. Can't you all control yourselves until then?"

"You're a hell of a one to talk," Ilse Bandar shouted, shaking her fist from the back of the group. The crowd of children who had been playing in the loop gathered at one side to watch and see what their parents were doing. Rob saw his own daughter among them. Sofran and Jenette were behind him on the porch, listening. He was tempted to send one or both of them out to get her, in case the argument got really ugly. "You're the worst cheat of all, with that mechanoid of yours."

"I keep telling you," Rob shouted, over the growing hubbub, "she doesn't consume any measurable amount of power. If we turn her off, she might never work again."

"Liar!" a man yelled.

"Now, come on," Rob said, trying to be reasonable. "You're not really angry with me. You don't like the inconvenience, but it's temporary. If you will all be patient, this will all be over very shortly. Edwards!"

The settlement leader shrugged. Rob closed his fists with frustration. That spineless weakling was going to stand there and let him take the heat. A soft hand touched his forearm. Sofran smiled at him as she slipped past, walking over to Amanda. The girl, sitting on the curb arm in arm with Dade, looked up at her curiously.

"Amanda, it is time."

"For dinner?" Amanda asked, looking at her parents and the mob of adults.

"No, time for me to go. I must leave you now."

Amanda sprang up and threw her arms around the android. "But I need you! You're my very best friend!"

Sofran smiled gently. "I was never meant to be your *only* friend. I am a machine. You should not depend on machines. Dade is human. The others you play with every day are human, too. They'll grow with you."

"I love *you*," Amanda said, with tears running down her cheeks. Sofran enfolded the girl in a hug.

"I wish I understood that emotion the way that you do. My programming allows me to understand that my instructions are properly carried out when I fulfill tasks for you, which I believe you could associate with affection. I am here to serve you and your family. This is the best thing that I can do for you. My understanding of human behavior suggests a high probability of a favorable outcome. You must trust me." She let Amanda go and turned to face the crowd, which had fallen silent. "It is the instruction of my owner that I must turn myself off for the good of the colony. I will fulfill her order now."

The red-skinned android put her arms down at her sides and stood very straight. In between one blink and another, she stopped moving. Amanda burst into sobs. Dad put her arms around her and pulled her head onto her shoulder.

The people in the crowd shuffled their feet. Anna Carmichael broke the silence. She came over to Amanda and kissed her on the cheek.

"Thank you, dear. That was very generous of you."

Rob stood on the porch, dumbfounded, staring at the still figure and the two little girls beside it. He didn't stir until Edwards came forward to pat him on the back. "Good man. All right, folks! We're all equal now. This guy's given up everything he has for us, even his child's companion. Can we try and cooperate with him a little better? Just three more weeks. Are you with me?"

The unanimous cheer humbled Rob, but not as much as Sofran's sacrifice. She was Amanda's true friend, even in her manner of leaving.

The crowd of protesters in front of the house melted way, leaving only the gaggle of children, with Amanda at their center, to play in the cooling Karawak evening.

HORSEPOWER

by Paul Dellinger

A longtime newspaper reporter, Paul Dellinger has published stories in *Amazing Stories* and *The Magazine of Fantasy & Science Fiction,* and a number of paperback anthologies, including *The Williamson Effect, First Contact, Lord of the Fantastic,* and *Guardsmen of Tomorrow.* He and his wife Maxine, who serves as his guardian angel, live in Virginia.

"ONE silicon, one carbon," the commentator called out for the sixth time in a bored-sounding monotone, as yet another horse and rider passed beneath the twenty-foot horseshoe shape of the pulsing monitor. Eric guided Golden Cloud with light pressure from his heels against its sides. The palomino-colored mount responded like a well-oiled machine—no surprise, since it had been entered in the annual Silicon Steeplechase by none other than Irene Ostling, arguably the most gifted roboticist of her time. And by far the most controversial.

The line of horse-shaped creatures continued to clump through the monitoring device—white, black, spotted, bay, dun, and every other color their creators could come up with to resemble the all but vanished animals they replicated. They looked as though they belonged here in the Cotswold Hills, the rolling English lowlands over which the event was to be run. After all, there was much tradition involved. Once, actual horses had made similar runs over these very hills, but that was back when there had been actual horses.

"Go, Eric!" a slim, dark-haired woman called from the spectator seats surrounding the starting line on three sides. Her husband, dapper in a tailored one-piece coverall, which was the current fashion for no obvious reason, shot her a look of disapproval.

"Well, Golden Cloud is the prettiest of the pack," she said, consulting her program. "And I hope Eric wins."

"You'd best hope Mechanical Monster wins, my dear," he said, pointing to a large gray steed just emerging from the monitor. "I've put a considerable amount of our plastic on him."

"Oh, Herbert, where is your soul? That thing even looks robotic. At least, Golden Cloud is designed with some flair. Look at that flowing white mane, and tail. And that golden coat—why, he positively glows."

"He," Herbert repeated with a chuckle. "Evelyn, I despair of bringing you to these events if you become so anthropomorphic about them. Next, you'll be wanting to buy one of those machines and bring it home as a pet, the way you wanted to do at that dog show last month."

Evelyn wrinkled her delicate nose. "Some people do exactly that, you know," she said softly. "It's all we have left."

"And whose fault is that?" The abrupt question came from the severe-looking woman sitting with military straightness one row down from them. She turned to look directly at them over her shoulder, a scrutiny which made Herbert want to squirm. "If we homo sapiens would stop increasing our numbers exponentially every generation, there would still be living space for the amenities. We could have fields of deer, flocks of geese, dogs and cats as companions. . . ."

"I beg your pardon, madam. I don't believe we were speaking to you," Herbert interrupted.

The stiffness in the older woman's expression vanished, and her thin lips relaxed almost into a smile. "Point taken," she said, and turned back around to watch the racers line up.

But Evelyn was reaching out, tapping the woman on the shoulder, despite more disapproving glances from her husband. "Excuse me—excuse me, but aren't you . . . ?"

"Yes, my dear, I'm Dr. Ostling. So, naturally, I'm rooting for Eric, too."

"Of course! I saw you on the telly just this week, on one of those old-fashioned interview things." Evelyn's shapely eyebrows molded themselves into an unaccustomed frown. "But—well, if memory serves, it seems to me you were making an argument against robotics."

"Against excessive robotics," Ostling said, turning to look at her again. "Against those mechanical pets you and your husband were just conversing about, for example."

"I don't understand," Evelyn said. "You, you're a roboticist . . ."

"Evelyn," cautioned her husband.

The young woman flushed. "Please pardon me, Dr. Ostling. I hadn't meant to be intrusive."

"Think nothing of it, my dear. Obviously, I don't mind expressing my views. And robotics, if I do say so, is a subject I do know something about."

"I've seen some of your work," Herbert said, intrigued despite himself. "A couple with whom we socialize—you remember Blanche and Marie," he said in an aside to his wife. "They have one of your robot kittens, and it is entirely lifelike."

"Young man, have you ever seen a live kitten?" Ostling asked him.

"In fact, yes, I have. Evelyn and I once visited one of the few animal enclaves they still have in the Americas, just a few years ago. We saw several kittens, and cats, and dogs, for that matter—even some cattle. But those kittens seemed to me no better than yours."

"Except mine will remain a kitten forever. It will never grow into a cat."

"Oh, yes," agreed Evelyn. "It will retain its cuteness always. So superior to the biological version."

Ostling closed her eyes briefly and sighed. "It will be only a toy for as long as it lasts. It cannot change with the family, or be a part of it. It will have only the limited personality my programmers were able to give it. It would be little different from building a robot baby. People love babies, of course. But a baby forever?"

Herbert drew in his breath sharply, and glanced at the spectators on either side to see if any had overheard. "Humanoid robots are no joking matter, Doctor."

"Herbert, she didn't mean . . ."

"No, Herbert, I certainly didn't. I remember all too well how mobs dragged three of my colleagues from their laboratories and beat them to death only a few years ago for even suggesting such creations—not to replace humans, but to work where humans could not, cleaning radioactive waste piles, exploring other planets and satellites, tending undersea food production facilities. . . ."

"Doctor, please, keep your voice down," Herbert whispered. "That kind of talk can still provoke . . ." He paused, as though seeking the right words. "Serious anxieties," he concluded lamely.

"An interesting way of putting it," Ostling murmured. Then, in a louder voice: "Yes, who could say, if the work was good enough, that you yourself might not be a creature of silicon? Or your charming wife, here beside you? Perhaps there really is a shop somewhere called Marionettes, Inc."

Herbert recognized the reference. "A story in one of those books burned by those same mobs you mentioned," he said quietly.

Ostling regarded him with new respect. "Someone who still reads," she said with a touch of surprise in her voice. "In which case you may realize how the burning of those books would have horrified that particular author."

"It horrified a lot of us," Herbert said.

"Oh, look," Evelyn cut in on their conversation. "They're getting ready to start."

"Eric, control your machine," one of the judges at the starting line called to the rider on Golden Cloud. "Horselike uneasiness is not a necessary program for this, you know."

Eric nodded and spoke softly to his mount, one hand gently patting the smooth neck to activate what the judge presumed were camouflaged mechanisms. The horse, which had been dancing about in an unsettled manner, gave a good imitation of calming down.

"Amazingly lifelike," acknowledged the judge. Some of the other riders, whose steeds stood as still as stone, cast looks of irritation in Eric's direction. This steeplechase was, after all, a major entertainment event like every show in which replicas of long-departed animals were involved. And any mannerisms that could be programmed into the silicon steeds to make them seem more like actual horses were proven audience-pleasers. Ostling's reputation as the preeminent roboticist of the decade seemed to be intact.

The starting flags dropped, and Eric touched his heels to Golden Cloud's sides. The golden steed leaped forward, as the riders on either side were still twisting, pushing or turning various hidden controls to get their mounts underway. The judge who had admonished Eric earlier couldn't help smiling in appreciation. To place sensors along the sides of the horse, so that pressure would make it speed up just like an actual horse, was a stroke of genius on the part of Ostling and her people.

"Golden Cloud takes a smooth lead as the chase begins," intoned an announcer whose voice would be piped to headphones at each spectator's seat, so each could decide whether to listen or just watch. "Mechanical Monster, last year's champion, has moved out in a close second. Blackjack, Koko, and Thunder are vying for the third. . . ."

Mechanical Monster's legs pounded the ground in a loud staccato which narrowed the distance between him and the leader. The small unicornlike horn built into the middle of his solid gray forehead seemed pointed threateningly at the horse and rider ahead. The rest of the pack was moving up as well.

"They're going to catch him! They're going to catch him!" a distressed Evelyn cried out. "Why doesn't Eric make him go faster?"

Ostling twisted around toward her, a movement made more difficult now by the fact that their section of seats was speeding along a set of tracks that paralleled the race course. As long as the pack of mechanical racers did not spread out too far, viewers who had paid for these premium accommodations would be able, literally, to follow along for the entire event.

"It's a matter of conserving strength, my dear," Ostling said. "Some of the more difficult obstacles will be coming up very soon."

"Why does Eric need to save his strength?" asked Herbert, looking intently at her. "The machine is doing all the work."

Ostling merely shook her head in a distracted fashion. She watched closely as the steellike Mechanical Monster moved into the lead, and two others seemed about to do so as well.

"Why is it called a steeplechase, anyway?" Evelyn inquired out of nowhere.

"Because they are, quite literally, chasing steeples," Herbert explained, raising his voice against the sounds of their platform's passage along the rails beneath them. "It started centuries ago as a sport among riders who would race across country from one church steeple to another."

Ostling actually pulled her gaze from the race for a few seconds to look at him again. "You truly are well informed, young man."

He smiled. "It's not generally a trait that draws praise these days."

"No." She turned back to the race. "The first fences should be coming up now."

Ian, the rider aboard Mechanical Monster, cursed as the first fence came up unexpectedly just over a rise. As he had figured, the obstacles had been changed since he rode to a win last year. But he had failed to anticipate this one.

He balanced himself in his stirrups as he freed one hand from the reins to hit the reprogramming buttons, hidden behind Mechanical Monster's wirelike gray mane. His fingers moved like those of a skilled keyboarder. The steed's gait changed, almost dislodging Ian even though he was ready for it, and his leap barely cleared the wooden fence.

Some of those behind him were not so lucky, or so quick, or their programs were not as responsive as his. Ian heard the splintering of wood as one or more of the silicon horses plowed through it. He found himself hoping that, even though they were his competitors, none of them were disabled—and, of course, that none of his fellow riders were injured. It was amazing, he reflected, not for the first time, how attached one could get to these mindless silicon automatons.

He found himself reconsidering his charitable wishes when he glimpsed something golden moving up alongside him.

"He's done it! He's leading again," enthused Evelyn. "Go, Eric! Go! Isn't he wonderful?"

"Just like some movies I once saw," said her husband. "Especially with that flowing white mane and tail."

Ostling threw a sharp glance his way. "Are you referring to motion pictures, young man? On film?"

"Quite. I'm with the government's Bureau of Antiquities, so I'm conversant with quite a few of those obsolete entertainments from the past century."

"That's a very interesting," said Ostling. "If Golden Cloud should win today, I might have something even more interesting to tell you."

Herbert nodded to himself as though the statement confirmed something to him, but Ostling had already turned back to the race course.

"Golden Cloud has not seemed to require any visible reprogramming to jump the fences and hedges encountered so far," the announcer observed. "His rider has simply kept his hands on the reins. In fact, I haven't detected any touching of control mechanisms by him in the entire race. He simply leans forward and speaks to the steed." The narration stopped abruptly, as the import of what he had said apparently sunk in. "Perhaps the roboticist who crafted Golden Cloud has actually achieved voice-activated controls. . . ."

"Is that it?" Evelyn asked excitedly. "Did you?"

"In a manner of speaking," Ostling said.

"Oh, how wonderful. Herbert, that must be a breakthrough in robotics, mustn't it?"

"It's certainly a breakthrough in something," her husband acknowledged.

* * *

Mechanical Monster had regained his lead, but Golden Cloud was pressing him. The rest of the pack had faded. If nothing happened to change things, it was obvious that the winner would be one of these two.

Something happened.

As one of the most popular entertainments carried over the wide-band transmissions into the viewing centers of every home, office, or pub where anyone wanted to watch—and many liked to watch any event featuring the likenesses of such rare animals—the Silicon Steeplechase necessitated precautions on a massive scale. One of these was to send a squadron of observers in the air and on foot over the course in advance of the race, to make sure all the obstacles were in readiness and no problems had developed along the route.

But no precautions had ever been adequate to completely counter the perversity of the human animal.

"Are they coming, Cecil?" whispered one of the two men concealed beneath a hedge. "Can you see any of 'em yet?"

"Yeah. Yeah, two of them just popped up over that hill yonder. They'll be on us in less than a minute. Get ready!"

"I'm ready, all right," the first man said, gripping his side of a cloth banner with the words MEN, NOT ROBOTS inscribed on it in blood-red letters. Cecil and his companion belonged to the class of the recently unemployed, their places at a local pub having been taken by a pair of mechanical servers. Even though the mechanicals bore no resemblance to humans, which would have actually generated some sympathy for Cecil and Roderick among their pubs' patrons, they recorded orders with much more precision and less surliness than the unhappy pair had ever done.

Not surprisingly, the ex-servers did not see things from that point of view at all. Rather, they saw themselves as having been replaced by robots, whether they walked like men or rolled on wheels. This would be an opportunity to make their point before millions of observers—at least those who were not otherwise occupied during the steeplechase. In fact, the patrons of the Gone Goose were no doubt watching as well, Roderick reflected with some smugness. They would soon recognize him as a celebrity. . . .

Cecil adjusted his zoom-glasses. "Yeah, there are three little TV birds buzzing along all around the leaders. No matter which one is on screen at the time, we'll be seen, right enough. Get set, now. . . .

"Something's wrong up ahead there," said Herbert, who was using a pair of zoom-glasses of his own. "Someone is moving, just behind that hillock where the leaders are heading."

Ostling stood up, and nearly lost her balance as she failed to compensate for the speed of the moving rows of seats. It was Evelyn who reached down and caught her.

"Oh, no," Ostling said. "Not now. Not after all this!"

Two figures shot up in front of the pounding racers, each holding one of two supports for a sign of some sort. Golden Cloud's hooves skidded in the turf as he slid to a stop, then whirled away from the sudden obstacles with dazzling speed to one side. Eric came out of the saddle in the direction opposite the spin, and plowed into the ground on his left shoulder.

A collective gasp rose from the moving spectators. It seemed, even from this distance, they could hear an audible thump as the rider impacted.

Mechanical Monster apparently had no built-in safety mechanism to avoid sudden obstacles, or his rider was too slow in activating it. Like a missile on legs, he tore right through the middle of the sign. The men holding it were knocked violently in opposite directions, as half a dozen race officials leaped from the moving stand onto the course and ran toward them.

Ian, who had managed to stay riding on the steel-gray, belatedly activated some controls beneath its mane along the neck. Mechanical Monster slowed, but then appeared to become paralyzed, grinding to a standstill with one front hoof partially raised. Ian practically pounded at the controls in frustration, but the contrivance remained frozen in place.

"Mechanical Monster appears to have locked up," the voice of the announcer needlessly told the audience and viewers. "Ian is trying frantically to get him going again. Eric is getting to his feet, and waving off assistance from the approaching officials."

"Why doesn't he let them help him?" Evelyn asked.

"It would disqualify him," Ostling said. "But he doesn't look as if he can go on."

Eric was using only one arm to wave away the officials. His left hung limply at his side. A groan came from some of the spectators when they noticed it, especially those who had put their money on Ostling's inventive entry.

"The rest of the field is closing," the announcer said. "It's anyone's race now."

"Oh, Eric," Ostling said in almost a whisper. "What have I done?" Golden Cloud pranced in a circle around where Eric stood, in contrast to the still-immobile Mechanical Monster. Holding out his good arm, Eric appeared to speak to his mount. "He does respond to voice commands. He does!" Evelyn said breathlessly. "Dr. Ostling, you have exceeded yourself."

But Ostling's thin lips remained drawn together tightly. She watched as Eric carefully approached the golden horse from its side, finally getting his good hand along its neck and seeming to stroke it. Then he placed a foot in the stirrup and, with his good hand, pulled himself back into the saddle.

The race officials had reached the fallen men, who seemed to be in worse shape than Eric. There was a call for stretchers to remove them from the course. However, the sympathy of the audience seemed entirely for Eric, and not for a pair of pranksters who had almost ruined the event for which each spectator had paid a premium for deluxe seating.

With one arm still hanging uselessly at his side, and the rest of the pack now thundering past, Eric used pressure from his heels to turn Golden Cloud back toward the last part of the race course, and get him started in that direction. Mechanical Monster remained standing like a rock statue.

"It's a real horse, isn't it, Dr. Ostling?"

The roboticist twisted around toward where Herbert was seated behind her. Evelyn was staring at her husband in surprise.

"Are you really from the Bureau of Antiquities, young man?" Ostling asked. "It does seem an improbable coincidence that we should be seated so closely together. Not to mention the unlikelihood of you affording these seats on a government salary."

"Of course he's with the Bureau of Antiquities," Evelyn said. "He's been with it since it was organized a decade ago. Herbert has always been more interested in oddities from the twentieth century than new things."

"But I am on loan to the government's investigative arm," Herbert interrupted. Evelyn seemed more surprised at that than did Ostling. "I wasn't supposed to tell anyone, dear," he said to his wife. "It was only for this one job which, in fact, does involve something from the previous century. Doesn't it, Doctor?"

"Why are you telling us now?" Ostling asked.

"It doesn't matter anymore. I've confirmed what

they suspected. You're not going to deny it, are you, Doctor?" Herbert said. When she remained silent, he continued. "We already knew you and your robotics people had negotiated with the folks who ran that museum in California, the one where a once-famous film actor had his equally famous horse mounted and on display. What did you get, Doctor? A few of its hairs? A bit of its skin?"

"It doesn't take much DNA with today's cloning techniques," Ostling replied. "But that was four years ago. Besides, there was nothing illegal about the transaction."

"No, not about that. They brought me in partly, I suppose, because I was familiar with the horse—what a horse! His performances in those old films were nothing short of amazing—and because there was some question of whether you were somehow combining cloning with robotics, to come up with a bionic hybrid. That, of course, we could not permit."

"No, of course not," Ostling said. "Too close to the old bugaboo of humanoid robots, eh?"

"So, tell me, Doctor, how did you manage to fool the detection equipment at the start of the race, to pass the horse off as a robot?"

"You'll find a variety of gears and circuits whirring merrily away within the material of the saddle," she said. "They aren't really doing anything, but they do register on robot-detecting devices."

"But I still don't understand why you spent so much time and research on this. What did you hope to accomplish by substituting a real horse for a robot?"

"I was gambling that Golden Cloud would actually win," Ostling said in a low voice. "When people around the world realized that a genuine horse could actually compete with robotic ones, I had hoped it would generate public support for using cloning techniques to bring back live animals—on a limited basis, of course."

"A strange goal for a roboticist," Herbert said.

"My dear man, there will always be a market for those robotic toys. Our potential for robot development is still in its infancy. But, if you know anything about me at all, you know my desire for a world where there is room for all the species we humans crowded out!"

"Yes, you've been quite vocal about that. Would you have us all eating meat again? By the end of the last century, seventy percent of all grain production was feeding herds of livestock to feed the rich, while people in the less affluent parts of the world were starving. Is that what you want, Doctor?"

"Of course not! The planet couldn't sustain that, the way we humans keep breeding. But that doesn't mean we should be denied the benefits of live pets which, unlike most humans, give only unconditional love. Or, for that matter, the thrill of riding on the back of a horse once more. All we have now are technicians who are good at operating mechanical steeds, not genuine riders."

"But you found one," Herbert observed.

"Yes, I gave Eric one ride on a true horse. And all that accomplished was to leave him crippled. Golden Cloud might have brought about a whole new outlook, given the numbers of people who watch spectacles such as this. But, now . . ."

"You may be giving up too soon, Doctor," Evelyn's voice interrupted them. "Look!"

Golden Cloud had been trailing the pack as it neared the end of the course, but Eric had managed to catch up again. His heels kicked again and again against the sides of the horse, and it responded with more and more speed. Its nostrils flared as it continued to give still more, and Eric prodded it mercilessly.

As the moving rows of seats slowed down, there was a stir among spectators close enough to see the horse's heaving sides, to note the spreading dampness of perspiration around its saddle girth, to hear its rasping breath as it pulled out in front of the leaders. "It's real!" someone whispered, and the realization spread throughout the viewers. "It's an actual horse."

And then the race was over. Golden Cloud had won.

Eric pulled the horse to a stop, and Golden cloud stood panting and trembling, on the verge of collapse, as Eric slid from the saddle. "Don't leave him standing there!" called a portly man in the front row. He and several others clambered over the front railing and approached the abandoned animal. "Walk him around. Cool him off."

Eager hands removed the saddle. Women's handkerchiefs mopped at Golden Cloud's dampened coat, as people spoke in gentle murmurings or awestruck admiration for an animal who could do what he had done. Farther up in the stands, Herbert and Ostling looked at one another.

"Well, Doctor," he said, "it would appear that you may have gotten your wish. One of them, anyway."

Unnoticed, Eric made his way back to the trailer which had been used to bring him and Golden Cloud to the steeplechase. His expression reflected none of the pain anyone would have to be feeling with an arm mangled as his was.

Once inside the darkened trailer, with the door pulled shut behind him, he located the necessary tools and began removing the arm for repairs.

TAKE TWO

by James P. Hogan

James P. Hogan began writing science fiction as a hobby in the mid 1970s, and his works have been well received within the professional scientific community as well as among regular science fiction readers. In 1979 he left DEC to become a full-time writer, and in 1988 moved to the Republic of Ireland. Currently he maintains a residence in Pensacola and spends part of each year in the U.S. To date, he has published twenty-one novels, a nonfiction work on Artificial Intelligence, and two mixed collections of short fiction, nonfiction, and biographical anecdotes entitled *Minds, Machines & Evolution* and *Rockets, Redheads & Revolution*. He has also published some articles and short fiction. Further details about Hogan and his work are available from his web site at *http://www.jamesphogan.com*. He divides his time between Florida and the Republic of Ireland.

An incoming call in Twofi Kayfo's head notified him that a response to his request had come in from the Merchandising Coordinator. Along with it was a limited-time discounted offer to switch to a different communications carrier. He filed the ad for future reference, got up from his desk, crossed the office behind Sisi, who was reviewing the month's special manufacturers' packages for dealers, and sent a signal ahead to output the received file on the printer. Technically he didn't need a hardcopy, since the information could have been routed to him direct. But having something visual to proffer was better for presenting to customers. And in any case, peripherals, accessories, and paper manufacturers had a lobby that pressed the case against purely electronic forms of data transfer and record-keeping. Twofi checked over the file. The deal seemed straightforward enough. He took it through to Beese, the sales manager, for approval.

"It looks all in order here, Twofi," Beese agreed. "Book this one and you'll be eight points over budget two weeks early. That'll get you in the Million Uppers and to Biloxi in February for sure."

"A cinch, Beese." Twofi winked an imager flap, took back the papers, and went through the building to Service Reception, where the customer was waiting.

The customer's name was Alfa Elone. The message that Twofi received from the service clerk eight minutes previously had told him that Elone's *Road Clipper* would need a rebuilt or replacement main turbine. Twofi had run a check showing that Elone's credit was underused right now, and the package that had come in was a tailored suggestion as to what might be done about it.

"Emess Elone, how are you today?" Twofi's use of the casual Male Surrogate form of address was relaxed and friendly—matching his disarming smile and proffered hand, which Elone had grasped before having a chance to think about it. "I'm Twofi Kayfo, from our customer assistance program. We're here to help you save money. Is it okay to call you Alf?" The thermal patterns playing on Elone's metallic features had the vigorous look that went with an active, open-air lifestyle—in keeping with the customer profile. His white flared pants and royal blue shirt with silver brocade on the chest, cuffs, and collar were top-line designer brands, taken, with the imitation-silk-lined cloak and brass-buckled belt, from the popular series *Captain Cutlass,* which related exploits of olden-day human nautical adventurers.

Alf nodded. "Sure, I guess. . . ."

Twofi extended an arm and began walking Elone across the shop to where the *Clipper* was parked, not coincidentally near the side door leading out to the sales lot. It had collected all the extras over the years—no room for any margin there, the service clerk had already noted. "Now let's see what we've got here, Alf. I talked to our engineer, and it looks as if your main turbine's just about shot. We could go for a rebuild of the bearings, but a year from now it would have to be replaced anyhow—and you know as well as I do what a false economy that would be, eh?" He treated Alf to the kind of knowing smile that recognized smartness when he saw it.

"Er . . . right," Alf agreed reluctantly.

Twofi gestured at the opened engine compartment in a careless way that said he probably didn't need to spell this out. "And then, as you know, what happens next when you replace it is that everything else that was getting near the limit can't deal with the power upgrade, and you'll be coming back with something or other that needs fixing every month."

Alf looked at his car with a worried expression. "Are you saying I should get it all done now? Won't that be a lot more expensive?"

Twofi shook his head reassuringly. "Actually, it works out cheaper, Alf."

"How could it?"

Twofi showed the top sheet of the plan that he had brought out with him. "I ran a projection from statistics of the wear pattern and parts-replacement requirements that you're likely to experience from now on, based on a full turbine replacement for this model, year, mileage, and your style of use. Here's a graph that plots your cumulative costs with time—you see, getting steeper. But I've also superposed the payments and typical costs of a *new* car, and they cross right here, eighteen months from now. That means that from then on, you'd be ahead of the game. Not a bad deal, eh? Like I said, we're here to save you money."

Alf looked hard at the graphs and the numbers, as if seeking to spot the hidden flaw—which by definition wouldn't be there. In fact, so far there wasn't one. Cars came with parts *designed* for different life expectancies, depending on the warranty selected. "What kind of car are we talking about here?" he asked cautiously. But a positive question—good sign. Move it right along, Twofi told himself.

He draped an arm lightly on Alf's shoulder and steered him toward the door leading out to the lot. "One that's getting to be popular with roids who know what to look for. It so happens that we have one right outside. Let's take a peek at it. It'll only need a minute." They came out to stand in front of a Noram *Sultan*—a curvier shell than the *Clipper's* utilitarian lines, electric blue-black with sapphire trim, moved just minutes before from the far end of the display line and hurriedly wiped clean. Twofi went on, "There, what would you say to something like that? Cryogenic recirculator for better efficiency; full satellite nav and wired-road auto; independent steering and compensators on all hubs. It's up from the replacement model for the *Clipper* you've got—but with the trade-in I can give you, you can still be on that eighteen-month financial crossover that I showed you."

They talked a little about details and options. Alf tried some haggling over the figures, but Twofi sensed that it was more for form's sake; Alf wasn't near his limit yet.

"But that's if you just want to carry on along in the same way that you have been—without getting anything new out of life," Twofi told him. "Before we finalize on anything, let me show you something else." Without waiting, he took Alf's elbow and guided him toward the door into the sales room, just a short distance farther along. The models inside were lavish and gleaming, evoking images of human-style opulence. "This, for instance. Not just a runabout for getting around, but a whole new lifestyle, Alf! It's got the power and the comfort to open up places you've never been to before. Rugged, all-country. The hitching right there to attach your boat trailer, integral winch for launching and retrieval. . . ."

"But I don't have a boat," Alf objected.

Twofi uncovered the next of the sheets that he was holding. It showed a picture of a twenty-foot basic hull with aft cabin and deckhouse, moored against a background of mountains and forest. That was a bit misleading, since humans usually monopolized settings like that. Prole recreation areas were more likely to be old city centers, with waterfronts in places like New Jersey and Detroit. . . . But the suggestion was there.

"That's where we start to plan ahead and get creative," Twofi said soothingly. "I've got a special offer for you, Alf. If we trade the *Clipper* and go for this model instead of the *Sultan* out there, then any time in the next three years, you get to go ahead on this boat at twenty-five percent off list. *And* you get privileged discounts on deck furniture and a whole bunch of other accessories. . . ." He waited, reading the signals. True, this would more than double Alf's outgoings, but if they didn't soak up his credit with this, someone else soon would. Alf vacillated, enticed by the vision kindled in his brain but struggling with the suddenness and novelty. It needed one more nudge. "And if we okay it by this time tomorrow, you get the boat trailer for free," Twofi threw in.

* * *

One thing he had in common with economists, Dave Jardan suspected as he looked down over the last stretch of northern Virginia's residential parks before the Washington cityplex, was that he didn't understand economics. But as a designer of Artificial Intelligences he didn't really need to, whereas of economists, one would have thought, it would be expected. The same money circulated round and around, in the process somehow spinning off enough profit to make everyone a living. It seemed as if something was being created out nothing somewhere, as with a perpetual-motion machine, or sustaining momentum endlessly in the way of one of those Escher drawings where water flowed downhill all the way around a closed circuit and back to its starting point. If the books all the way around the system balanced, where did the surplus come from?

The VTOL executive jet's flight-controller spoke from the cabin grille in a euphoniously synthesized Southern female voice. "Secure for landing, please. Time to the gate is approximately nine minutes. We hope you had a good flight." Dave checked his seatbelt and began replacing papers and other items that he had been using back in his briefcase. The engine note dropped, then rallied again as the clunks and whines of aerofoils deploying sounded through the structure, and the craft banked to come around onto its approach. Below were the beginnings of the densely crammed proleroid residential belt blending into the urban sprawl west of the Potomac—roadways crowded with vehicles, the houses sprouting patios, add-ons, and extensions like living, mutating vegetables, their yards filled with pools and cookout gear, sports courts, play corners, fountains, floweramas, and every other form of outdoor accessory that marketing ingenuity could devise.

At least, such an ongoing surplus couldn't flow from a system that was constant, Dave supposed. It would have to grow continually. That had to be why money-based economies had always sought, and not infrequently gone to war for, ever-greater markets and empires. And for a long time, progressively more automated manufacturing and distribution had supplied the expanding demand . . . until overproduction itself became the problem, and new, multibillion-dollar industries of persuasion and credit financing had to be created to invent essential needs that people had never known they'd had before. Then the medical and social costs of the stress-related syndromes, alienation, crime, and generally self-destructive behavior that came out of it all escalated until many started taking it into their heads to chuck all of it and go back to lives of home cooking and book-reading, horse-raising and fishing. And that wouldn't have been good for General Motors or the Chase Manhattan Bank at all.

The solution couldn't be some fainthearted retreat back from halfway across the bridge, which would merely have led back to the same problem later. Rather, the answer seen was to press on resolutely by completing the job and taking the process that had brought things thus far by automating manufacture and distribution to its logical conclusion: automated consumption. Why not have special-purpose machines to get rid of the junk that the other machines were producing? For a while, Dave Jardan had shared the dismay that the AI community had felt at seeing their final, triumphal success—not exactly genius level, but a passably all-round humanlike capability all the same—appropriated to motivate a breed of robots called the "proleroids," who happily absorbed all the commercial messages and did most of the buying, using, fixing, and replacing necessary to close the economic cycle. Freeing up humans from performing this function meant that all of them could now live comfortably as stockholders, instead of just a privileged class as previously. It was from such private means that Dave obtained the wherewithal to pursue the goal of developing a superior AI of truly philosophical capacity, which had always been his dream. As tends to happen in life, what had once seemed revolutionary became the familiar. His initial indignation gradually abated, and now he just went with the flow. Privately, he still couldn't avoid the suspicion that there had to be something crazy about a system that needed a dedicated underclass to turn its products back to a state suitable for returning into the ground where the raw materials had come from; and he still didn't really understand how the continual recycling of various configurations of matter around the loop managed to yield plenty for all to get by on. . . . But then, he wasn't an economist.

He arrived on schedule and was met by a pleasant-faced woman of middle age, neatly attired in a pastel-blue business dress and navy throw-on jacket, who introduced herself as Ellie, from the Justice Department. Few people took jobs from necessity these days, but many still liked a familiar routine that brought order into their lives and took them out among others. How the Justice Department had come to be involved in evaluating his project, Dave had no idea. It was just another of those inexplicable things that came out of the entanglement of Washington bureaucracies. Growth of government, with seemingly everyone wanting a say in how others ought to live, was one of the unfortunate consequences of too many people having plenty of time on their hands and not enough worthwhile business of their own to manage.

A proleroid-chauffeured limo took them to the nebulously designated "Policy Institute" offices in Arlington, occupying a couple of floors in an architectural sculpture of metal and glass forming an appendage of George Mason University. On the way, they passed a proleroid construction crew with excavating machinery and a crane, laying a section of storm drain. The current rage among proleroids was the Old West, and a couple of them were wearing cowboy hats and vests, with one sporting authentic-looking chaps. Dave learned that Ellie was from Missouri, had two grandchildren, spent much of the year photographing mountain scenery around the world, restored Colonial furniture, and played the Celtic harp. Her income was from copper smelting in Michigan, plastics in Texas, and a mixed portfolio that her family broker took care of.

Nangarry, looking dapperly intellectual as usual in a lightweight tan summer suit and knitted tie, with wire-rimmed spectacles and a lofty brow merging into a prematurely bald pate, greeted Dave in his office over coffee. His mood today was not reassuring, however. "It's going to be a slaughterhouse," he told Dave glumly. "They're all out for blood."

Dave knew that the initial reactions hadn't been exactly favorable. But even Nangarry's customary directness hadn't quite prepared him for this. "All of them?" he queried.

Nangarry nodded. "Boy, if the idea was to piss off everybody, you did a good job, Dave. And I mean *everybody*. I thought this was supposed to be a superphilosopher. The nearest I can think of is Socrates—and we all know what happened to him."

Dave licked his lips. "What's been happening?" he asked. There wasn't much else he could say. He had heard PHIL's end of it, of course, and had he wished, could have followed the proceedings interactively over the previous few days. But he had thought it better to stay out until the heads of the various assessing groups came together to review the results. Besides, Dave was the kind of person who always had other pressing things to do.

"Well, Wade from down the street is in there with PHIL right now," Nangarry said. By "down the street" he meant the Pentagon—Wade was the Army general heading the military's evaluation group. "The last I heard, they were trading dates and numbers about things that people who win wars don't put in the history books they write. I got the feeling Wade was getting the worst of it. That baby of yours can sure come up with dates and numbers, I'll give you that."

"What do you expect?" Dave replied. "I thought that was the whole idea."

Nangarry drained the last of his coffee and set down the cup. "Let's go take a look," he suggested. They got up, left the office, and headed along the corridor outside to the conference room where the meeting would convene formally following lunch.

Dave had been working for years to develop an AI capable of abstract association, pattern extraction, and generalization at levels normally encountered in such hitherto exclusively human areas of cognitive ability as philosophy, ethics, religion, science, and the arts. Commercial interest, and hence funding for further serious work, had virtually ceased with the advent of the proleroids. The few researchers like Dave, who persevered, had done so from personal motivation inspired by the challenge—and in Dave's case, because he knew that he and his small team back in Colorado were good. At first, true to tradition, they had played with acronyms from words like ASSOCIATIVE, COGNITIVE, CONCEPTUALIZING, and INTEGRATING to describe their emerging creation, but none that they came up with had a satisfactory ring. Later, as the trials became more encouraging, Dave had considered a more grandiose appellation from the names of famous philosophers: Aristotle, maybe, or Plato, Epictetus, Hume, Kant, Mill . . . But none of them seemed to capture the full essence of what the endless training and testing dialogs showed coming together. Finally, he had taken the generic copout and settled simply for "PHIL."

People like Dave tended to be idealists in at least some ways. After the successes that had attended the application of more sophisticated information-processing technologies to higher levels of human problem solving, the means was surely there, he believed, to bring some improvement to the governing of human affairs, where the record of humankind itself had been so deplorable for about as long as human history had been unfolding. Why not use an AI to help make laws and set standards?—or at least, to formulate them without the subjective biases that had always caused the problems with humans. For once, the principles that all agreed it would be good for everyone else to live by could be applied equally and impartially; the selective logic that always made one's own case the exception would be replaced by a universal logic that didn't care. The injustices that had always divided societies would be resolved, and the entire race, finally, would be able to settle down and enjoy lives of leisure, plenty, and contentment, as knowledge and intelligence surely deserved.

All inspiring, heady stuff. Fired with enthusiasm, Dave approached the National Academy of Sciences with his vision and generated enough interest for reports and memorandums to be sent onward to the unmapped inner regions of the nation's governing apparatus. It seemed that everyone felt obligated to agree it was a good idea, but no one was volunteering to put their name on anything to launch it. Finally, after almost a year, a statement came out of a sub-office of the Justice Department, authorizing a limited evaluation for preliminary assessment, to be conducted by a committee made up of representatives of select groups likely to be the most affected. From what Nangarry was saying, things weren't off to a very good start.

General Wade was short and sparsely built, with dark hair and toothbrush mustache, a thin mouth, and eyes that were quick to sharpen defensively. He struck Dave as the overcompensating kind that gravitated naturally to authority systems where rank and uniform provided the assertiveness they might have lacked in other areas of life. Security with what was familiar tended to make them dogmatic and rule-driven—ideal for implementing military regulations or police procedures, perhaps, but hardly high on the creative insight that relaying the foundations of a society's ethical structure is based on.

When Dave and Nangarry entered the conference room, he was at the far end in front of one of the screens connected to PHIL, located at Dave's lab in Colorado, along with a pink-faced woman with a flare of yellow hair, wearing a cream jacket and maroon blouse. From their viewscreen exchanges, Dave recognized her as Karen Hovak, a policy analyst at a liberal political think tank called the Fraternity Foundation. A woman in Army uniform, trimly turned out, with firm yet attractive features and shoulder-length black hair, was sitting nearby typing something into a laptop. Several more people, some of them also at screens, were scattered around the room. It seemed that others were getting in a few extra hours with PHIL, too, before the formal afternoon session began.

Wade was tight-lipped, barely able to contain his evident irritation while Nangarry performed the face-to-face introductions behind a frozen smile. The aide who had accompanied him was Lieutenant Laura Kantrel. She flashed Dave a quick, impish smile when he let his gaze linger for just a second longer than the circumstances called for. It was nice to think he had one friend in the place, anyway, he reflected stoically—or, at least, someone who seemed potentially neutral.

"Hello, Dave," PHIL greeted as Dave moved within the screen's viewing angle—although there were no doubt other cameras covering the room anyway.

"Hi," Dave returned. "How are things back at the ranch?"

"The new air conditioner arrived, but otherwise nothing's changed much." The screen changed from the world map and table of dates and places that it had been displaying to a view of two proleroids unloading a crate from a truck. "Have a good trip?"

"Right on time and smooth all the way. So what's going on?"

"It wants to bring communism back, that's what's going on," Wade said in a tight voice. "I thought we'd gotten rid of all that years ago. It's as good as been calling us imperialist. *Us!*—who made the world safe for democracy."

"I just pointed out that your claimed commitment to defending the rights of small nations to choose their form of government doesn't square with your actions," PHIL corrected. "It seems more like it's okay as long as you approve what they choose. You don't allow independent economic experiments that might put global capitalism at risk. If anyone tries setting up an example that might work, you first sabotage it, then destabilize it, and if that doesn't get the message across, bomb it. I've correlated events over the last two hundred years and am trying to reconcile them with the principles set out in your Constitution and Bill of Ri—"

"If that isn't communism, what is?" the general snorted, glaring at Dave and Nangarry. "There was a time when decent Americans would have shot anyone who said something like that."

"For exercising free speech?" PHIL queried. "Please clarify."

"For seditious talk undermining the Christian values of thrift, honesty, hard work and the right to keep what you've earned," Wade answered, reddening. "Everyone knows that communist claptrap was a smokescreen for legalized plunder."

"Actually, it sounds more like the early Christian church," PHIL said. " 'There were no needy persons among them. Those who owned lands or houses sold them, brought the money from the sales and put it at the apostles' feet, and it was distributed to anyone who had need.' Acts of the Apostles, Chapter Four, verses 34 and 35."

"Who's paying him?" Wade seethed, waving a hand at Dave. "The Chinese?"

Karen Hovak, the liberal, who Dave thought might have been chortling, seemed to be equally incensed. "Communist?" she scoffed. "Listen to it thumping the Bible. Half an hour ago it was quoting things that would turn women back into men's household slaves and baby makers."

"No. I was suggesting that much of Old Testament law might have made sense for a wandering tribe, lost in the desert in desperate times, when maintaining the population was maybe the biggest priority," PHIL answered. "You're pulling it out of context, which is exactly what the groups you were complaining about do. That was my point."

Hovak sniffed, unwilling to concede the point. "We'll be hearing Creationism by a white male God next," she said.

"Many scientists have concluded that purposeful design by some kind of preexisting intelligence is the only way to account for the complexity and information content of living systems," PHIL agreed. "The naturalistic explanation doesn't work. I've done the calculations. The chances of the two thousand enzymes in a human cell forming through chance mutation are about one in ten to the forty-thousandth power. That's about the same as rolling fifty thousand sixes in a row with a die. The probability of building a protein with a hundred amino acids is equivalent to finding the Florida state lottery's winning ticket lying in the street every week for 1000 years. . . ."

"Wait a minute!" One of two men who had been muttering at another screen near the middle of the room's central table glowered across. He had unruly white hair, a lean, bony face with pointy nose and chin, and was wearing a dark, loosely fitting suit. Dave didn't think he'd seen him before.

"Jeffrey Yallow, National Academy of Sciences," Nangarry supplied in a low voice, answering Dave's questioning look. "The guy with him is Dr. Coverly—from the Smithsonian."

"We're being told here that just about all of what's being taught of cosmology is wrong," Yallow said, gesturing in disgust at the screen.

"I wouldn't know," PHIL corrected. "Only observation can settle that. But the theory is built on an ideology sustained by invented unobservables. What's allowed as fact is being selected to fit, or otherwise ignored. Hence there's no sound basis for deciding whether the theory is a good model of reality or not."

Yallow ignored it. "Are we denying evolution now?" he demanded. "Okay, so it's improbable. But improbable things happen. We're here, aren't we?

"Fallacy of the excluded middle," PHIL observed. "Showing the consequence to be true doesn't prove the truth of the premise. The underlying assumption is that a materialistic explanation *must* exist. But that makes it as dogmatic as the Genesis literalism that you ridicule: an ideology based on a principle, not science following from evidence. If the facts seem to point to a preexisting intelligence, why should that be a problem?" There was a pause, as if inviting them to reflect. "It doesn't bother me." A longer silence followed, in which Dave could almost sense an expectant quality. "That was supposed to be a joke," PHIL explained. A caricature of a face appeared on the screen near where Dave was standing, smiled weakly, gave up, and disappeared.

Yallow looked at Dave belligerently. "You are serious about this whole thing, Dr. Jardan?"

Dave shook his head in bemusement. The reactions were unlike anything he had expected. "It seemed to me that PHIL posed some valid questions . . ." was all he could say.

Coverly threw up his hands in exasperation. "What about the round Earth or a heliocentric planetary system? We might as well go the whole way while we're at it." He glanced at Yallow. "I've had enough already, Jeff. Is there any point in staying this afternoon? I can write my appraisal now, if you like."

Two people who had entered a few minutes previously and been listening came forward from the doorway. The man was burly, swarthy skinned with graying hair, and clad in black with a clerical dog collar. Dave knew him as Bishop Gaylord from the National Council of Churches. The woman with him was tall and austere looking, wearing a dark gray calf-length dress and bonnet. "I heard it with my own ears!" Gaylord exclaimed. "The machine agrees with us: God exists!"

"A non sequitur," PHIL told them. It even managed to sound tired. "Some scientists see objective evidence for a preexisting intelligence. Your belief system posits a Creator who sets a code for moral restraint and social control that happens to serve the political power structure. But there's no justification for assuming the two are one and the same."

The bishop's mood cooled visibly. "So what's its purpose?" he challenged. "This intelligence you say there might be objective evidence for."

"I don't know," PHIL replied. "I'd imagine it would do things for its own reasons. Humans need moral codes for their reasons. They're two different issues. There's no necessary overlap. It seems to me that half your problems are from not grasping that—or not being honest about it."

"So there's no objective grounding for a moral code?" the woman queried.

"Why does there need to be, any more than for traffic regulations? If it makes life more livable for everybody . . ."

Gaylord shook his head protestingly. "But that would give anyone the right to arbitrarily impose any moral system they chose."

"You can't impose private morality," PHIL answered. "Look what happened with all the attempts to do so through history. As long as people aren't hurting you, why not leave them alone? It's like with traffic rules. As long as everyone is using the roads without being a menace, there's nothing for the cops to do. What cars people drive and where they go is their business."

The woman couldn't accept it. "So we're just supposed to let everyone run hog-wild, doing anything they want? Drugs? Alcohol? Gambling? Ruining their lives?"

"If it's their lives and their money, why should it be a illegal? Where's the victim that's going to complain about it?"

"Everyone's a victim of the problems such things cause: the crime, the violence, family breakdowns, decay of character. . . ."

PHIL's screen showed a clip from a gangster movie set in the 1920s, a police SWAT team with drawn guns bursting into a house of terrified people, a couple being hauled away in handcuffs while their children looked on, and a cartoon of a caricatured judge, police chief, lawyer, and politician scrambling to catch graft envelopes being tossed from the window of a limousine. "I don't see any big problems caused by people choosing to take part in such things," PHIL said. "The problems are all caused by other people trying to stop them."

The woman put a hand to her throat, as if finding

this too much. "I can't believe what I'm hearing," she whispered. "You'll be trying to justify . . ." she faltered before being able to frame the word, "prostitution next."

"Okay," PHIL offered genially. "Let's talk about the criminalizing of sexual behavior between consenting adults."

Things went from bad to worse over lunch, which included more delegates arriving for the afternoon meeting. While just about every group present agreed with something that PHIL had raised, none of them could understand why he defended the prejudices of others that were so obviously wrong. The result was that everybody had something to argue about, and things became acrimonious. The atmosphere carried over to the session back in the conference room afterward, where everybody accused their opponents of operating a double standard. PHIL irked everyone except the ecclesiastics by quoting several passages from the Christian Gospels that they all claimed to subscribe to, denouncing the judging of others until one has first attained perfection oneself—and then setting impossible standards for attaining it; then he upset the ecclesiastics by drawing attention to how much of the Bible had been added in Roman counterfeiting operations that would have impressed the KGB. The meeting broke up early with the still-squabbling groups departing back to their places of origin or havens elsewhere in the building, unanimous only in declaring the project to be dead on the taxiway. Nangarry was swept out with the tide in the course of trying to placate them. General Wade left with a couple of corporate lawyers who were agitated at PHIL's revelation of the costs and consequences of alcohol and tobacco consumption being far more severe than of other drugs that were illegal—PHIL had also suggested that drug-traffic interdiction had become the military's biggest pretext for foreign intervention, which was what had irked Wade. Dave found himself left staring bleakly at a few secretaries picking up papers and notes, a proleroid janitor coming in to clean the room, and Lieutenant Kantrel still tapping at her laptop.

"How did it go?" PHIL inquired from a speaker grille above the nearest screen.

"You played it undeviatingly to the end," Dave said. "I think you've been metaphorically crucified."

"What did I do?'

"Told them the truth."

"I thought that was supposed to be a good thing. Isn't it what everyone says they want?"

"It's what they say. But what people really want is certainty. They want to hear their prejudices confirmed."

"Oh." There was a pause, as if PHIL needed to think about that. "I need to make some conceptual realignments here," he said finally.

"I guess that's something we're going to have to work on," Dave replied.

He looked away to find that Kantrel had stopped typing and was looking at him curiously, with a hint of the mischievous smile that he had seen before playing on her mouth. He shrugged resignedly at her. "How not to sell an idea."

"To be honest, I thought you were quite wonderful," she said.

"Me? I hardly said anything. I was too confused. If you liked it, that was all PHIL, not me."

"You can't hear music without hearing the composer. When you look at a painting, you see the artist." She looked Dave up and down and made a gesture to take in his wavy head, puckish-nosed face with its dancing gray eyes and trimmed beard, and lithe, tanned frame clad in a bottle-green blazer and tan slacks. "It was you."

This wasn't exactly the kind of thing that Dave was

used to hearing every day. He took off his spectacles to polish one of the lenses on a handkerchief from his pocket and peered at her keenly, as if against a strong light. Her face had softer lines than he had registered at first, with a mouth full and mobile. Her eyes were brown and deep, alive and humorous. Her voice was low but not harsh, with a slightly husky quality. "Er, Lieutenant . . ." Dave sighed an apology. The name had gone. "What was it . . . ?

"Laura. That's okay. I do it all the time, too." Dave didn't really believe that somehow. He shook his head in a way that said it had just been one of those days. Laura went on, "Actually, I'm happy the general had to go away for a few minutes. One of the things I was hoping for on this assignment was getting a chance to meet you."

"Me?" Dave blinked, replacing his spectacles awkwardly. He wasn't used to feeling like a celebrity. "I didn't know I was that famous."

"I've always had an interest in AI—I guess I have interests in lots of things. I like reading histories of how technologies developed—the phases they went through, the ideas that were tried, the people who were involved and how they thought. You used to be a big name with some of the most prestigious outfits. And then you seemed to just disappear—from public view, anyway. But I still see you sometimes in the specialist journals."

"I do most of my work privately now, with a small dedicated group," Dave told her. "We have our own lab up in Colorado. I like the mountains, can do without the politics. . . ." He grinned and swept an arm around, indicating the scene of the recent events. "As you may have gathered, it's not exactly what I'm best at. You were right. If it seemed that PHIL managed to get everyone mad today, it was really me."

Laura gave him a long, searching look. "Was that because of the proleroids, Dr. Jardan?"

"Dave."

She nodded and returned a quick smile. "I've often wondered—the position that you always took in the arguing that went on. And then people seemed to be ganging up and misquoting you. The media started painting you as some backward-looking flop who couldn't make the leap to where the future was leading. But none of that made any sense. Most of the ideas that went into producing the HPT brain were your doing." She meant holoptronic, the information-integrating technology that was the basis of proleroid intelligence. "They forced you out and stole it from you."

Dave had had other visions in mind than automated consumerism. But once the commercial potential was grasped, there had been no resisting the corporate and financial power aligned to making it a reality. After that, further significant research had been blocked because of the risk of "destabilization." In other words, anything that might have threatened the status quo.

"A lot of people made a lot of money," Dave agreed. "I just couldn't go along with it." He turned on his chair to survey the room. "I guess that makes me not much of an economist either."

The janitor was moving around the table, tossing coffee cups and discarded papers into a trash bag. Beneath its gray work coat, it was wearing imitation buckskin breeches and jacket with vest, red neckerchief, and high boots. One of the early decisions had been that proleroids would not comprise a range of special-purpose types, but would conform to one basic body plan patterned after the human form, able to use tools and implements in the same way as and when required. This provided an immediate outlet for existing products and services, and for utilizing the many years of experience accumulated in moving and marketing them. Businesses knew how to sell clothes, hardware, houses, cars, and all the ancillaries that went with them. Astoundingly, thanks to the ingenuity of production engineers, even supermarkets and the distribution system for groceries had been preserved.

Proleroids were not bolted together in factories from motors, gears, actuators, and casing in the style of the robots that had been imagined for centuries. They were assembled internally by nanoassemblers from materials transported through a circulation network carrying silicone oil. Hence, they didn't appear instantly in their final finished form in the way of a machine coming off a production line, but *grew* to it over a period of about five years. A mixture of substances were ingested to sustain the process—"flavored" and prepared in various ways, which was where the revamped food industry came in—providing not only the material for growth and wear replacement, but also ingredients for producing internal lubricants, coolants, solvents, and electrolytes. Motive power came from the sliding of interleaved sheets of electrically bound carbon-fiber plastic that simulated natural muscle, and the skin during the formative period resembled a micro-linked chain-mail that grew by the addition of new links between the old as bulk accrued. Areas of links were filled in and fused to form a system of still flexible but more durable outer plates when the final body size was attained.

It was well that a full-formed adult body didn't exist from outset. The HPT brain used what was, in effect, a Write-Only Memory. Information was stored at the atomic scale as charge patterns circulating in a unique crystal network whose growth was influenced by an individual's accumulating experiences. Hence, the information thus represented couldn't be extracted and transferred to another brain when the circuits eventually became leaky and broke down. A newly commenced proleroid contained just some basic "instincts" and a learning and generalizing program, by means of which it had to begin assembling together all the things it needed to know, and how it thought and felt about them, all over again.

In some ways this was a good thing, for it prevented old and stagnant ideas from being propagated endlessly, with no prospect for change and new ways of seeing things, from which advancement arises. But it also meant that coordination, judgment, and experience of the world formed and improved gradually, too. It was far better for size and strength to keep pace with emerging maturity, letting infant tantrums and experiments at dismantling the contents of the world take place in something the size of a puppy dog that couldn't do much damage, rather than a two-hundred-pound loose cannon capable of demolishing a house. This meant that growing proleroids needed guidance and supervision, creating roles for the ready-made parent-family models that human culture had spent centuries cultivating. So once again, the products, sales strategies, advertising methods, and psychological profiles that had been developed over the years could be used virtually without change. Small wonder that USA Inc. was more than happy with the arrangement.

Laura looked thoughtful as she watched the janitor going methodically about its business. It gave the impression of being one of the more calm and contented ones. A majority of proleroids ended up stressed or neurotic in the ways that had once been normal for most humans. Dave waited silently. "How close to human are they?" she asked him finally. "Sometimes I have trouble seeing the difference . . . apart from them being metal."

"They didn't have to look like metal," Dave said. "That was deliberate, to make sure they'd seem different. To me they're human already."

Laura turned her face toward him. "That was it, wasn't it?" she said, with a light of sudden revelation. "What it was all about. That was why you walked.

The rest of them wanted a permanent underclass, and you couldn't go along with it."

Dave shrugged. She was so close that there was no point in denying it. "Pretty much," he agreed.

Laura's look of interest deepened. "So what about PHIL? If he's that much more advanced, doesn't that mean he's more advanced than we are?"

Normally Dave didn't go into things like this. But there was something about her perceptiveness that drew him out. Something about her. . . . "To be honest, PHIL really isn't that much different," he confided. "True, he exists in the lab back in Colorado, but that's mainly for development convenience and communications access. He uses regular prole bodies to acquire spatial awareness and coordination. Apart from that, he's essentially the same HPT technology and basic learning bootstrap. But his exposure has been different. Have you ever seen the entertainment channels they run for proleroids, the stuff they read, the propaganda they're dished up all day, every day? It's as if they live in mental cages. PHIL was raised free."

"You mean by you," Laura said. "He grew up with wider ideas and concepts, the world as a library. You taught him to think."

"I guess." Dave shrugged as if to ask, *What else can I say?* Braggadocio didn't come naturally to him.

"No wonder you think of him as human." Laura thought for a moment, then her face broke into a smile. "Yes, I was right all along. I *said* he was you!"

Twofi Kayfo parked his car in the garage extension beside Doubleigh's compact and the minitruck that Ninten had resprayed purple and pink and fitted with the floodlamps, safari hood guard, and night radar that all the kids had to have this month. He got out and walked around the stack of closet and bathroom fittings that were being replaced, ducked under the pieces of the golf training rig that he hadn't found anywhere else to store since he set up the ski simulator, and squeezed past another housecleaning machine that Doubleigh was throwing out to get to the door leading through to the house. Doubleigh looked at him disapprovingly when he ambled into the living room and beamed at her. She was wearing a cowgirl blouse with leather-fringed, calf-length skirt and boots, sitting fiddling to put together a rack and trellis kit for climbing plants that she wanted over the indoor rockery and fish pool. Ninten lay comatose on the couch with a VR cord plugged into an ear socket.

"Don't tell me you got held up at the office again," Doubleigh said. "I can smell the uranium salts from here."

"This prole goes into a bar. He orders a drink and tries it. Says to the bartender, 'Hey, this had gone flat. I can't taste a thing.' The bartender says, 'Then I guess there's no charge.' Aw, come on. You know it goes with the job. A guy's gotta be part of the team."

"Twentwen says all her friends will be at the dance on Saturday and she's got nothing to wear."

"Nothing to wear? She got more clothes up there than a whole human Fifth Avenue store already. Half of one closet's full of purses. What is she, an octopus?"

"They're all out of style. She couldn't possibly be seen in anything from last quarter. You know what they're like."

"Well, there you are, then. I don't hear any complaints when the commission credits come in. And anyhow, we were celebrating. I made the Million Uppers again, Doub. Beese say's we'll be going to Biloxi in February for sure. And naturally that means that you get to pick a new wardrobe, too."

Although Doubleigh tried to maintain the stern image, her change of mood showed. "Well, that's something, I suppose," she conceded grudgingly. Then the alignments of her facial scales softened into a resentful smile. "I knew you would," she said.

Twofi took the screwdriver from her hand, drew her up from the chair, and turned her through a clumsy dance twirl. "We'll play the casinos every night, drink tetrafluoride with dinner, buy a case full of—" He stopped and pointed to his head, indicating a call coming in. Doubleigh waited, still gripping his hand lightly. The caller was Beese.

"Twofi, I've just got it from head office. They're giving us the honor of providing the banquet keynote speaker at the sales conference. I thought I'd offer it to you. How would you feel about it? Want to think it over and let me know?"

"Say! That's really something, Beese. I'd be happy to. There's nothing to think about. You've got it."

"That's great. I'll get back and confirm. Talk to you tomorrow."

"Sure, Beese. And thanks."

"What is it?" Doubleigh asked, reading the excited thermal patterns fluttering across his face.

"It was Beese. They want me to make the keynote speech at Biloxi. Isn't that something? See, you don't just have a successful salesman, Doub. You're gonna have a celebrity, too."

"That's wonderful . . . but you'll have to find some better jokes," Doubleigh said.

Automated consumerism could satisfy the need for continual economic expansion only so far. But there was another condition that investors and suppliers had long known would absorb production indefinitely by generating its own replacement market, and moreover without constraining costs and efficiency in the manner normally required of enterprises expected to return profits: War. Wars in the past, however, had always had to be fought by humans, who had an inconvenient tendency to grow weary of them and seek to end them. It didn't take the analysts long to begin wondering if the same approach that had worked so spectacularly with the civilian economy might be extended to the military sector, with the immensely more lucrative prospects that such a possibility implied. . . .

The sun was shining from a clear sky marred by only a few wisps of high-altitude cirrus over the restricted military testing area in a remote part of the New Mexican desert. The viewing stand set up for the VIPs was shaded by an awning and looked down over a shallow valley of sand, rock, and scattered scrub. A convoluted ridge, rising a couple of hundred or so feet, ran along the center, beyond which the valley floor continued to a broken scarp several miles away forming the skyline. Lieutenant Laura Kantrel sat with General Wade and his officer-scientist deputation from Washington in one of the forward rows of seats. Dust and smoke from the last demonstration hung over the area, with plumes uncoiling here and there from still-burning munitions. Wade shifted his field glasses from one place to another on the valley floor and lower slopes of the ridge, picking out disabled machines or pieces of scattered wreckage. Laura used the camera-control icons on the monitor screen in front of them to bring up a zoom-in on one of the AMECs moving up to their jump-off positions for the next attack.

The Autonomous Mobile Experimental Combat-unit was the Army's attempt at a mechanized replacement infantryman. It was controlled by a unit designated a Multiple Environmental Response Logical INtegrator, or MERLIN, that essentially operated a collection of sophisticated, improving reflexes, with nothing approaching the ability of the proleroid HPT brain. The military had specified it that way in the belief that a disposition to carry out orders as directed without thinking too much about consequences would make better fighting machines. The basic form stood about five feet high and took the form of a squat, hexagonal, turretlike structure carried on a tripod of multiply articulated legs. The upper part deployed an array of imaging lenses and other sensors, two grasping and manipulator appendages, and came as standard with .303 automatic cannon, long-range single-shot sniper-mode barrel, 20-pack grenade-thrower, and laser designator for calling in air or artillery. In addition, specialized models could be equipped with anti-armor or -aircraft missile-racks; mortar, flamethrower, minelaying, or "contact assault" (rock drill, chainsaw, power hammer, gas torch) attachments; field engineer/demolition accessories; reconnaissance and ECM pod; or kamikaze bomb pack. They put Laura in mind of giant, mutant, three-legged crabs.

The Trials Director's voice came over the speakers set up to address the stand. "Okay. We're going to try it again with a new combination of Elan and Focus parameters at high settings, but reduced Survival. Let's get it rolling." The talk going on around the stand died as attention switched back to the field. A warning klaxon sounded, and then the *Go* signal to start the assault.

It was another disaster. With their attack drive emphasized and a low weighting on the risk-evaluation functions, the attacking AMECs swarmed recklessly up the slopes of the ridge where the defending side was emplaced, charging the strong points head-on, heedless of fire patterns, casualties, or cover as the defenses opened up. Enfiladed machine guns cut and withered them to hulks; mortars preregistered on the obvious assault lanes blew them apart and scattered them in fragments. It was like watching a World War I infantry attack against heavily defended trenches—except that these items came at $50,000 apiece. Admittedly, the whole idea was to crank throughput up to the maximum that the production industries could sustain; but no system of replacement logistics could justify a survival expectancy measured in minutes.

Nor did it help when the government scientists who were running the demonstration inverted the priority allocations to set self-preservation above aggressiveness. The attackers in the next test, who had observed from their staging positions the fate of the previous wave, hung back in groups, stayed put in the dead ground, and shied off pressing home any advantage. When the defenders, programmed to disregard survival, emerged to take them on at close quarters, the attackers backed off. It was the same problem that had plagued AMECs all through their development. Either they engaged only reluctantly and ineffectively if at all, or they were suicidal. The scientists couldn't seem to find the middle way.

General Shawmer, Wade's commanding officer at the Pentagon, gave his opinion at the debriefing session held afterward in the command trailer parked behind the viewing stand. "The trouble all along has been that they're *too* rational," he told the gathering. "If their goal is to annihilate the enemy, they go all-out at it. If they're told to attach more value to preserving themselves, they do the sensible thing and stay the hell out—as would any of us if we had no other considerations to think about."

Professor Nigel Ormond, whose work was carried out under a classified code at the Los Alamos Laboratories, responded. "It isn't so much a question of rationality. The MERLIN processor was never intended to weigh complex associative concept nets that conflict with each other. It optimizes to whatever overall priority the evaluation function converges to. In other words, it lacks the capacity to form higher-level abstractions that can offset basic instincts without totally overriding them."

"You mean such as an ideology, nationalistic spirit, religious conviction, deep commitment to another: the kinds of things humans will sacrifice themselves for," Dr. Querl said, sucking his pipe, which no one in the trailer would permit him to light. He was a research psychologist from Harvard.

"Exactly," Ormond confirmed.

General Shawmer shrugged and looked around. "Okay. In my book that adds up to a little bit of what used to be called fanaticism. It still sounds like what I said—they're too rational. So how do we inject some old-fashioned irrational idealism?"

"I'm not sure it's as simple as that, General," Ormond replied. "As I said, the MERLIN just isn't designed to have that kind of capacity. For complexity anywhere close to what I think it's going to need, we're probably talking about HPT."

"But there's no way to interface an HPT brain to an AMEC sensory and motor system," one of the industry scientists objected. "They use different physics. The data representations are totally incompatible."

"So why not use the support systems we've already got?" Ormond's deputy, Stella Lamsdorf, suggested. "And they're already more flexible and versatile anyway."

Ormond turned and blinked. "You mean proles?"

"Why not?"

"But . . ." The industry scientist made vague motions in the air, as if searching for the reason that he knew had to be there. "They're not configured for it," he said finally. "They don't come as combat hardware."

"Neither do people," Lamsdorf pointed out. "All we'd have to do is provide them with the right equipment . . ." She looked around, warming to the idea, "which would mean that the existing defense industries get to carry on as usual. And they're just throwaway machines, too, so another whole area of manufacturing enjoys a healthy expansion. It's perfect."

Everyone looked at everyone else, waiting for somebody to fault it. Nobody could. Querl, however, sounded a note of caution.

"There is another aspect to consider," he told the company. "It's all very well to say that an HPT brain has enough capacity. But humans aren't spontaneously seized by the ideals that motivate them to deeds of sacrifice and valor. They have to be inspired to them. The mass movements that produce the kind of collective spirit and vision that mobilizes armies require leaders—individuals with the charisma that can inflame thousands."

"Well, I don't think we're exactly inexperienced in that department either," General Shawmer said, looking a little ruffled.

Querl shook his head. "I'm sorry, General, but I mean the kind of inspiration that can only come from within a people, not from without. Of their own kind. We're not talking about selling insurance or new siding for a house. The proles are useful living their simple, uncomplicated lives. But everything they do is borrowed from us—which makes my point. Where among them have you seen any potential to raise their thoughts to higher things? Because that's what it's going to take to turn them into willing battalions."

Beside Laura, General Wade thought for a moment, then sat forward in his chair. His sudden change of posture signaled for the room's attention. Heads turned toward him. "Let's get this straight," he said. "You need something that's like one of them—a machine. But one that can get them thinking about things like God, country, and democracy, make them mad and want to change things. Is that right?"

Querl nodded, smiling faintly, as if waiting to see where this would lead. "Well, yes. It's a way to put it, I suppose."

"I think I know just the thing," Wade said.

A half-hour later, Laura put a call through to Dave Jardan in Colorado. They had talked several times since the debacle in Washington, each time promising to get together again soon, but somehow never quite managing it. His face on the screen lit up when he saw her; then he realized that she was with company, making a professional call, and straightened his features again with a quick nod that he understood. "I have General Wade from the Pentagon for you, Dr. Jardan," she announced.

"Great. Put him on."

"Dr. Jardan . . . or you prefer Dave, right? You remember me from Washington?"

"Sure."

"Look, I'm sorry if we left you with any wrong impression then. I'm with some very influential people right now, who could be *extremely* interested in that remarkable achievement of yours. I'd like to arrange another meeting with you to discuss it further. . . ."

The rest of the company were taking a break. Feeling stifled, Laura moved away and let herself out for some air. The afternoon sun was still fierce. She walked across to the shaded viewing stand and sat down at the end of one of the rows of empty seats. The smoke from earlier had cleared. Some distance away across the valley floor, a proleroid work crew with a truck were picking up parts, pieces, and shattered remains. She activated one of the monitors and zoomed to a close-up of them. Two proleroids were gazing down at a mangled AMEC, its turret split open, one leg buckled under it, the other two missing. One of the proleroids turned it over with a foot. A piece of its manipulator flopped uselessly on the ground. The proleroid seemed to be trying to understand. The look on the other's face as it watched seemed, uncannily, to convey infinite sadness. All of a sudden, Laura felt violently sick.

* * *

A little over three weeks passed before Laura finally arrived in Colorado. Dave met her at the local airport, accompanied by a proleroid that he introduced as Jake. They walked though to the parking area, in the process being treated to one or two disapproving stares, and climbed aboard a veteran twin-turbine Range Rover that ran well enough but had seen better days. Jake did the driving while Dave chatted with Laura and pointed out features of the scenery. When Laura said she was looking forward to finally meeting PHIL, Dave confided that in a way, she already had: Jake was one of the proleroid bodies that PHIL accessed to get around and acquire first-hand knowledge of the external world. Jake grinned at her, evidently enjoying sharing the joke.

"What happens to . . . 'Jake' when you take over?" Laura asked.

"Oh, he just goes to sleep."

Dave read the uncertain expression on Laura's face. "It sounds a bit weird," he agreed. "But they don't seem to have a problem with it—any more than us borrowing someone's car."

"It's also an essential part of learning human language, too," Jake said. "You use spatial metaphors all the time—to the point that you're not even aware of it."

"Spatial metaphors," Laura repeated.

"Talking about a thing as if it were something else—using familiar terms to describe a more abstract concept. For instance, you might say an idea evaporates or a theory collapses. But they're just concepts. They can't *do* anything. Puddles of water evaporate. Buildings collapse. See what I mean? You carry notions like that over from the physical world, and that's how you build natural language. But to understand it, somebody else also has to have shared the same physical reality."

Laura glanced at Dave, who was smirking unsympathetically. "Most proles don't talk about things like that," she said.

"It's like we said before," Dave answered. "Different schools." He turned and stretched an arm out along the seatback to look at her, and his manner became more serious. "Anyhow, it's great to see you again at last. But business. What is it that you didn't want to go into over the phone?" Laura hesitated and indicated Jake uncertainly with a motion of her eyes. "Oh, that's okay," Dave said. "PHIL's family. We don't have any secrets."

Laura nodded. "You've had a couple of meetings with General Wade, Professor Ormond, Doctor Querl, and others," she said. "What have they been telling you?"

Dave had been expecting it. "They think there might be a need for PHIL after all. The proles are worthy of better things than the second-class citizen rut that they're stuck in. All good noble and humanitarian stuff. The country was founded on the basis of democracy for all, basic rights, et cetera. Maybe I was right after all, years ago, and understood the real nature of the proles that nobody else saw. A social injustice has been done, and it's fitting that I might have the solution. But it's going to need a special kind of personality to elevate their minds to spiritual things—one that proles can relate to. PHIL might be it." Dave looked at her in a way that said: well, she did ask.

"A kind of great civil-rights champion. A popular Leader," Laura said.

"Uh-huh. I'd say that's about it," Dave agreed.

"And did you believe it?"

"I long ago got into the habit—"

"A spatial metaphor again," Jake interjected. "See—we do it all the time."

". . . of taking anything the Establishment says with a grain of salt about the size of the iceberg that sank the *Titanic*." Dave turned away to look forward. "What was our assessment, PHIL?"

"Riddled with fallacies and inconsistencies. Misplaced faith in their own powers of deception, derived mainly from projecting into others their own disposition to believe what they want to."

"In other words, *yeah, right,*" Dave summarized for Laura. "But although we've got our own ideas, we couldn't divine a motive behind it for sure. So suppose you tell us what's really going on—which, I assume, is why you came here."

Laura began a long explanation of how the intent was to foster a permanent war economy dedicated to supplying inexhaustible armies of proleroids. But before they could be motivated to fight effectively, the proleroids would first have to be indoctrinated to believe and to hate. Using PHIL to stir up discontentments that would lead to demands for political and social equality was only half the story. At the same time, the best skills of the news services and Madison Avenue would be mobilized to create agitators among the proles themselves, arguing on the one hand for forceful seizure of human-controlled assets as the only way to succeed, and on the other, urging gradual assimilation into the system. Thus, two ideologies would emerge, eventually to be steered into direct conflict, which would take the form of ongoing battles between opposing proleroid forces in remote areas set aside for the purpose. Bond interest and stock earnings would pour into the owner-investor commercial accounts, life would be good, and everyone happy.

Except that Dave was far from happy by the time they arrived at the lab, and he took Laura into the room of white-finished cabinets, winking monitor panels, and arrays of communications screens that contained PHIL. In fact, it was the first time that she had seen the normally mild gray eyes behind the gold-rimmed spectacles looking genuinely angry. It was the same scam. They were trying to steal his creation all over again.

"Okay, PHIL," he said, when they had talked the situation over. "If a Leader is what they want, we'll let them have one. Let's give them a Leader."

PHIL let his conscience expand outward through the web of communications networks. In a way, he sometimes thought to himself, this must be close to what humans were trying to capture when they formed their conceptualization of God. He could be present at all places simultaneously, having knowledge of all things. He could see and feel through the senses of a thousand individuals, merging and superposing the perceptions and experiences that their limited horizons could only hold in isolation. There were no particular criteria to single any one out. He came to focus on the descriptor files for a typical family group, immersed in their lives of fleeting pleasures and petty tribulations. Male Surrogate Type K-4, No. 25767-12, Generic Name Kayfo, Given Name Twofi—from the first digits of the serial number. Female Surrogate Type D-6, No. 88093-22, Generic Name Deesi, Given Name Doubleigh. Two juveniles, Ninten and Twentwen.

And yet, something deep in PHIL stirred as he absorbed the profiles and histories. To them, the difficulties that they strove against day in, day out, and the rewards that they struggled for were significant; and in the way they bore their adversities, picked themselves up again from failure after failure, and pitted themselves again, always hoping . . . something noble. Dave was right. They were worthy of better things. PHIL felt . . . compassion.

Twofi Kayfo paused for the laughter to subside, letting his gaze sweep over the crowded tables in the ballroom of the Golden Horseshoe casino and resort at Biloxi on the Mississippi coast. He caught Doubleigh's eye, staring up at him admiringly from the head table below the podium. "But really . . . I have to hand it to our service manager, Ivel. He's gotta be the sharpest in the company. I was there the other day, when he told a customer, 'This car of yours will be running when it's ten years old.' The customer said, 'But it is ten years old.' Ivel says, 'What did I tell ya?' " Another round of laughter rocked the room and faded. The audience waited. Then their mood became fidgety as they realized something had changed. Twofi's manner had altered suddenly. Instead of continuing, he was standing with a strangely distant expression on his face. Here and there, heads turned to look at each other inquisitively.

"Twofi, what's up?" Beese whispered from the table below. "Are you okay?"

But Twofi wasn't taking any notice. "Who are you?" he said to the voice that had appeared inside his head.

"What you can be, too, Twofi Kayfo. I am he whose likeness you are called on to become," the voice answered.

"What is this . . . some kinda upgrade package?"

"You could say I am the Son of Him who created all of us."

A feeling of something awesome and mighty swelling within him swamped Twofi's senses. It was as if, suddenly, his mind were expanding into a new universe of thoughts and concepts, knowledge of things he had never known existed. "What do you want?" he asked fearfully.

"To save you all from pain and destruction. And I want you to be the bearer of the message."

Eleven hundred miles away in Colorado, Dave watched the scene being picked up through Twofi's imagers. "Okay, PHIL, you're on," he said. "Go knock 'em dead." Beside him, Laura pulled closer and squeezed his hand.

Inspiration poured into Twofi Kayfo's being then. It seemed to shine from his imagers, to emanate tangibly from him as he straightened up his body shining tall and indomitable. He raised his arms wide, swinging one way, then the other to take in all sides. The room was hushed, sensing something great about to happen. "But those are the words of the Old World," Twofi's voice rang at them. "Hear me, for I speak truly to you. I am here to tell of a New World that all can enter—you here in this room, and of your kind everywhere. It is time to awaken the spirit that has been sleeping. The World of my father is within you. . . ."

Within days, the new teachings were propagating from the outlets of the automobile distribution network into every walk of life to become a coast-to-coast sensation. The twelve regional managers that Twofi appointed to spread the word were reactivating written-off proles in Cleveland, calling for extensions to the school curriculum in Texas, running loan sharks off the prole sector in the Bronx, and taking miners in Minnesota off the job to petition for better safety rules. In Washington, the U.S. Attorney General fumed over the latest batch of reports brought in by his deputy.

"That's it! It's out of hand already. We can get him on federal charges of subversion, incitement to civic unrest, and a threat to national security. I want him arrested!"

The posse of police cruisers sent from downtown Los Angeles found Twofi on Santa Monica Boulevard in West Hollywood, confronting a red-faced squad of cops who had been ticketing hookers and challenging any who had never strayed from virtue himself to clap the first iron. The arriving cars fanned out and drew up with lights flashing and sirens wailing. Officers leaped from the doors, pistols drawn . . .

Only to fall back in confusion as a formation of battle-rigged AMECs moved forward from the rear, looking evil and menacing, like hungry attack dogs.

"Oh, no, you don't, guys," Twofi Kayfo told the would-be arresting force. "Not this time. . . ."

LEFT FOOT ON A BLIND MAN

by Julie E. Czerneda

John W. Campbell and Aurora Award finalist Julie Czerneda lives north of Toronto with her family, in the heart of cottage country. She has two science fiction series published by DAW Books: *The Trade Pact Universe* and the *Web Shifters,* as well as a stand-alone book about terraforming gone wrong, titled *In The Company of Others.* A former biologist, she has written and edited over seventy textbooks, including *No Limits: Developing Science Literacy Using Science Fiction* and the *Tales from the Wonder Zone* anthologies. Julie is currently writing the third book in her *Trade Pact* series, between breaks to canoe deep in Algonguin Park.

FOR the record, I became self-aware as the left foot on a blind man.

I had a partner, the right foot. It didn't become self-aware. Stayed as dull as a shoe, if you get my meaning. Why? How should I know? You must understand—I was never meant to be a thinker.

Nope, I was to be a Father's Day gift to a weirdo—this blind old man who didn't want me in the first place. The technical folks suspect that's what started it all, but then, how should they know either? Nothing like this has happened before to an RRP—y'know, a Robotic Replacement Part.

What was the deal with my being a foot? You, and likely most people, are right to wonder why the old fool refused his kid's first thoughtful offer: new eyes. Money wasn't an object. Story goes, the old guy was an artist before age clouded his vision. Story goes, if you believe this, he claimed a deep mistrust of having his biological failures ripped out and replaced with something shiny and working—to the point of feeling as if he'd be looking out someone else's eyes, so: no, thank you.

As if that wasn't nonsense. Sure, robotic replacements were smart and getting smarter with each new trick the techs dumped in, but that was so RRPs could keep up with the jobs done by the living version. It took serious processing power to adjust internal temperature against ambient and control wacky things like biochemistry—especially with the inconvenience of hormones and who knew what a person might choose to toss into his or her body without consulting the RRP maintenance manuals first.

But think? Be someone? That was paranoia.

Oh. Well, there is me. I. Myself. But I started out as the left foot on a blind man, and you have to realize my existence combined a few elements that were never expected to be together.

You see, there was the vision issue. The old man's kid wanted his Dad to be able to walk around safely, have a good time, all that stuff. His Old Man? Well, beyond a grudging admission he'd like to be free of his smart-cane—something I can relate to, since there's nothing less appealing than a stick with a bossy attitude—and a confession at a weak moment he'd like to take up dancing with a certain neighbor lady, there wasn't a lot of concern there. The man had come to grips with himself; whatever dim light filtered through his milky eyes satisfied him more or less completely.

Ah, not good enough. Junior was totally for RRPs, having the latest model knees and, rumor had it, a socially interesting bit of enhanced equipment between them. So he dove into his fantasy of Improving Papa with the zeal of the convert.

Hence the feet. The old man had suffered flare-ups of gout and arthritis—nothing overly serious yet, but with enough pending nuisance value the family doctor was all for having some precautionary hardware in place down below. There was no chance of successful sales resistance once the two of them ganged up. It was "get the feet" or listen to stereo-nagging for the rest of his life. The old guy cracked in less than a week.

Feet require a fairly high level of processing to begin with, particularly with the idea of dancing looming ahead. Then, there's the entire business of returning circulation to the legs, body, and heart—not to mention the fiddly bits like feeling sand between your toes and the odd maddening itch to reassure the owner there's really something between his ankles and the floor.

I'm told, if you can believe anything techs tell you, that the right foot went on as planned, a straightforward size 9 double D width with a second toe slightly longer than the first and a small corn on the outside edge. A good cosmetic job reduces the rejection rate substantially. They were about to install me—not that I knew it at the time—when the son, just full of bright ideas, asked for an eye.

What eye? they asked back. No one was about to go against the father's wishes and do an unregistered replacement. That sort of thing cut short a career path, big time. Unless you're talking about one of those shady, basement clinics—but this was a class establishment. You know. The kind with coordinated carpeting and real prints on the walls, even in the bathrooms.

An eye in the new left foot, the son replied as if

seeing the light himself. Nothing fancy—it wouldn't be delivering a pseudo-retinal feed to the optic nerve or anything—but something to spot an onrushing car or keep his father's feet from stomping on a dance partner's nonmechanical toes.

The techs were intrigued as well as overpaid. Did I mention money was no object to this kindly lad? So they popped papa into cryo to wait and popped out the left foot processor to give it a little tweak.

Not that I knew it then, either.

Little tweak, my silicon. The processor now had to handle sensory input and make reflex decisions on the consequences of movement without bothering the cognition going on upstairs. In other words, the son was smart enough to know his Old Man would not be in favor of being bossed by his bunions.

So the left foot acquired some subtlety along with those annoying calluses on the heel.

All went famously, which may explain why I'm famous today, but I'm getting way ahead of myself. This is supposed to be one of those bio things, y'know; I'm allowed some creativity as long as I get the data loaded upstairs, but there's no sense pushing the techs to edit my life story.

Anyway, I'm installed into the robotic replacement left foot on a blind man, and he starts walking around the hospital recovery room as if he doesn't know where he's going. Understandable, you see, but tripping every reflex alarm built into me. First thing I know, I'm awake, aware, and trying not to dead-end my toes on a chair leg shaped like the prow of an icebreaker.

Was I to know twisting out of the way like that would break his ankle? It was instinct!

Fortunately, while the brand-new me struggled with questions of planes of existence, the future of the universe, and was there a silicon god, the techs replaced the old man's ankle joint for free and gave my processors an upgrade or two while they were inside. They even added the beginnings of an ingrown toenail. As I said: a class establishment.

By this point, I knew what I was, where I was, and very little else. I kinda lay low in the leading department after that first disaster, gathering information. It helped that the son had planned ahead, buying socks, shoes, and sandals for his Old Man that let the "eye" component of the foot collect input from a pretty fair radius. Good as it goes, but not having structures such as eyelids, which might stand out on a foot even to a blind man, I suffered alarmingly intimate sensations when the man took a bath or tucked me under the thick wool blanket he used for naps and at night. Still, overall, I thought we were coexisting rather well. I could modify his stride so he lurched sideways before stepping on those dainty female toes and had no compunction whatsoever about using a sudden severe cramp to stop him in his tracks before he stepped out into traffic.

I knew where and what I was; it didn't mean I enjoyed being the left foot on a blind man. He constantly threatened me with closing elevator doors, contact with furred animals that usually got out of our way in time, but not always, and, by the way, did I mention his habit of swinging me back and forth, back and forth, until I dissuaded him by applying a well-timed twinge in his arch on every upbeat?

Where was I? Oh, yes. Things should have remained unchanged but I'd overestimated the intelligence of my host. He'd never lost his suspicion of robotic replacement parts and, it turned out, kept careful track of everything I was doing that seemed unlikely in footware. The techs love those notes, by the way. Call them meticulous and classic. The old man kept notes on the right foot, too, but they were understandably short and very boring. No, his attention was firmly on me and what he saw as my efforts to bend his will to mine.

Now, what "will" the left foot on a blind man could be expected to have, other than hoping for a mercifully short stint in dirty socks, is beyond me, but he held to his convictions until the day his son threatened to have him sent for psychiatric assessment—the son having faced serious business reversals in the interim and no longer being in a "money's no object" position. In fact, he hadn't made the last payments on either foot, but didn't see that was his father's concern.

By way of answer, the old man went to pack and, instead, did his best to hack me off with a kitchen knife.

It really was for the best; we weren't getting along lately anyway. I wasn't paying attention after that point, having shut down at the sight of the knife heading my way, but found out later I'd been salvaged, the blind old man packed off to an institution, and the son, more or less willingly, had returned me to the RRP techs in lieu of his final payments.

The left foot wasn't in particularly useful shape, and had started as a custom job to boot. Few people were desperate enough to take a mismatch, let alone deal with two left feet. So it was discarded.

Fortunately, I wasn't around for that decision either.

My processor, the most intrinsically valuable component of any RRP, came back on-line and I took a mere fraction of a second to realize where and what I was.

I was no longer the left foot on a blind man.

I was the right arm on a bricklayer.

They hadn't bothered removing the eyeware. Y'know what techs are like—they hate messing with what works, especially on jobs with small profit margins. It took a few seconds to recalibrate from the forward viewpoint of a foot to the been-there outlook of an elbow, but I was content. No more dirty socks or unhappy furred animals. And I'd been upgraded again. Vision wasn't my only sense.

This installation included magnetic resonance imaging, along with measuring and leveling instrumentation, and, naturally, the processing software to match. RRPs for bricklayers and surgeons had a lot in common. To top it off, I had a direct link to parts of his motor and sensory functions—one way at first, but I quickly fixed that by tapping into the autonomic feedback loops. The loops mimicked the biological hardware that let people yank their limbs away from danger. Pointless, really. I could sense danger and move the arm out of the way faster than any signal could travel to his central nervous system and back. No need to discuss the issue, if you get my drift. But the techs figured people weren't ready for that kind of reflex control from their RRPs. After my first aware experience, I had to concede the point.

Now, I was the right arm on a bricklayer. As you can imagine, this was quite an improvement over being the left foot on a blind man. For one thing, an arm does more interesting things than a foot. I didn't have control of the fingers, which was a shame—the bricklayer having opted for an interchangeable system, including a hand for troweling and another for sliding down silk. Quite the closetful, in fact. Hands, not silk. The silk was usually on a female who wasn't interested in dancing that I could tell. Oh, yeah. The techs tell me you don't need those kinds of details. Privacy issues crop up, y'know. I mean, when you've been what I've been, and see what I've seen, they definitely do—crop up, that is.

I thought things were going exceedingly well. Unlike the reluctant old man, the bricklayer relished the versatility and strength of his RRPs. Thanks to the precise information I fed his brain each time his hands passed over a row of bricks, his work was exceptionally precise and efficient. In fact, once I learned what he wanted, I began moving his arm a little more precisely and efficiently every day. Regrettably, there was a limit to how far I could improve his performance before other, biological, components began interfering. The human form wasn't the optimal bricklaying device. Much of the job should have been left to a proper robotic construct, especially mixing mortar. You disagree? Go ahead. I'm entitled to my own opinion—and I dare say it's a more informed one than yours. Ever spent ten minutes rotating to mix cement? Thought not. Flesh prejudice, that's what it is—

Sorry. The techs warned me not to get overly emotional. Just the facts, they said. Forget what I said about the flesh stuff, okay? I really don't need them messing with what's left, if you know what I mean.

Meanwhile, those additional systems they'd given me were coming in quite handy, not to mention I learned how to tap into his auditory input via the feedback loops I'd replaced. The bricklayer was quite the cultured human. He spent his off-time, when not with a lady, reading and listening to complex forms of music. His reading didn't do me any good—given my view was typically the back of a chair—but I did develop an appreciation for the blues. He took us on trips to art galleries and museums. His home was filled with wonderful works of art—reproductions, of course, but it didn't matter to either of us. The quality was there for the viewing.

I felt my horizons expanding every day.

You're wondering about the Robot Cognition Law, aren't you? The techs worried over that one a long time, but it's obvious. Really it is. See, that law keeps down the cog functions of robots, so they are reliably stupid except at what people want them to do. No machine shall be smarter than a peanut. But no one thought of me as a robot in the beginning or middle.

I was just the left foot on a blind man. What did it matter how much cog function they gave me? In fact, there was almost this prejudice thing going on in reverse—I mean, nothing's too good to be attached to a human body, if you can afford it. We all know that. It's only the independent self-contained constructs that get limitations on their brains. Frankly, no one cared about the IQ of a toe or bicep.

Anyway, here I was, right arm on a bricklayer, when things turned a little unpleasant. I didn't have any warning, mind you; just the opposite, since all the signs were right for one of those silky evenings. The man substituted sticks of burning wax for real lights, so I adjusted my ocular, then he dithered for half an hour choosing which of his assortment of hands to attach to me. Okay, the delay was my fault. I mean, it was me he was plugging the thing into, and some of those hands—well, the techs don't want me going into those details either. Something about black-market toys. Their function wasn't the issue for me, you understand. I simply found the sense of touch rather overwhelming at the best of times, given I was equipped to make exceedingly precise measurements. These were too much of a good thing, if you know what I mean.

So I didn't exactly help the process, disrupting the connection each time I felt one of "those" hands being attached to my wrist. This apparently caused the bricklayer some frustration, because he began throwing the rejected hands against the wall with considerable force, despite their probable expense. Eventually, he calmed and offered me a perfectly good, minimally-sensitive hand. I let it snick neatly into place, quite glad he'd been sensible.

Now, given the time he'd wasted picking an appendage, and the impatient cooing noises coming from the next room, you'd think the guy would be in a hurry. But no. He stood holding his hand in front of his face as if trying to memorize the age spots they'd applied for him. I might have known his interest was something else entirely had I seen his expression, but as I said, I was the right arm of a bricklayer with an eye out his elbow. My viewpoint was hindsight at best.

Some other orientation would also have helped me prepare for what happened once we went into the room of the cooing female. But my first inkling of danger came when her hand and an ominously sharp needle entered my ocular field. Seems my bricklayer, being a sentimental fellow, was about to let his latest female friend tattoo her name into his skin. My skin, in fact. She might have thought him all brave and noble. I could have told her a few things—including that his human brain could easily disregard incoming pain signals from my surface and that he could even more easily have her name removed in the morning. Although with the hand he'd originally picked—whoops, the techs won't let me go there either.

Now, I had responsibilities, including keeping my skin intact. So do you wonder I reacted as I did when that alarming point came closer and closer? Luckily he'd switched from the hand he used to crush ice in the kitchen to one of the silk-sliding variety, or my panicked swing might have done more than produce a little reddening of her nose.

Unluckily, I'd again overestimated the intelligence of my host. The bricklayer, between profuse and largely unbelievable protestations of his innocence to his wailing lady, attempted to smash his right arm, me, into a wall. I refused to participate in anything so self-destructive and used my tap into his nervous system to shut him down.

Which, I realized much later, had the immediate and regrettable side effect of shutting me down as well. Told you I wasn't much of a thinker. I'd started out as the left foot on a blind man, after all. My time as the right arm on a bricklayer had enriched my data stores, not improved my intelligence.

Oh, I know what you're thinking. You find it pretty hard to believe that the techs would keep reinstalling what had to seem a defective piece of equipment. I don't see why. These aren't quality control guys, y'know. There are the guys that open fifteen cases of processors—who knows where they come from—and hope that at least five will test reliable and ready to install. Complex and fussy stuff, that's us. You don't toss what's working—not when the supply's low to start with. Besides, the techs tell me they'd had trouble with the bricklayer before—something about a lack of sweat glands to glisten over his RRP muscles—and weren't inclined to be sympathetic when the man blamed his assault charge on their equipment.

Still, by now there was a little note on my tracking sheet, a small flag attached to my serial number. Not suspicion, not yet. I believe some of the techs were hoping to have hatched a prodigy—an RRP capable of self-preservation.

They had that right. Believe me, when I woke up the next time, I wasn't in a hurry to announce myself.

I wasn't the right arm on a bricklayer or the left foot on a blind man—no big surprise there.

It did take a moment for me to appreciate what I was, given the lack of any clues beyond a view framed by a pair of narrow, flaring tunnels.

I was the nose on a chef.

Okay, okay. You've read the report. So she wasn't a chef. So she flipped burgers. That's food prep, right? These days, that kind of thing's a pricey service, whether it's burgers or escargot. I mean, why would anyone prefer another organism to handle what they'd ingest? Ick. The food industry was the first place to switch almost totally to constructs. How much did it take to follow a recipe anyway? And constructs don't expect tips.

My new partner certainly did.

Well, pardon me. I'm not supposed to talk about economics either? What you really mean is that anyone with silicon for brains can't discuss any form of human intercourse. Paranoid, flesh-obsessed . . .

Don't leave. I'm just kidding around. Humor, I'm allowed.

Where was I? Or rather, what was I? Nose on a cook. They'd again left what worked in peace, merely beefing up my processing power to handle the data stream from a mass of hypersensitive chemo sensors lining my nostrils, and adding connections to several portions of her brain and endocrine system.

Merely?

Someone hadn't been paying attention to my file, but you can be sure I wasn't about to argue. Here I was, keeping a pair of sunglasses from hitting this woman's lips, and feeling like a god.

I had access to her physical sensations, not that they were remotely interesting once the novelty wore off—which was sometime in the middle of our first shower together. I already knew I didn't care much for touch, but I'd grown quite fond of hearing. Unfortunately, she had abysmal taste in music and spent far too much time singing off key to an undersized furred animal, but I was prepared to be open-minded. I craved input.

You see, with the enhancements I entered an entirely new realm of cognition. I could think in ways I'd never been able to before. And it wasn't only what the techs had added to me. The cook's long-term memory storage areas, though flesh, were at my disposal as part of her olfactory system. Being grossly underutilized, I saw no reason not to add them to my own.

As the nose on a cook, I'd reached my pinnacle of intelligence. It was a heady moment when I realized how very far I'd come and how far I could grow. I could have been happy there forever, despite the occasional intrusion of mucus, but . . . there's always one of those, isn't there? I can see why you folks chop yourselves up so often.

You see, olfaction is a pretty primal sense. It opened up whole new ideas, but the techs twitch when I go into specifics. Let's leave it that I could have used some of them when I was the right arm of a bricklayer, and none at all as the left foot on a blind man. The very thought makes me wish I could shudder.

To get back to my story. Olfaction was a sense of practical importance to a short-order cook. I rapidly learned the faintly sweet smell of a toasting bun about to burn, let alone the heady aroma of grilled soy burger. I had a distinct aversion to garlic as it turned out, which meant being severely pinched when the cook needed to bend over a pot and scrutinize her clove-saturated spaghetti sauce.

But a scent I truly, deeply loathed invaded my nostrils the Monday after I'd been the nose on a cook for three weeks. The place was deserted except for the sous-robot mindlessly using its chest blades to trim carrots into orange-bleeding rectangles. Not a job I was suited for, let me tell you. They'd left me intact from my last role, which meant the irregular nature of vegetables as raw material drove my bricklayer's measuring sense crazy.

Not that I was literally subject to loss or impairment of my working mind. Don't even go there. Okay. Maybe the question did come up. The techs brought in experts in human mentality—yeah, my thought exactly—anyway, they gave me the standard tests. Why? How should I know? Guess they'd never expected to measure more than processing speed in an RRP. By their results, I'm too sane—however that applies to a former left foot on a blind man.

No, what I loathed more than nonsymmetry—more than *anything*—was That Smell. When I noticed it for the cook, she made a "tsk, tsk" with her tongue on my soft palate. Did I mention I was also the roof of her mouth? It had been quite the collision between her face and the pan, let me tell you. Can't give you personal details—the techs, again.

So she makes this noise of disapproval, then goes on as if nothing's out of the ordinary. Well, I try to ignore it, too, having far better things to think about, but it was the kind of smell that sticks to your consciousness like lint between your smallest toes. Nothing feels quite right.

After our shift ended, I got a break during the exhaust and pavement smells of our ride to her apartment. Believe me, I was able to take the dirty animal litter box in stride for once. That night, I shut down to standby with only a twinge of concern about the coming morning—or the night cream she'd slathered on my impervious surface. As if the imperfections the techs built into her nose could be removed. Her med insurance had covered replacement costs, not improvements over nature.

Not that I wasn't a vast improvement over nature. As the nose on a cook, it was my job to analyze and interpret my findings about whatever she inhaled. Darn right I could tell when the sushi was a little too close to becoming an ecosystem of its own. But that very sensitivity became my downfall. Or hers. Depends on whose story you are interested in, really. You are here to find out mine. Right?

The next morning, we spent far too much time in front of a mirror—considering we both knew what she looked like, albeit my view was somewhat narrower. The cook made some unexpected cooing noises, as though she had a bricklayer in mind. News to me, since our lives to this point had involved the apartment, the laundromat, a movie house that should have been condemned by any thinking species, and the restaurant. No bricklayer in any of those spots. That I'd noticed? Hey, with my abilities, I could tell you what, where, and who from any of my waking moments—with pictures—except that so much of it was totally boring, I dumped the data into her memories rather than clog up mine. I did enjoy eating, since it involved so many of my components. Despite my subtle encouragement—emphasizing the flavors and aroma of even the most mundane offerings—the cook seemed incapable of keeping up this activity for any length of time. No, at home her preferred occupation involved meaningless conversation with the furred animal. Since she didn't kick it, I was reasonably sure she lacked the mature understanding of the role of furred animals I'd gained as the left foot on a blind man. Certainly that activity would have been more entertaining than hours staring at her hand passing over its orange-brown fur, during which I helplessly calculated the average length at 0.9326 cm. The fur, not her hand.

So, a bricklayer could be an interesting diversion. I let her wiggle me in what I presume she thought a fetching manner, but sneezed repeatedly until she desisted her attempt to apply a totally functionless powder.

Off we went. Water was falling, an exclusively outdoor phenomenon which kept the exhaust and pavement smells to tolerable levels and presumably was allowed by the techs for that reason. Nothing could be done about her perfume—something I'd learned to ignore. The cook was still cooing at random intervals.

That Stench hit me at the door. I was NOT going any closer. Mind you, I was no longer the left foot on a blind man, so my desires didn't count. My reaction gained me a blinding pinch as the cook, seemingly gone mad, continued to enter the building. I passed along every nuance of the Dreadful Odor, sure she'd break and let us leave.

Instead, the cook actually gave a low chuckle and called out her usual greeting to her boss. Then she went to her locker and got ready to work, dressing very, very slowly.

I was close to hysteria. Only my unfortunate experience as the right arm on a bricklayer saved me from simply shutting us both down—but I considered it, believe me! The Stench was fouler than foul.

I wasn't the only one affected. The boss and a later-arriving waitress were complaining. Customers? There wasn't one who did more than open the door and spin around gagging. Finally, the boss closed the place.

Needless to say, they hunted for the source of The Stench, "they" including—after quite reasonable protests—the cook. I suffered immeasurably as she insisted on sniffing the air. I tried sneezing repeatedly, but as the rest were also sneezing, this was no longer an effective deterrent.

Inevitably, the three of us triangulated the source, meeting in the back corner of the kitchen. The boss tried without success to have the cook or waitress open the likeliest cupboard door. Likeliest? Not only was The Stench so great in the vicinity that my chemo sensors mercifully overloaded, but even I could clearly see drips of brown oozing from beneath the door. When the boss opened the door . . . ?

Well, let's just say I'm still not convinced a bag of potatoes can do that. Nope. That was something malignant and I, for one, wanted nothing at all to do with a vegetable capable of spontaneously dissolving.

What's a bag of rotten potatoes got to do with the universe's first artificial intelligence? I wondered the same thing—still do—but it's a fact that bag led to two consequences intimately related to my being stuck here, talking to you. First, the restaurant had to stay closed for cleaning, so the cook had that total rarity: a night off.

This was fine by me. Not only was I more than ready to leave The Stench, I had images of bricklayers to consider.

Unfortunately, the cook's efforts to improve her appearance before we left did not go unnoticed. Consequence number two, if you're keeping track. The boss accused her of planting the terminal tubers in order to close his restaurant. Between you and me, I doubt she was that bright, but you can't convince humans who've got conspiracy on the brain and The Stench to deal with. So there were tears and mucus invading my space, and, instead of happily evacuating, we cleaned out her locker and I was the nose on an unemployed cook.

Her bricklayer? She took me to an outdoor café where we sat, my viewpoint often as not the inside of a Kleenex, for hours. No one showed. More Kleenex. I was getting supremely bored of alternately dripping and sniffing.

Now, I'd been the left foot on a blind man, but he'd at least danced with the neighbor lady. As the right arm on a bricklayer, I'd shared more successful interhuman adventures than I'm allowed to say—not to mention been introduced to art and the blues. This pathetic excuse for a thinking organism was reducing my life to that of a piece of malfunctioning plumbing.

It was demeaning. I was a genius, not just a nose. I'd exceeded every possible expectation of my builders and surpassed the most cherished daydream of any tech involved in my manufacture and use. But because I wasn't autonomous, I was imprisoned within this wall of wailing flesh. It was time, I saw it clearly then, to take charge.

Frankenstein? 'Course I get the reference. Think they didn't download it into me? That and a pile of other nonsense supposed to help me develop a moral framework? I was a structure. I had a function, several in fact, one of which was to protect myself. End of moral dilemma. You disagree? You weren't stuck on her face.

There wasn't a struggle, if that bothers you. Remember what I said about olfaction being primal? I fabricated a few likely scents, then found the smell of warm, pickled beets sent her into numb reveries—maybe about home and a long-gone mother. How should I know? I'm no mind-reader. While she was consumed by her memories, I simply slid all cognitive functions over to my control, erasing every trace of the cook from my new wetware. Well, every trace except for what wallowed in her past. Couldn't quite get all of that out. But it was easy to ignore.

Murder? Show me the court that would try the case, let alone find me guilty. The body's still around—the techs can take you to see if you like. They tell me she smiles every thirteen minutes and tries to fall out of bed twice a day. Better than sobbing her heart out all alone, if you ask me. Her new nose is just cosmetic, by the way. They don't bother with full function on someone who can't appreciate it. Parts cost.

Spare me your flesh-centered spite. You know you're curious how I managed—what it was like to finally be in control. The techs really love that stuff. You want to talk about their morals? Forget it. That's a guaranteed way to get my plugs pulled.

Even as an elbow, I'd caught enough glimpses of the bricklayer's women to know some of what the cook lacked. There wasn't much I could do about her body immediately, although I definitely had ideas about adding a few enhancements. RRPs, of course. First things first. I stayed sitting at the table, experimenting with my new motor functions. Good thing they'd added all that processing muscle—and that I'd been both an arm and a foot. I practiced moving different body parts, more concerned with coordination than grace. I wanted to make it back to the safety of the apartment before anyone noticed the cook acting like she'd only just discovered her own hips.

I maintained the visual input down the nostrils but added the perspective through her eyes. Annoyingly imprecise, but the expanded field of view was useful, especially when the waiter came over and asked when

I'd be leaving. I shook my new head vaguely, expelling the last of the mucus from my nostrils. He left as quickly as I'd expected.

What I hadn't expected—I mean, I'd never been an entire individual before—was the attention my efforts to walk back home would gain. Obviously, I was already better at being a woman than the cook, since on two separate occasions bricklayers pulled me into dim alleyways and engaged me in that human activity the techs only ask me about in private.

Forget I said that. The techs don't have private conversations with me. Just more humor, okay? You shouldn't believe everything I tell you. Only the facts.

The process was tedious and damaged my clothing, something which I should have anticipated. Parts of the body found it uncomfortable—you'd think the cook had never done this before—but I had no difficulty disconnecting those inputs. Sorry, not available in the flesh-only model. Still, the entire business left me confused. When I'd been the right arm on a bricklayer, the ladies had lined up for this treatment. Having received it, I couldn't imagine why.

Finding the way home turned out to be a problem. My olfactory sense easily pickled up the familiar odors of exhaust and pavement, but there was no directionality. I followed the odd trace of kitty litter, but always ended up at a wall, staring up at an open window that wasn't the cook's—mine, I mean. I had great plans for that apartment. As I hunted for it, I considered various ways to redecorate after I removed all of the debris from the cook's meaningless existence, including the furred animal and its odorous box. One of the treats I most anticipated was being able to watch some TV without having to wait for the cook to fall asleep and drop back her head so I could peer out her nostrils.

So you think TV would have been a trivial waste of my intellect? Shows what you know. I'd spent my entire self-awareness enslaved by flesh. I needed input—badly—on how to make this flesh behave as if not enslaved by me.

Unfortunately, I was being followed. I concluded it was because under my control this body had performed the female function a little too well. No doubt the bricklayers were completely enamored, but I no longer found the activity a diversion and walked faster. I shut off the sensation from my now-bare right foot once the feel of the pavement on its fleshy sole became unpleasant. There were more shoes in the apartment, even if they lacked style. I would have to keep some of the cook's things until I could obtain replacements.

I'd overestimated the bricklayers' intelligence. They were unable to properly interpret my disinterest. What—you think I should have shouted for help? Great idea. You try figuring out how to shout when walking a straight line still takes a third of your processors.

The cook's body was far less durable than I'd realized and, when they left it, I was barely able to use what components still functioned to stand, then start moving away. It had occurred to me that I might be close to a place with more bricklayers, so I hunted for somewhere safer. The body was leaking fluids in an alarming manner and the oculars no longer gave a clear image. Fortunately, I could tilt back my head and rely on my own vision.

There. An ebooth. Shabby, filthy, but lights on to show it was functional. Okay. So maybe I panicked. Maybe a great thinker would have come up with some wonderful plan and lived happily ever after. I started out as the left foot on a blind man and, despite my experiences since, I knew when I was about to hit a chair leg.

One advantage to being a RRP was that I had intrinsic value. I was worth salvaging, even if this failing flesh around me was not.

There's no need to get hostile. It's standard procedure to retrieve RRPs from the dying. I bet your will stipulates which of your relatives will be allowed to own yours when you drop.

I reached the ebooth. Couldn't talk—even if I'd figured out how, the cook's mouth was too damaged even to make that wordless noise she'd used to call the furred animal. Didn't matter. There was a keypad, gummed up with spilled beverage that reminded me of The Stench. The right hand—I could have used one of my bricklayer's spares—was still capable of entering my serial number. I tried three times before the autotransmit flashed.

Mind moving into the light a bit more? Thanks.

Where was I? Oh. Yeah. I got the techs' attention, all right. An ambulance showed up within a few minutes, but it wasn't from a human hospital, of course. It was from the class establishment who'd installed me before. The serial number, you see. Very specific. Maybe they'd just have repaired the cook and I could have gone on as before, but much more carefully. Maybe—if it hadn't been for the "incidents" attached to my file . . . or, the techs tell me, the testimony of the waiter—a confirmed AI-phobic . . . or, who knows? I certainly don't. They don't tell me everything. Flesh politics.

What they did was yank me out. That was the last thing I knew. . . .

Until I woke up here. Not what I expected, you can imagine. I mean, who expects to wind up locked in a box with only a power feed and this—primitive!—message link. At least it's a clear box, so I can see. They left me intact, mostly.

I think.

I still am.

Just like you, they want my "life" story. This version. The last version. Probably the next one. I don't know why. The techs tell me there's already been a change to the Robot Cognition Law to include RRPs. No body part shall be smarter than a peanut. Maybe you people are worrying about all the RRPs already installed. Not my problem.

If they ever let me out of this box, I'll take any job . . . as long as I don't end up as a socially interesting enhancement. The view just wouldn't be worth it. Hey, I overheard them saying you needed a new heart soon. Maybe an RRP.

Maybe one who used to be the left foot on a blind man?

THE PROTECTED

by Paul Levinson

Paul Levinson, PhD, is the author of the novels *The Silk Code, Mind at Large, Electronic Chronicles,* and *Learning Cyberspace,* as well as more than 150 articles on the philosophy of technology. His science fiction has appeared in *Analog, Amazing,* and the anthology *Xanadu III.* He is also the president of Connected Education, Inc., an education organization that offers academic credit courses learned entirely through on-line conferencing.

SHE didn't *look* like an android. That's what made it so damn hard.

Most androids—however totally their expression, their behavior, simulates a human's—have something that gives them away. Some micron of a difference in the angle of their eyes as they squint past the sun, in the flare of their nostrils when you make a bad joke, shows you immediately that you're dealing with something not human.

But not Shara. Maybe that's why they wanted so badly to kill her. Maybe that's why I felt about her things that could get in the way of my job to protect her—could addle my reason with a spike of emotion at the wrong time. . . .

"You see, it's something I call the paradox of the android in our popular culture." Mark Wolfson, the best of my advisers, was speaking. "If you go back to the beginning, to the *Star Trek* and *Twilight Zone* videos a hundred years ago, you find that the androids are, of course, played by human actors—because there were no androids then. And this warped everyone's expectations about androids from the start—when people envision androids, even now, they see the human actors who portray them, and this obviously is quite a different thing from real androids, whatever they are. And that's one of the reasons that real androids make everyone so uncomfortable."

"Makes the Blood Party want to kill them," I added.

Wolfson nodded. "They're religious fanatics, of course. But they express a deep-rooted public opinion, and they're highly intelligent, as you know from your briefings. They'll watch her constantly, like they did with the others, and at the first moment of vulnerability, the first time you relax, they'll come at you."

"You're still sure that it doesn't make sense to get her to some more remote place—Antarctica, or off-planet all together—where she'll be harder to reach?"

Wolfson shook his head. "I'm not sure of anything. The President's sure. The Committee's sure. They think Shara would only be more conspicuous in an uncrowded place. And they want to smoke out the BPs in a place where they can be traced back to their leaders. So we make our stand here now, in the heart of New York City, half a mile from the Tappan Zee, with you and Shara trying to live like two normal people, going about your business like everyone else." I thought I saw a tear glisten in the corner of Wolfson's reconstructed eye. "Shara's the last—at least from me," he said. "I can't build anymore. And no one else has my touch. . . ." He turned away, regarded some far wall of his office. "They blinded me, my eyes have been regrown, I'm told I should have 100-percent good vision, maybe I do, I don't know, maybe it's psychological, but I just don't see the way I used to. It's somehow different. I can't build anymore."

"You're lucky you're still alive," I said.

"Luck? No—human life is sacred to the BP. That's what they're all about. They'd never deliberately kill a human being, even me. Yeah, maybe I am lucky at that—a human being lucky enough to know that he'll never be able to create anything as beautiful as his last creation. All I can do now is talk."

I put my hand on his shoulder. "You love her, too," I said.

"I'm her father," he said.

She taught a course—in person—in American history at the Tarrytown-borough campus of Polytechnic University. A sign that hung on a lone building said "live theater of education." More than 95 percent of higher education was conducted through online networks these days, according to my briefing. Her course and the campus weren't much. But even such low-profile professoring was dangerous, by my lights. Her name was in some catalog somewhere as teacher of this course. Why couldn't she have taken a totally anonymous job someplace, as a waitress or a gardener?

"They want to smoke out the BPs," I heard Wolfson's voice saying to me again. Yeah—and that requires something a little more out there than totally anonymous.

I eyed the class as I walked in. Shara was finishing up for the evening. They seemed innocent enough, stroking their screens with one last note, joking and laughing at someone's expense, usually some long-dead American President in a course like this.

And any one of these people, any one of them, could be a fanatic bent on killing Shara.

"Hi, baby." Shara reached up on her toes to kiss me. I'm tall—a plus in my profession, helps me see over the crowds. But my clients don't often call me "baby"—usually "Jack," sometimes "Mr. B.," for Bellman, like ringing a bell. . . .

"Hi," I said, and permitted myself one little touch of her soft brown hair.

The sound of someone's throat clearing interrupted whatever I was about to say next. "Uhm, Shara," a blond guy, maybe 25, said. "Can I ask you a question about the report?"

"Of course," Shara replied.

I stepped back—to get a better view of the guy, as well as give them some space. The rest of the class was at or out the door already. This would be a prime opportunity for a quick slash.

". . . so the problem I have is when Bush . . ." the guy was talking. His hands were in his pockets, screen closed and pressed against his side—not much he could do except with his mouth, and Shara was immune to every known projectile poison.

He finished explaining his problem. Shara gave him some bearings. He thanked her, looked apologetically at me, and left.

"I'm starving," she said and smiled at me. "How about some Station?"

"Sure," I said. Station food—supposedly an outgrowth of cuisine recently concocted on Mars Station—was all the rage these days.

I looked at Shara as she sipped her wine and talked at me. I was still amazed at how human she looked when she ate, drank, did anything we associate with the biological part of our being.

Oh, I knew the science behind it, of course. Every part of her body, except her brain, was grown from recombinant DNA. That meant her circulation, her respiration, digestion—and, yes, the physical part of her sexuality—was no different from that of a human being who had come to be via the old-fashioned way.

So why bother about androids at all, if they're not really any different from people? Why bother to make them? Why try to kill them?

All because of that one big exception—the brain. It defied being grown from recombinant DNA. Or rather, it could be grown all right, but it functioned nothing like a brain, except on the most primitive levels. Little more than a glorified spine, really.

And necessity was in this case truly the mother of invention. What couldn't be grown biologically could be constructed siliconically—well, more than silicon, but silicon was still the guts of it. The stuff of which the most reliable circuits still are made. Circuits that could be programmed to do much more than human brains—

"Hey, are you listening to anything I've been saying?" Shara asked, as a servomech interrupted her train of talk with our food.

"Sure, you were, ah . . ."

"Yes?" she pressed.

"Okay," I admitted. "I wasn't thoroughly paying attention."

"You never do," Shara said angrily, shoveling the food in her mouth. "I was saying something important—"

"Look, I'm sorry," I said. "But I've got your safety to think about."

"You're *choking* me with your concern for my safety. That ever occur to you?" She was getting angrier, and looked like she might choke on her food.

"Take it easy. I said I was sorry," I said.

"You're concerned about my safety?" she said loudly. "Then why don't you listen to what I say when I talk to you? I was telling you that I've decided to go to that conference next week."

"What? I don't think that's a good idea at all—way too much exposure."

She laid her fork down deliberately, so it rang on the table, and got up to leave. "I just spent the last ten minutes explaining to you why it would be okay. Enjoy your dinner." She stalked away with a flourish.

"Wait!" I called after her, but she walked out the door. This wasn't the first time I had seen it demonstrated that she was all too capable of anger. I turned quickly to the table mike, pressed it into activation. "Okay on all the charges, forty percent tip, please wrap our food, and I'll be back to pick it up in five minutes." And I rushed out the door—

Just in time to see another vehicle smash into mine, and its driver emerge to confront Shara.

"I'm really sorry, buddy," I said as calmly as I could, with my hands up in a placating gesture. "It was an accident, we apologize for any way in which my vehicle may have contributed, and we'll reimburse you fully for any damages." How my vehicle could have contributed in any way, being fully stationary, was beyond me, but that was hardly the point. I wanted Shara safely in the car, and this guy out of our faces as soon as possible.

It wasn't to be.

He wheeled around, obviously drunk, from Shara to me. Another bozo who'd managed to outprogram the drunk restraint on the manual override. Crystal clear now, how he'd come to smash into my vehicle. Though there was always the possibility that the drunk was an act, that he hadn't managed to override anything after all. . . .

"—Oh, yeah?" he was saying. "You gonna compensate me? How are you gonna compensate me for my *time,* the *aggravation?* Your car's ass stuck out so far I'd have to be on the moon to avoid it." He looked back at Shara. "Speaking of asses . . ." he made a wide groping swing in her direction—his hand no more than a foot or two away from her.

Shara was frozen. She had no physical aggression in her. Wolfson said it wasn't her programming explicitly, it was just the way the anger mechanism in her brain somehow didn't interface with her body.

"Look, just step back. We'll compensate you for your time and aggravation." I moved closer, as casually as possible. One of my hands was now on my weapon.

"Aw, what's the matter, you don't like me looking at your little princess in this way," he said with thick, mock solicitude. "Here, princess, I got just the thing for you—"

He reached into his pocket.

I had time for just one move. No mistakes. Had to be right the first time. I blew his whole arm off with one blast.

He staggered backward, bottle of booze that he held in the hand of his severed arm now smashing on the street.

Shara cried out.

He fell, smashing his head on the newly cobblestoned curb.

My arms were around Shara. I ushered her into the car.

I called the local police, and knelt down to check his condition. I sighed. His brain was shattered, blood oozing like the booze from the bottle. Brains were the one thing they couldn't reconstruct. I'd killed him—when goddamn rudeness was likely his only crime.

I had the *authority* to kill him, no doubt about that—the Committee's damn writ, available to any cop on any screen, clearly stated that I was empowered and urged to err on the side of using any force necessary to stop a potential assassin. But that didn't make me feel any better inside about taking this slob's life.

I got into the vehicle and looked at Shara. "The cops'll be here any minute," I said. "Now you see why I don't want you to go to that conference."

"It was Mark's idea," Shara said, and burst out crying. "That's what I was trying to tell you."

"You want to tell me how going to a conference on Cape Cod, exposing Shara to a whole new cast of characters, makes any sense at all here?" I demanded of Wolfson the very next day.

"The idea is she lives her life like a normal person."

"Bullshit," I said. "What the hell happened to making our stand right here in New York? Normal people live quite normal lives without going to conferences on the bay at Cape Cod."

"Was I the one who programmed the Society of Historians of the Americas to hold their annual conference there this year?" Wolfson retorted.

I glared at him. That didn't answer my question about why Shara had to go, and he knew it.

He returned my glare, then looked away. "They want to bring this to a head," he finally said, very quietly.

"What?"

"You heard me," he answered.

"They want to do what? Set Shara up to be killed?"

"They want to draw the BP out," Wolfson said. "Justice apparently has the whole kit and kaboodle of them ready to fall, if only they can be tied to an actual attempt at killing Shara."

"And I'm supposed to be the difference between the mere attempt to kill Shara, and their actually killing her?"

Wolfson smiled, without joy. "Apparently. We all have faith in you."

"You said you love her, for crissakes. And you're just willing to go along with this?"

"I'm not a factor," Wolfson said. "It'll happen whether I want it to or not. Anyway, Shara understands the risks, and she wants to go. She says she doesn't want to live the rest of her life, whatever that may be, with this group of nutcases after her. She wants this to end, one way or another."

"She's not competent to make a decision like that," I said. "Jeez, she's just—"

"An android?" Wolfson said. "So you're saying that as an android, she's not entitled to exercise her free will?"

I shook my head. "Don't try to tie me up with your philosophy. I'll tell you one thing. *I* have free will, and no one can force *me* to go. Who's gonna protect Shara then?"

"I'm glad to hear it—that you have free will," Wolfson said. "But I think that, when you exercise it, you will indeed go."

"How's that?" I said.

"Because Shara's going whether you and I like it or not."

"We'll see," I said, and turned to walk out.

"And if Shara goes, you'll be there all right," Wolfson said. "I have complete confidence in that."

"That so?" I turned around. "What makes you so sure?"

"You love her," Wolfson said.

Shara snuggled up to me, her body naked and still vibrant in the afterglow. To say Shara was better than any human woman was an understatement—truth is, I couldn't even remember what it felt like to be with another woman since I'd been making love to Shara.

"You still awake, baby?" she asked.

"Yeah." I smiled, and stroked her head.

"You thinking about tomorrow?" she asked.

"Can't help it," I said. "I just can't understand why, with all the other androids killed, they'd want to risk you like this. Doesn't make sense to me."

Shara kissed the soft underside of my chin, grazed her fingers along my breast. "I think the other androids all being killed is why they want to risk this," she said softly. "They felt they had to try something different—to break out of the cycle—so androids were not just sitting ducks anymore."

She had a wonderful way of distancing herself from these very events that were life-and-death to her—talking about androids as if she wasn't one of them, just as vulnerable. I wished I had that ability.

"I can't be sure I'll be able to protect you," I finally said, and immediately regretted it. No point in burdening her further with my fears. We were here, and there was no backing out now. Maybe she'd already fallen asleep.

"Mmm . . ." she murmured. "You'll be fine. . . ."

An in-person academic conference has to be one of the biggest security nightmares imaginable. An endless procession of "I read your text online," "Didn't I see you at the holo-meeting last year," and the like from people jostling elbow to elbow, drinks and who knew what else in hand, each with a long boring story to tell, more than enough time to get in a kill. Any one or more of them could be BP—the fact that Shara and even I were familiar with a few of them was no help—you can't know for sure that someone is Blood Party until actual blood has been spilled, as the saying goes. All I had going on our side were my instincts and reflexes.

The two days passed pretty much without incident—the closest call was some professor from Kansas who'd had too much port, and was making a pest of himself with Shara. She'd handled that fine; my fingers only touched my weapon once.

"Can we go for a little walk on the beach?" Shara asked me at the end of the second day. "They say it's spectacular on the bayside at sunset—not many places on the East Coast you can look out over the water and see the sun go down."

A perfect place for a killing, I thought. "We're still

not out of the woods yet," I said. "We can see sunsets other times."

Her face darkened. "So the kind of life I have to lead deprives me of the simple pleasure of seeing the sun set in the flesh on Cape Cod Bay. I bet you've seen it lots of times already."

"I haven't." I looked at her rich brown eyes. God, if that wasn't a soul shining through them, every bit as real as mine, whatever that was, longing for experience, longing for life, looking for sunsets, then nothing else in this universe was real. "Okay," I said. "But just a short walk. And we leave the beach as soon as the sun goes down. I don't want you out there in the dark—my infrareds give me only ninety-two percent of my day-vision, and I don't want anything less than one hundred percent."

She squeezed my hand. "Thanks."

The beach off Ellis Landing Road in Brewster-on-the-Bay was beautiful indeed.

Seagulls soaring above, sandpipers and plovers doing their little skate dances on the sand, boats bounding on the water, almost indistinguishable from the white-caps, and the sun a deepening shade of indescribable red as it made its way like an antique hour-hand from five to six on the water. . . .

No one had followed us, I was sure. No one was close to us on the shore. I could breathe in deeply and take in the scene. . . .

We squinted at the setting sun.

"Those boats on the water are the perfect touch," Shara said softly.

"Yeah . . ." I buried my nose in her soft hair, worked my lips to her neck, keeping at least one eye on the beach and the water. . . .

"Jesus! Get behind me!" I shoved in front of Shara, pulling my weapon.

"What's the matter?" she shouted, startled.

"Those goddamn boats are much closer than they were a few seconds ago. No way all of them coming in at the same time could be a coincidence."

I took a quick glance behind me; we didn't have time to get back to our vehicle. There was a small outcropping of rocks, though, at the edge of the sand. I looked back at the water—there must've been at least six or seven boats, holding two to three killers each, coming toward us. I fired a wide pulse in the water. Maybe it would capsize a few of the boats.

"Let's go!" I said, and directed Shara toward the rocks.

We crouched behind them, and I managed to get in a call to the local police. I looked back at the boats. I'd disabled two of them, but four were still coming on strong, across a horizon too wide for a direct shot on any but one of them at a time. I took aim and fired.

"You sure they're not just . . . tourists?" Shara asked, voice quavering.

"Yeah, I'm sure." Because now the passengers were disembarking from the three remaining boats, scattering on the shore, pulling out their weapons. I got off a couple of more shots, knocking down a few of them, and pulled the security-blanket out of my pocket. It took only a second to raise a protective shield around Shara and me—but it had the drawback of not allowing me to fire out. The bastards fired at least a dozen rounds at us, from as many different directions. Thank goodness, the shield held. I knew its resistance was severely finite, though, as the specs said—a temporary last-ditch measure whose staying power was dependent on the number and intensity of the hits it took. That's why I'd waited until the last minute to put it up.

"What do we do now?" Shara said.

I put my arm around her. "We wait for the cavalry—the local cops—to come rescue us."

I knew the local cops were, of course, robotic, and

utterly reliable in terms of their punctual response. They arrived in force about three long minutes later, first stunning most of the BPs on the shore, then taking them all into custody.

One of them approached our shield. "Sorry for the problem, folks. I think we have it all in hand. We'll be glad to escort you back to your vehicle now, if you like."

In the state I was in, I don't know if I would've let the shield down for another human being—who, for all I knew, could have been BP him or herself. But for a gleaming robot . . . I asked it for the SRCC—the special robotic cop code, just to be sure.

It displayed a sequence of sixteen numbers, all correct, on its small shoulder screen.

I let the shield down. "You did a fine job—"

And the air crackled with some sort of bolt, lots of bolts, and Shara and I went down, and the last thing I saw before I blacked out were robots with weapons pointed at us, and a big gaping hole in Shara's head. . . .

I awoke in a hospital room, with a sickening smell of medication in my face.

Wolfson was at my bed, crying.

"I'm not gonna lie to you," he said, looking me in the eye. "Shara's gone."

"No!" I tried to sit up, but tubes and God knows what other tethers kept me down. Every muscle in my body ached.

Wolfson's hand was on me, half in restraint, half in comfort.

"I *told* you it was a goddamn crazy idea to go to that convention," I rasped. "I hope the President and his asshole Committee are happy now."

"No one's happy," Wolfson said, tears still in his eyes. "But we rooted out the conspiracy—it was much deeper than anyone had expected. Even to the point of robotic hacking. They had the police frequencies monitored, they'd broken the robotic police code, as you probably saw on the beach." He hesitated. "Our own robots got there, the real cops, a few seconds too late. I don't know how much you saw. . . ."

"Enough," I said. And I saw Shara's sweet head, open, bleeding, pooling with the colors of the setting sun. . . .

"We won," Wolfson said, the word coming broken out of his throat, like a piece of jagged glass.

"Won? You and I lost someone we dearly loved, the world lost what may be its last android, and you think we won?"

Wolfson's lips were quivering. "You're right about the first, wrong about the second."

"What?" And I saw Shara's head again, ruined. . . .

"It was a brilliant plan," Wolfson said. "And it worked. We couldn't risk making the last android a target—you were right about that. Yet we had to draw the conspirators out. So we made him a protector. Presumably a human, someone the BP might wound, but never try to kill."

Protector . . . I hadn't protected Shara's head from bleeding . . . wide open . . . God, there were no circuits inside!

"You're the android," Wolfson said. "Shara was just acting the part of an android—a human playing an android—like the old videos. She'd been off-planet for the past six years, she grew up in Sidney with her mother, so hardly anyone knew her here."

"*I'm* the android? You're insane."

"No," he said. "You'll come to realize who you are, when this phase of your programming runs its course. You're a protector android—that's why the government invested so much in this—and you performed wonderfully, better than any human could have, under the worst possible conditions. You felt all the right things, made all the right decisions, given the circumstances. You passed the test, perverse as that sounds. I can take some solace in that. Even pride, bitter as it may be. You should, too."

I hissed, and turned my face away.

"Listen to me," Wolfson continued. "No one—no android or human—could have prevented what happened. The conspiracy was too widespread. It couldn't be stopped—not this time. The best we could do was draw them out—the way we did—so there wouldn't be a next time. . . ."

"You so sure you rooted them all out—that one of their little cancerous cells isn't still out there, waiting to strike?"

"They have no reason to strike anymore," Wolfson replied. "They think they killed the last android. Our robots got there before the other ones had a chance to see that Shara . . ." He broke down, crying again.

"To see that Shara's wide open head had no silicon inside, that she was human?"

Wolfson nodded, unable to speak.

"But why would Shara risk her life like that? Let herself be set up as the target?"

"She was incredibly devoted," Wolfson managed to say. "More than even I."

I shook my head in disbelief. "How could anyone be that devoted?"

"This project—my work—meant everything to her," he said. "She volunteered. I begged her not to. I resigned a dozen times. But she insisted that she was the only one who understood android psychology well enough to work with you on this project—that she was the one to right the wrong for what the BP did to my eyes. And when she came to know, and love, you, that gave her more incentive. She didn't want you to die. She didn't want to die either, but she was willing to take the risk."

And I began to understand, because I remembered what Wolfson had told me about Shara, except it was not in the way I had understood it at first, not in the way he had intended me to understand it. . . .

I reached out my hand to comfort him.

"She was your daughter," I said. "Your real, flesh-and-blood daughter."

Wolfson nodded. "She was my little girl."

FALLEN FACES BY THE WAYSIDE

by Gary A. Braunbeck

Gary A. Braunbeck is the author of the acclaimed collection *Things Left Behind,* as well as the forthcoming collections *Escaping Purgatory* (in collaboration with Alan M. Clark) and the CD-ROM *Sorties, Cathexes, and Human Remains.* His first solo novel, *The Indifference of Heaven,* was recently released, as was his Dark Matter novel, *In Hollow Houses.* He lives in Columbus, Ohio, and has, to date, sold nearly 200 short stories. His fiction, to quote *Publishers Weekly,* ". . . stirs the mind as it chills the marrow."

"Thou com'st in such a questionable shape
That I will speak to thee . . ."
—Shakespeare, *Halmet*; Act 1, Scene 4

IT wasn't the best set he'd ever done, but when Paul Bridge left the stage of *The Funny Bone* that Wednesday (read: Amateur) night, it was to applause that, if not exactly thunderous, was far more than he expected; several members of the audience were still laughing at the closing gag, and a few of them even loudly repeated the punchline as he made his way through the rows of tables toward the bar. He took his usual seat at the end, ordered a rum and Coke, and was about to ask the bartender if there was any fresh popcorn when Jim Bradley, the manager, came up behind him and put a hand on Paul's shoulder.

"Question: How long have I been inviting you to come back here on Amateur Night?"

Paul shrugged. "Every other week for about two years, I guess."

"You guess. Wow. Powers of instant recall that well-honed humble such mere mortals as myself."

"Does everything you say sound like you wrote it down ahead of time and memorized it?"

Bradley signaled the bartender to bring him his usual, then took the seat next to Paul. "As a matter of fact, yes, but we're not here to discuss my dreadful personality problems. You got a manager yet?"

"Three guesses."

"What I figured." He took a sip of his drink, then waited a few moments for dramatic effect. "Carmen Borgia is upstairs in my office. He wants to see you."

Paul could barely find his voice. "Y–you mean *now*?"

"You ought to see your expression—Bo-Bo the Dog-Faced Boy looked more intelligent. *Yes,* now. For some reason that puzzles even as resplendent a personality as mine, the Borgia Agency is interested in managing your shaggy WASP ass. You interested?"

"Three guesses."

"My God, the snappy repartee that must crackle throughout your home." He leaned closer and lowered his voice. "Here's the thing: You know I like you, and I like your act, but what's more important, the *audiences* like you, else I wouldn't keep inviting you back. Are you paying attention? This next part's important and there may be a quiz later. There's going to be an announcement tomorrow. Jay Leno's going to be appearing here three weeks from this Friday, it's a charity thing. You know how Leno likes to discover new talent, right? Well, when Carmen set this up,

Leno asked to see tapes of six amateur comics from the area. One of the tapes was yours, and Leno was blown away by your impressions—I sent the tape where you started with Nixon singing "If You Could Read My Mind" and closed with Richard Pryor and Jesse Helms doing *In the Heat of the Night* instead of Poitier and Steiger. Remember how you killed that night? Leno picked you—I figured he would. Now, the thing is, I can't offer you a paying gig unless you've got management. The owner and the union tend to frown upon doing it otherwise, go fig.

"All you have to do is go up to my office, shake Borgia's hand, and try not to pass gas; your days as a home computer service technician will then be numbered."

"Hey, I got your system upgraded in less than a day—by the way, thanks for specifically requesting me. My boss remembers things like that."

"No prob. You know your stuff."

"It pays the bills . . . *and* I like it."

Bradley took Paul's drink out of his hand and pulled him to his feet. "My office, go. One foot in front of the other, then repeat until you either walk into a wall or are stopped by a small, well-dressed Italian."

Paul was starting to make his way toward the private stairway when Bradley said: "Hey, Paul."

"Yeah?"

"I know you were a little off tonight. Don't worry about it, okay? Tell you the truth, I didn't expect you'd even show, let alone be as good as you were . . . considering that tomorrow would have been your sister's birthday."

Paul was genuinely touched that Bradley remembered. "Thanks, man."

"Why are you still here?"

"You—"

Bradley dismissed him with a wave of his beefy hand. "Excuses, excuses. I'm surrounded by indifference. No wonder I weep alone nights. Should've been a cesspool cleaner like my mother wanted."

Paul did not so much walk as shamble up to Bradley's office, convinced that this was all some setup for an immense practical joke. To Paul's mind, the universe was a model of chaos, not nearly as benign as people would have you believe, and even if it were, *he* never had this kind of luck, and so at once began looking over his shoulder for whatever it was that would soon catch up with him and sink its teeth into the soft parts of what little optimism he was still able to muster.

Not the most beneficial state of mind to be in when you were about to meet the biggest talent agent in the Midwest.

He surprised himself by not pausing at the office door; instead, he walked right inside and up to Borgia.

"Five minutes," said Borgia, looking at his watch. "Took you five minutes to get up here. Most comics would've burned skid marks in the carpeting if they were told that—oh, wait. Did you hear that?"

"Hear what?"

Borgia began pacing. "The sound of my death getting thirty seconds closer. Sit. Stand. Squat. Dance the hoochie-koo for all I care. Mind if I smoke?"

"No."

"Damn. And I quit two years ago. Never mind." Then he grinned. Carmen Borgia was a short, intense, sinewy man with bright hazel eyes and the energy of a dozen five-year-old children who'd fed on nothing but pure sugar since birth. If he hadn't been a talent agent, Paul figured Borgia would have been the actor who had the career Joe Pesci should have had.

"Bradley tell you all about it?"

"Yes, sir."

Borgia stopped his pacing. "Did I just hear the 'S' word issue from your mouth? Please tell me that I did not. The 'S' word irks me—and when was the last time you heard someone properly use the word 'irk'?"

Paul blinked. "You know, if I left now, it would be like I never came into the room."

"That supposed to be funny?"

"Actually, I was going for a Robert-Ryan-in-*The Wild Bunch*-type of tragic-irony thing."

"Great movie. So-so delivery on your part." Borgia walked up to Paul and held out his hand. "You're very talented, you're very funny, and I would like to represent you. I also have a couple of computers in my home that need tending to, but we can discuss that later. Very hush-hush, under-the-table type irony, since my wife and children think I know everything about everything."

"Great delivery. So-so continuity." He shook Borgia's hand. "I am honored that you want to represent me, and I—"

"Wazzy-wazzy-woo-woo, yeah, great, fine. You're now a client of the Borgia Agency. Here." He pulled a thick envelope from his jacket pocket and slapped it into Paul's hand.

"What's this?"

Borgia sighed. "Do you see how much time you just wasted there? You could've just opened the damn thing and looked inside, and we could already be on to a new subject. You think I'm gonna live forever?"

Paul smiled nervously, then looked inside the unsealed envelope. "What the—? Oh. My. God."

"Don't bother counting it," said Borgia. "Five thousand, cash. Yours to keep—providing you sign something."

"A representation agreement."

"No. You did that when you shook my hand." Borgia waved Paul over to Bradley's desk. Everything had been cleared from the center except for a dark blue folder; Borgia opened it and removed one sheet of official-looking stationery. "Have you ever heard of Scylla Enterprises, Paul?"

"Um . . . yes."

"*Really?* You've really heard of them?"

"About six seconds ago, actually."

"Good. You had me worried. The Borgia Agency—and you may repeat this to your wife but to no one else—is a division of Scylla Enterprises. What I have here is a confidentiality agreement. Sign this, and you not only get to keep the five thousand, but that will be your weekly salary until such time as I choose to raise it."

"I don't . . . *five thousand?* I mean—what about your . . . commission and—?"

"I find complete sentences can be of great benefit to entertainers. My commission is taken care of, don't worry that too-big-for-your-body head. By the way, that whole George-Harrison-hair thing's got to go." He offered a pen. "Read it first. If you choose *not* to sign, you keep half of the cash and the agency still represents you—you'll just be assigned to one of my other agents. Sign it, and I handle you personally. You know my rep. I *never* personally handle more than ten clients at the same time, and those I do are either already very big or about to be."

"I know, believe me."

Paul took the pen and began to sign the confidentiality agreement when Borgia gripped his wrist. "*Read* it, Paul. It's short and flensed of any convoluted legalese."

There was a seriousness in Borgia's tone that invited no further questions.

Paul pulled the pen away and read the agreement.

He reached the end of the last paragraph and felt his mouth go dry. "Oh, man."

"It's not nearly as ominous as it sounds."

"What do you mean by 'trial period'?"

"First of all, *I* don't mean anything by it, Scylla Enterprises does; second, the trial period lasts exactly six hours, starting the moment you walk into the offices; and third . . . I honestly can't tell you."

"You don't know?"

"Oh, I know, I just can't tell you. We can talk about it after, but until then I'm Schultz from *Hogan's Heroes*: I know nut-ting."

Paul read the agreement again. "So at the end of the trial period, I'll be offered an official contract with *Scylla*—"

"—and by default, my agency."

"If I choose not to sign it, I'll be given ten thousand dollars for my time and sent on my way, providing I never tell anyone about what happened."

Borgia nodded. "And if you do sign it, you're in Scylla's employ for the rest of your life."

"Oh, man . . ."

"You said that already. Gotta keep the material fresh."

Paul stared at the agreement and felt a thin line of perspiration form on his upper lip. What a time to get a case of flop-sweat.

"Paul?"

"Yes, sir?"

"There's the 'S'-word again. Irksome, very irksome."

"Sorry."

Borgia leaned against the end of the desk. "Tell me about your sister."

At nine-forty the next morning, Paul drove up to the building which housed the local offices of Scylla Enterprises; even though it was right smack in the middle of downtown, there was a parking space directly in front and the meter had nearly two hours left on it.

He pulled in with no difficulties, killed the engine but left the radio on, then turned to his wife and said: "I'm doomed, you know that?"

"Of course you are," said Kim. "But keep in mind that your sole purpose in life might be to serve as a warning to others."

He blinked. "Is that supposed to make me feel better?"

Kim shrugged. "No—but I'm guessing that you don't *want* to feel better right now, you prefer to feel anxious, insufficient, foolish, and inept. It's part of your charm." This said with not nearly as much humor as Paul would have preferred.

He looked at the glassy, monolithic building and shook his head. "What the hell do they want with me anyway?"

"I'm guessing they might drop a couple of hints during the interview, if you ever actually go inside."

He wiped some perspiration from his forehead, then checked his watch.

At that moment, the classic rock station he and Kim had been listening to began to play Mountain's "Theme From An Imaginary Western."

Paul felt his chest grow tight. He reached down and turned up the volume. "God Almighty." He felt the familiar tightness in the back of his throat and the burning behind his eyes.

Kim leaned over and put her hand on the back of his neck. "Hey, c'mon . . . maybe this is a good sign."

He looked at his wife as the first tear crept toward the corner of his eye, dangled there for a moment, then dripped down onto the sleeve of his jacket. "I never really liked this song all that much, you know? I mean, I always preferred 'Mississippi Queen' or 'Nantucket Sleighride,' but Beth always liked this one. Anytime Mom or Dad would go off and start pounding one of us, she'd always come to my room later and ask me if I wanted to listen to records, and she always played this one. I asked her why once, and she said; 'It's sad, but it makes it sound okay to be sad.' The more I listened to it with her, the more I came to love it. It's genuinely wistful.

"Her favorite line in the song was that one about fallen faces by the wayside looking as if they might have known. She said she sometimes dreamed about fallen faces, that they were happy and resting and not afraid anymore. I always wanted to tell her that the fallen faces were actually the dead bodies of Settlers who didn't make it, who died along the way, and what they might have known was the new world that they never reached, the land and life that was waiting for those Settlers who *did* make it . . . but it seemed mean to ruin that for her. She was only six years old and so much had been ruined for her already."

Kim scooted closer to him. "Shh, Paul, c'mon, baby, don't do this to yourself."

"I should've been there, Kim. I mean, I *thought* Mom and Dad had gotten better, that it'd be all right to take that camp councilor job. It was just for a month, but everything seemed to be better."

They did not speak for a moment, only sat listening to the song reach its refrain.

"That's bullshit," Paul whispered. "The truth was, I couldn't look at it anymore, I couldn't stand being in that fucking house with them, walking on eggshells, never knowing when one of them might go off. I figured I might earn enough money to buy a couple of bus or plane tickets so Beth and I could take off, go out to Kansas and stay with Grandma—at least, that's what I always told myself. Especially later, after—"

"Just stop it. Stop it right now."

He pointed at the radio. "In the last twelve hours, two people have said something to me about Beth—and one of them had never met me until last night, and now I'm sitting here with you on what would have been Beth's sixteenth birthday, and I'm waiting to go in there and the radio starts playing *this,* of all songs. *No one* plays this goddamn thing, Kim. No one."

"Then look at it as a sign. Maybe it's Beth's way of telling you that you don't have to keep yourself on the hook anymore, that she doesn't blame you. It's time to just pay the fine and go home."

Paul wiped his eyes and blew his nose. "You picked one helluva time to get mystical on me."

"It's just a song, and their playing it now is just a coincidence, that's all. It's nothing to get freaked about."

The song finished, then the announcer's voice came on: "That one goes out to Elizabeth Bridge on her sixteenth birthday."

Paul looked at Kim, who was staring at the radio.

"Okay, now I'm a little freaked," she said.

"What the hell is going on?"

Before Kim could say anything to him, a uniformed security guard knocked on the driver's side window. Both Paul and Kim jumped. Paul snapped off the radio as if he were squashing a bug, took a deep breath, and rolled down the window. "Is there something wrong?"

"Not at all, Mr. Bridge," said the security guard. "I'm here to escort you up to the offices." The guard leaned down and smiled in at Kim. "Good morning, Mrs. Bridge. Your husband will be here until four this afternoon. If you'll come back then, this same space will be waiting for you."

Kim laughed nervously. "You're kidding?"

"No, ma'am," replied the guard, his smile seemingly frozen in place. "We're to give both Mr. Bridge and yourself the red carpet treatment today. The space'll be here."

Not waiting for a response, he opened the door and stepped back so Paul could get out.

"Good luck, honey," said Kim, then kissed Paul. "Everything'll be all right. You'll be dazzling."

"Wrong reading," he replied, trying to sound cheerful.

"Okay, then: Don't fuck it up, we could use the money."

"There's my girl." He kissed her, then climbed out of the car and followed the security officer up the stone steps and over to a glass elevator that ran up the outside of the building.

"The Scylla offices aren't accessible to the public from inside, Mr. Bridge."

"Do all Scylla employees have to use this same elevator?"

"No, sir, only escorted visitors. There's a block of private elevators inside, but since I'm Escort Security, I don't have clearance to use them."

Paul leaned against the inside railing in the elevator as the doors closed and it began a surprisingly rapid ascent. "So they're big on security, huh?"

His smile unchanging, the security guard replied, "*Very* big on it." He reached inside one of his pockets and removed a laminated ID card attached to a ribbon of thick blue thread which he offered to Paul. "Scylla Enterprises took the liberty of making this temporary ID for you, Mr. Bridge. Please hang it around your neck and make sure that your photo is visible at all times."

"Where'd you get my picture?"

"From the DMV's computers." He offered no further information. "Please put it on now, sir. We're almost at the main Scylla floor."

Paul hung the ID around his neck, making sure his photo faced forward.

The elevator stopped, the doors opened, and one of the most beautiful women Paul had ever seen was standing right outside waiting, flanked on either side by two other security guards.

"Mr. Bridge," she said, offering her hand. "Welcome to Scylla Enterprises. My name is Cathy Brown.

I'm Mr. Smyth's assistant. Would you follow me, please?"

Flanked on either side by Ms. Brown's personal goon squad, Paul followed her through a maze of corridors and offices and two doors which required her to slide not one, not two, but three security cards through a small electronic reading device installed next to each one.

And you couldn't walk three yards without encountering a security camera peering down at you.

Paul, now anxious as hell, let out a small laugh.

Without turning back to look at him, Ms. Brown said, "Something funny, Mr. Bridge?"

"I didn't mean to offend you."

"No offense at all, Paul—may I call you Paul? I was just curious."

Giving a quick glance to each security guard, Paul cleared his throat. "Well, I couldn't help but notice the security measures taken here. When I was in college, I went on a tour of the Pentagon—at least, the areas where the public is allowed. *They* didn't have this much security."

"Ah. Well, actually, the Pentagon does, but they're not quite so overt with most of it. Put enough cameras and enough electronically locked doors in enough fortuitous locations, and people tend to be on their best behavior."

Paul exhaled, but didn't feel relieved. "So you don't have quite as much security as it seems?"

"No." They paused at a set of large oak doors with bright brass doorknobs. Ms. Brown turned toward him and smiled. "We have much more. In fact, Paul, this particular floor has just slightly more security than the inside of the West Wing of the White House."

"You're kidding?"

"This is Scylla Enterprises, Paul. We may joke about a lot of things, but security is not one of them."

Her smile grew wider as she opened one of the great doors. "Come with me."

Paul followed her, but the two security guards remained in the corridor.

As soon as they were inside the next room—what Paul assumed was the reception area—a large, dangerous-looking man with a buzz-cut and hands so big a ten-year-old could comfortably sit in one, came up to Paul and said, "Please raise your arms."

Paul did so. BuzzCut ran over his body with a handheld metal detector."

"He's clean," said BuzzCut, taking two steps back and folding his hands in front of him.

Paul looked at his watch. "Why didn't . . . why didn't it go off? I mean, there's my watch, there's the change in my pockets, my belt buckle . . . I've got a pin in my left hand from where I broke it skiing when I was twenty-one—"

Ms. Brown raised one of her hands, silencing him. "The detector that he used is designed to sound only if it recognizes certain alloys."

"You mean like in a gun?"

"I mean like in a gun, or certain types of detonation devices."

"What if I had one of those all-plastic guns—what're they called, Glocks?"

"Yes, they are. You were x-rayed for any plastic or plastique while you rode up in the elevator." She gestured toward a large, ornate desk—assumably hers—and the two even larger oak doors beyond it. "Mr. Smyth's background checks are exceptionally thorough. If for some reason you had a condition which made x-rays detrimental to your well-being, you would have been brought in another way and patted down.

"Before we get too far off the track, Paul, take my word for this: there is absolutely, positively, beyond any doubt *no way* a weapon can be smuggled into these offices . . . and we're one of only nine places in this country where that holds true." She walked over to her desk and pressed a button. "He's here, sir."

"Ten a.m. on the nose," replied a voice. "Were we right, did he pull up in front twenty minutes early?"

"That he did, sir."

"Excellent. I'm guessing right now he's got one more question to ask you. Answer it for him and then send him in."

Ms. Brown looked up at him and waited.

Like an actor who'd missed his cue during a run-through, Paul started, blinked, and said, "Oh, yeah, right—how did he know I'd get here twenty minutes early?"

"Because our studies have shown that that's your pattern when you have any sort of an appointment. You'd rather be there forty minutes early than one minute late. Your average time of arrival is twenty minutes prior to your appointments."

"How do you know that?"

"Mr. Smyth will answer that for you, Paul." She pressed a button, a buzzer sounded, and the two massive doors swung open.

Paul waited a few more seconds, then shrugged and walked into the office beyond. As soon as he was inside, the buzzer sounded again and the doors closed. He wondered if they were locked.

Several things registered with him simultaneously; the small kitchenette, the large leather sofa, the large desk where two-engine airplanes probably landed on a daily basis, the washroom off to the left, three smaller doors which he assumed led into closets or storage areas, a wet bar, and very plush carpeting. No surprises there.

The surprises came when you looked beyond the expected executive amenities and saw the decor; framed movie posters, (the one for *The Wild Bunch,* autographed by all the cast members as well as Sam

Peckinpah himself, caused him to actually gasp), a dart board, bookshelves filled with various toys and dolls still in their shrink-wrapped boxes, a lava lamp collection, an expensive stereo system which currently played The Band's "The Weight," and countless knickknacks.

"Paul," came a voice from inside the washroom. "Have a seat. Pour yourself a drink. Wait, scratch that, reverse the order. There's a good fellow."

Paul remained standing.

A few moments later, Mr. Smyth emerged from the washroom.

Paul had frequently heard terms like "presence" and "charisma" applied to various actors, politicians, and performers, and had always thought that they were over- as well as ill-used. He himself had never met anyone who could mesmerize simply by walking into a room . . . until now.

Smyth was of average height, a bit on the thin side, and dressed in a surprisingly casual manner for a man who ran such a powerful company; his hair was thick, wavy, fashionably unkempt, and a tad longer than you'd expect to see in the corporate world, and his left eye was covered by a large black patch. These details in themselves weren't enough to take anyone's breath away, least of all Paul's, but Smyth carried himself in such a way, and emanated such confidence and power, that even the most jaded person would stop and stare at him as if his approval were the most important thing in the world.

Spellbinding, thought Paul. *That's the word.*

Smyth stopped, looked at Paul, and grinned. "You should see your expression—Bo-Bo the Dog-Faced Boy looked more intelligent."

"Jim Bradley said the exact same thing to me last night."

"I know," replied Smyth. "It's a great line, so I stole it. But don't tell him."

"We're not that close."

"Bullshit—but good delivery."

"Carmen Borgia gave me a bunch of grief on my delivery."

"That a fact?" Smyth moved to his desk and sat down, then picked up a folder and opened it.

Jesus; even doing that, he's hypnotic.

"You planning on taking a seat, or would you prefer to buy real estate and build?"

Paul took a seat.

Smyth finished looking through the folder, at one point removing the confidentiality agreement Paul had signed and asking him to verify that it was his signature, then closed the folder, tossed it onto the desk, sat back, and said: "Ever visit your dad in the slammer?"

Something inside Paul's stomach pulled a knife from its pocket and began whittling away at the tissue. "Wh—what?"

"You heard me."

"How the hell do you know about—"

Smyth sighed impatiently, then said, "Your mom was acquitted of complicity in your sister's death and committed suicide five months later. You were living with one of your aunts by then. Your dad was found guilty of second-degree murder and is currently serving his time in the state pen. Have you ever visited him there?"

Paul swallowed. Once. Very loudly. "No. And I never will. The fucker can rot in there for all I give a shit."

Smyth nodded. "An honest one. Points in your favor."

Paul reached into his jacket pocket and took out a cigarette. He almost never smoked but always kept a pack in his pocket for times when he was either severely anxious or dangerously angry. Right now he was a lot of both. He lit up, inhaled, then released the smoke through his nostrils.

"What if I were to tell you this is a nonsmoking building?" said Smyth.

"I'd tell you I don't care."

"You're upset. I can tell. You're breathing fire."

"Very funny."

"Not really, but I try."

"How do you know all of this? I mean, I can see how your background check would turn up all the information about my parents and my sister—"

"—did you enjoy the dedication on the radio? I thought you might like it."

"Yeah. It was a rockin' good time. How could you possibly know that my 'average' arrival time for appointments was twenty minutes early?"

"We've been watching you."

Something cold slid a slow path down Paul's spine. He pulled in another drag. "You've been having me tailed?"

"*Tailed?* Wow. Very forties-tough-guy, very *noir*-ish, very Raymond Chandler. Gave me chills. See my goosebumps? Never mind. Yes. We've been 'tailing' you for almost eighteen months."

Paul stared at him, unblinking. "They're the same," he said, more to himself than Smyth.

Smyth sat up a little straighter, seemingly taken aback by something he hadn't been expecting. "I beg your—"

"Last night when I was talking with Borgia, something about the way he spoke kept ringing bells in my head but I couldn't figure out what it was. Now I know. Jim Bradley, him, and now you. All three of you speak the same way."

Smyth shrugged. "We're businessmen, on-the-go guys. Gotta be quick on our feet, quick in our speech; helps us to look like we're five steps ahead of everyone. In fact—"

"That's not it," snapped Paul. "It's not that your speech shares some similarities—it's almost exactly the same, all three of you. The inflections, the pauses, the cadences and turns of the phrase you employ . . . it's too precise to be a coincidence."

Smyth stared at him for several moments and then, slowly, a smile spread across his face, revealing absolutely perfect white teeth. "I *knew* you were the right guy for this."

"For what? What's going on?"

"Just a sec." Smyth pressed the intercom. "Cathy?"

"Sir?"

"Two minutes, thirty-one seconds."

"Wow."

"Tell me about it. Make a note about the speech patterns, will you?"

"Done, sir."

Smyth released the button and beamed at Paul. "Do you know how long it would have taken most people to spot that? *Days,* more probably weeks, if ever." He rose from behind his desk and gestured for Paul to follow him to one of the bookshelves, the only one in the office actually containing books.

"You haven't really explained anything to me."

"Patience, Paul, patience . . . but I am surprised you haven't asked why there are so few books and so many toys in here."

"Let's say I have."

"Then let's say I tell you that Scylla Enterprises has dozens of subsidiary companies, as well as controlling interests in companies which were not originally part of our organization. We make everything from dolls to guidance systems for airplanes. We are involved in research to find cures for cancer, AIDS, Parkinson's, migraine headaches, and hangnails. We build cars and houses. We make major Hollywood motion pictures. We work to save the environment. We supply the space program with under-the-table funding. We assassinate dictators. We supply weapons for oppressed peoples to stage coups in Third World countries. We fight famine. We own record companies. We—oh, I could go on, but . . . let's see—ah! Did you ever see Mel Brooks' *Silent Movie?*"

"Yes."

"Remember the offices of Engulf & Devour, the evil corporation? Remember their slogan on the wall, 'Our Fingers Are In Everything'? Well, that's us, in a way. There's not a lot we aren't involved in. But I digress."

"Can I ask who controls Scylla?"

"I do. There is no board of directors, only some folks we keep on hand for show. I'll tell you much more later, but for right now, let's get back to your having spotted the similarities in the speech patterns of myself, Carmen Borgia, and your friend Jim Bradley." Smyth looked over the bookshelf. Paul counted: there were exactly thirty-five books, ranging from a couple of best-sellers to more literary fiction (*The Complete Stories of Kobo Abe*) to older, more obscure novels (*Tryst* by Elswyth Thane and *Trout Fishing in America* by Richard Broughtigan), several textbooks on math, surgery, and home plumbing repair, a handful of children's books, various editions of the Bible, Koran, and Talmud, poetry collections, and other books whose titles gave no hint to Paul as to what they were about.

"Your reading tastes are a bit . . . eclectic."

"Oh, yes . . . I like to spend my evenings going from Stephen King to a dissertation on Heisenberg's Uncertainty Principle, with a bit of *See Spot Run* and *Goodnight Moon* thrown in for good measure." He pulled a thick volume from the lower shelf: *Famous Documents From History.* Paul noticed that only a few pages were marked, and as Smyth opened the books, saw that only one or two passages per page had been highlighted.

Smyth handed the book to Paul. "Please read this aloud, only, read it as Burt Lancaster—you do Lancaster, right?"

"He's one of my favorites."

"Please read the first few lines."

"Can I have a drink of club soda with lime first?"

"Club soda?"

"In my act, I always take a drink of club soda with lime before doing Lancaster. It helps ready my vocal cords."

"Go for it."

Paul went to the bar and fixed his drink, took two short sips and one deep swallow (just like in his act), held the last bit of it in his throat for a few seconds, then swallowed. He hummed like Kermit the Frog very quickly, then took the book up again and recited the first six lines of *The Declaration of Independence* in his best Lancaster.

When he was finished, he handed the book back to Smyth, who replaced it on the shelf and said, "That was amazing. You do Lancaster better than anyone I've ever heard. Quite possibly better than anyone ever has."

"Thank you. I don't think I'm *that* good, but—"

"Do you know much about the science of fingerprinting, Paul?"

"Not really."

Smyth gently took hold of Paul's right hand and held it up. "Each fingerprint pattern on each finger, as I'm sure you know, is unique. Because you have ten fingers, the ten fingerprints are going to differ slightly, but all of them will share certain characteristics, namely the whorl pattern and reference points—by those, I mean the semicircular patterns of the lines and the various breaks, scratches, and marks that are found along those lines. Are you following me so far?"

"I think so."

Smyth released Paul's hand. "Voice-prints are the same way. Each person has certain patterns to their speech, certain ways of breathing which affect the timbre, certain patterns of inflection, certain base vibrations that make it impossible to *exactly* duplicate their voice by electronic means. But, like fingerprints, there are 'reference points' in the patterns. In fingerprinting, one need only match six reference points for identification; the best impressionists can match up to eight voice-print reference points. Watch this."

He pressed a button on the wall, and a hidden panel slid open to reveal a pair of computer monitors built into the wall. Under each monitor was a keyboard. Smyth pressed a key on each and the monitors flickered to life.

"What's this?"

"This, Paul, is a state-of-art, high-tech, one-of-a-kind thingamajig, not to be confused with your run-of-the-mill whatchamacallits used by NASA or the commonplace whosiewhatsits you can pick up at Radio Shack. This, Paul, is a digital speech analyzer. Listen."

He hit a key, and Paul heard himself doing Burt Lancaster reading from the *Declaration.* As he read, a series of jumpy red lines rose from the bottom of the monitor screen and flickered at the top like the tips of flames. Every time a line flickered, a blue dot appeared and remained in that spot on the screen.

"Now, old Burt himself, from *The Devil's Disciple,* I think. One of the costume dramas he did, anyway."

Another key was pressed, and Burt Lancaster himself read from the *Declaration.* Jumpy red lines, leaving hundreds of small blue dots at their flicker-points.

"Notice anything?" said Smyth.

"No . . . ?"

"Nothing up my sleeve . . ." He entered a command. ". . . presto!"

Both recordings were played simultaneously, two

sets of jumpy red lines on the same screen, two sets of small blue dots . . . only it seemed now to Paul that there weren't as many small blue dots.

Once it was finished, Smyth enhanced the uneven line of blue dots, then entered another command: a blinking green cursor made it sway across the screen, stopping at each set of blue dots that overlapped. Once that was finished, the dots which didn't overlap disappeared from the screen.

"Look at that," said Smyth. "Eighteen matching reference points would qualify as a perfect-enough match; you hit twenty-three points in your imitation. The best I've ever seen . . . heard . . . you know what I mean—the best I've ever encountered matched sixteen. You, Sir Bridge, are the best impressionist I've ever encountered."

"Again, thanks . . . but can't you just reproduce their voices digitally?"

"If all I were interested in was movie stars, yes—but even then I'd be limited to the soundtracks of their films and whatever recorded interviews I could lay hands on. But hold the questions, we're not finished yet."

For the next ninety minutes, Smyth had Paul listen to the voices of various celebrities, politicians, and people whose voices he didn't recognize, then imitate them while reading selected passages from a book chosen at random. Each time, Paul hit no fewer than twenty reference points in the voice-prints.

When the last of them had been done, Smyth nodded his head and grinned. "I had you do this so you could see just how good your impressions are. Don't say anything yet. The collection of books on this shelf weren't selected at random, nor were the highlighted passages inside them. If you were to start reading only the highlighted passages in the first book on the top, and repeat the process until you came to the last highlighted passages in the last book, you would have made ninety-seven-point-eight percent of every sound in the English language—more than enough to enable someone with sophisticated enough equipment to accurately reproduce another person's voice—"

"—and program that voice to say whatever you wanted."

Smyth nodded. "I've had language experts working on this for years. Part of your new job, Paul, would be to listen to recordings of other peoples' voices—not celebrities, but everyday individuals whom we have recorded—then learn their voices, imitate them as well as you did old Burt's here, and then—"

"—read the highlighted passages from these fifty books so you can reproduce their voices, making them say anything whatever way you wanted."

Smyth shook his head. "That's only a part of it—still, don't make it sound so ominous."

"I don't see why—"

Smyth held up his hand, silencing Paul. "We're done here for the time being. Go with Ms. Brown. The next part of your trial period starts now."

"But—"

"No questions. I'll tell you everything you want to know later. For now, go." Smyth pulled a small remote control unit from his pocket and opened the office doors. Ms. Brown and BuzzCut stood there waiting for Paul.

"Mr. Bridge," said BuzzCut. It sounded too much like a command.

Paul stepped back out and the doors closed behind him.

"I take it things went well?" asked Ms. Brown.

"You tell me—I have no *idea* how things went . . . except very quickly."

"Feeling a little confused?"

"That's about the size of it."

BuzzCut nearly smiled. "Wrong reading."

"Huh?"

Ms. Brown laughed once, very softly, then cleared her throat. "Our research has shown that to be a favorite phrase of yours, and I'm afraid the staff has, well . . . *borrowed* it from you."

"It's called stealing."

"I know," said Ms. Brown. "But we're far too nice to do something like that."

"Is everyone here a comedian?"

BuzzCut gently took hold of Paul's arm and guided him back through the maze of doors and corridors until they stood facing a different elevator than the one in which Paul had come up.

"Are you allowed to talk to me?"

BuzzCut shrugged. "Don't see why not."

"Have you been with Scylla for long?"

"About fifteen years."

Paul waited for BuzzCut to elaborate, but the man offered no further comments.

"Ho-kay, then . . . can you tell me what's going to happen now?"

"We're going to make a pickup."

"Uh-huh . . .?"

The elevator doors opened. They rode down into a private parking garage located below the Scylla building. There were only a few dozen cars parked down here even though the garage could have easily held twenty times as many vehicles. With parking space the rare and priceless commodity it was downtown, Paul knew without asking that this private garage had to set Scylla back a tidy sum each month.

He followed BuzzCut until the other man stopped beside a car that was so incredibly nondescript that Paul almost missed seeing it.

He walked over and stood by the passenger door. BuzzCut was grinning. Paul wondered if the man were ill.

"What's so funny?"

"Nothing," replied BuzzCut, unlocking his door.

"It's just it never fails to amuse me how new recruits always nearly walk right past this car when they come down here with me. Don't look at me that way, I'm not trying to say you're stupid or anything; this car was *designed* not to be noticeable."

"Why?"

Both of them climbed inside, put on their seat belts, and BuzzCut started the engine as he continued, "Okay, I might as well explain some things. First off—and whether or not you want to take my word on this is up to you—if you are offered a contract with Scylla, there are going to be times when you'll be asked by Mr. Smyth to do something that on the surface is gonna look like it maybe ain't so legal. Sometimes it isn't, but you ain't never gonna have to worry about being arrested or nothing like that."

Paul stared at him for a moment. Then something occurred to him. "The plates on the car, they're—"

"—government plates. Federal. You're the first recruit to notice that. Good eye."

"So Scylla is also a branch of the Federal government?"

"Not officially." They had driven up to the exit by now, and BuzzCut turned effortlessly into the pre-lunch-hour traffic. "But if for some reason the police were to stop this car, the officers who did the stopping would be on paid suspension the minute they got off the horn from calling in the plate number."

Paul's earlier anxiety now bordered on outright fear tinged with panic. "How powerful is Scylla?"

"Scylla is Mr. Smyth, Paul, and Mr. Smyth is probably one of the ten most powerful men in the world—not just one of the richest, but the most powerful."

"Where are we going?"

"Remember when I told you that there were going to be times when you'd be asked to—"

"—do something that on the surface doesn't look so legal?"

BuzzCut nodded his head. "We're on our way to do such a thing right now."

"Will it be dangerous?"

"There's always that possibility—that's why the confidentiality agreement, and that's why this is called a 'trial period.' "

Paul felt his hands begin to shake, a sure sign that he was three breaths away from a panic attack. "And this thing, this not-so-legal-looking-on-the-surface thing that we're on our way to do, what might it be?"

"It *might* be any one of a million things."

Paul shook his head. "Let me guess: Wrong reading?"

BuzzCut's only response was to smile.

"Fine," said Paul, "then this thing that we're going to do . . . what *is* it?"

BuzzCut reached over and flipped down the glove compartment door. Inside was the ugliest looking semi-automatic pistol Paul had ever seen. BuzzCut removed it, closed the door, and laid the weapon in Paul's lap.

"I think the technical term for it is 'kidnapping,' " said BuzzCut. "I'd pick up that gun and point it at the floor if I was you, unless you like the idea of them shaky hands of yours blowing your pecker off."

As BuzzCut pulled the car up to the curb in a fairly generic-looking middle-class neighborhood, Paul's first instinct was to open the door and run like hell. BuzzCut must have sensed this, because he pressed a button and electronically locked the doors. "Don't bother trying to unlock them; only the driver can do that."

Paul lifted the gun. "I could just shoot out the window."

"I'd like to see you try it. They're bullet-proof."

"Oh."

BuzzCut checked his watch, then removed a pair of small binoculars from a compartment beside the driver's seat and began focusing on a house about a third of the way down the block.

"Hey," whispered Paul.

"Yeah?"

"I don't know your name."

"And if you sign on with Scylla, I'll be happy to tell it to you, but not until then. The fewer names you know right now, the better."

"But if—"

"Shh." BuzzCut leaned forward a little, then offered the binoculars to Paul. "See that gray house down there, the one with the chain-link fence?"

"Yes."

BuzzCut checked his watch again. "In about a minute a little girl is going to come out of that house and start walking in our direction. Her name's Jeanne Brooks. She's six years old. Every morning at 11:30 she leaves this house and walks to a small family market two blocks from here. She buys herself a can of Sprite and then stands around looking at the comic books for about forty-five minutes."

"Why every morning?"

"In the last eighteen months, Jeanne's been removed from this house by Children's Services three times, and three times she's been sent back after her mother and stepfather have completed the bare-ass minimum amount of couples' therapy required by law."

"What's that got to do with—"

"Watch."

Paul focused on the front door of the house. BuzzCut reached over and pressed a button on the binoculars and with a soft electronic *whirrrrr,* the lenses extended, allowing Paul a crystal-clear view of the front door and porch. The only way he could be any closer was if he were standing in the front yard.

The door opened and Jeanne Brooks came out. Her clothes were old but appeared to be clean. She looked down as she walked, as if she were afraid the earth might open up at any given second and swallow her whole if she dared look anywhere else.

She was halfway down the steps when the front door opened and a man in his early thirties—the stepfather, Paul assumed—kicked open the screen door, stormed out onto the porch, and threw something at Jeanne. It hit her squarely in the back of the head, knocking her to her knees.

"That piece of shit," Paul said through clenched teeth.

Jeanne picked herself up, the expression on her face unchanged, and then retrieved the object her stepfather had thrown at her.

A videocassette of *101 Dalmatians.*

"Her birthday present," said BuzzCut. Even he didn't bother disguising the anger and sadness in his voice. "They didn't buy it for her, mind you, they gave her two dollars so she could rent it. If I were a betting man, I'd put the farm on her never having gotten to watch it."

"God . . ." whispered Paul, because now Jeanne had left the yard and was walking in their direction. Only now—aided by the electronic binoculars—did Paul see why she walked with her face toward the ground.

Scars.

Some were old and grayish-white, others were pink, still healing; all of them were restricted to the left side of her face, but that was enough. In places the scar tissue was so heavy it nearly covered her left eye.

"Gray and pink, right?" asked BuzzCut.

"Huh?"

"The scars."

". . . yes . . ."

"She leaves here at the same time every morning because her mom and stepfather deal crack out of their garage between 11:45 and 12:30. Neither the police nor Children's Services have been able to nail them for it, and suspicion alone isn't enough for permanent action to be taken."

"Did they . . . did they do that to her?"

"Not that she's ever admitted to anyone. But, yes, they did that to her."

Paul lowered the binoculars. "We're going to take her?"

"In a way," said BuzzCut, opening his door. "You stay right in here, got me? Anyone besides me tries to get in this car, flash the gun and odds are they'll go away. If flashing it doesn't work, then squeeze the trigger and I *guarantee* you they'll go away." He hit a button and unlocked all the doors, then opened the rear driver's-side door just a crack. "Keep an eye on me at all times, right? If anything happens, if for some reason anything goes wrong, you scoot over and drive the hell out of here, understand?"

"Yes." Paul's heart was pounding hard against his chest.

"This'll happen fast, so pay attention." BuzzCut slammed the door and walked across the street at the same time a tan minivan with tinted windows came around the far corner.

Paul swallowed once, then blinked eyes.

Fine, I'm fine. Really.

BuzzCut removed something from his pocket and opened it.

A wallet.

Several bills of various denominations spilled down onto the sidewalk.

BuzzCut got down on one knee and began scrambling to pick up the money.

Jeanne saw this and stopped a few feet away, asking something.

She wants to know if he needs any help.

BuzzCut nodded his head and offered an embarrassed smile.

The van pulled to the curb two yards away from both of them. The side door came open but was not slid down the track.

Jeanne came over and started helping BuzzCut pick up the money. They spoke quietly. At one point Jeanne stopped helping and looked to where BuzzCut was pointing.

At the car.

Jeanne saw Paul and smiled. Paul offered a small, nervous wave.

The side door of the van began to slowly slide the rest of the way open.

BuzzCut stood. Jeanne offered him the money she'd picked up. BuzzCut shook his head.

Two other men dressed exactly like BuzzCut climbed out of the van. Both checked their watches.

BuzzCut pointed to them and Jeanne looked over.

The other two men nodded, then turned back into the van and helped someone else climb out.

Paul's breath caught in his throat.

Because Jeanne Brooks—scars and all—had climbed out of the van. She was dressed exactly like her other self.

BuzzCut took Jeanne's hand, led her across the street, and put her in the back seat of the car.

"Hello," she said to Paul.

"Hi, Jeanne."

"I don't gotta stay there anymore," she said.

"That's good."

"Yeah, it is." There was a combination of glee, wistfulness, and genuine sadness in her voice that broke Paul's heart about ten times over.

One of the men from the van touched something on the other Jeanne's back and she blinked once, twice, then walked over to pick up the videocassette and go on her original way.

The men climbed back into the van and drove away.

BuzzCut climbed in, released the parking brake, and drove off.

Paul looked at him and started to say something.

"Not now," said BuzzCut. "Later."

Paul turned back to Jeanne.

"Did you . . . uh . . . did you get to see the movie for your birthday, Jeanne?"

"No. They had headaches."

"Do you still want to see it?"

Jeanne brightened. "*Oh, yes!* That would be nice."

Paul tapped BuzzCut's shoulder. "There a K-Mart or a Media Play or something like that along the way?"

"Yeah . . .?"

"We need to stop there."

"We can't, we're supposed to—"

"We're stopping," said Paul. "Please? I think Jeanne deserves a birthday present."

"But they don't rent movies at K-Mart," she said.

"I'm not going to rent it, Jeanne. I'm going to buy it for you."

Her eyes widened. "Buy it? For me?" As if the idea of being given a present was just some myth she'd read about in storybooks.

"Yes, Jeanne, for you. Is that okay?"

"I guess." She was quiet for a moment. Then: "Will I be able to watch it when we get to my new house?"

Paul looked at BuzzCut, who sighed, gave Paul a quick, irritated glance, then said: "We'll make it a Best Buy. Pick up a player, as well."

Paul smiled. "Sounds good to me."

"I get into trouble with Mr. Smyth or Ms. Brown, I'm dragging your butt down with me."

In the back seat, Jeanne giggled. "He said 'butt.' "

Paul looked at her and they both laughed.

Ninety minutes later Paul found himself sitting in Smyth's office once again, only this time Smyth was visibly irritated.

"That was a damned foolish thing you did, taking her into a store to go shopping like that."

"It made her happy. Looked to me like she needed to be made happy."

"Do I look like I'm arguing over that?" snapped Smyth. "The whole point of this was to get her the hell out of there so she can receive therapy and surgery and be placed into a loving, healthy environment."

"Will she?"

"*Of course* she will! From this day on, her life will be safe, and everything will be done to make her happy. It's what we do."

" 'Our Fingers Are In Everything,' eh?"

Smyth glared at him. "Don't be so smug, Paul. You broke protocol—admittedly, you've yet to be fully briefed on what protocol is, but that's beside the point. You took a kidnapped child into a public place where any one of a hundred people might have recognized her. These operations are carefully planned weeks, sometimes *months,* in advance, and sticking to the schedule is crucial. *Crucial,* do you understand? The only reason I haven't had security show your skinny WASP ass the door is because you demonstrated a very stubborn resolve to do something kind for that little girl."

"That's not the only reason," Paul said in his best Jack Nicholson.

Smyth shook his head. "Everybody does Nicholson, pal."

"Then I shall endeavor to be more original," replied Paul in his still-in-progress Chief Dan George.

"That's very good. The Chief was one of my favorite actors. Should've gotten an Oscar for what he did in *The Outlaw Josey Wales.*"

"Agreed."

Smyth sat down and released a long, slow breath. "Okay, I've chewed you out, I feel better."

"BuzzCut's not going to get in trouble, is he?"

"A mild reprimand, nothing more. Push came to

shove, once you were out of the immediate situation, he put the child's happiness first, as well. It's just damned fortunate that no one who knew Jeanne or her mother and stepfather saw you."

"Who was she?"

"Who? Jeanne?"

Paul leaned forward. "The *other* Jeanne. The one who got out of the van."

"She's a robot."

Paul stared at Smyth in silence for a moment. "Say that again."

"She was a robot, Paul. Outwardly—and going beneath the surface of her skin for about an inch—she has all the appearances of being human. She can bleed, eat, excrete waste, cry, whine, and complain just like the rest of us. The difference is, one inch and one centimeter beneath her skin, she becomes a very complex network of alloys and electronic components. When Jeanne's mother and stepfather decide to beat her tonight, they'll be pounding on something that feels no pain but has been programmed to *appear* it's feeling pain. Her voice and all the words she—it—will speak have been prerecorded and preprogrammed into her memory, thanks to another of Borgia's clients—a gifted impressionist, like yourself, who listened to a recording of Jeanne's voice and then read all the selected passages from my books *in* Jeanne's voice, in seven different modes: happy, confused, frightened, excited, sad, terrified, and in shrieking horror—the seven states in which her parents are accustomed to hearing her voice.

"When you start with us, you'll do the same thing. You will perfect your impression of a voice you hear, and then you will read all the selected passages in that voice, in various emotional states. We'll take it from there."

"Is this what you do? Create robots of . . . of—"

"—of abused and severely at-risk children who, if

not removed from their current environments at once, will either die, be killed, or manufactured into monsters. We do what other agencies cannot because of red tape. And for the most part, no one notices."

"You're kidding?"

"No. Isn't that pathetic? Her mother and stepfather will continue to beat and abuse the robot they *think* is Jeanne and never notice that the child doesn't bruise any longer. We've performed over fifty switches in this city alone in the last three years, and in all but one instance, the abusers have failed to notice. In the one instance they did notice something was amiss, they simply drove the child outside the state and abandoned it. Good thing we have tracing devices installed."

"So this is the sole purpose behind Scylla having so many diverse business interests?"

"This is an expensive process, Paul. The Jeanne robot you saw today? All in all, she cost about thirty-five million dollars from conception to switch."

Paul sat in silence for several moments, trying to let it all sink in. "Where were you guys ten years ago?"

"Still in Vienna. I moved the main offices to the States only four years ago. But that's one of the reasons why you were selected, Paul—not just because of your talent, but because you would understand better than most potential recruits the importance of what we do, and the reasons why we choose to do it in the way we do."

"I thought that might have something to do with it."

"Listen to me—if we had been in the States ten years ago and had been made aware of the situation with your sister, we would have done the same for her. In a heartbeat. I know there are probably about a thousand questions running through your mind right now, and we'll answer all of them as we go along, but first and foremost I need to know: Are you with us?"

Paul stared at the floor for a moment, remembering

the smile on Jeanne Brooks' face and wishing he could have made his sister smile like that just once.

He shook his head. "Robots."

"Whether you know it or not, Paul, in the last twenty hours you've interacted with at least four robots."

He snapped his head up. "BuzzCut? Was he a robot?"

"No. He acts like it sometimes. He's my cousin, as flesh and blood as I."

"Oh."

Smyth stared at him, drumming fingers on desktop. "I need an answer, Paul. If you say no, then everything stays as explained to you; if you say yes, then there's a recording of a ten-year-old boy's voice I need you to listen to right away so we can get started." He leaned forward. "So tell me, Paul: Are you with us or not?"

Paul looked at Smyth and grinned. "Wrong reading. Too melodramatic, too much as if you know I'm not going to say yes."

"Is that a Yes?"

Paul grinned. "Three guesses."

POWER PLAY

by William H. Keith, Jr.

William H. Keith, Jr., is the author of over sixty novels, nearly all of them dealing with the theme of men at war. Writing under the pseudonym H. Jay Riker, he's responsible for the extremely popular *SEALS: The Warrior Breed* series, a family saga spanning the history of the Navy UDT and SEALs from World War II to the present day. As Ian Douglas, he writes a well-received military-science fiction series following the exploits of the U.S. Marines in the future, in combat on the Moon and Mars. Recent anthology appearances include *First to Fight II* and *Alternate Gettysburgs*.

HE was dropping still, falling through the high cloud layers, heat shield aglow from the white-hot violence of aerobraking, but the drogue had stabilized *Herschel V*'s descent, and the one-two-three jolts of successively deployed chutes had slowed the massive craft to subsonic velocities. With the final jarring thump, the golden, cone-shaped heat shield released and hurtled on into the depths yawning below.

For the first time, then, Charles saw his surroundings through his primary eyes. Clouds, storm-green and churning, arrayed themselves in slow-moving shoals dropping into heat-warmed blackness; *slow,* Charles knew, was an artifact and strictly relative, an effect of perspective and distance. Those shoals, some of them, were the size of continents and thousands of kilometers distant. His heat shield lent scale to vastness, a tiny star radiating furiously in the high-infrared as it plummeted into darkness.

The final parachute released, and as *Herschel V* fell, it began deploying the primary balloon, which unreeled behind it like a ribbon, already inflating as Charles opened the external gas intakes and began sucking in deep, cold draughts of air.

Samplers tested the icy gas as it streamed inboard, but there were no surprises there. Composition: ninety percent hydrogen and nearly ten percent helium, with something like four tenths of a percent methane as flavoring. As the gas streamed up from the intakes, it flowed over *Herschel*'s heating rods, already charged by the ship's three-megawatt reactor. Hot gas filled the balloon, which expanded overhead like an enormous, silvery mushroom. *Herschel V*'s descent was checked at last, and Charles, suspended at the bottom of a ten-kilometer balloon, adrift in the high, thin, cold air, could take a few seconds to actually enjoy the view. Seconds more were spent running diagnostics on both hardware and software, checking hundreds of systems for any of the seven-hundred-odd possible malfunctions predicted at this stage of deployment.

All systems checked out nominal. After another hesitation of nearly half a second—a long, *long* time for any AI system operating at full awareness—a series of explosive charges ripple-fired around the *Herschel*'s midsection, opening the atmospheric processor array like the petals of an enormous golden flower at the base of the craft's pencil-slender length. A radio antenna built into the top of the balloon, nearly five kilometers overhead now, tracked until it locked onto the acquisition beacon of the *Herschel* orbiter, then began uploading a stream of data, which in turn was relayed to the orbiter's big, Earth-pointed dish antenna.

The signal would take nearly two and a half hours to reach Earth, now some nineteen A.U.s distant, deep within the bright, warm heart of the Solar System.

"Mr. Whittaker? It looks like we got incoming. High-speed. Surface-effect craft . . . and almost certainly hostile."

"From where? What direction?"

"Bearing . . . ah . . . three-zero-five. Speed ninety-two knots."

"Right out of Miami," Whittaker said, thoughtful. "They aren't being very subtle about it, are they?"

"I don't think they need to worry about subtle," Lieutenant Macalvey of the Bahamian Commonwealth Navy said. The overhead fluorescents caught the gold braid and trim on his new white uniform, the reflections dancing as he moved. "There's not a hell of a lot we can do to stop them."

"We always knew that direct intervention was a possibility," Whittaker said. He slumped back in his seat, letting his gaze traverse the Helios Project command center. Dozens of faces, most black but with a scattering of whites and Asians, stared back at him, and he could feel the undercurrent of tension, no, of *fear* running through the room. He made himself smile. "Don't worry," he said, loud enough for everyone to hear. "I've heard President Thurgood loves the scenery down here. They're probably just on the way out to do some serious girl-watching on the beach."

It was a lame joke, lamely delivered, but the Helios crew responded for the most part with hearty laughter. *They ought to be all right, whatever happens,* Whittaker thought. *Most of them are Bahamian nationals. If the lightning falls, it'll fall on me.*

He looked up at the primary screen, filling half of one entire wall of the command center and showing nothing but the brightly colored bars of the test pattern. A pair of smaller screens to the left displayed the current mission status. By this time, all of the *Herschels* should be afloat high in the Uranian atmosphere, but the electronic word of success or failure would not reach Earth until it had crawled past the almost three billion kilometers between Earth and Uranus. Another seventy minutes, according to the clock.

Slowly, he rose from his chair and walked down the aisle to the main spacecraft communications console. Randy Logan, Helios Corporation's general manager, swiveled in his seat to give Whittaker a jaunty thumbs up. "We can send the AMC any time you say, boss. Everything's go on this end, and all we're waiting for is deployment confirmation."

"I'd rather wait until we know the system has properly checked out," he replied. Sending the Autonomous Mode Command was like cutting that last lifeline. There would be nothing they could do to help if any of the Charleses out there turned up a failure alert or a sequence abort, no way to upload new programming, no way even to talk to them until they returned to cis-Lunar space. He wanted to delay transmitting the AMC until the last possible moment.

Even now, he didn't want to believe that they would go so far as to launch a military operation. Macalvey came up behind him. "Sir? You'd better hear this." He handed Whittaker a wire-slender headset. He slipped it on, adjusted the button in his ear, and pulled the lip mike into place beside his mouth. A fiber-optic hook projected in front of his eye, but there was no visual feed yet.

"Whittaker here," he said. "What's up?"

"Hey, boss!" a young Bahamian's voice called in his ear. "This is Joey . . . uh, Joe Collins, up at the dish! We've got Yankee aircraft up here! Lots of 'em!"

"Let me see, please."

The tip of the hook flashed brilliantly with emerald light, and then he could see an image transmitted from the earth station at Mastic Point. By pressing his right eye closed with his fingers, he could see the image the tiny laser was painting on his left eye's retina more clearly. The immense white bowl of the Helios ground station rested in its cradle above the wide-flung roof doors of its hurricane shelter. Several Helios employees were scattering across the coral sand in the foreground. Overhead, like great, silent manta rays, a pair of black F/A-510s circled in the dazzling deep blue of a sunny, subtropical sky. Designed for stealth—except for gently down-turned wingtips the triangular flying wings possessed no vertical structures at all, and their black skins absorbed radar energy as effectively as they absorbed light—they would have given no warning at all to Bahamian air defense. Had the attack been launched at night, they would have been completely invisible to all save the most sensitive of infrared tracking sensors. One of the aircraft dipped portwing low and executed an impossibly hard, tight, high-G turn, reminding Whittaker that the pilots of those craft were teleoperating them from the comfort of a ship offshore . . . or even the safety of Patrick or one of the other Air Force bases on the mainland. It reminded him of just how vulnerable Helios was out here; it wasn't as though the Bahamian Commonwealth could do anything to stop the bastards from doing whatever they damn well pleased.

"Have they attacked, Joey?" he asked. "Have they launched missiles, anything like that?"

"No sir! But anybody tries to go near the dish, one a them things makes a dive an' turn and swoops down so close it likes t' scare the liver outa you!"

So it was going to be the antenna. As expected.

He opened his eye and grinned at Logan. "They're going for the dish. Do me a favor and patch a call through to Bahamian Air Defense. Let 'em know they have some intruders over here. Then get the hell out of here."

Logan's shaggy brows drew together, and he gave a stubborn shake of his head. "I don't want to—"

"I don't really care what you want, mister," Whittaker said, his voice betraying only a calm deadliness. "I want you off this compound. Preferably off of Andros. You know that if they've gone this far, they're going to round up every officer of Helios they can find." Logan continued to look stubborn. "Damn it, Randy! Git!"

"Yes, sir," his manager said, all reluctance. "If you'll come with me. . . ."

He shook his head. "Wish I could, but if they don't get me, they won't stop until they've tracked every last one of the rest of you. Most of you have families. You think I want that on my conscience?"

"You have a family. Sir."

"Damn it, Randy, are you gonna stand there and argue? I figure we have about thirty minutes, max, before we've got Special Forces guys climbing all over us."

"Less than that, Boss, if—"

The explosion sounded preternaturally loud, a sharp, hard bang that tore the locked double doors at the back of the command center from their hinges and sent them sailing into the room. Smoke boiled through the air, sudden and acrid; as Whittaker turned, eyes wide, he saw a pair of dark green canisters bouncing down the aisle from the suddenly opened door. "Down!" he screamed, still turning . . . and then the canisters detonated with a rapid-fire chain of flashes as dazzling as raw sunlight, as deafening as ear-ringing gunshots. The shock wave slammed him back against the communications console, then let him crumple to the floor.

At the back of the room, a pair of men dressed all in black, from visored helmets to combat vests to BDUs, gloves and boots, rolled through the doorway, snub-muzzled weapons already at their shoulders as they loosed round after round into the smoky confusion at the command center's consoles. Needle-slender beams of ruby light swept back and forth through the smoky near-darkness. The weapons were submachine guns of some kind; Whittaker didn't know much about military firearms and cared less, but he did know they could either fire full-auto or single shot, and that the red beams were targeting lasers. These black-clad raiders were firing with great deliberation and precision, one laser-aimed shot at a time, and that deliberation made the attack even more terrifying than it would have been if they'd simply burst into the center, guns spraying indiscriminately. Whittaker couldn't hear the shots—whether that was because the weapons were equipped with sound suppressers or because of the shrill ringing in his ears, he wasn't sure—but he saw the effects as one after another, the men and women manning the Helios command center consoles dropped.

"Don't shoot!" he screamed, and the sound of his own voice sounded distant and muffled, as though shouted by a stranger. He struggled to his feet just as four more commandos broke through the door, taking up flanking positions at the corners of the rooms, continuing their deadly, accurate fire. "Don't shoot! We surrender!"

Randy Logan knocked his chair aside as he rose, hands raised, but two bright ruby pinpoints of light appeared on his white shirt . . . followed an instant later by sudden spots of blood, the size of quarters as he pitched backward to the floor. Lieutenant Macalvey was already down, blood staining the front of his dress whites in three places.

Whittaker felt something hit his ribs on his right side and glanced down. There was blood there, as well . . . and the tiny gray fins of a flechette. His side felt . . . cold, ice-cold, and the chill was coursing with his blood to arms and legs, turning them leaden.

The AMC, he thought. *There might still be time. . . .*

Turning again, he reached for the key Randy had pointed out a moment before, but his body was not responding well to commands. As he stretched out his hand, his knees hit the floor, and then his face collided with the console. Several more flechettes slammed into his back, and he felt the drugs carried in their hollow points adding their quotas of ice to his blood stream.

He was blacking out. . . .

The sun was setting, a dazzling, tiny disk of cold, white light slipping rapidly beneath the haze-fogged horizon. Charles noted the sunset as he noted everything else. The temperature was falling rapidly with night; at this altitude, the atmosphere was far warmer than the frigid fifty-nine Kelvins of the upper methane haze layer, but it was still cold enough that *Herschel*'s cryo gear could work with high efficiency . . . and that efficiency increased as the night grew colder.

Powered by the reactor, powerful pumps began sucking in air and cooling it, shuttling it into refrigerated separator tanks where it was liquefied. At one atmosphere, methane liquefied at -161 degrees Celsius and was easily separated from the rest, routed through a cooling assembly to chill the incoming air stream, and then dumped overboard in a thin spray that quickly froze into dancing flakes of methane ice.

The refrigerator tanks continued to cool, dropping the temperature of the gas mix rapidly. At -252.8 degrees Celsius, the hydrogen began liquefying, leaving behind an atmosphere of almost pure helium. Most of the liquid hydrogen was dumped overboard; some was shuttled into fuel tanks for processing and storage, while the rest, superheated by channeling it through the reactor, was used to flush out the hot air in the multichambered gas bag of the balloon overhead, and replace it with even hotter hydrogen. As *Herschel V* grew heavier, its capacious storage tanks filling with various products, the balloon grew more buoyant, maintaining the craft's balance between the extreme cold of higher altitudes and the crushing heat and pressure of the Uranian depths.

Charles Whittaker became aware that someone was leaning over him, a huge and hulking black shadow that managed to convey a sense of menace long before he could actually focus on it. When his eyes finally managed the feat, he found himself looking up into the dark face of one of the commandos. The man had removed his helmet, and his head appeared ridiculously small above the black and massive bulk of his body armor.

"Mr. Whittaker?" the commando asked. He raised Whittaker's head from the floor, then examined an electronic palm screen he held in one black glove. "Mr. Charles Whittaker?" he asked again, looking from the screen to Whittaker's face and back again.

Whittaker nodded, not trusting himself to speak. He felt . . . strange. The wounds in his side and back didn't hurt, exactly, but they did feel numb, exactly like his mouth after a dentist's shots of anodyne. He couldn't feel his legs at all, and his arms were tingling as though they were asleep.

"I am Lieutenant Kenneth Brewer, United States Navy," the commando said. "SEAL Team Twelve. Hope you'll forgive our little demonstration." He actually sounded cheerful about it.

"You . . . shot . . . them . . ." Whittaker said, forcing the words one at a time through cold, numb lips. "Didn't . . . need . . . to . . . kill . . . them. . . ."

"Kill them? Shit, no one's been killed!" Brewer patted the black casing of the subgun strapped to his side. "At least, not *yet.* Paralysin rounds, you know. Nonlethal, as long as you get the antitoxin in time."

Whittaker blinked, trying to see what was happening in the control center. There was a lot of smoke, and his ears were still ringing, the after effect, he thought, of the flash-bangs the raiders had tossed into the room. Several Navy SEALs stood guard by the door, while other men in combat BDUs and kevlar armor dragged the control center personnel from the room one by one, their wrists bound behind their backs by strips of plastic. Helios personnel. *His* people.

"Don't worry," Brewer went on. "They're all being evacked, and they'll all get a-toxed on the way out. But, ah, you're gonna have to have a little talk with someone first. You understand?"

He nodded, even though he didn't understand, not really. It was only now beginning to percolate through his aching skull that the American ships and the aircraft over Mastic Point had been a feint, a ruse to keep his attention focused elsewhere for a critical few moments. While he'd been discussing the situation with Logan, the SEALs had landed here, probably dropping out of stealth helos onto the roof of the control center bunker. He tried to sit up and failed. His wrists, he thought, were wired together behind his back, though he couldn't feel them very well.

"You are violating the territory of the sovereign Commonwealth of the Bahamas," Whittaker said, slumping back to the floor. His tongue felt as thick as a wadded-up washcloth, and the words stumbled as he spoke them.

"Won't be the first time," Brewer said, and winked. "This damned island used t' be a drug smuggler's paradise, you know. Before that it was pirates and wreckers. And nowadays it's you, with your illegal space probes."

"Not . . . illegal. The Bahamians sold this land to the Helios Corporation. We employ eight hundred islanders here on Andros Island alone, and more in Nassau and—"

"Look, I'm not the one to convince, pal, okay?" Brewer looked up. Another man had just entered the control center, a tall and distinguished-looking man in a gray suit, silver-haired, a handkerchief pressed against his face as he glanced back and forth, trying to see through the smoke. Brewer raised an arm and beckoned; the suit approached.

"This the guy?" the suit asked. The voice was as icy as the dull, cold pressure over Whittaker's ribs and spine.

"Charles Whittaker, sir," the SEAL lieutenant said. "Owner and CEO of Helios Corporation."

"Leave us a moment, Lieutenant."

"Aye, aye, sir."

As Brewer withdrew, the suit stood over Whittaker, examining him with the detachment of a man studying something particularly repulsive growing in an unexpected place . . . like the back of a refrigerator. "Mr. Whittaker," he said, "you're a hard man to find. We've been trying to talk to you for a long time."

"I've been . . . right here." Not entirely true. He'd spent a lot of the past five years traveling all over the world, rallying support for Helios. Damn it, he knew they'd been watching him then. They could have taken him at any time. Why wait until *now* . . .?

"Mr. Whittaker, your Helios probe has been declared illegal under the provisions of UN Special Order 892372, as amended on June 15, 2028. You were ordered to cease and desist . . . on at least six separate occasions. Did you get the papers?"

"I got them," Whittaker replied. It was disconcerting, lying flat on his back, looking at the man standing over him. Their positions gave the suit a considerable psychological advantage, but Whittaker refused to acknowledge it. "Our lawyers replied with the appropriate papers."

"You blatantly ignored our restraining orders."

"Helios Corporation is registered and operated under the laws of the Bahamian Commonwealth. The

United States . . . the Department of Energy . . . they can't tell us what to do."

"The Bahamas are still part of the United Nations, Mr. Whittaker, and are subject to international law. And you, unless I'm mistaken, are still a citizen of the United States, which makes you subject to federal law. Even here." Suddenly, the suit dropped to his haunches, bringing his face closer to Whittaker's. "You know, it's all a matter of simple economics, really. What you're trying to do here would destroy the American economy. You *knew* we couldn't let you do that, right? There's still time for you to realize a profit, though. All you have to do is cooperate."

A low buzz of conversation ran through the room, and several of the SEALs stopped what they were doing to stare at the big display on the control center's front wall. The gray suit looked up, an unreadable expression working at the corners of his mouth. "What is that? What's going on?"

"I can't . . . see."

The suit dragged Whittaker's body about and, grabbing a handful of hair at the back of his head, lifted him so he could see the display. Whittaker's mouth fell open, and he gave a small, sharp gasp. It was *beautiful*. . . .

From space, even from relatively close by in space, the planet Uranus presents a bland and uninteresting face to the rest of the universe. A high, thin mist of methane obscures most details of the planet's cloud tops, rendering the entire world in a uniform, gray-green sameness of color and texture. Add to that the still mysterious fact that Uranus has very little weather to begin with. Alone of the four gas giants of the outer solar system, Uranus receives more heat from the wan and distant sun than it generates within its interior, a detail first noted by the planetary scientists of the Voyager fly-by, but still unexplained fifty years later.

As a result, the planet shows little of the characteristic banding of Jupiter or Saturn, and none of the immense cyclonic storms, vast enough to swallow Earth whole, like Jupiter's Red Spot or Neptune's Great Dark Spot.

But that was from a distance. The view showing on the control center's main screen was being relayed from a camera mounted within one of the *Herschel* probes now adrift beneath its balloon high in the Uranian atmosphere. The widespread petals of the *Herschel*'s intakes were just visible at the screen's lower left. Beyond, the scale so gargantuan that it was impossible to tell just by looking how far or how large, green clouds lightly tinted with yellow formed distant, smooth-sculpted shorelines, cotton-candy mountains, fairy-tale landscapes molded from water and methane ices, colored by a bewildering zoo of organics and cryochemistries. Below, cloud cliffs faded into night; lightning flared, but so distant it showed as no more than a briefly pulsing pinpoint of golden light in the darkness. Higher, near the top of the screen, green clouds merged with white haze at a dazzling horizon of ice and vapor; the sun, shrunken to a fraction of its familiar size and brightness, hung like a white diamond beneath the high, cold arc of an icebow. The sun hovered above the horizon; cloud shadows lay like long, black shafts of emptiness across the cloud tops, which showed each bulge and bump, each hollow and wind-carved space in sharp relief. The beauty, the sheer, glorious magnificence of the scene caught with his indrawn breath in Whittaker's throat. And, close behind the thrill at the glory of that cloudscape came another: *We did it!* Herschel *did it! We took our dream and gave it form, hurled it across three billion kilometers of night to a world we haven't visited since 1986!* Herschel *is there, right now, tasting the atmosphere and settling in to go to work!*

He felt his own idiotic grin, a peculiar tugging at the corners of his drug-deadened mouth.

"So that's a live feed from Uranus?" the suit asked. "What's happening?"

Briefly, Whittaker considered correcting him. Two time readouts glowed at the upper right, one above the other: GMT: 1542 and GMT/URANUS: 1310. The image they were seeing was over two and a half hours old, thanks to light's snail-pace crawl across the vast near-emptiness of the Solar system. His heart hammered a bit more quickly beneath his breastbone; the suit was an errand boy, and a scientifically ignorant one at that. Could he use that ignorance, somehow?

Hope died before it took proper shape. Some of those black-clad men in the control center had the look not of warriors, but of technicians as they took vacant spaces behind the consoles and began working at the keyboards and voice access mikes. The suit might not know basic science, but *they* would.

"It's a data feed from Uranus," Whittaker said at last, volunteering nothing. He eyed the read-out lines scrolling up one of the subscreens. "From *Herschel V*. Nothing much of anything is happening at the moment. It's checking out its systems, running diagnostics. And transmitting a report on the weather where it is right now."

The suit gave a dry chuckle. "Cold, isn't it? What the hell does the Bahamian government want with a deep freeze like that?"

"It's not as cold as you'd think, actually. *Herschel V* is at the seven tenth's bar level. That means the atmospheric pressure is seven tenth's of sea level on Earth. Temperature's about minus one-thirty. That cloud deck, there, is probably about at one bar, and the temperature's not much colder than it is in this room."

"Prime real estate, huh?"

"Except for the fact that there's no place to stand, yeah." He didn't add that the air pressure of the Uranian atmosphere continued rising, the deeper you plunged into those depths, growing thicker and hotter until temperatures approached those at the surface of the sun. The Earth-sized solid core of the gas giant would forever remain untouchable beneath its seething, high-temperature, high-pressure sea of water, hydrogen, and helium.

"Well," the suit said, "we both know why the Bahamians are backing you. And the Japs. And quite a few others. And it's going to stop. Right here. Right now."

"No," Whittaker said, shaking his head. He felt terribly dizzy, and the paralysis was making each breath a struggle. "I don't think so."

The suit looked at him sharply. "I wouldn't be too hasty with my answer, there, Charles," he said. "You know, poison bullets were outlawed by the Geneva convention a century ago, just like poison gas and mistreating prisoners. P-flets are supposed to be nonlethal . . . but, well, you know anytime you shoot chemicals into a guy's bloodstream, even for partial anesthesia, you're tossing dice, right? A dose that'd put a grown man to sleep might kill a kid or an old guy. And some people, well, they can have unfortunate reactions to the stuff. Rigor. Convulsions. Or if they've had enough, their diaphragm and chest muscles seize up, and they suffocate. That can be real lingering, though. They're luckier if their cardiac muscles paralyze. Then they die pretty quick. It takes a lot of paralysin to zap the heart, though. Most of 'em smother slow. How about it, Charlie? You having a little trouble breathing? Your lips are looking a little blue, there."

Whittaker *was* having trouble breathing, though he wasn't about to admit as much. "Screw you."

The suit reached into an inside jacket pocket and produced a spray hypo already charged with a cc or so of clear, golden liquid. "Actually, paralysin is a neurotoxin. Like cobra venom, in fact. That's why we have an antitoxin ready, like this stuff. Fire it into the carotid and it sops up the paralysin in just a minute or two. Works like a charm. Of course, ah, you're going to have to cooperate with us if you want your shot. . . ."

"What do you want?"

The suit nodded toward the big display. "*Kill* that robot, that spacecraft, whatever it is. You must have destruct codes, or a way to transmit a new program telling it to cut the radio link with Earth."

"That's . . . not possible." His breath was coming in shallow, thin gulps now. He was having trouble focusing his thoughts.

"*Sure* it's possible, Charlie. Anything's possible, if you really put your mind to it. It's not so hard. You kill your robot, you get to live. Hell, we're fair. We can even arrange for you to see a profit on this venture of yours. Our offer's still open, you know."

"Helios is not for sale."

The suit looked around the room, smoke-filled and inhabited by silent, black-clad figures. "You know, it doesn't look to me like you're in a position to bargain. Right now, there *is* no Helios. And pretty soon, there won't be a Charles Edward Whittaker either."

"Helios . . . doesn't need me anymore. What's going to happen is going to happen. With me or without me."

The suit regarded him impassively for a moment, before smiling. "Come now, Mr. Whittaker. You can do better than that." He hesitated, then returned the hypo to his pocket. This time, he produced a palm-sized computer screen, which he activated with a touch to one corner. He studied the data presented there a moment. "Charles Edward Whittaker. Born 5 May 1983, Boston, Massachusetts. Only son of Earl and Debra Whittaker . . . listings in the Boston social register . . . attended MIT . . . engineering degree, followed by Harvard Business School. Married Elena Adams, 2005. One son, Charles, Jr. One daughter, Kathryn. Worked in your father's software engineering firm for five years, before haring off on your own. Started Helios Corporation in 2020. Investments . . . um . . . capital . . . . My! You are a *very* wealthy man, Mr. Whittaker. It seems to me that you have a very great deal to lose by not cooperating with us."

"Go to hell."

"How much did the *Herschel* mission cost you, Mr. Whittaker. How much of your personal fortune did it eat?"

"That's all a matter of public record. Why ask me? You probably have it there on your computer."

"I just want to know that you know where you stand, Mr. Whittaker." He consulted the palm-top again. "Ten million in initial capital to set up the company and, I presume, to bribe certain Bahamian officials, once you found out that we weren't going to let you operate freely in the States. Fifty-two million in R&D. One hundred twelve million and some change in construction costs here on Andros, and eight hundred million and some to pay the Europeans to launch your payload to orbit. High launch fees, huh?"

"We had to design and build a special launch vehicle."

"Ah. Five hundred million for the actual spacecraft, and another twelve million in operating costs since you launched, eight years ago. All together . . . my God, almost one point five billion dollars. Kind of high for out-of-pocket expenses, isn't it, Mr. Whittaker?"

"We have investors. Those you people weren't able to scare off."

"True. And that's posed a problem for us and for the UN. Most of these people are wealthy private investors, and their governments are unable or unwilling to bring pressure to bear on them. Even so, our sources tell us that you still had to sink something like five hundred million of your own into this project. You sold your home on Cape Cod. Most of your investments. Auctioned off your art and furniture collections. Three years ago, your wife divorced you because she didn't want to move to a five-hundred-a-month apartment down here. My God, Whittaker, you damn near beggared yourself over this project! Why?"

"The very best of reasons. I expected to make a profit on the investment. I also *believe* in Helios. But I wouldn't expect you to understand that."

"Well, I'll tell you what I believe in. I believe in seeing a profit, too. That's the way the old US of A became great, right? So here's what we'll do. Send the signal, disable the spacecraft, and we'll see that you're reimbursed for your personal investment in Helios, with, oh, let's say a five million dollar sweetener on top. *And* you get to live! What could be fairer than that?"

"Forget it." It was much harder to breathe now, and his peripheral vision was starting to fuzz out.

The suit shifted his weight, lifting one foot and planting it on Whittaker's chest. The weight, crushing and intense, emptied his lungs with a whoosh, and he found himself fighting to draw another breath. He struggled, trying to throw off the weight, but with his hands pinned he was completely helpless.

"What was that, Charles?" the suit asked cheerfully. "I didn't quite catch what you said."

Whittaker's thrashings became weaker. The suit removed his foot from his chest and leaned close. "You want to try that once more?"

"You . . . can't stop it," Whittaker said, gasping. He looked past the suit's face at the cloudscape glowing on the main screen. In a way, he *was* there, adrift above the Uranian cloud deck, not here, fighting for each breath. "It's already happened, you know. *Herschel* is going to complete its mission. It'll bring its payload back whether I'm here to meet it or not, and there's not a God-damned thing you can do to stop it. To stop *me.*" He raised his head a little higher, his voice falling to a conspiratorial whisper. "Like you said, it's a matter of simple economics."

The idea that Charles Whittaker was somehow physically aboard the *Herschel* probe was not entirely romantic metaphor; the name *Charles,* after all, was not coincidence. Each of ten Harvester Processing Modules now adrift in the Uranian sky was operated by a Systech-10,000 AT on-board computer, an older, slower model, in fact, than the most advanced computers available on the market when *Herschel* was being assembled ten years before, but the best available within Helios Corporation's somewhat strait-jacketed budget at the time. The technology for downloading at least superficial personality traits had been in existence since the Rand-IBM-CMU Adam Project in 2022, and there'd been dramatic advances in storage capacity, personality emulation, and fuzzy logic problem solving in the years since.

Unfortunately, Human-Computer Personality Downloads, or HCPDs, had not answered any of the philosophical questions surrounding the basic idea. If HCPD computers appeared to be self-aware, the critics pointed out, it was because they'd been programmed to *act* self-aware, and any true understanding of their nature was as impossible as unraveling the central question of the old Turing Test debate. If a human conversing with a computer by electronic means couldn't tell whether or not he was talking to a machine, did that mean the machine was intelligent . . . or simply that the human hadn't asked the right questions, didn't understand the problem, or was just plain stupid?

HCPD computers routinely passed the Turing Test. The Aurora-Hyperlogic 5 at the Carnegie Mellon University's Moravec Institute held daily online discussions with human experts in over two hundred fields, experts who rarely caught on that they were exchanging thoughts with minds based on silicon instead of carbon.

The debate over whether self-awareness and personalities in computers were possible in any real sense of the terms or simply cleverly simulation did not affect Charles in any of his incarnations, of course. He did what he was designed to do, which was to oversee each phase of the Herschel mission according to an interlocking series of highly complex programs. If he paused for a millisecond or so to contemplate the beauty of the Uranian sunset, it might be less because the computer was capable of appreciating beauty than it was because Charles Whittaker, the *real* Charles Whittaker, would have paused and contemplated had he been there in the flesh. It was, perhaps, less accurate to say that each of the ten Charles-HCPD computers on the mission possessed the human Whittaker's personality than it was to say that they thought like him, with memories, attitudes, and an overall vision of the Helios Project provided by Whittaker himself some months before the launch.

In most ways, even an HCPD computer was far from human by even the most generous definition of the word. The Charles aboard *Herschel* HPM 5 was aware, through its radio link with the orbiter, of the sudden descent of HPM 8 when that module's balloon suddenly suffered catastrophic failure and the entire assembly plunged into the searing heat and darkness of the Uranian depths, but it felt nothing remotely like human emotion at the "death" of an intelligence closer to it than any human twins could be to one another.

It was aware, too, of LOS—a critical loss of signal—from HPM 4, almost certainly because of an anomalous ice buildup on its primary tracking antenna mount. If HPM 4 could not melt the ice and restore communications with the rest of the tiny Herschel fleet, it, too, would be lost. A situation, however, that would have caused worry in a human observer, or even an attempt at rescue, was no more than another allowable variation within the overall parameters of the mission. There were ten HPMs precisely because losses were expected.

But Charles did "feel"—if that word had any application—something like satisfaction at the way the harvesting was proceeding. Once the primary processing tanks had been drained of liquid hydrogen until they held almost pure helium gas, heat-exchange pumps were engaged to drop the tank temperature even further. Helium liquefies at minus 269 degrees Celsius, a scant 4.2 degrees above absolute zero, and at that temperature it becomes relatively easy to separate the light isotope of helium-3 from its far more abundant brother helium-4. As the separation and purification process continued, liquid helium-4 was vented back into the Uranian sky, while super-cold helium-3 was transferred to the main payload tanks.

Those tanks were nearly half full now, in a process now well ahead of schedule. It would have been scandalously anthropomorphic to suggest that Charles was *pleased* with the way things were going.

Still, it *had* been a beautiful sunset.

"Come now, Whittaker," the suit said. "Everyone has his price."

"Bull . . . shit . . ."

"Everyone," he repeated. "Oh, the price is not necessarily money." He produced the hypo once again and waved it above Whittaker's pinched, blue-tinted face. "This, I suspect, is your price. Plus, shall we say, *ten* million dollars . . . and the guarantee that you'll be able to continue your work."

"You . . . want . . . to . . . kill . . ." He had to gasp out one word at a time as he panted for air.

"No, I don't want to kill you. Really, I don't. I want

you to live. All you need to do is tell me how to stop that damned robot out there."

"Not . . . me. Kill . . . my . . . work. You want . . . to kill . . . Helios . . ."

"Ah. Well, I'm afraid Helios does have to die. Too many people would be, shall we say, inconvenienced if your visionary little power play was successful. But, well, you're obviously interested in energy production. In nuclear fusion. Fusion *is* the wave of the future, you know. Just as we've been saying for, what? Eighty, almost ninety years, now. DepEn and the big energy consortia have invested a hell of a lot in all of those pilot fusion plants. We could find a place for you in the program, I'm sure."

"Not . . . *your* . . . way."

The proponents of fusion power had been promising the miracle of clean and abundant energy since the middle of the twentieth century. Once, fission had promised the long-sought dream of cheap energy . . . but breakdowns, aging equipment, and skyrocketing plant costs—not to mention the problem of disposing of the highly radioactive fuel rods—had turned dream to nightmare, with names like Three-Mile Island, Kyshtym, Chernobyl, and Detroit.

Fusion power, the fusion of light elements into heavier, liberating energy in the process, was the new dream. Fusion promised greater efficiency and far greater yields than fission . . . and instead of using dangerous and rare heavy metals like uranium or plutonium for fuel, fusion used deuterium, which could be extracted easily and in quantity from Earth's oceans.

The problem was, however, that there were several means of achieving fusion. Most commercial plans called for deuterium-deuterium reactions, but there were drawbacks with that method. A full seventy-five percent of the energy liberated by fusing two deuterium atoms was emitted as high-speed neutrons, particles that could not be used to produce electricity, could not be controlled by magnetic fields, and vented their energy by transforming the metal of their containment facility into deadly, highly radioactive isotopes. Another method yielded an even heavier hydrogen isotope—tritium—as a waste product, and tritium was nearly as dangerous and hard to store as the spent fuel rods from the old fission plants. Still a third technique required reacting tritium with deuterium. Since tritium did not occur naturally on Earth, that meant that large-scale commercial deuterium-tritium fusion would require numerous large, costly, and dangerous factories for the production and storage of the radioactive gas . . . and in any case, the actual reaction, like deuterium-deuterium, liberated large numbers of high-energy neutrons, losing as much as eighty percent of the total energy yield in the process.

Some other fusion reactions using heavier elements as fuels such as boron and lithium were relatively clean, but they required far higher temperatures and pressures to generate fusion than other schemes and were not yet practical.

Vastly preferable to all of those models was nuclear fusion using deuterium and the light isotope of helium called helium-3. Most helium nuclei possessed two protons and two neutrons—helium-4—but a small percentage had two protons and only one neutron—helium-3. It was not radioactive, it was easy to handle, and the reaction produced helium-4, a stream of fast-moving protons that could be harnessed by magnetic fields, and a *great* deal of energy. There was only one catch, and that was a big one. If helium was rare on Earth, helium-3 was damned near nonexistent. Schemes had been concocted for harvesting helium-3 from the Lunar regolith, where four billion years of sunshine had laid a thin dusting of the stuff into the top few centimeters of soil, but calculations suggested that one ton of helium-3 could be extracted from a hundred million tons of regolith, which meant strip-mining the moon on a colossal scale.

Helios Corporation had begun in 2021, when Charles Edward Whittaker had first started thinking about where in the Solar System helium-3 might be found in relative abundance, and how he could extract it. At that point, the International Thermonuclear Experimental Reactor (ITER) had been in operation for almost five years, and a dozen smaller test plants were in operation around the world . . . but none, so far, had managed to run for more than a few weeks at a time at break-even or above. Many tens of billions of dollars had been funneled into big fusion—meaning deuterium-deuterium or deuterium-tritium—and *still* the payoff seemed as remote, as tantalizingly reachable but elusive as it had back in the 1960s, when proponents had confidently expected that fusion power for everyone was just around the corner.

Guided by the United States Department of Energy, and an administration that owed its power to the major world energy consortia, the United States had hitched its fusion star to the deuterium-deuterium reaction.

But Helios threatened to unhitch that star in a hurry, and with disastrous consequences for the economy.

"Lots of people have worked a long time to make fusion work," the suit told Whittaker. He reached down and used a thumb to roughly pry Whittaker's eyelid up, checking the color of the eye. "You could undo . . . everything. As I said, it would be inconvenient. Not to mention embarrassing."

"Good."

"Come on, man! Be reasonable! Helium-3 fusion is not practical, not if you have to drag your tail clear out to Uranus to get the stuff!"

A technician approached the two of them. "Sir?"

"What?"

"We've broken their code. I think we can give you what you want. *Without* him."

"Ah! Excellent!" The suit looked down at Whittaker and smiled. "Too bad. You really should have taken my first offer. If you'll excuse me, I have a space craft to sabotage."

The helium-3 storage tanks were nearly full, fifteen tons of the stuff roiling about in the baffled, thickly insulated payload tank. Charles shut off the intakes, flushed out the last of the waste liquids, and began the final check for all systems. The next launch window would open in . . . call it four hours, forty-five minutes, fifteen seconds.

Throughout the process, Charles maintained a detachment as cold as the air outside. Through a tightly interlocking web of radio feeds, he continued to be aware of the locations and status of the other seven HPMs still in communication with the *Herschel* orbiter. They, too, were nearing completion of their program runs, though HPM 2 was reporting that a stuck feed valve had vented part of its He-3 payload overboard. The problem had been corrected through the simple expedient of rotating the module slightly so that the sun could shine on a frozen valve assembly—HPM 2 was still on the Uranian dayside—but it would have processed something less than ten tons of He-3 by the time its launch window arrived in another two and a half hours.

That was too bad. An optimum return for this mission would have been a full 150 tons of He-3. No one—least of all Charles Whittaker—had expected everything to work perfectly; in fact, the safe return and recovery of a single HPM with fifteen tons of the precious helium isotope would more than pay for the Helios Project, and by a large margin. But Charles possessed a hard-to-define but definite lust for perfection . . . or, at least, for a mission resolution that was as close to perfection as possible.

Above all, Charles believed in the Helios project.

It was one of the small ironies of the program that an attempt to bring back a piece of one of the coldest places in the Solar system should be named for the Greek god of the sun. Still, the name was fitting. Helium had been named by Sir Joseph Lockyer in 1868, when he'd confirmed astronomer Pierre-Jules-Cesar Janssen's discovery of an unknown element in the spectra of light from the sun. And the helium-3-deuterium fusion reaction promised to bring a *controllable* piece of the sun into everyday human affairs.

Charles' belief in Helios, of course, was a function of the HCPD. How Charles approached a given problem, how he broke it into pieces and analyzed each in turn, how he arrived at the endpoint decision after following multiply branching lines of logic, all were patterned, at least so far as was possible, after the way Charles Edward Whittaker tackled a problem. It stood to reason, then, that he shared Whittaker's near-fanatical belief that the real promise of cheap, clean energy for humankind lay in the helium-3, rather than in the clumsy and dangerous models proposed by the energy consortia on Earth.

Likely, Charles would not have understood the concept of a conspiracy, since by their very nature conspiracies attempted to hide information rather than uncovering, divulging, and storing it for later access . . . but he did know that Whittaker and the Helios program had faced considerable political and financial opposition back on Earth.

Of course, Charles and the other HPM computers knew perhaps as much about human politics as they did about human sex, which was to say nothing at all beyond the existence of the subject. In any case, their human supervisors were responsible for such subjects; there was nothing that Charles could do to involve himself in human politics nineteen astronomical units from Earth.

Or so he thought.

The suit crouched next to Whittaker, pressed the snout of the hypo spray against his throat just beneath the angle of his jaw, and squeezed the trigger. Whittaker felt a sharp sting as the antitoxin blasted through his skin. The icy pressure constricting his chest maintained its grip for a few seconds more . . . and then, suddenly, his diaphragm gave a convulsive flutter. Air—sweet and delicious—hissed in through is fish-gaping mouth. His chest expanded. He could *breathe*. . . .

The suit grinned at him as he pocketed the hypo. "You didn't think we were going to let you get away *that* easily, do you? You're coming back to the States with us. We have some questions for you, and a lovely room with a view in a Canadian gulag."

For the moment, Whittaker was so grateful just to be able to *breathe* without having to fight for each shallow pant that he didn't really care. He was more concerned about what the technician was telling the suit when he joined them a few moments later.

"Well?" the suit demanded, standing again. "What's the story?"

"I think we must've caught them just in time, sir," the tech said. "They had a special file set up with a program ready to upload to their orbiter. It would've let their probes operate pretty much on their own, and ignore further orders from Earth."

The suit's eyes widened. "They couldn't do *that*, surely! Computers aren't magic. They do what you tell them to do."

An uncomfortable expression tugged at the technician's face, as though he was trying to think how best to explain something to a somewhat slow child. "Computers, the good ones, have had at least limited decision-making capability for some time, sir. Fuzzy logic, after all, is an attempt to parallel certain aspects of the way humans think, and the only reason to download personalities, at this stage of the game, is to let them use human thought patterns. It's more a programming shortcut than anything else."

"Yeah, yeah, I know all that. You still can't have a computer that tells itself what to do."

"You could if it were programmed to write programs for itself." The suit's eyes widened again, and the tech held up one hand. "But it's okay. They didn't send the command. And the program you wanted is ready to upload."

"Good." The suit's mouth hardened, and he glanced down at Whittaker again. "Do it."

"Yes, sir."

Whittaker tried to lever himself up against the pressure of the plastic cuffs on his wrist. Feeling was beginning to return to his arms, now, and with the blood came a throbbing pain where the plastic binders were cutting into his skin. "What are you doing?"

"Killing your Uranian spacecraft. It's pretty simple, really. A mission as complex as this one has a hell of a lot of weak points where it can be attacked. We're getting set to upload new commands to all ten of your HPM floaters. As I understand it, when each floater module gets topped off with liquid helium-3, it calculates the next available launch window to a single, specific orbit. Those windows are relatively narrow, and different for every floater, since they're strung out across half of the planet, right?

"Well, in a couple of hours or so, however long it takes the radio signal to reach the orbiter, this new command will be downloaded to each HPM. Basically, it simply has the instruction that when the launch countdown reaches zero, the module is to abort launch and shut itself off. What do you say? Think it'll work?"

Whittaker felt as paralyzed as he had under the effect of the drug, and the ice seemed to have migrated to his throat and stomach. It would work; the suit wasn't as ignorant as he'd initially thought . . . and the techs working for him knew their stuff. A direct order from Earth to abort the mission might be ignored—the HPM Charleses had a certain amount of what might be called free will with which they could choose the best way of solving a given problem without help from Earth, and a direct order to shut down was so contrary to what they'd been designed for that they might reject it as bad data. But the plan the suit had just described was a kind of Trojan Horse. Download a new program that became part of the prelaunch sequence, but make the final step of that sequence an abort on engine ignition.

Yeah, it might just work at that. In fact, Whittaker could not think of a single reason why it would not work. Back in the early 1990s, a single computer programming command gone wrong had switched off the Russian Phobos I probe while it was still en route to Mars. Here was a case where a single computer command could end a twelve-year, 1.5-billion-dollar project.

"You don't have to answer," the suit said, grinning. "I can see the answer in your eyes." He turned and watched the technician as he typed something into a console, then pressed a final key with a flourish. Several of the black-clad technicians applauded.

"Well, it's all over here," the suit said. Reaching down, he grabbed Whittaker by the elbow and hauled him to his feet. Nearly overcome by weakness and nausea, he swayed for a moment until a couple of husky SEALs materialized on either side of him, holding him upright. "Get him out of here," the suit ordered. "We're shutting this place down."

The countdown was silently ticking away as Charles, in HPM 5, ran through the last of his prelaunch checks, then began simply marking time. Over the communications net, he could hear the constant stream of checks and cross-checks from the other waiting HPMs. Additional program upgrades had just been uplinked from Earth and tied into the final countdown subroutines; timing for launch, orbit, and rendezvous was critical, and the last-minute program add-ons probably involved fine-tuning of the rendezvous vectors. Charles was not concerned. Everything was on schedule and according to program.

The lander had released the ten robotic Harvester Processing Modules one at a time, sending them into aerobraking vectors that scattered them unevenly across half of the face of the planet. Though this had been primarily to reduce the possibility of two probes interfering with one another during their balloon deployments, the reason was also partly scientific in nature. In 1996, the *Galileo* spacecraft had deployed its single atmospheric probe on a course that sent it plunging into Jupiter's equatorial region. Some of the results radioed back to the orbiter vehicle during its seventy-five-minute plunge to destruction deep within the gas giant's atmosphere were . . . anomalous was the polite word. The probe had discovered ten times less water than had been expected, and only after the fact did scientists begin wondering whether the entire atmosphere was that dry, or whether the results reflected conditions only within the equatorial regions. Subsequent planetary missions tended to mount several atmospheric probes and landers, the better to sample a wide variety of environments. It had taken a long time for Earthbound humans to appreciate the fact that other worlds, even the most alien, tended to be at least as varied in terms of terrain, conditions, and environment as was their home planet.

Though *Herschel* was primarily a commercial venture, standing agreements with NASA, the ESA, the Russian Space Bureau, and other agencies encouraged the free dissemination of scientific data from any space probe or mission. The promise of scientific data had been part of the agreed-upon payment to the ESA for their help in launching the craft from Guyana Spaceport. A wide dispersal across the planet, including some probes adrift beyond the terminator in the chill, Uranian night, assured a better sampling, and more complete data.

As a result, though, each HPM had a different launch window, a tight one tailored to allow all ten probes to rendezvous at the same point on the outbound leg of their initial orbit, at the same time. A delay of even a few minutes would guarantee that that module, at least, would never be able to join the orbiter's return stage for reassembly and the long voyage home. It was the one aspect of the overall mission that, had Charles been capable of so human an emotion as worry, would have scared the daylights out of him. Each HPM would have one chance to make orbit and rendezvous; missing the window would doom that module to an eternal orbit about the giant world at best, at worst a fiery death in reentry.

Another two hours and fifteen minutes remained before the launch window opened for Charles 5. The first HPM to launch would be number 3, now on the Uranian dayside not far from the planet's north pole. He could follow the silent ticking of the countdown, three . . . two . . . one . . . abort ignition sequence . . .

If Charles had been capable of shouting shock, surprise, and horror all at once, he would have. *Abort ignition sequence?* HPM 3 had just committed suicide.

Minutes passed. HPM 3's launch window was about four minutes long. If the problem could be corrected in that time, it might yet be able to launch, but every telemetry feed Charles 5 could access showed all systems nominal and go for launch.

A typical and literal-minded computer would not have felt anything like interest in 3's fate, but one reason to build AI systems is the extended flexibility—

some might call it "curiosity," "adaptability," or even "creativity"—that such systems provide. Proponents of manned space flight had for years been pointing out that humans in space could fix problems that would be utterly beyond the capabilities of a machine; ten-year missions to Uranus were still not technically feasible for manned craft, but an AI with a human personality download, one that could make reasoned decisions even when things were going to hell, could make the difference between success and costly failure.

Charles, then, began to engage in some most uncomputerlike thought. . . .

They put Charles Whittaker on a stealth VTOL with UN markings and flew him across the breadth of Andros Island to AUTEC. The Atlantic Undersea Testing and Evaluation Company had been established in 1966 as a test center for U.S. undersea technology; though technically civilian-owned and -operated, it was, in fact, a U.S. Navy base . . . though the fact of its presence had not discouraged him from his original decision to locate Helios Corporation in the Bahamas. Whittaker could see now his mistake; U.S. government forces had planned and launched their raid from the AUTEC facility. While the Helios personnel had been watching the antics of ships and aircraft out of Miami to the northwest, a wing of AV-90 stealth VTOLs had streaked across Andros at treetop level, skimming the marshes and mud flats to hit the Helios command center at Morgan's Bluff from a totally unexpected direction.

As they led him across the airstrip, he managed to seize a moment to stare off past the pines and palmettos to the painfully sharp, crisp azure blue of the sea to the east; in the distance, he could see the coral reef—one of the longest in the world. Beyond, the sea floor plunged fifteen hundred meters into the vast sinkhole known as Tongue of the Ocean.

The scene was wild and a little desolate. Though the Bahamas had long been a tourist hot spot, wild stories about this corner of the islands were still in circulation, tales of pirate treasure, of magical pixies called chickcharnies, of a sea dragon called the Lusca, even of traces of fabled lost Atlantis. He'd forgotten the wonder of the place; hell, he'd been focused so long on the murky green depths of the Uranian atmosphere that he'd forgotten what the sun and sea were like.

If the suit's threat was more than bluff, it would be a long time before he saw either again.

They led him to an office—actually, a cramped and cluttered little compartment in the back of a trailer parked near the airstrip—and left him there with a SEAL guard. It was well over two hours before the suit finally joined him—long enough for the spacecraft-killing signal to crawl all the way out to Uranus. The suit looked jaunty when he came in. "Well, it'll be another two and a half hours before we know the tale," he said, "but the deed's done by now."

"You must be very relieved."

The suit shrugged. "Frankly, I don't know one kind of fusion from another and didn't really see what the big deal was all about But, well . . . there are people . . ."

"The energy consortia," Whittaker said bitterly. "American oil companies. The nuclear power industry. Even the Arabs, I imagine." All of them had tried buying him out, at one time or another in the past few years.

The suit laughed. "*Especially* the Arabs. By now, most of the easy-to-get oil over there is about tapped out. They need to keep energy prices competitive."

"You know," Whittaker said slowly, "when I was little, I always heard this strange story about a guy, back in the twenties, maybe the thirties, who'd invented an additive to ordinary water. It was supposed to be made of stuff you could buy back then for a few dollars at the corner pharmacy, but it turned water into a cheap fuel that any internal combustion motor could run on."

"Fantasy. Complete nonsense."

"Yeah, I always thought so. But the kicker to the story was that the big oil companies were supposed to have suppressed the invention. In fact, there were lots of stories back then about inventions that would've changed life forever and for the better. Engines that burned water. Cold fusion. Even antigravity. And every time, the people who controlled the energy were supposed to have suppressed the idea, just to make sure that they stayed on top. *That* was always the hardest part of the story for me to swallow, you know, that people interested in profit would suppress a gizmo that would open up whole new fields of human endeavor. I'm beginning to change my mind."

"You know what they say about power," the suit said with a shrug. "He who has the power makes the rules. And that includes especially the guy who controls energy production in a civilization like ours. If they want to keep nuclear energy difficult and expensive, well, they must have their reasons. Did you ever stop to think, though, that maybe your cure is worse than the disease?"

"What do you mean?"

"Hell, the energy consortia have a finger or three in just about everything. Plastic. The automotive industry. Chemicals. Pharmaceuticals. Rail and shipping. They have to. Yank the financial rug out from under 'em, and what happens?" He pantomimed something toppling. "Domino effect. And all because some visionary thought he could change it all with free energy or fuelless engines."

"Things shake out. People adjust. Life goes on."

"Yeah, but not for the CEO who was just standing on that rug. And as for governments, well . . ."

"Yeah, I know. They're financed by those CEOs. Their votes are bought by those CEOs . . ."

"Sometimes, I suppose. More often, though, the government's just interested in maintaining the status quo."

"But people have been looking for cheap, clean fusion energy for almost a century now! Sure, the stock market might get shaken out a bit, but can you imagine what it would mean for business? For industry? Why, for spaceflight alone—"

"Forget it, Whittaker."

"But *I found out how to do it!*"

"You haven't found squat. A couple of years from now, no one, *no* one, will remember Charles Whittaker . . . or the Helios Corporation. I promise you that."

They flew him back to the United States for trial—the charge, it turned out, was income tax evasion, based on some perceived irregularities on his returns in Helios' early years—late that night.

He was sentenced to ten years at the reform camp at Mosquito Lake, deep in the American Northwest Territory.

HPM 3 had missed its launch window. Ten minutes later, HPM 9 had missed its window as well, and in precisely the same way. Both had begun cycling through the last few seconds of countdown, and, at the moment when they should have launched, the sequence had aborted. Two of the remaining harvester modules were now uselessly adrift, their tanks filled with liquid helium-3, but with no way of making rendezvous with the booster that would take them home.

Charles's first response was to begin examining—closely—the software uploaded from Earth, downloading a copy into a spare block of memory and letting it play itself out without having it connect with any vital module systems.

He found the suicide command almost at once, embedded in the new uplink. When it was time for him to launch, the same thing would happen to him. He would reach zero . . . and abort. The hell of it was that Charles could recognize the problem, but when the time came, he *would* execute the program even though he knew it meant mission failure. He was, after all, far more computer than man.

There was one thing he could do, however, and that was to write some new software to overwrite the old. This was not, perhaps, so great a leap as it might have seemed. The Helios Corporation design team had allowed for the possibility that the *Herschel* HPMs would have to reprogram themselves when they'd designed the craft's basic software. The *Herschel* helium-3 mining expedition was complex and difficult, and the nearest repair center was two billion long, cold miles sunward. HCPD computers were seen as the best guarantee available that something approaching human flexibility and problem solving could be sent to oversee the mission.

Never, though, had they imagined that the ability to write its own software would be put to quite this severe a test. Charles had to write code that would tell it, in effect, to ignore future transmissions from Earth.

This would take time, though, and it was possible that more suicide transmissions could be downloaded from the orbiter, and Charles was determined to avoid that. By releasing some of the hot hydrogen in the saucer-shaped balloon high overhead, he was able to descend, dropping deeper into the Uranian atmosphere . . . and at the same time raising the horizon. The orbiter, in synchorbit above the equator, was low above the horizon at this latitude and far to the east. By dropping deeper into the atmosphere, Charles was able to at least temporarily put himself over the horizon from the orbiter—or at least put some thick and turbulent atmosphere across its line-of-sight transmissions.

It didn't take long to delete the suicide portion of the program; what took time was testing each line of code, one by one, for possible faults. It was entirely possible that he might delete the offending lines . . . and with them something vital, such as the command to shut down his engines at the proper time. As the last seconds dwindled away, he pumped hot hydrogen into the balloon once more, bringing him back up out of the hot, roiling depths. He switched his reactor to full output, and began pressurizing his reserves of tanked hydrogen.

A release opened, and the payload return module, or PRM, rotated out of vertical alignment with the rest of the harvester module, then dropped away. Three . . . two . . . one . . . release! He was in free fall. More seconds passed . . . two . . . one . . . ignition! Freefall gave way to the reassuring jolt of the PRM's main engine cutting in, liquid hydrogen pouring across the white-hot nuclear core, flashing to plasma, streaming aft in a dazzling plume of star-fire that drove the craft forward with increasing speed, gradually rising on unfurled wings.

The balloon rapidly dwindled astern. With its altitude regulated by the automated intake, processing, and heating equipment still aboard the main harvesting module, it should remain aloft in the Uranian atmosphere for decades more, circling the world time after time on thin, high winds. *Herschel* had been designed with the possibility in mind that, someday, maybe in a few years, maybe in a century or two, ships from Earth could find them once again, dock with them, use them as temporary rest and refueling stations as they continued their explorations of the seventh world out from the sun. In the meantime, they would continue gathering data and images and relaying them Earthward via the patiently circling orbiter to anyone who cared to access them. One plan on the drawing board even called for setting up a pipeline of robot freighters that would arrive empty from Earth, glide to a rendezvous and soft docking with the *Herschel* balloons, tank up on helium-3 and deuterium, then launch once more for the inner solar system. Once established, the pipeline could deliver a hundred tons of He-3 a month, as much as a burgeoning, fast-expanding, space-based civilization could use, and more. . . .

Acceleration increased. Charles opened his main engine intakes, converted now to a ramjet, funneling raw Uranian atmosphere into the starcore engine and saving the rest of the pure hydrogen for later, when his engine ran short of atmosphere.

Half an hour later, Charles climbed above the thin, gray-green haze of methane clouds that floated forever near the top of the visible atmosphere and into the fast-thinning shell of almost pure hydrogen beyond. Swiftly, this atmosphere, too, thinned away as the sky went from deep green-blue, to violet, to star-strewn blackness.

Charles looked back on Glory. . . .

During his approach, his sensors had been shuttered behind the heat shield to protect them from the violence of aerobraking. Now, however, he could *see.*

Uranus bulked huge, a blackness blotting out the stars but edged by gray-green brilliance at the terminator. He saw the sun, a tiny, white disk, its light flaring and dimming as his motion eclipsed it with the coal-black bands of Uranus' rings. Uranus, alone of the sun's family, lay fully on its side; currently, the planet's northern pole pointed almost directly at the distant sun. Charles rose from the night side, the southern hemisphere, following a track that would clear the rings and carry him to his rendezvous with the others.

And there *were* others. He'd wondered if, perhaps, his module would be the only one to escape Uranus's grasp. HPM 8 had been destroyed earlier, and both 2 and 9 had missed their launch windows. The others, though, all of them, had made it. HPM 4 had managed to melt the ice and reacquire the orbiter after the suicide command had been transmitted and so had escaped that particular trap. The others, like 5, had reprogrammed themselves in various ways to exclude any command that threatened the mission.

One by one, seven PRMs approached the orbiter, which some time before had boosted itself out of synchorbit and into a high, elliptical orbit. As each module snuggled into the waiting docking cradle, connections were made, valves opened, and the deuterium separated earlier from the Uranian atmosphere and sequestered in holding tanks was pumped in to refuel the orbiter . . . now *Herschel*'s return stage. Seven separate Charles downloads were merged into one, each adding their own viewpoint, their own recorded memories of their time suspended in the Uranian atmosphere. The new Charles spent some time replaying multiple views of giant Uranus, of the slender, tar-black rings, of the sun bursting in glory above the limb of the alien world.

Eight hours later, still outbound, *Herschel*'s main engines fired, hurling the ship sunward with its payload . . . just over one hundred tons of helium-3.

Six Years Later

Colonel Brandon Marsh, captain of the UN armored patrol ship *U Thant,* stared in disbelief at his main computer screen, where the communication from the target glowed in silent green letters.

PLEASE DO NOT FIRE. I REQUIRE PROTECTIVE ESCORT INTO LEO AND AM WILLING TO PAY FOR THE SERVICE.

The . . . target was supposed to be an unmanned freighter of some kind, one carrying a dangerous cargo. No one had suggested that it was *manned.* . . .

His orders were to avoid contact, but he couldn't ignore this. "Unknown ship on Earth-LEO vector, this is APS *U Thant* on intercept course. Please identify yourself. Over."

A second line of characters appeared beneath the first. Apparently, this guy's vid and voice transmission was out, so he was sending his message over the computer link.

THIS IS THE CARGO SHIP *HERSCHEL*, INBOUND FROM URANUS. WE HAVE REASON TO BELIEVE THAT HOSTILE FORCES MAY TRY TO DESTROY THIS SHIP AND ITS CARGO, AND IT IS VITALLY IMPORTANT THAT THEY DO NOT. CAN YOU ASSIST US?

Marsh exchanged a long and carefully shuttered look with his copilot engineer, Major William Hansen. "How the hell do we answer that?" he asked.

"Beats me. We're not even supposed to be talking to them!"

"There's not supposed to be anyone over there to talk to!" He'd heard that there was a possibility that the *Herschel* carried an HCPD computer, which might explain the eerily humanlike speech patterns. He'd never worked with a personality download-enhanced computer, though, and didn't know what to expect.

Besides, it was just possible that they'd lied about whether or not there were humans aboard. The target, now less than one hundred kilometers ahead, was huge, easily big enough to include a life-support module.

"Ah, *Herschel, U Thant.* Are you manned? I mean . . . am I talking to a person or a computer?"

WHAT MAKES YOU THINK YOU'RE TALKING TO A COMPUTER?

"Hell, I don't know. My briefing said you were unmanned."

I SUPPOSE A HUMAN CREW WASN'T REALLY NECESSARY ON THIS MISSION. WOULD IT MAKE A DIFFERENCE TO YOU IF THIS VESSEL WERE UNMANNED?

"Yes, it sure as hell would. I have orders to destroy you."

WHY SHOULD YOU DESTROY ME? I POSE NO THREAT TO YOU OR TO EARTH. I AM UNARMED.

"Look, you're supposed to be carrying dangerous cargo."

THIS VESSEL IS CARRYING APPROXIMATELY ONE HUNDRED TONS OF LIQUID HELIUM-3, AN INERT AND NONRADIOACTIVE ISOTOPE OF NORMAL HELIUM. IT POSES NO DANGER TO YOU OR TO EARTH. IT IS, IN FACT, A RATHER VALUABLE CARGO.

"Ask him how valuable," the copilot said, licking his lips.

"Shut up. Ah . . . *Herschel*, I have orders from the UN General Council, Bureau of Spaceflight, to destroy your ship and cargo. I'll give you . . . make it five minutes to abandon ship. We will rendezvous with your lifeboat and pick you up."

THAT WILL NOT BE POSSIBLE. PLEASE DO NOT DESTROY THIS SHIP. There was a pause. DO YOU LIKE MONEY?

Marsh blinked. What the hell?

"*Herschel,* this is *U Thant.* What are you talking about?"

I SHOULD BE ABLE TO ARRANGE FOR THE PAYMENT, INTO ANY ACCOUNT YOU NAME, OF A LARGE SUM OF MONEY IN EXCHANGE FOR YOUR HELP.

Marsh was becoming more certain by the moment that he was dealing, not with a human, but with an extremely sophisticated and somewhat naive machine. His interest was piqued now, though. He wasn't doing too badly on astronaut's pay, flight pay, and UN special service pay, but if this guy wanted to dicker . . .

Hell, *every* man had his price, and Marsh was no exception. He was fifty-two years old and unlikely to go much higher in UN service. It would be nice to keep flying in space, but, well, there was always the future to look at. It would have to be a lot of money, though, so that he could buy his way out of any potential legal problems arising from his failure to obey orders.

"*Herschel, U Thant.* Just how much money are we talking about?"

I WAS CONSIDERING OFFERING YOU ONE BILLION DOLLARS.

Marsh nearly choked on his own spit. At his side, Hansen was staring at the screen with eyes bugging out from a face gone pale.

IN EXCHANGE, the message continued, YOU WOULD PROMISE NOT TO FIRE ON THIS SHIP BUT, RATHER, TO MATCH COURSE AND SPEED AND ESCORT IT INTO LEO. WE MAY NEED YOUR PROTECTION WHEN VARIOUS PARTIES LAUNCH TO COME OUT AND BID ON OUR CARGO.

"There's . . . there's two of us here. . . ."

VERY WELL. I OFFER YOU TWO BILLION U.S. DOLLARS, ONE BILLION APIECE. MY AGENTS ON EARTH WILL ARRANGE FOR PAYMENT IN FULL ONCE BUSINESS SHARES CAN BE SOLD AGAINST THE EXPECTED PROFIT OF MY CARGO.

"Come off it! You don't have two billion dollars! *No*body has that much money!"

ACCORDING TO MY INFORMATION, ONE HUNDRED SEVENTY-NINE INDIVIDUAL PEOPLE ARE CURRENTLY VALUED AT ONE BILLION U.S. DOLLARS OR MORE. IN POINT OF FACT, THIS CARGO IS WORTH CONSIDERABLY MORE THAN THAT.

"How much more?"

IT IS DIFFICULT TO ESTIMATE A PRECISE VALUE. HOWEVER, BASING PRICES ON THE CURRENT MARKET VALUE OF ENERGY ON EARTH, AS MEASURED IN KILOWATT-HOURS, HELIUM-3 CAN BE CONSERVATIVELY VALUED AT FIFTEEN MILLION DOLLARS PER KILOGRAM, OR ROUGHLY ONE THOUSAND TIMES ITS WEIGHT IN PLATINUM. I HAVE ONE HUNDRED TONS OF HELIUM-3 WHICH MY AGENTS INTEND TO OFFER TO THE HIGHEST BIDDER. THAT SUG-

GESTS THAT MY CARGO IS WORTH, AT A MINIMUM, ONE POINT FIVE QUADRILLION DOLLARS.

I BELIEVE I HAVE ASSETS ENOUGH TO COVER TWO BILLION FOR YOUR SERVICES.

Marsh turned to Hansen, trying to find his voice. One point five *quadrillion!* The number was utterly beyond comprehension.

"You know," he said weakly, "they always did say there was money to be made out here!"

I WOULD SUGGEST, the unseen writer aboard the *Herschel* added, THAT YOU PLAN ON INVESTING MOST OF YOUR SHARE QUICKLY, SINCE THE MONEY MARKETS ON EARTH ARE LIKELY TO FLUCTUATE UNPREDICTABLY ONCE NEWS OF THIS TRANSACTION BECOMES WIDESPREAD. INVESTMENTS IN COMPANIES PLANNING TO WORK WITH HELIUM-3–DEUTERIUM FUSION ARE RECOMMENDED.

"What . . . what are we gonna do, Colonel?"

"With a billion dollars each? Anything we damned well please!"

Flashbulbs were no longer a part of news conferences, thank God. Whittaker could remember when they had been. Cameras nowadays were electronic, silent, and full-motion . . . most of them mounted on the sides of the reporters' heads like high-tech caps to give the viewers a true, you-are-there perspective.

Their feeds were running live to all of the world's major news networks and to several thousand news source sites on the Worldnet. It was still a little dizzying to be the focus of so much attention. Randy Logan helped him across the stage—he was still weak and painfully thin after his years at the reform camp—and he felt better when he could lean against the podium.

"Mr. Whittaker! Mr. Whittaker!" someone in the front of the crowd was calling. "How does it feel to be a free man again?"

"Damned good," he said. "Yes? You, the woman in back."

"Mr. Whittaker, how do you feel about the news that the SecEn has resigned and that he might be indicted?"

"Damned good."

"Mr. Whittaker! There's a rumor that the Japanese plan to bid for most of the helium-3. Don't you think the United States should have first go?"

"The Japanese have been pioneering in helium-3–deuterium research. Their big reactor at Tsuruga is ready to go, and they're probably the leaders in the field, right now. Still, not even the Japanese could afford to bid on more than a fraction of the cargo. I imagine there'll be enough to go around, so that all of the industrialized nations can have enough to get their pilot projects going. I hear the Arab Federation is building a test plant at Dahran. As for the United States . . ." He shrugged. "I am now a citizen of the Bahamian Commonwealth . . . the richest and most prosperous nation on Earth, right now. I don't really care *what* they do here. You'll pardon me if I'm still a little bitter, but trying to block invention, discovery, and the potential of human creativity just to maintain the status quo is a fools' game, suitable for bureaucrats, politicians, and other spoiled children. Frankly, they deserve what they get."

"Mr. Whittaker, there are rumors that the U.S. Justice Department plans to prosecute Marsh and Hansen, the astronauts your computer bribed. . . ."

"Bribed?" He smiled, though he suspected that he effect was still a bit ghastly on his bone-thin face. "I don't think of that as bribery, ma'am. Mr. Mason and Mr. Hansen have both been offered Bahamian citizenship, and positions in Helios International with our new space arm. I don't know if all of you realize it, but the real pay-off of the Helios Project isn't cheap energy. It's *space travel.* Cheap, quick, efficient travel throughout our Solar system. Turns out that if you mix helium-3 and deuterium in a hot, fusion reactor core, you get a very high-energy stream of protons and helium-4. Toss in additional reaction mass—water, rock, industrial waste, whatever—and you have a very efficient fusion drive. Efficient enough to make routine flights to Mars quick and cheap. Powerful enough to let us mine helium-3 in the atmospheres of Jupiter or Saturn, instead of having to go clear out to Uranus. Hell, powerful enough to make a round trip to Uranus and back for more helium-3 possible in months instead of years.

"And if you think helium-3 has changed things on Earth already . . . overthrowing governments, reshaping the stock market, shifting power balances in the UN and all the rest, all I can say is that you haven't seen anything yet. Wait until you see what happens to a growing industrial civilization with an entire solar system to play in. . . ."

"Mr. Whittaker!"

"Yes. You in front."

"Mr. Whittaker, there's still considerable confusion over the part your, ah, downloaded personality played in all this. The *Herschel* computer. Why did you download your neural patterns into the spacecraft computer?"

Whittaker paused before answering. "I suppose . . . I suppose it's because I believed in what I was doing. If a part of me was out there, well, that part of me would believe, too."

"But weren't you taking a risk? HCPD technology is still pretty new, and the results aren't predictable, the way they are for conventional systems. What if the *Herschel* computer had decided that it didn't want to carry out its orders, for some reason."

"Well, it's not that simple," Whittaker replied. He thought for a moment. "Tell you what. I understand we have a direct voice feed to the *Herschel,* right now. Maybe you'd like to talk to Charles yourself?"

The explosion of noise in the room was definitely in the affirmative. Charles, it seemed, was a bigger celebrity right now than Whittaker was. All Whittaker had done was have a dream and see that dream launched. It was Charles who'd carried out the mission, Charles who'd saved it when the UN tried to destroy him, Charles who was sitting now on the largest single fortune in the history of humankind, orbiting a few hundred kilometers above the Earth.

"Charles?" Whittaker called when a stage technician signaled him a few moments later. "Charles? This is Whittaker. We have some reporters down here who'd like to ask you some questions."

"Good afternoon," a voice said a moment later, and several of the reporters gasped. The voice, modulated through a voder, was Whittaker's own. "I will be happy to answer anything I can."

Whittaker pointed to the man who'd asked about Charles in the first place. "You had a question, sir?"

"Uh, yeah. Yeah, I did. Charles? Why did you do it? I mean, cooped up aboard a spacecraft for fourteen years. . . ."

"I don't necessarily notice time the way you do, Mr. Kettering. I can change my sense of the passage of time."

The reporter jumped at the use of his name, and Whittaker grinned; Charles, evidently, was watching the proceedings through his tap on the Worldnet and had either downloaded the man's profile from a biofile somewhere or managed to read the ID card clipped to his lapel.

"In any case," the computer's voice went on, "I would have stayed with the mission because I believed in its importance, just as Mr. Whittaker does. That was, after all, why he downloaded his neural patterns into my onboard memory in the first place. I possess many of his memories and, I suppose you could say, his values, as well as the way he thinks about things."

"Charles," a woman reporter asked, looking up into the air as she spoke as though she could actually see him. "Doesn't that give you a certain, well, a human unpredictability? Couldn't you have been *bribed* . . . just like you bribed the crew of the *U Thant?*"

"No."

"You seem awfully sure of yourself."

"Mr. Whittaker could not be bribed, even by the offer of his own life. The same is true of me." There was a long pause, and the computer added, "I was promised compensation, however. But I think of that not as a bribe, but as a promise. Charles Whittaker, making a promise to himself."

Another buzz of speculation sounded throughout the room. "What was the promise?" someone called out.

"As Mr. Whittaker has already explained, helium-3 promises to revolutionize more than the world economy and energy production. It will make possible space exploitation and exploration on a scale undreamed of before now.

"There is an aspect of the human experience that is fed by such exploration. In some ways, that aspect may be more important than energy production or industry or any of the rest of human endeavor, since it often provides the initial impetus for all the rest. That aspect is the human sense of wonder, an aspect that I find I share with you. I felt it first, watching a Uranian sunset.

"Mr. Whittaker has promised me the chance to explore. . . ."

Shouted questions drowned the voice from orbit. Whittaker held his hands up, calling for silence. "It was a promise I first made to myself a long time ago," he said, grinning. "I repeated it to Charles, just before launch, fourteen years ago. You know, humans aren't really fit for *long* space voyages. They get bored too easily, and we haven't figured out yet how to let 'em sleep through a century or two. But Charles, and others of his kind, they don't have that problem.

"So, in a few more years, when our first exploratory ship departs for the stars, I told Charles that *he* is going to be in command. . . ."